SUZANNAH ROWNTREE

A Day of Darkness

Watchers of Outremer, Book Three

For all the single men who are kind to more than just the pretty girls—
For all the taken men who still have friendship for single women—
For all the older men who listen first and speak second—
With all my love.

Prologue

Cairo, A.D. 1288

Soraya awoke to find a dead man in the bed beside her.

An arm was slung over her waist, cool and slack. Feeling the weight, she jolted away in alarm. The sudden movement made her head pound and when she opened her eyes, blinding morning sunlight pierced her head like a knife.

Groaning, Soraya blinked down at the corpse. He was a youngish man, well-made and whip-lean, with a black beard trimmed so neatly, it looked like velvet. He was also very undeniably dead. The myriad little motions of life were gone, and a greyish tinge had begun to transform his face into a waxlike mask.

Dread, cold and slippery, crawled up her back. *Not again.*

Soraya couldn't tell where the thought had come from. She blinked again, trying to focus. Last night. What had happened last night? Could she even remember?

She was still kneeling on the bed, frozen, when a knock sounded at the door and instinct took over. Ignoring her pounding head, Soraya dived from the bed and grabbed at the clothes spread across the floor. Kaftan, sash, turban and trousers. A curtain of figured silk looped across the centre of the room and Soraya took refuge behind its tail, breathing hard as the door opened.

The servant cleared his throat respectfully as he entered. "My lord?"

My lord. Fear slithered unpleasantly in her gut. It didn't take a great intellect to deduce that this luxurious apartment—furnished with rugs, curtains, and potted citrus, its furniture carved of some gleaming dark wood—must belong to a very rich man. She'd known that as soon as she opened her eyes.

But there was only one man this could be. His name bubbled to the surface of her memory.

Al-Malik al-Salih Ali.

The sultan's eldest son and trusted heir, and she had killed him..

Beyond the curtain a wail split the air and the breakfast tray crashed to the floor with an explosion of fine pottery.

Soraya jolted, and as the servant raced for the door wailing for help, she began pulling on her clothes with muttered curses.

Remember, Soraya. Remember. What the hell were you doing last night—

Oh.

Most of Soraya's past was missing, her memories lost, but she still had last night; it was surfacing now, through a haze of drink.

Her master had dragged her from her prison, given her a small vial of poisoned honey and a series of commands. She was to dress as a dancer to attend a feast. There, she would make sure the honey got into the future sultan's food, using whatever inducements necessary.

Afterward she must make her escape, allowing the prince's mamluks to see her fleeing, but giving them no indication of her true nature.

There was no refusing the command, and so Soraya had done what was necessary. In the process, she'd drunk herself into a stupor. Drink was far from her favourite mode of dissipation. Food, with all its subtle flavours, was her indulgence of choice. Motion—the dance, the hunt, the fight—was a close second. Lust—well, that part recurred to memory with a shudder; she used her body like a tool, shaped and discarded it like a tool, and invariably came to despise it like a tool too. But drunkenness, along with hashish and poppy juice, was the very worst: it deadened sensation, dulled reflex and got between herself and her body. Again.

The only benefit to getting drunk was that it made it easier to forget you'd just poisoned a man in cold blood.

Again, some ghost from a past life whispered to her. *This wasn't your first murder.*

It won't be your last.

Beyond the chamber door, the servant's alarm was spreading. Booted feet pounded the floor in disciplined unison and armour jingled as the prince's mamluk guards raced towards him.

As slaves purchased from across the sea—usually Circassians, Turks, or Tartars—a prince's mamluks were raised in his household to be his most elite warriors and loyal servants. With their loyalty proven, mamluks would eventually be freed to act as officers in the army and administrators in the government. Most would start collecting a mamluk army of their own; some would grow strong enough to challenge the sultan for his throne. Although a man's fortune would go to his natural sons after death, his rank could only be inherited by his mamluks. It was a system built upon fierce bonds of loyalty for the purpose of forging the finest warriors in the world—half a dozen of whom were racing straight towards her.

Soraya hissed and continued to yank on her clothes, fumbling with drawstrings and buttons.

Is this who I really am? she wondered. *What happened, to make me like this?*

Her memories, like her freedom, had been stolen from her. This morning, that felt like a mercy.

From a latticed wooden window floated the muffled sounds of the city and, nearer at hand, the tinkle of a fountain and the song of caged birds. If her instincts were correct, the door at the back of the room would lead downstairs to a private bath room, and beyond that would be a door onto the garden. Giving up on the multitude of buttons on her green kaftan, Soraya tied the jacket shut with her sash and hurried across the room toward the private door.

She didn't make it. As Mamluk guards burst through the door behind her, Soraya hit the floor, scrambling beneath a table of dark wood.

"Dead," their leader said after a moment's terse silence, "he's dead. Oh, God!" He pulled his hands down a face that had quite suddenly become haggard.

A short, puffy-faced man in civilian robes appeared in the main doorway, breathing hard. A chamberlain, most likely. For an instant, silence reigned as he digested the mamluk's words.

"He can't be. He was getting well again."

"He left last night with a dancing girl," the mamluk said, tight-lipped. The bedclothes rustled, and Soraya's neck prickled as he leaned over the bed and slipped a hand between the covers.

He stiffened like a dog coming to point, and Soraya mouthed a soundless curse. The bed must still be warm.

She backed beneath the table, judging the distance to the far door. Her orders had been to allow herself to be seen, but on no account to be caught. Despite the prince's mamluks swarming across his room, escaping wasn't going to be a problem. Doing so without revealing her true nature, however, would be.

She came out from beneath the table and rose silently to her feet as the mamluk emir signed orders to his men. His eyes widened as she appeared.

Time splintered.

Instinctively, Soraya looked at the emir and smiled.

He flinched as though she'd pointed a crossbow his way.

Soraya wheeled in a flutter of silk and reached the door before the emir recovered enough breath to call the alarm. Under the brush of her fingers, it flew open. Behind her, the emir's shout propelled his men into motion. Soraya took the stairs three at a time and burst into the empty hammam, its atmosphere thick with steam and the faint scent of rosewater.

From here, a service passage led to the kitchens, and a door opened onto the garden. Soraya turned to the door, which was almost certainly locked to maintain the young prince's privacy. Footsteps and shouts echoed behind, but the hunt was not yet in sight. Soraya curled her fingers around the iron barrel-lock and yanked, dragging at the latch. Nails popped out, tinkling across the tiles. She threw the door open and fled into the greenery beyond.

Where now? A massive wall surrounded the garden—one that only a prodigy could climb. Beyond the garden, in the barracks where the dead prince kept his slave warriors, a horn blew. Behind, her hunters spilled from the door, yelling at her to stop or die.

It wasn't them she feared.

Soraya spotted a jasmine vine crawling up the wall and raced towards it, ensuring she did not too obviously outdistance the men behind her.

Al-Malik al-Salih Ali. She couldn't help remembering the look of shock and despair on the faces of the prince's men as they saw her handiwork. She'd learned a little about the heir to Egypt in the last day or two. He was trusted by the sultan to rule and well-respected by the high-ranking mamluks in the government. With all the makings of a capable ruler, Ali might not have made life *better* for the people under his control, but at least he would have shielded them from misgovernment or war.

Now, because of her, he was dead.

How many others? The thought put a terrible ache somewhere under her breastbone. The best she could say for herself was that the honey was a quick and painless killer.

She reached the vine and scrambled up it, supporting herself precariously on its fine tendrils and the seams of the rough stones. Below, the mamluks yelled and attacked the vine with their swords, hoping to bring the whole thing down. But Soraya was quick and strong; stronger than they could guess.

With one last effort, she reached up and got a hand over the top of the wall. Her feet scrabbled at the vine, hoisting her up. *Catch me now, if you can.*

Maybe she ought to have attempted to leave last night, before she had confirmation that the honey had worked. Certainly she had been a fool to get drunk. But in the end, her master had wanted her to look guilty; fleeing the scene so publicly in the morning would certainly send the right message.

Soraya jumped to her feet, blowing her pursuers a mocking kiss as she balanced on the narrow parapet. She glanced down into the street below. A striped awning to the right offered a plausible place to land, and the narrow alley opposite would provide sufficient cover to—

Pain blazed through her gut, a sharp impact from one side. She looked down in shock to find a fletched arrow protruding from her belly.

They had an archer.

Her arms windmilled in a useless attempt to steady herself. The world reeled, the sky spinning beneath her feet. For one blinding moment, the terror of freefall enveloped her.

Her body slammed against stone and broke.

Her lungs gasped one last agonising breath. As Soraya flew free, a memory surfaced from the torment. A name. A place.

Yarmouk.

For a fleeting instant, the thought filled her with warmth; the impossible sense that once, at least, she had done the right thing.

But that was long ago now.

So very long ago.

Chapter I.

Syria, A.D. 636

Upon arriving in Antioch that evening in late summer, John Bessarion found that he was not the first to bring news of the great defeat.

"The Emperor knows about Yarmouk already." The Isaurian barbarians of the emperor's personal guard loomed over John forbiddingly.

The Isaurians could not have known who he was, or they would never have attempted to intimidate him. "Will you tell the Emperor I'm here? He'll want to see me."

"The Emperor is busy."

John sighed, rolling his shoulders back. It had been a long week's travel, and he had hastened to the city's great palace as soon as he had secured safe lodgings for his family and the invaluable relics with which Patriarch Sophronius of Jerusalem had entrusted him. With the holy city expecting a siege and the armies of Rome in shreds, it was only wise to send the True Cross and other relics to safety.

He said, quietly, "I am the Praetorian Prefect of Jerusalem."

The Isaurians glanced at each other dubiously, but stood their ground. "Beg your pardon, my lord. But the Emperor has commanded that we not disturb him."

Still a few years the right side of forty, John was young to be the emperor's governor in Palestine. The post required a sharp mind and proven loyalty. A man of his age would not be appointed to that position unless Emperor Heraclius thought very highly of him…but apparently, the guards needed that spelled out for them.

"The Emperor knows me. I fought beside him at Nineveh." John sighed. As the praetorian prefect he'd tried to build a different life for himself, a peaceful life; yet the past was difficult to leave behind and impossible to change. "My name is John Bessarion."

That got their attention. The younger of the guards turned slightly pink. *"You're* John Bessarion?"

The other snapped to attention and reached for the latch. "I beg your pardon, sir! I'll ask him."

While he waited, the younger guard eyed John with breathless admiration. "Is it true, sir, what they say about—?"

"Certainly not. For one thing, you can see for yourself that I don't have the scars."

"But our Domestic, Ashot was there—do you know Ashot?—and *he* said…
"

This time, the interruption came from the returning guard, and a quiet cough from the emperor's chamberlain. "Lord Prefect?"

John nodded to the young Isaurian. "Don't believe all the tall tales you hear from the battlefield, son."

He followed the emperor's chamberlain into a dark peristyle overlooking the palace garden, faintly illuminated by the last faint glow of sunset in the evening sky. In daytime, this place would come alive: the muted colours of marble and porphyry, the silken billow of curtains and cushions, the gleam of frescoes adorned with gold leaf, all of it lit up with threads of dancing light reflected from the fishpond near the foot of the steps leading into the garden. But the lamps went unlit tonight, and all that could be seen of the peristyle was a dark lowering roof and the harsh black lines of the square arches and fluted columns leading to the garden. Cloaked courtiers murmured in the shadows, their voices hushed as though someone had died.

John paused, taken aback by the funereal atmosphere. But the chamberlain led on towards the place where Emperor Heraclius sat in a chair at the foot of one of the pillars, little more than his outline visible.

John walked forward five steps and sank to his knees, pressing his forehead against the cool stone of the floor.

"John Bessarion."

John lifted his head. "Many and good years to you—"

Heraclius growled. "What have you come to say to me, Prefect? I know what happened at Yarmouk."

"I've come for the sake of Jerusalem, my lord. I've come to tell you that we are preparing for a siege."

"A siege." Heraclius' voice lifted incredulously. "Why, in God's name?"

That boded ill, but John set his jaw. "The heresiarchs from the south did not come to Syria for their health, my lord. They came to make a conquest of us."

The Emperor gave an impatient jerk of the head. "So much is clear."

"I come to you for aid. We may resist them for a time, but without your help, we must fall."

The Emperor looked away from him. "And your strategy, Prefect?"

John had been at war for most of his life. The armies of the Persian empire had taken Jerusalem when he was a boy, and Alexandria when he was a youth. He had seen his emperor face defeat and despair before, but he'd never known Heraclius like this: old. Tired.

Hopeless.

"The same as last time," John said, choosing his words carefully. "The Persians dominated the countryside, my lord, but the cities remained faithful to Rome, and because of that we were able to fight our way back from nothing. More than, that, my lord, this time I have a weapon..."

"Weapons be damned—I need the dragon's teeth with which Cadmus sowed the fields of Thebes, and reaped soldiers in the morning. What are firespouts and scorpions without men to use them?"

"What if I told you it was the weapon which won Yarmouk for the heretics?" John said when the emperor's question died away.

"Go on."

"It was a spear," he said slowly. "The one who used it was mighty beyond measure in battle. It never broke, it never faltered. In the moment when victory was within our grasp, it turned the tide of battle and broke our momentum. At that moment our defeat began."

"So one of their warriors was in league with demons? I could have told you that."

"It was the weapon. I—when another man used the same weapon, he was every bit as powerful as the first."

In the dark John felt, rather than saw, the emperor's eyes narrow. "What are you telling me, Bessarion?"

Again, John picked his words carefully. "I mean that we may have lost the battle, my lord, but we won the weapon. It's here with me, in Antioch now."

There was a short silence. Heraclius grunted. "You won the weapon, but lost the battle?"

"I—yes, my lord." John swallowed, his mind flinching away from the nightmarish memories. "But with the spear, and a little hope, we can retreat, rebuild, and reconquer. Just as we did when the Persians invaded."

"So this is your strategy," Heraclius said after a bleak moment. "You're nothing but a fool, Prefect. You can't make a victory out of hope."

"Perhaps not, my lord, but we surely can't make a victory without it. You taught me that."

"Then you should stop dwelling in the past, John. I am not who I was then. None of us are, not even Rome. We cannot help it if the future takes a shape beyond our control."

"Beyond our control? What are these desert tribes compared with the might of Rome?"

"What is Rome compared with what she was?" Heraclius sighed heavily. "Persia weakened us, and now one blow could shatter us like glass."

John swallowed. "My lord, I promised the Patriarch and the good citizens of Jerusalem that I would return with help for them."

"Then take your magic spear back to Jerusalem. Call your Watchers. Pray and fast. Hold the gate shut, or open it, as you like. It comes to the same thing in the end."

This couldn't be real. John let out a slow, controlled breath, and asked the question he thought he would never ask. "Are you abandoning us?"

No answer.

"We only ask for a little help. If we can hold Jerusalem—"

"You won't. Don't you understand?" The emperor was nearly shouting. "Do you think me a fool? It is because of our sins that this has happened!"

"Evidently, my lord, but—"

Heraclius pressed his fist to his mouth again. "This is because of my wife," he said very softly.

The Augusta Martina was, notoriously, also the emperor's niece. The whole empire, up to Heraclius himself, knew what the law said about such unions.

"Then let her depart, and be absolved of it, my lord, while this judgement lies yet light upon you." The words escaped John unthinkingly. Around the peristyle, the courtiers hushed their conversation, letting his words ring clear in the evening air.

His blood ran cold as a shadow detached itself from the darkness and glided forward. There was a muted flash of jewels as the Augusta went to Heraclius and put her hand on his shoulder. Heraclius reached up and took her hand, leaning his cheek against the plump arm. For a time, there was silence. John stared at the polished stone floor, trying desperately to think of some way to convince the emperor.

Before he could think of anything, the door opened, and a soft voice called, "My lord?"

"It's time," the Augusta murmured.

The emperor sighed and took hold of the arms of his chair to rise.

"Wait!" John pressed his forehead to the floor again. "My lord, the good people of Jerusalem are ready to fight and to die for the sake of their liberty, and out of love for you. Have you no words of comfort to send them? Will you really forsake us?"

Please don't deny me. Oh, my lord God, please don't let him deny me.

"I have no choice," Heraclius said harshly. "My men are scattered and my strength broken. If I send any man to Jerusalem I send him to his death."

"And Antioch? Will Antioch stand any longer if Jerusalem falls?"

"No."

The flat answer took his breath away. "You would give up Syria as well as Palestine?"

"Have I any choice?" Heraclius stood. "I am going back to Constantinople tonight. My horse and servants are waiting, and my ship is in harbour at Laodicea. If you survive the siege, bring your magic lance to me. I could use you at Constantinople."

"But—my lord—"

"They are waiting, Prefect."

He felt numb, punch-drunk. "What will I tell them in Jerusalem?"

"No more than this: *Farewell, my fair province, thou art an infidel's now. Peace be with you, O Syria! Such a beautiful land you will be for the enemy.*"

This was happening. He no longer wondered that the lamps were unlit and the peristyle in darkness. Night was falling, with no dawn in sight.

"Farewell, Prefect. Many and good years," the Emperor added with irony as he passed out of the room. In the darkness, there was a swish of robes and clank of arms as his attendants followed him, and then silence.

* * *

"What are we doing here, anyway?"

Two days' travel out of Antioch, high in the Syrian mountains, stood the small provincial town of Oliveta. Built of honey-coloured limestone, the town saw harsh winters and mild summers. The high plains were dry and unbeautiful at this time of year, the red earth pocked with tufts of scorched grass, and only hints of green in the shabby grey of olives and the harshly dark foliage of cypresses.

In one of the rooms they had been given in the town's most opulent villa, John ought to have been sorting through his pack in search of clean clothes. Instead, he found himself staring sightlessly at the neatly-folded linen tunics.

In the crowded marketplace as they had arrived in the town, he had glimpsed a face he thought he knew. A face he was half convinced he'd seen at the battle of Yarmouk. A face that reminded him that the heretic invaders were not so far away, occupying Emesa less than a day's ride to the south.

Fool, he berated himself. Two days ago he had hidden the spear in Antioch and left his armour and weapons as the guarantee for a loan to hire donkeys and a cart for his family to ride up into the hills. It had seemed sensible at the time; after all, there was no way he would actually *need* his arms. Surely the heretics could not have traced him from Yarmouk.

"Abba?" His eldest son's voice cut through his thoughts. Lukas stood at the window, silhouetted against the square tracery with stubbornly folded arms. "What are we doing here?"

John straightened, his temper fraying. He was coated in dust and sweat, and he wanted to find a bath and feel clean linen next to his skin again. He did not have the heart for this argument.

"The Syrian Watchers are meeting here at Oliveta tonight," John said with careful patience. "We've come to ask for their help."

"We're asking the *Watchers* for help?"

Lukas' voice lilted up in incredulity. Most Watchers were simple labourers or craftsmen, humble laymen dedicated to doing good deeds. Watchers built hospitals, took in orphans, and gave to the poor. They commanded no armies and wielded no immense treasuries. John understood his son's doubt—he'd had the same doubts himself, late at night as he lay in begged, borrowed, or hired rooms, worrying about a future he couldn't control.

"Yes," he said shortly. "We are asking them for help."

"We have no other choice, Lukas." Rahel Bessarion entered from the adjoining room holding their youngest, a sleeping Elisa, on her hip. A soft, vivid little woman with dark hair, olive skin, and a cheerful smile, John's wife might not be the most beautiful woman he'd ever seen, but she was the one he most loved to look at. She walked over to Lukas and squeezed his shoulder comfortingly. "The Watchers may not win battles, but winning battles is not the true test of a ruler. No matter how hard we fight, we don't deserve to win unless we do justice and love mercy. Where princes and armies fail, the Watchers may succeed."

"What about emperors?" The muscles in his jaw twitched. "Are we going to talk about what happened in Antioch at all? What did the Emperor say?"

John sighed, knowing how his son would react. "Heraclius went back to Constantinople. He's not sending us any help."

Lukas sucked in a sharp, pained breath. At the doorway to the adjoining room, curtain-rings rattled and John glanced over to meet his daughter Marta's huge, shocked eyes peering from behind the partitioning curtain. Beside her, six-year-old Paulus glanced from one face to another in worried confusion. John hadn't told them until now; he didn't want to see that look on their faces. Their whole world was crumbling, and they were too young to do anything about it.

He swallowed. "I'm afraid the emperor plans to sacrifice Jerusalem."

"He can't do that. It's our *home*." Marta's sense of justice was outraged.

"Not any more, I'm afraid." John sighed. "Not if the heretics want to take it. Heraclius feels he has no choice. After the Persian wars, the empire is too weakened to face another struggle."

And the great Bessarion legacy, built by generations of warriors, statesmen and diplomats, would be dispersed into the hands of strangers.

He had meant to do *such* good with it, too.

"So we give up?" Lukas spoke huskily. At seventeen, the boy was old enough to fight, and John wondered if his son would ever forgive him for going off to the wars without him. "You *promised.* The night we left, you promised we'd go back to Jerusalem and defend it."

"I promised them *I* would return," John answered, letting some steel into his voice. "*Your* job is to take care of your mother, Lukas. After tonight, I'm sending the rest of you by ship to Constantinople. I have a little property there, enough to keep you in a quiet way, and I'll send more if the invasion takes that long. You'll be safe and comfortable."

"I don't *want* to be comfortable," Lukas broke in. "I don't want to be *safe!*"

His shout startled three-year-old Elisa, sleeping in Rahel's arms. At once, she burst into tears. Rahel pulled the little girl closer, shushing her. Lukas, shame rising in his cheeks, looked almost as though he wanted to burst into tears himself. Instead he turned his face away, awkwardly patted Elisa's back, and then grabbed a clean if rumpled tunic from his bedroll. "I'm going to have a bath," he muttered.

The door slammed behind him. John sent a harried look to Rahel, but it was Marta who moved first. "I'll go and talk to him," she whispered, flitting after Lukas.

With the two older children out of the room, Rahel shook her head. "He wants to fight, John."

John felt his jaw clench as stubbornly as his son's. "I've seen too much war to wish it on my son." He looked down at his scarred hands. "It's all too easy to solve problems with a sword. Maybe it's too late for me, but he needs to find a better way."

"He feels like a coward."

"If he knew anything of war, he'd know it isn't cowardice to flee a battle you can't win."

Rahel said, quietly, "Then why do *you* go back?"

He looked up into brown eyes that shimmered with tears. Something in her voice had cracked and fallen away—that hard bright shell of cheerful resolve that she'd built up around herself over the last year or so.

"Dear heart," he sighed, feeling unanchored now that she was questioning him, too. Sometimes he forgot just how good Rahel was at putting a brave face on things.

She signalled to him to wait, and took the two youngest children into the next room. When they were settled for a nap, she returned and walked into his arms. "The children don't want to leave you. Nor do I."

"Please let me send you away," he begged, twisting his fingers into her hair. Although it had been a day or two since she'd last bathed, a faint scent of rosewater still rose from the glossy dark waves. "Who am I if I can't protect you?"

"Who am I if you send me away?" she countered, pulling back to look into his eyes.

He didn't know the answer to either question. Instead, he brushed her hair away from her soft brown skin. There was a little brown mole there, right on the nape of her neck where the fine silky black hairs began. There had been times during the last two weeks—on the afternoon the heretic army had cut off their retreat and got them backed up against the cliffs over the Yarmouk river, for example; or on that last terrible day of all, when bodies fell from the cliffs like falling stars at the end of the world—yes, there had been a few times when he was sure he had no hope of ever seeing that mole again. He pulled her nearer and kissed the spot gently. For the last time?—The premonition fleeted through his thoughts, making him shiver.

Rahel pulled away from him, still too distracted to lose herself in his caress. "Lukas is right, though, isn't he? You haven't been telling us everything."

There were reasons for that, good ones.

Not-so-good ones too, if he was being honest with himself. John let go of her and went over to the window, feeling somewhat distracted himself. "What did you want to know?"

"You never told me about the battle."

He bit his lip, then turned from the window. "There's not much to tell. It was six days of hell."

"Then tell me about that."

He didn't want to relive the defeat. He didn't want to think about all the ways he'd failed his fatherland, his family, himself.

There was a terrible sense of inevitability about time; he felt it sometimes if he broke or injured something. One brief moment ago the thing was undone and there was hope; now the thing was done and would never be undone again. And it never seemed right that with only heartbeats between the two, there could be no turning back to try again.

Every choice he had made had brought him to this moment, where Rahel was waiting. If he said nothing then she would know there was something to hide.

"It was a bad start," he began. "Romans, Greeks, Armenians, Arabs—none of us agreed on what ought to be done. Later, some of the Arabs went over to the enemy. They were Monophysite heretics themselves, and their pay was in arrears. Vahan the Armenian was commander, and he decided to risk a pitched battle with the enemy despite the Emperor's orders otherwise. It wasn't treachery; it was sense. While the heretic armies were massed, we had one chance to smash them with our superior numbers. It was a sure thing—it *ought* to have been a sure thing. And we couldn't hold off forever: our supplies and pasture were running out.

"On the first day there was skirmishing. Some of our champions challenged their commanders to duels."

"Did you fight?"

Nine years before, the skirmishing before the battle of Nineveh had made John Bessarion into a legend. He had been a younger man then; he had not yet learned what a terrible burden it was to hold the power of life and death over another mortal.

"Not this time, but I watched the fighting." Watched it, and saw the heretic spearman who had fought like a demigod. John cleared his throat. "On the second day we attacked them bodily and nearly broke them, before they rallied somehow and regained the original lines."

Again, he had seen the heretic spearman at work. John sighed.

"After that, the men were discouraged. The battle went on for four more days, hard fighting back and forth, until they cut us off from our fortress and got us pinned against the cliffs over the river. Vahan asked for a truce, and the heretics scented victory. They refused the truce, massed their cavalry and pummelled us until our horse broke. We had our backs against the precipices over the river Yarmouk. I don't know how many men we lost falling from the heights. Some of us fled down the gorges, and the rest were taken prisoner." He sighed. "That's all. I failed you."

She slid an arm around his waist. "You did what you could."

He couldn't help stiffening. "Perhaps."

Most certainly he had not. He'd had the means of turning the tide right there in his hands—if not for the dust and the chaos of battle. While he was fighting to repel the heretic attack at the rear, the flank and front shredded. He'd never even seen it until the tide of the retreat washed him away like so much flotsam.

Rahel frowned up at him. *"Perhaps? What is that supposed to mean? That one man should have been able to turn the tide?"*

"Maybe."

"You had all the numbers on your side and you said yourself the strategy made sense. What more could you have done? Are you God, to give victory and defeat?"

"Maybe I could have been more deserving." After all, he was a Watcher.

"You can't wipe out others' faults, John."

She might be right, but that hardly seemed to make it better, when he had so many faults of his own. He turned to her, shaking his head. "You had a vision. Seventeen years ago when Lukas was born, you *saw* the future that awaited our fatherland. How can we build that future when we're slaves?"

"The same way slaves built the world we live in now." She gave a bittersweet smile, and her hand tightened on his arm. "We don't need victory, John; we need truth. Your children don't need to see your power; they need to see your courage. As for the vision, I'm not afraid of failing it. I don't believe we *can* fail it." She smiled up at him encouragingly and went to her pack, bringing out a small packet sealed with a thick coating of red wax. "I prepared this before we left Jerusalem. I had a feeling we'd need it."

Rahel's feelings were rarely wrong. John took the packet, mystified. "What is it?"

"It's that formula of Isidore of Miletus—the one you sought for so long."

His fingers trembled a little as he nestled the packet into the pouch he wore at his belt. Rahel was always considerate, and if there was one thing in his whole library that he valued above anything else, it was this.

He couldn't imagine what possible use it might be now that he was losing his whole future. But that Rahel had felt compelled to bring it—that gave him hope.

"And tonight?" he asked. "What do you feel about tonight?"

"I think we'll need Paulus and Elisa wide awake for the council tonight." Rahel peered around the curtain. "Both of them are asleep; good."

The council. That was something else to worry about: he suspected the Watchers weren't going to be happy with him. Not after that letter. "You still think you'll need to substitute Elisa?"

"I'll be ready for it if I must." Rahel looked at him with sympathy.

"Constans seemed welcoming."

"I hope he'll stand with us."

"There's no use worrying about it. Try to get some rest."

Somewhere, he found the energy for a teasing grin. "Only if you'll join me."

"All right, but first you bathe." She wrinkled a nose at him, and he laughed.

Turning back to his pack, John found his clean tunic at once. It was the good one with embroidered claves to denote high military status, and it was folded at the top where he'd left it. He must have been looking straight at the garment without seeing it. The two others were dirty, and he shook them out of their neat folds and threw them out onto the bed to await laundering. The thought momentarily occurred to him that he might avoid the Watchers' Council altogether and spend a soothing evening doing laundry, as he'd occasionally had reason to do on campaign in his youth. Instead, he sighed and walked slowly to the baths. His eyes scanned the thinning crowd in the marketplace, but he caught no second glimpse of the heretic.

It had been in his possession barely a fortnight, but already he felt naked without the spear.

Chapter II.

"As Watchers, we're supposed to see to it that justice is done with mercy, in peace and humility to all. And yet, both as the emperor's soldier and as his prefect, it was my duty to coerce and destroy." John took a deep breath, glancing around the shadowy faces that watched him.

None of them seemed very happy with his defence. Before the great battle, John had written to the Syrian Watchers' council to propose a radical act of penance. He had expected the letter to provoke lively discussion, but now he felt as though he was on trial.

If this was to work, he could not try to conceal his sins. John swallowed, forcing himself to go on. "When the emperor resolved to cleanse the state of heretics, I obeyed. Jews, Monophysites, and Nestorians—I confiscated their property, I forced them to be baptised, I prosecuted them when they resisted, even to death. I believed it was God's will. But then the Emperor himself embraced the heresy of the Monothelites, and ordered me to persecute the orthodox with equal vigour.

"I couldn't do it. I asked myself: if it is wrong to destroy the orthodox, why is it not also wrong to destroy the heretics who have lived among us so long in relative peace?"

Silence fell within the small basilica where the council had gathered. The night was hot and still, full of flickering torches and brooding shadows. In the semidome of the apse, a mosaic of the Christ Pantocrator looked down with a half solemn, half smiling face, one hand upraised in judgement. The smile and the frown, John thought; mercy and judgement met together. For when the proud and haughty of the earth were humbled, the poor were lifted up, and so it ever had been.

But which was he? Which was the Watchers' Council of Syria?

Behind him, Rahel touched his hand, reminding him that she too was on his side. He laced his fingers between hers.

A throat cleared. Constans, the Presbyter of Syria, once his fellow-student in the tutelage of Patriarch Anastasios. *"But though we, or an angel from heaven, preach any other gospel unto you than that which we have preached unto you, let him be anathema.* The emperor made an error of doctrine, John. But true heresy must be stamped out lest we all be accursed."

"Heresy is a dreadful thing," John said tiredly. "It is a thing so dreadful that I am not sure mortals like ourselves should be permitted to wield the sword against it; not even the emperor. For months I studied this, fasted and prayed and wept. But in the end there was no way to escape the truth. I had sinned. The emperor had sinned. All of us have sinned in doing these things. The heretics committed no crime, no strife, no sedition, and we had murdered them."

"Blasphemy!" someone muttered in the shadows. Another of Anastasios' old students, once a friend.

John closed his eyes, suppressing a sigh. Was it not enough that those he had killed still haunted his dreams? A clean kill in battle was one thing—one armed man against another, when the other fellow was certain to kill you if you did not kill him first. It was quite another to harass harmless men, women, and children to recite creeds they did not believe. The heretics he had fought at Yarmouk had come as invaders, and he meant to offer them only hard blows, but the heretics he had persecuted for the emperor had deserved no such cruelties.

"The Presbyter of Palestine has given us much to think about." The silence was broken at length by a Watcher from Mesopotamia, who mopped his shining forehead and smiled brightly. "I suggest that we postpone future discussion until the next Council."

"*Next* Council?" Lukas burst out. Caught off guard, all John could do was watch as his son shoved forward through the crowd, fists clenched with frustration. "We came here for help! We're in the middle of an invasion!"

John caught his elbow. "Not now, Lukas."

The Presbyter's eyes flickered towards Lukas, then away again, and John was chilled by the dispassionate annoyance in Constans' voice as he continued. "An excellent idea, Nicephorus. If there's no dissent…"

Lukas surged forwards again. "*I* dissent!" He shoved up his sleeve, showing the Watcher's Mark tattooed on the inside of his arm beneath the elbow. A thick black *I* and *X* superimposed on each other like the spokes of a rimless wheel, a Watcher's Mark was a trusted sign across the known world, an identifying mark John and the rest of the family shared.

"Don't you understand?" Lukas went on. "We don't have the time to delay. By next year's Council we'll all be *dead.*"

"Nevertheless, this is an issue that shouldn't be decided hastily," said the Watcher from Edessa. "I support an adjournment."

"Then it's decided," Constans said. "Let's move on. Call the Messenger."

John's shoulders slumped in defeat. His suggestion hadn't received a warm welcome at the Council back home in Jerusalem, either. He should have known the Syrians would be no different. But Constans had been his friend. Surely, he'd thought, surely he of all people would understand.

Defeated, John turned to his wife. "Rahel?"

Rahel was already taking Elisa from Marta's arms and carrying the young child onto the council floor. "Let me forgo the Message tonight." She bent down, setting Elisa on the floor. "The child will speak."

Elisa burst into tears and John tried not to let his dismay show on his face. Rahel was a Messenger, a Watcher with the gift of making judgements and foretelling the future. Calling one to ask for a message was part of the procedure of every Watcher's Council, although Messengers, like Portentors or Healers, were rare giftings.

The problem was that Rahel was John's wife, and after the recent debate, any message she delivered would fall under suspicion. It had been her idea to substitute Elisa, and John fought not to show the doubt he felt as the other Presbyters stared at the wailing little girl.

"Are you sure of this, sister?" Constans asked.

"I have the right to appoint my replacement, Presbyter. I appoint Elisa

Bessarion."

Constans lifted an eyebrow at John.

John set his jaw and nodded. Perhaps it was wrong, but all that was keeping him going right now was sheer obstinacy.

Constans returned his nod reluctantly and cleared his throat. "Elisa Bessarion, I name you Messenger for the Council of Watchers. If you have the words, speak."

Elisa kept her face hidden in Rahel's skirts.

"This is useless," the Watcher from Edessa snapped. "Let me send for my slave."

"Hush!" Rahel said.

The basilica fell silent as Elisa lifted her head to stare at the Watchers. When she spoke, her voice had changed: it had become unchildish, relentless. "Heart of stone! Even the ancient Jews must release their slaves at the end of seven years. But you have kept yours years upon years without recompense, without reparation. There are even some that you have maimed in anger."

The Watcher from Edessa fell back a step. John wrenched his gaze from his tiny daughter and glanced around the room: the Council froze as though they had been turned to salt, their faces pale.

Surely they would listen to him now. Surely they would hear and join him in repentance, and the future might yet be saved for them.

"If you will not confess your sins, they will be exposed before all." Elisa turned, pointing. "*You* have dealt cruelly with the strangers which God has sent you to welcome and protect. *You* have dealt treacherously with your wife. *You* have made false accusations of heresy for the enrichment of your own coffers."

With that, the finger landed on Constans and all the anger went out of John in a rush. *Constans* had done this? Oh, *God*.

"You have the witness of your own hearts against you," Elisa continued. "You have had warning after warning and you have refused to heed them. Therefore the guardianship of these provinces is taken from you and given to John Bessarion and his heirs, in whom there is no deceit. The Council of Watchers is disbanded, and the land has vomited you out."

There was a silence as loud as a trumpet. Sweat trickled between John's shoulders. *Am I truly a man of no deceit?* he thought. There were promises he had not yet kept. *But I will. I promise.*

Elisa burst into tears again, her wail loud and startled as though the last few minutes had frightened her as badly as everyone else. Rahel swept the little girl into her arms, hushing her gently.

The Council turned to each other, filling the basilica with a clamour of shock and indignation.

Oh, God, John thought as her final words began to sink in. *How can I protect these lands all by myself?*

Lukas shouldered forward to put a protective arm around his mother. "Let's go," he growled.

Rahel blinked, nodded. "I should take Elisa home."

With an effort, John wrenched himself back to the moment. The distance to the villa was short, but he didn't want Rahel out there on her own. He must have been imagining the heretic in the marketplace; but still. "Lukas, will you...?"

Lukas was only too willing to leave, shepherding his mother out of the shadowed church. As relieved as he felt to have the rash boy away from the Council, John couldn't help feeling a spark of pride. Lukas had seen through the Watchers. His heart was in the right place, but he still had much to learn...John found himself wondering if he should take his son back to Jerusalem with him after all.

He turned, searching the shadows for his second child. Marta was waiting there patiently as usual, watching everything with big expressive eyes. As he turned, she picked up Paulus and balanced the sleepy boy on her hip, although his weight bent her fourteen-year-old frame like a field mouse on a blade of grass.

"I'll stay with you, Abba," she whispered.

"Marta, you don't have to do that. You should go home."

She only smiled at him. If Lukas was a young man of outspoken indignations, Marta was characterised by loyalties no less fierce for their silence. He knew instinctively that she could not bear to leave him alone to face the Watchers' ire on his own, and although there was nothing she could do to help him, he was glad she stayed.

"Bessarion." Constans had gone red in the face, his hostility now open for all to see. "I never would have dreamed it of you, but I must ask: did you tamper with the Messenger?"

The other Watchers stared at him with equal hostility, sending a chill running down John's spine. Elisa had spoken as no mere child could, and it meant nothing to them? "My daughter is *three years old*," he snapped. "Her mouth cannot even shape half the words you just heard her say!"

"Can you really expect us to believe that?"

"Why not consider the possibility that she may have spoken the *truth?*" He lifted his voice, determined not to be drowned out by their objections. "God knows I do not claim any particular righteousness for myself, but as Watchers it is our duty to shield our people from the wrath of heaven. If there is no need to repent of our sins, then how is it that our land lies at the point of conquest for the second time in a generation?"

In the centre of the council, Constans took a deep breath and stepped forward to meet John's gaze. "My friend," he said, and for a moment John thought he really was trying to regain the friendship they'd once had. "My friend, this is not seemly. I think we must ask you to leave."

All the fight went out of him. So he was being thrown out of the Syrian council as he had been thrown out of the Jerusalem council.

"Please," he begged. "*Please* imagine for a moment that you might be wrong. God is gracious. We can still save our future—but only if we are willing to change our ways."

Constans' eyes flickered to his feet. "I understand, Presbyter. You have given us much to discuss and now we must discuss it."

There was nothing else he could say, nothing else he could do. He turned numbly, signalling to Marta. As she and Paulus followed him out of the church, John heard whispering start behind him.

So, he thought, they had failed the test. They could not find compassion for the heretic neighbours who had lived among them and served them so long; and now they would be ruled in turn by the heretics from the desert. His hand, poised against the shadowy door of the basilica, was shaking a little. He took a deep breath and pushed the heavy door open.

Outside, the stars shone on a sleeping town, the day's heat still radiating from the tessellated pavement in the basilica's courtyard. John stood on the church steps, staring up at the sky. *What now?* Would the invaders be kind, at least, to those he had wronged? He shuddered, once again seeing the dust and chaos of the battle. It was doubtful.

Paulus was the first to speak. "Are we going home?"

Both the children were looking at him, waiting for an answer. "We're going back to the villa," he said at last. Constans' villa, two rooms of which he'd loaned them for the duration of their stay in Oliveta. A stay which no doubt would be cut short in the morning. John couldn't help but feel relieved. Tired and aching as they might be from the journey, he wouldn't sleep easy until he knew his family were on their way to Constantinople and safety.

Marta nodded and let Paulus down to the ground, kissing his head affectionately; John put out a hand to ruffle the little boy's hair with a twinge of worry.

Once he said goodbye, would he ever see his children again?

He was becoming morose as he aged. John shook his head and beckoned the children across the pavement, but they hadn't made it more than halfway across the courtyard when footsteps echoed through the street beyond and Lukas pelted through the archway.

"Mother's had a vision," he gasped. "Heretics. A raid."

Between one heartbeat and the next all his fears came to life.

Before he'd been a husband, father, or Presbyter, John Bessarion had been a cataphract in the Persian wars, and he had seen enough destruction to know how vulnerable Oliveta was. He was back at the door of the church almost before Lukas finished speaking, seizing the latch. "Heretics! Heretics! Raise the alarm!"

The latch resisted him. Locked.

John fell back in disbelief. No sword; he'd left it behind as a gesture, to show he came—for once—as a man of peace. His heart almost stopped, then started again, beating like the drums of doom.

He turned, waving to the children. "Lukas. Marta. Take Paulus and run to the hills. Find your mother, go to Antioch, and get a ship for Constantinople. *Don't return.*"

Lukas looked stubborn. "What about you?"

"Don't wait for me."

"Abba, no," Marta whispered.

Her words were drowned out by Lukas' eruption. "Do you think I'm a coward? I'm going to stay with you. I want to fight."

Marta touched her brother's sleeve. "Shh. Listen."

A sound like distant thunder rolled toward them, resolving into the beat of hooves.

They had found him.

Why, *why* did he bring his family to this benighted place?

"I should have told you." He stepped forward, grabbing Marta and Lukas by a shoulder each. "I know who this is. I know why he's here. He won't stop until he finds me. You have to leave."

There was still a chance, he reminded himself, just a chance that this was not who he feared it was. Since the great defeat there must be thousands of heretics in the eastern parts of Syria. Any one of them might have chosen this moment for a raid on a small unwalled town.

But then the hoofbeats rolled to a stop, and a shadow appeared in the archway. A tall man in a dark cloak, appearing like a spectre in a dream.

All hope died.

"Abba?" Marta whispered as he went stiff with dread.

"I am not here to fight, John Bessarion." From the gateway, Khalil ibn Hassan spoke accented Greek. "You know why I am here."

His fists clenched uselessly. All he could do was step forward, putting his children behind him in a futile gesture of protection. "Yes. I know."

Beyond the courtyard, Oliveta stirred to the clack of hooves, banging doors and shouts.

The heretic spearman moved forward a pace and swept out a slim straight sword, levelling it at John's face. Behind the blade, the heretic's eyes were just as keen and sharp. "Be wise. Surrender the weapon without resistance."

John barely heard the words, but the slight rustle of fabric as Lukas shifted his weight struck his ear like a shout.

"Lukas," he snapped, "don't be a fool!"

Khalil gestured, signalling his men forward to surround them with levelled spears.

"The weapon. Where are you hiding it?" the heretic demanded.

Starlight glittered on the blades that surrounded them. John closed his eyes a moment. If it had only been himself facing these men, his course would have been obvious. He would throw himself upon their blades, and die as he had lived, a man of the sword.

The spear in Antioch was Jerusalem's last hope. With it, he would have had a fighting chance, but let the heretics get their hands on it, and all hope would indeed be lost. The best he could do was try to bargain with this man, try to come to some agreement. If he had to give up the spear, at least let him try to save his children's lives and the Watchers. "Knowing I held such a thing, do you think I would willingly put it in the hands of my enemies?"

In the street outside, someone screamed. Behind John, Paulus gave a terrified sob.

"You have not destroyed it," Khalil said. "I should have known if you had."

"Perhaps I might," John said. "Perhaps it is too dangerous a thing to exist."

Khalil smiled. "I think not. You need it too much."

"But *you* do not. Your armies have conquered Arabia and most of Syria. The armies of the orthodox have perished. So what brings Khalil ibn Hassan through miles of enemy territory with only a handful of men to retrieve it? Answer me that. Then perhaps, I will know how to answer."

Khalil's eyes were hard. "He who has the strongest weapons holds power over men. But you spin out the time to no purpose, John Bessarion. Lead me to it."

John fought back the urge to speak: Khalil must not guess that he was desperate to make a bargain. The man was stubborn, fanatical. If he decided to slaughter the whole town and John along with them, there was nothing John could do to stop him. Best to give in—

The despairing thoughts touched his mind like the brush of wings. Instantly John knew they were not his own, but even so it took a moment to shake them off. He occupied his mind with other things.

By some sorcery Khalil had followed them to Oliveta, but that sorcery could not have shown him where the spear was hidden. If John died, he would take the secret of the spear's hiding-place to the grave with him. Khalil's threat was empty.

As the night beyond the courtyard filled with the sounds of pillage and violence, John looked into the heresiarch's eyes and smiled.

It was a mistake. Khalil's eyes were suddenly cruel. "Kill his children."

The ring of blades around them tightened like a garotte, and John's gut clenched. "No," he barked, as though the heretics were his own men. He narrowed his eyes at Khalil. "Touch them and I promise you'll never find the weapon."

Khalil raised a hand, halting his men. Behind John, a scuffle sounded at the door of the basilica as the Watchers within finally heard the sounds of battle without and tried to get out. There was a confused shout and a scream of pain as the heretics at the door thrust them inside again, locking the Watchers within.

They would have been no help anyway. Few of the Watchers were fighting men, and those who were, like himself, left their weapons behind when they gathered.

Khalil bent his head to speak in his own tongue to a raider who had come from the town with a message. John caught a few of the words, and a shake of the man's head; and again, he permitted himself a grim smile.

Khalil turned back to him. "The town has been searched. There is no sign of the weapon." He paused. "Tell me where to find it, and I'll spare your children."

Lukas erupted: "Don't tell him. Whatever it is, that weapon should belong to *us.*"

"Peace, Lukas." John kept his relief hidden; the bargain was not made yet, but at least the man was willing to deal with him. "How can I trust you to keep your word?"

"You can trust me to kill them if you refuse."

Khalil narrowed his eyes at John, and the assault on his mind intensified. This time not fear but rage was the tactic: *It's no good. He's too powerful. Why bargain? Why die crawling on your belly? You have a knife, draw it and charge. Buy a quick death, a warrior's death, a red death.*

It was a voice he'd heard far too often in his life. Heard, and listened to. As if by its own will, John's hand inched towards the knife at his belt. The raiders surrounding him edged closer, their eyes watchful, but all John could hear, echoing in his head, was that voice of honour and bloodlust.

How many of these heretics could he take with them? More than one, for all their armour and weapons. Or he could throw his knife. He heard it in his mind, thwacking wetly into Khalil's unguarded throat. He could die avenging himself. A red death. A warrior's death.

His fingers brushed the hilt as bloody images flashed through his mind. The broken bodies of the heretics who'd died at his command, the detritus of the towns he'd sacked. If he did this he would doom his children. Perhaps the whole town.

John recoiled a step, yanking his hand from the hilt as though it burned him.

"It isn't in Oliveta," he blurted. "I left it in the heart of Antioch, hidden with the bones of my old tutor, the Patriarch Anastasius. Look for it in the great basilica—if you dare!"

The bloody thoughts vanished like foam in the backwash of a wave. The pent-up tension washed through John's body and he found that he was laughing almost hysterically.

Khalil's self-command shattered. Baring his teeth, he swore in his own language and threw himself on John with knotted fists. Seeing him coming, John dropped to his knees and curled over, shielding his head with his arms. Feet and fists pummelled him, pain bursting like sparks behind his eyelids. *Dying on my belly, like a worm, after all.* He suppressed the thought at once. John had lived thirty-six years and seen war for thirty of them; he ought to have learned long ago that highborn honour was all very well, but sometimes it was better to take a beating and live.

He'd rather his children saw him like this and live to remember it, than let them die watching him throw himself on their enemies' swords.

The beating stopped as abruptly as it began, leaving him gasping with pain. Close by, bells were ringing. The Watchers in the basilica had sounded the alarm at last.

Would anyone hear? Would anyone answer? Bara, the nearest town, was three hours' walk. A fast horse could do it in half an hour. If someone *had* a fast horse. If someone set out at once.

He must go on talking, try to delay, try to make the bargain. John got to knees and elbows, wheezing. "Rage all you like, it will not open Antioch's gates to you."

"No," Khalil agreed. Still breathing hard, the heretic turned, signalling to soldiers outside the courtyard. The gate darkened with people as the citizens of Oliveta were herded through, sobbing and limping. Raiders at the church door hauled the Watchers out as others lit torches, flooding the courtyard with glaring red light.

Why were they being herded into this one place? Suddenly, a chill of fear slid down John's spine, and he found that he was covered in cold sweat.

He'd seen enough of war to know what came next.

"Rage may not get me into Antioch, but power will," Khalil said. He gazed around them at the sobbing people packed into the courtyard. "Those who inhabit the waste places, the silences of the desert, know that there is power to be found in destruction. But the ritual requires blood and perversity. I do not know if there is enough in this whole town."

He'd gone too far; and now Khalil was about to do...what? Something that set his scalp prickling, and more of those voices whispering in his spirit.

Behind John, Marta moved suddenly, swinging her arm out. There was a red flash as her own knife left her hand and shot through the air, directly at the heresiarch.

Khalil twisted aside and the blade clattered harmlessly on the tessellated pavement.

Somehow, John found himself on his feet again. "I can get you into Antioch," he shouted. "Don't be a fool, Khalil."

Khalil took no notice of his pleas. Instead, he took a brush and a pot of whitewash from one of his lackeys, bending to draw an intricate sigil upon the colourful geometric patterns underfoot. The design was more or less diamond-shaped, a point towards each cardinal direction. Working in methodical silence, he traced ancient symbols, words in an incomprehensible flowing script.

John smelled smoke, a thin eddy on the air. By degrees, a red glare filled the sky around them and beyond the courtyard, flames began to lick the sky. Seeing the flames, the terrified people crowded into the courtyard began to wail in fear.

"Khalil," John bellowed again. "You don't have to do this. We can bargain!"

Khalil straightened, surveying his design in pride. Then he stepped over to John and looked him in the eye.

"Does the lion make bargains with the worm?"

Hands fell on John's shoulders, wrestling him to the easternmost point of the design. With a few quick yanks, his limbs were tied together and he was shoved to his knees at the eastern point of the design. The heretics grabbed his children, dragging them to each of the compass-points, forcing them to kneel within painted circles at each point: Marta south, Paulus north, and Lukas west.

Stepping into the sigil, Khalil moved to each of them in turn, marking them on the forehead with a finger dipped in paint. "There are many *djinn* and *afrit* in the deserts and mountains, from the hairy jackals that inhabit lost cities to the Pestilence by Day and the Destruction by Night. For a sacrifice, they will give me the power to destroy Antioch. You have sealed your fate, John Bessarion." He stepped into the centre, lifting his hands. "Poison Mother, to you I make this sacrifice." The firelight flickered in his eyes. *"Kill them all."*

Helpless, John looked at his children. All the fight had gone out of Lukas, and tears stained his cheeks as he stared up at Khalil in dread. To his left,

Marta knelt in her ring staring at Paulus with her lips moving; praying for him, perhaps willing him to be brave. To his right, Paulus lay in his circle firmly trussed, his body shaking with terrified sobs.

There was nothing, nothing at all, that he could do to protect them.

"Don't look. Cover your eyes," John tried to say, but his throat had gone dry and his voice was lost among the screams of the people of Oliveta as the heretics moved among them cutting throats.

It was worse than any battlefield he had known. As their bodies fell, thin streams of blood traced the knotwork and labyrinths of the pavement. Khalil threw his arms out as he began to chant, his voice a loud rumble beneath the awful, piercing sound of the massacre.

For a slow, agonising minute there was only a nightmare of sound, the hot metallic scent of blood—and then a blistering wind screamed down on them, making sheets of flame billow from the embers of the town. Amidst the firestorm, whirling shapes appeared.

Malice poured down, a chatter and snick of blades like the feathers of massive birds. Voices clamoured in his head—terror, agony, rage—and his mind drowned beneath their roar. Above him, Khalil thrust out his arm, baring the skin, calling a name three times; and one of those black and birdlike shapes settled upon it.

A harpy with the head of a black-haired woman, its claws sank into Khalil's arm as it leaned down to press a kiss upon his mouth.

The sound of retching stole John's attention. In his own circle just beyond reach, Paulus convulsed with fear; then, flailing like a fish, he pushed himself across the white painted lines.

The still-wet paint smeared.

In that moment's silence, as heaven and earth drew breath, John could have sworn he could hear the spell crack, heard gleeful voices shrieking in the wind. *Mother! Let us feed!*

Khalil's voice faltered. Then he screamed; the whole earth was screaming.

The bladed wings chattered as black shapes poured down in a deadly torrent.

Chapter III.

Soraya hated dying. One moment she was alive, poised atop the wall in a world of laughter and wind and sunlight, the next she was a spirit of smokeless fire: blind, deaf, and mute to all but the other spirits around her. They flickered like bright flames as her soul tether snapped taut, whisking her across the city.

The shadowy shapes and muffled voices of the bright world of matter streamed helplessly past her, then vanished as she was sucked back into her prison. It was a narrow place; voiceless and eyeless, where she could only *be* and *remember.*

And that was the worst thing. Although she had no access to her memories, she could still sense them somewhere beyond the spells that held her. She knew she had lived in this prison for uncountable ages, allowed to emerge only when it suited her master. A free djinn could see and interact with the other spirits around her. A djinn trapped within, say, the ring of a sorcerer, however, had even that denied her.

There was only one sense Soraya could use here: taste. Sometimes dust, sometimes water, sometimes grease; but most of the time she tasted blood, and right now her prison was foul with it. With the first metallic taste, more memories flew back to her.

Blood—she had drunk it until she was sick. Armed men flooding through a city on fire, a dead caravan in the desert, every man and beast lying huddled and shapeless; the congealed memories washed over her, making her shiver with the closest thing to nausea that she could experience in this form. Blood sticky and hot on her hands, sweet and cloying in her nostrils.

Instinctively Soraya fought against the unseen bonds that held her.

Let me out! Let me free!

There was no give in her prison, but she sensed a jolt of awareness through the soul tether. For once her scream had got through to him. Instinct readied her to be commanded into dormancy but instead, the taste of grease wiped away the blood; and the command, when it came, was unexpected.

Come out, then, and take form.

Obedient, she flashed from her prison. Around Soraya, the city flickered with millions of spirit-fires, but one burned bright and steady nearby, its light intensifying as her master took a stronger grip on the soul-tether.

Soraya had only a few days' worth of memories, but it was clear already that he didn't trust her. She couldn't fault him on that. Somehow she knew he never had—in the same way she knew she had never trusted him either.

Compelled by his command, she reached out blindly and *pulled.*

She never quite saw what happened in this process, but she could imagine it. First the air moved, creating a vortex. Dust and water-droplets flew in, creating a funnel of raw elements. Connections sparked between the tiny particles. More and more links formed; the wind grew stronger. Sensation grew as she merged with the whirlwind, fashioning bone, blood vessels, organs.

Unlike most djinn, Soraya did not need to possess a mortal in order to assume physical form. Instead, she was able to create her own vessel from her surroundings. Within moments she was embodied again. Smooth flagstones stretched across the great dim underground room in which she found herself, cooling her newly formed feet. Light filtered in through high windows, gently illuminating the racks of swords and spears lining the walls. A young man who stood opposite her wiping bloody hands on a greasy rag—her master.

"Explain yourself," he said tightly.

Soraya tilted her head experimentally. "Oh, how nice. I'm not hungover anymore."

He moved forward, throwing down the rag in disgust. A carnelian on his finger glowed like the door to hell, and Soraya stared at it hungrily. The ensorcelled ring. Her prison. If only—

"God have mercy! You got *drunk?*"

Soraya blinked with mock innocence. "Oh, it was the *drink?* Should I have known that? Why didn't you tell me?"

"I didn't think you'd be that foolish," he said, completely missing the sarcasm dripping from her voice. "You were supposed to kill the prince—"

"I did!"

"—and *maintain your disguise,*" he continued, furious. "Instead, after indulging yourself in liquor, you vanished in a cloud of dust in front of the whole marketplace. Now everyone knows it was magic." He paused. "Well?"

"What can I say? Violent bloody death—can't get enough of it. I see a man waving a crossbow, I leap in front of it. Why don't *you* try it sometime?"

"I have."

"Missed you, did he?"

"Quiet," he snapped and Soraya's mouth locked shut.

That was just another lovely feature of being enslaved—she was incapable of disobeying any of her master's commands. As her mouth sealed, Soraya's heart plunged. This had happened a thousand times before, she could feel it. How often had she killed for this man? How long had this been going on?

He glared. "This is exactly why I can't trust you, Soraya. Each time I ask you to do something useful, you end up stuffing your face or drinking yourself senseless or stealing a racehorse."

That last one sounded like fun. *Still, you'd know better than me,* Soraya thought bitterly. With her memories stolen, he must know her better than she knew herself. The one thing she held onto, with a knowledge engraved deep on her bones, was that escape had become a consuming passion for her. Locked in her prison, she had nothing else to dream of.

Soraya studied her captor for a moment in silence. With an aquiline nose, a carefully-trimmed beard and smooth, unwrinkled skin, her master could have been any age between eighteen and thirty-five. His fine silk tunic and impeccable grooming suggested that he was a man of some wealth and standing; his stance proclaimed him either a dancer or a fighter.

Given the spear in the crook of his arm, certainly a fighter.

A pretty man, though mortal men held little appeal for her. As for this one, he only filled her with bitter resentment. What had made him purge her memories two days ago? She must have learned something, something important. Maybe how to escape him. There was no recovering the memory now, but once again Soraya's eyes fastened on the carnelian ring on his finger.

His eyes—a pale, intense grey-green—narrowed. "What is it? Speak."

The command almost forced her to reveal her thoughts of escape. In the nick of time, she substituted another question: "Why have me kill the future sultan? He would have been a wise ruler."

"I only act on orders of my own," he said, a little too quickly.

So there was someone controlling both of them. "But *why?*"

"What difference does it make?" He crossed to one of the racks, selected a spear, and tossed it through the air to her.

As Soraya's hands closed around the shaft, knowledge flowed through her body and she sank into an instinctive crouch. "I had to pour poison down his throat," she hissed. "I'd like to think there was a reason for it."

He looked at her with surprise and perhaps a little dawning respect as he came on guard. His voice rang sincere: "I don't know the reason. All I know is that things will be better this way; for Egypt, for everyone, God willing."

"Really?" Soraya slid forward in a lunge, her spear darting in and out like a snake's tongue. "I asked about the next heir last night. Al-Ashraf Khalil. A pleasure-seeking idiot."

Her master parried her strike and pressed back with a lightning-fast attack. "He'll change now."

"Oh?"

He lunged forward, his spear aimed squarely at her chest. Soraya bent backwards in a dancer's move, letting the blade pass harmlessly through the air above her. In the same moment she whipped her own spear around one-handed, bludgeoning her master in the ribs. Not expecting the blow, he stumbled aside with a gasp.

Soraya rebounded upright, breathing hard. "And you? Who did *you* kill this morning?"

He regained his balance and paused, staring at her with a hand pressed to his aching side. "What?"

"You get a lot of blood on your hands, don't you?" she asked tightly. "Who was it this morning?"

"That's none of your business."

"Are you trying to make this master of yours sultan?"

"You ask too many questions."

"Only because I don't have enough answers. I don't even know your name," she added bitterly. *"You* saw to that."

He let go of his aching ribs and charged at her again. Soraya stepped aside deftly and parried, watching his hands, his footwork, the ring on his finger.

Perhaps, if she could injure him badly enough…

Soraya made the same attack three times, lulling him into a pattern. On the fourth attempt, she feinted. When he parried, her spear wasn't there to meet it. As his own weapon flew wide, Soraya lunged, pinning him in the right shoulder.

He groaned and staggered back a step, leaving her blade glistening with blood. Soraya lunged again, expecting an easy victory with his right arm crippled. Instead, he batted her spearpoint away and fell back a few steps, shrugging casually as though stretching a knotted muscle.

The soul tether pulled on her, loosening her grip on her body and making the room swim dizzily before her eyes. Soraya's gut churned with dread as she guessed the true extent of her connection with this man.

He smirked and pulled off his shirt, showing smooth unmarked skin where the wound from her spear should have been. "You know, this happens every time. Each time I purge your memory, you're unhappy till you've put a blade in me."

She ground her teeth. Well, of course if she could actually *hurt* him, he'd never be sparring with her like this, with sharps. It was the soul tether that was keeping him alive, of course. Her own immortality, her own strength and speed flowing to him through the ring that connected them. Without that connection, her power would have ended this fight before it began.

He twirled the spear, still smirking. "So. Are we done yet?"

Soraya bared her teeth. "No."

She launched herself forward, all her focus on the ring. As he lunged to meet her attack, she whirled his spear to one side and dropped her own, throwing all her weight at his midriff. He collapsed under her onslaught and she snatched the knife from his belt, grabbing for his wrist.

So he could steal enough of her power to heal instantly from his wounds? All right. Let him regrow a finger.

Without warning, dizziness clogged her vision, sending her stroke wide. Beneath, he bucked and rolled. Now he was on top. Soraya gasped as his hand crushed the bones in her wrist, forcing her to drop the knife.

The soul tether. He's drawing on my strength.

Two could play that game. Focusing on the tether, Soraya gritted her teeth and yanked. A measure of power flowed back into her before he tightened his own grip—too late to stop her. Soraya lunged up, cracking her forehead against his nose. She heard the cartilage snap, and he reeled backwards with a cry of agony. Soraya followed. Though he was immune to injury, he was still vulnerable to pain, and that she could use. She landed on his chest and brought an elbow down hard on his throat to disable his vocal cords and prevent him issuing more commands. His body spasmed and he dropped the knife, just out of her reach. Soraya dove for the blade, but as her weight left his chest he dragged strength back through the tether and lunged after her.

She drove the knife towards his hand again. He grabbed her wrist, and for an instant they wrestled, evenly matched over both knife and power.

Then slowly he began to get the upper hand, wrestling more and more strength through the soul tether. Feeling her arms weaken, Soraya let go of soul tether and knife both at the same time. Caught off guard, he nearly toppled to the side, just catching himself.

She lunged up at him with bared teeth just as he found his voice again.

"No biting," he rasped. "Fight's over."

Soraya's teeth snapped shut, and she stared up at him mutinously.

The ghost of a smile crossed his lips. "This is the point at which I usually introduce myself. Al-Mukhtar Saif al-Din. Most of the time you call me Saif. You aren't very respectful, God have mercy on you."

There was something in his eyes that was almost affectionate. Almost. He'd forbidden her to bite and he was holding her leash so tight that he was nearly pulling her spirit away from this constructed body. As though she was a dog, a plaything to be praised when obedient and whipped when otherwise. Suddenly, passionately, she could imagine one person whose blood she *did* want on her hands, slick between her teeth.

Instead, Soraya did the only thing she still could: she leaned up and kissed him forcefully, spitefully. Saif recoiled with a sound of horror. The next instant she was able to grab enough strength to jump to her feet and face him, breathing hard.

"Did I surprise you that time?" she snarled.

Every hint of affection was gone, his face like a chip of granite. "You will await further orders in—"

All defiance evaporated. "No," she whispered. "Don't lock me away again. *Please—*"

"You will await further orders in confinement," he repeated, louder. He stamped the butt of his spear on the flagstones, and Soraya's body fell away as she was drawn back into the dark, stifling narrowness of her prison.

Chapter IV.

John must have blacked out a moment, for he jerked into consciousness with a yell that bubbled away from his mouth. Water was everywhere: cold, dark and impetuous, spinning him like a grain of sand in a storm. His lungs ached, craving air as he searched hopelessly for sunlight, moonlight, anything to show him the way up.

Everything was black as night, suggesting an alternative explanation for his predicament. *I'm dreaming,* he told himself with a sharp sense of relief. For an instant John stopped fighting, allowing the water to carry him where it willed.

The next instant he broke surface and the will to fight rushed back like a flood. John gasped for air before the angry water spun him into an eddy and pulled him down again, rushing in on his indrawn breath. His lungs spasmed, immobilising him as he tried to cough it back up.

This was no dream. He was going to drown.

No sooner did the thought flash through his mind than a strong current grabbed him, tumbling him over and over until suddenly he was thrown against a bank of soft earth. With a sob of relief John latched onto the deeply-rooted waterweeds and clawed his way out onto a reedy bog. He stayed there for a moment, waist-deep in water, gasping, coughing, and shivering in the unseasonal cold.

In the dark, there was not much he could see. The sky was clear and full of stars, the river was a wide torrent behind him and the reeds blocked out most of the landscape ahead, although the black bulk of a large hill seemed to face him further inland. Apart from the rushing water and the sounds of animals hunting, there was no sound at all.

Where *was* he? What had happened at Oliveta?

How could he have been such a *fool* as to take his family there?

John thrashed through water and mud, aiming for the higher ground. Soon, the earth firmed under his feet and he crawled onto a soft, grassy bank shadowed by trees. Exhausted, he collapsed gratefully into the lush grass. He'd only rest a moment—then he'd get up and move on, find someone who could tell him what was going on. He closed his eyes, waiting for his heart to slow; but he found little relief. Flames danced behind his eyelids, blood trickled through the knotted pavement, and Paulus was crying on the ground…

"Children?"

John lifted his head.

Beside him, sitting in the grass, was Rahel.

"Children?" she called again, her voice wobbly with anxiety.

"Rahel?" John pushed himself to his elbow. At first he thought he hadn't slept at all, but the stars had changed place in the sky like a necklace pulled askew by a child, and the moon peeked above the shoulder of the great mound behind. He and Rahel sat beneath the spiky shadows of flax and cypress, and far away an owl hooted.

A faint nimbus of light hung around her, barely visible in the bright moonlight. John reached out to take Rahel's hand, but his fingers passed through her as though she were a spirit. No! He wouldn't believe that. Instead, he fell back onto the grass, covering his face with his hands. "I am only dreaming," he whispered firmly.

"What is this place?" she asked. "Are we in paradise?"

This wasn't the sort of thing a dream would ask. John pulled his hands from his eyes and sat up. "Rahel? Is—is it really you?"

A shadow passed across her face. "I don't know. I thought *I* was dreaming. Are you?"

Rahel Bessarion, the only person he knew who'd question her own existence on a dreamer's word. "Saints, dear heart! It's really you." He reached for her again, but just as before, his hands passed through her like smoke, and she shivered.

"You're alive," she said shakily. "Did they hurt you?"

He moved, testing the aches and pains from the beating Khalil had given him. "Nothing permanent."

"Where are Lukas and Marta? The other two are with me."

Relief cut through him like a knife through a puppet's strings. She was no spirit; she was alive. "Paulus is with you?"

A tight smile, too worried to be completely genuine. "He's well. Lukas and Marta?'

"I wish I knew." John dragged his hands down his face. "After the…after whatever happened, I woke up in the river there. One moment I was in the courtyard in Oliveta with the three elder children; the next, deep water."

What could have happened to Lukas and Marta? He didn't want to imagine.

"I feared you were dead." Rahel's voice wobbled.

"I fear not," he said with grim humour. "And you? How did you find the little ones? Are you safe?"

"You don't have to worry about me," she said quickly. "Tell me what happened to you."

"Not much. I got ashore and fell asleep."

"You *just* fell asleep?"

"Yes, why?"

Rahel touched the tip of her tongue to her lips. "Oliveta was the night before last."

"Impossible."

"Someone must have carried you away from the town," she suggested. "Perhaps you were drugged. What *is* this place?"

John laughed sharply. "I nearly drowned in it. That's all I can tell you."

"Salt water or fresh?"

"Fresh." John briefly considered the possibility that he had somehow ended up in Orontes, the river of Antioch. Impossible. That was a trickle compared to this river.

Rahel stared at the water visible through the reeds, now silvered with moonlight. "The Euphrates, then? But you *couldn't* have gone so far in a single night."

John rubbed his eyes. "One does hear strange stories," he said at last. "Mortal bodies transported from one end of a province to another in the blink of an eye…"

"There's no need to think that," Rahel interrupted, her voice ragged with strain.

"No," he admitted. "Not yet. No matter where this is, Rahel, I promise I'll make my way back to you." He rubbed his temples, thinking. "Try to get to Antioch, and I'll meet you there."

Her brave smile quivered, sending a jolt of dread through him. "What's wrong?"

Her eyes dropped to her hands.

"Rahel, what is it? Don't break it gently."

She shuddered and put a hand to her mouth as though stifling tears. "Oh, John. There were other survivors from Oliveta. Other *raiders.* They carried Paulus out of that inferno, and they found me and Elisa. Now they want us to take them to Antioch so we can hand over some weapon you hid there."

She might as well have punched him in the gut. "Strife," he whispered after a moment.

"Paulus told me you said it was hidden in the crypt of the St. Peter basilica." Her voice was ragged, accusing. "You never told me you had something that people would kill for."

But he didn't have it. He'd left it in Antioch like a fool, and took his family out into the mountains with no protection. Now his wife and children were prisoners of those barbarians.

"How many raiders?" he whispered at length.

"Two."

"Is either of them called Khalil ibn Hassan?"

She shook her head, and John's shoulders slumped in relief. Then there might still be hope. "You mustn't let them have it, do you hear me? *You can't let the heretics lay their hands on that weapon.*"

"But Paulus said you told their leader where to find it."

"I was stalling! I never thought he had a chance of retrieving it!" His voice was rising, too loud. John covered his mouth with his hands, staring at the reeds without seeing them.

"Then what am I supposed to do?"

"I meant to come back for it. I *will* come back for it. But if the worst should happen—if I don't make it back to Antioch—you must make sure it gets to someone who can use it. Even after Oliveta there'll be a few Watchers left. Or, failing that, you must take it to Constantinople and cede it to the emperor."

Rahel was staring at him, uncomprehending. Now her lips thinned. "I meant *how am I supposed to keep myself and the children alive*, John."

Her words cut through him like a knife. It was a time of war, and she shouldn't be on the frontlines like this. "Saints, Rahel. God knows I always meant to protect you from this, but..."

"Is that why you never told me? To protect me?" She couldn't hold back a sob. "It's only been one day, but with every minute that passes, I'm just amazed we're still alive. If I refuse to give them the weapon, we're all dead. Is that what you want?"

"Rahel, *no*. I couldn't—how could I *ever*—" Instinctively, he reached out to pull her into his arms, wanting nothing more than to kiss her tears away and then teach those barbarians a stern, bloody lesson.

His hands slipped through her and he pulled back, biting his lip. Seeing her in such need of him was torment. He was her *husband;* he was the only one who could protect her.

He forced his mind back to the mission. Back to the spear.

"All right. We'll think of some alternative. We'll get you away from them somehow. I'll find out where I am and ride back to you. The one thing we can't do is hand it over to them. This weapon could be our only hope of protecting Syria and Palestine, of keeping any more Olivetas from happening."

Rahel wiped her eyes. "It must be powerful."

"Beyond imagination, and the reason Oliveta perished, the reason we both lost so much, was to keep it *safe*." He lifted a hand to her cheek, more carefully this time, imagining he could feel the smooth soft warmth of her skin. "Sweetheart. I can't dictate to you. I *won't* dictate to you. But if you give up the weapon, that sacrifice will be for nothing."

Her face was tight with stress, but she nodded, putting that brave face on again. An instant later, she abruptly disappeared. John dropped his face into his hands, battling his anxiety. *God, protect my wife and children.* He repeated the words over and over again until they lost all meaning, an endless stream of sound without sense or faith.

John woke abruptly some time later, shivering in the dawn wind. The sky overhead was a crystalline dome of silver-blue. Birds were singing. He was still sprawled in the grass where he had fallen last night, his stomach growling and his body stiff from last night's beating. His embroidered tunic was wet with river-water and dew, holes burned through the thin linen from last night's fire. He got up and stumbled to the river's bank to wash. When John rubbed his forehead, a smear of whitewash came away: remnants of the mark Khalil had made on his brow.

Home. He had to find his way home. How many hours had he already lost?

John glanced around to get his bearings. The sun was rising behind the great mound this side of the river, outlining the small squat shape of the squinch-domed basilica which crowned it. Green pastures washed up the hill's slopes, verdant as midwinter. There was no other building in sight.

Something about this place was somehow familiar. It looked like—

John broke into a run, heading uphill towards the basilica. The slope steepened, making his heart pound before he came upon a path snaking obliquely to the slope. He turned onto it, but didn't stop running until the path lifted him above the cypresses growing by the river.

The great river itself was an intense ribbon of blue bordered with green, snaking its mighty way through a dusty landscape. On the opposite bank to the great mound lay the ruins of a town, jutting skyward like broken teeth. There, a few thin trickles of smoke still rose to the sky, hinting that some inhabitants remained.

John felt dizzy; perhaps from hunger and exertion, perhaps from simple shock. He fell to his knees on the path and his gaze fell on a stone that bordered it. Bearing the marks of ancient chisels, its chipped surface was decorated with a blurred relief of rosettes. The capital of an ancient Assyrian pillar; he would have known it anywhere.

Just as he would know that squinched dome on the hill.

"Nineveh," he breathed.

For the second time in his life, he was standing on the ruins of ancient Nineveh. The river must be the Tigris, hundreds of miles beyond even the river Euphrates. The basilica above was the shrine of the prophet Jonas. That meant the ruins across the river must be Mepsila—but when John had been here nine years ago after the great battle in which Heraclius smashed the Persian armies, Mepsila had been a thriving town.

He didn't understand.

From Oliveta to Nineveh was a journey of hundreds of miles and at least a week on horseback, closer to two if you had no remounts. It had been, at most, two nights since he'd been in Oliveta.

His skin prickled. It *had* been magic: instantaneous transportation across hundreds of miles. It was going to take him weeks to rejoin Rahel—what would happen to her and the children in the meantime?

And why, for the love of God, was Mepsila in *ruins?*

On the river, a flat-bottomed raft had left the far bank and was making its way across the water towards the old ferry point. John hurried down the path again in a dreamlike daze, for the landscape was both familiar and changed. Within ten minutes he was under the cypresses that bordered the river, heading for the crude wooden jetty.

Half a dozen countrymen, with their sheep or donkeys, were waiting on the shore for the ferry. They looked much the same as peasantry anywhere, the men in striped homespun tunics and turbans, the women in shady dark veils. They watched John approach with suspicion, and stopped talking amongst themselves when he said, in Persian, "Good morning."

Feeling their scrutiny, he glanced down at himself ruefully. Alone like this, deep in land contested between Rome and Persia, he would have preferred to pass as a countryman. Instead he stood out in the rumpled linen tunic he'd been wearing to the council at Oliveta. Despite the mud-stains ruining the fabric, the embroidered claves running from shoulders to hem marked him as a man of high status, to say nothing of his gold signet ring and a very good pair of leather sandals. In comparison with the small stature and sunken cheeks of the hard-living peasants, he was tall and well-fed with sinewy arms and legs.

He cleared his throat, gestured toward the ruins on the other side of the river. "Can anyone tell me what happened to Mepsila?"

They stared at him in silent distrust. Further off, there was a splash and bump as the ferry touched the jetty and began to tie up.

"Fares to Mosul!" the ferryman shouted. "Half a dirhem each way, children free!"

John turned sharply, every nerve screaming alarm. It took a moment for his conscious mind to catch up with his reflexes: the language the ferryman had spoken was one he knew, one he'd learned on espionage missions during the Persian wars.

Not Persian, not Greek. Arabic.

No one had noticed his surprise. John took a deep breath, forcing his heart to slow as he followed the peasants down the jetty and onto the boat. Now that they weren't staring at him in hostile silence, he caught snatches of their conversation.

They didn't *look* like the desert tribesmen. It made no sense. The heretics hadn't made it as far north as *Mepsila,* and even if they had, there was no way they'd already have the peasants speaking Arabic.

The ferryman asked him for his fare. He dug into his pouch, his heart in his throat as he extracted one of the few small silver coins left within. The ferryman frowned at the strange coin with its Greek inscription, and John breathed long and slow, preparing for action. He might toss the man into the shallows, run for the trees and the sanctuary of Saint Jonas—

"I can't give you change for it." The ferryman offered the coin back to him.

John released his pent-up tension. "Keep it; I don't mind."

"Come on then, I don't have all day." The ferryman's hands hovered on the mooring-ropes. With a deep breath, John stepped aboard.

His uneasiness only worsened as he followed the other passengers off the ferry and up the gravelled riverbank to ruined Mepsila. Even in ruins, everything was wrong: those brick horseshoe arches, that crumbled bit of tunnel vaulting; this wasn't the Mepsila he remembered. Feeling more disoriented with every step, he passed through overgrown streets to the central square where a market had been set up. A small caravan had taken over one side of the open forum. Peasants seemed to have flocked to meet it and each other, trading food and drink for small items from the merchants' wares—pottery, tinware, broadcloth.

Here at last John saw something undeniably familiar: the roofless hall of the city's great basilica. Memory struck him, bittersweet, as he made his way between the awnings of two merchant stalls and entered beneath the round arch and denuded tympanum of the door. Beyond, he paused with another twist of the gut. The caravan had chosen the basilica as a pen for its camels and horses.

It was hard to believe he had once attended Divine Liturgy here. Frescoes, mosaics, plaster, gilt and altar were all long gone, leaving only weathered stone in their wake and the gentle whicker of horses, the grumbling of camels. John took a deep breath, fighting back his anger. The merchants were not at fault for this sacrilege and destruction; clearly it was not they who had destroyed his people's future.

A boy was busy carrying water to a makeshift trough for the camels to drink—a great stone bowl which John recognised, sadly, as the old font. As the boy poured another bucket into the bowl and straightened, he caught sight of John and his eyes widened in fear.

Hastily, John pushed back his sleeve to show his Watcher's Mark. "Don't be afraid, son. I'm looking for anyone else who carries this mark. I'm a Presbyter, John Bessarion—"

Footsteps crunched in the doorway behind him. "You're trespassing, stranger."

Startled, John turned and found himself facing a dark-haired man as pale and massive as the Varangian mercenaries of the far North. Evidently some sort of caravan guard, his hand rested casually on the hilt of the biggest sword John had ever seen.

The boy edged past them with his buckets, and the young giant thumbed his sword loose in its scabbard. He watched John with eyes that missed nothing—not the way John moved into a fighter's crouch when startled, not the way his hands had gone to his waist to find a weapon, nor how his eyes skimmed his surroundings for something to fight with.

John forced himself to back a step, straighten, show his hands. "I beg your pardon," he said, making swift deductions. The other man's Arabic was good, but not quite native. That pale, with raw northern features, there was a good chance this man was in truth a Varangian, possibly in the emperor's service. "My name is John Bessarion."

"That supposed to mean something to me?"

So, maybe not everyone in the Roman army had heard the stories. Who was this man, this far east, speaking Arabic, and amidst some sort of desert tribe or merchant caravan to which he clearly didn't belong? A renegade? Or an imperial spy? It had to be one of them. Never mind that the man's commanding officer was crazy sending someone so obviously foreign on a mission deep into Persian territory.

John lowered his voice. "You aren't one of these people, are you, friend?"

The guard's eyes narrowed. "What do you want from me?"

"I only want to go home." John spoke clearly, softly. "If you're playing a dangerous game, I don't want to spoil it. I just need some help."

"Who are you working for?"

"At present? No one. I just want to go home to Antioch."

John caught a flash of…*something* in the guard's eyes. The hair on his neck prickled, but after a fractional pause the other man stood aside, motioning towards the doorway. Every sense on alert, John murmured his thanks and moved toward the market outside.

The attack came exactly when he expected it, at the moment he stepped past the northerner and lost sight of him.

A rustle of quick movement. Steel humming in the wind. A hand grabbing at his shoulder—missing. John was already diving forward, somersaulting across the hard ground and springing to his feet again on the other side of the arch, among the market stalls. To his left, a striped awning was held up by a slender pole and John twitched it away, dumping the awning onto the heads of the merchant and shoppers beneath.

At the door of the church, the guard recovered his balance and blinked at John in surprise. John smiled tightly back at him. In this fight, what he lacked in comparative height and bulk he made up for in speed, maneuverability, and a whole lifetime's worth of battles.

He'd outlived many of his friends, and there were few tricks he hadn't learned. John let the tip of his makeshift lance touch the ground, but he kept his knees soft and his balance centred. If he needed to move again, he'd be ready.

"Is something wrong?" he asked, not disagreeably, for part of him felt as though it was waking up again after a long sleep.

The northerner snarled. "You've been following me."

"Certainly not."

"You're spying for the Egyptians."

That left him speechless. Egypt wasn't a power; it was only the breadbasket of the Roman empire. Simply another province, like Syria—he'd said *nothing* about Egypt.

The northerner growled and strode forward, transferring his knife to his left and drawing his sword. John lifted his tentpole. Made of springy wood, it was a laughable weapon against a man in mail shirt and padded gambeson.

For the moment, the sputtering merchant beneath the awning had not yet fought his way free, and this part of the square was less full of people; there was a clear way behind to retreat. The other man had the advantage of power; John, merely of reach. As the northerner advanced, John backed away, waiting for his moment.

When the guard lunged, John stepped back and whipped his tentpole through the air, dealing a stinging blow to the face. The guard roared with pain, his sword flailing wide. John withdrew again, careful to let neither his weapon nor his body get in the way of that massive blade. "Really, my friend, I'm not working for anyone, and I don't want to hurt you."

The northerner only roared again and advanced, sword held high, ready to strike. John shifted away from the basilica, into the square, attracting attention from the onlookers—some cheering the skirmishers on, others crying shame on them.

"Stand and fight, you coward," the guard yelled, making another useless lunge.

"I don't want to fight you!" *Trust me, friend: you do not want to know how I made my name.*

Another lunge and the northerner paused to catch his breath, giving John his first opening in several stances. A few more paces, and his back would be up against a wall. With limited mobility, he'd be helpless under that sword. It was a stupid quarrel, a stupid reason to kill a man; but it was that, or die and leave Rahel and the children without protection.

In the heartbeat that the guard hesitated, John lunged, this time wielding the tentpole like a spear.

He aimed for the guard's Adam's apple, apart from his face the only vulnerable point on him. A difficult target, requiring precision to be effective. Had the guard moved an inch to either side his blow would have gone wide, but once more the northerner's sluggish weight worked against him. John's tentpole stabbed home and his opponent reeled, dropping his sword and clutching his throat.

"Butros! Simmer down!" A merchant pushed his way through the crowd, hobbling vigorously on a crutch. A dark-skinned, stocky man with a black beard, his turban had fallen from his head in the struggle with the awning. Recognising him, John returned the tentpole with a bow.

The merchant glanced at John in surprise before using his crutch to shove Butros' sword out of reach. "What are you doing, friend? What have you done to Butros?"

John sighed. If he'd been thinking straight he would have hidden his gold signet ring, at least.

Beside the merchant, the northerner was still holding his throat, choking. Now he collapsed onto his knees, his eyes wide and panicked, his chest heaving in a frantic bid for air. Only strange, desperate grunts escaped his lips as he reached out in some wild appeal.

"What's wrong with him?" the merchant insisted, clearly worried.

"I collapsed his windpipe. He can't breathe." He had shed enough blood in his life, and he meant not to waste any more lives if he could help it. John scanned the market-place and pointed. "Get me the Persian water-pipe from that stall. Now!"

"Do as he asks!" the merchant implored the onlookers, as John stepped over to the frantic Butros and shoved him down onto his back in the street. Within moments, someone had dragged the entire brass contraption over to John. He yanked one of the small brass pipe fittings from the water-pipe's mouthpiece, and fell to his knees straddling the northerner's chest.

"Lie still if you want to live." Sticking the mouthpiece between his teeth, John drew his dagger with his right hand and grabbed the man's forehead with his left. His jab with the tentpole had merely bruised and collapsed the windpipe rather than puncturing it. Now, John traced a finger down the labouring throat, positioned his dagger and carefully punched it through the skin, inserting the small brass pipe. Butros made a sound of pain, fighting him as he tried to get the pipe through the welling wound. For an instant, John was afraid that it might be too late already—that he might have killed the man.

But then the pipe went in. Beneath John, the man's chest expanded. Air whistled through the brass tubing.

John rose to his feet, careful not to let his bloody hands drip on his tunic. "There. He ought to live. I'm terribly sorry."

There was a moment's silence. John realised that he was surrounded by Arabic-speaking strangers, all of them staring at him in something between awe and horror.

His attacker—Butros—elbowed himself to a sitting position, breathing noisily. "Who *are* you?" His voice was faint and rasping, but it was still there.

John sighed. "My name is John." He held out his arm, showing the Mark. "I'm working for no one but myself, and I'm a Presbyter of the Watchers.

That's all."

The sight of the Watcher's Mark had a peculiar effect on the ring of bystanders; as though it was a leper's sore, they backed away and dispersed, muttering. Only Butros snorted—in something that bordered on amused incredulity. "Prester John? You don't say."

"Easy there, friend." The lame merchant drew him aside into the shadow of a ruined wall. "I'd keep that mark covered if I were you, John."

John blinked in polite bafflement.

"People who show that mark east of the Lebanon tend not to live very long." The man's right hand touched his own left forearm. "Good to meet you, friend. I'm Thomas Zakar, fine plain silks, from Tripoli."

Tripoli, in the Lebanon. John blinked again. Another Watcher? And with *that* name, too—for the first time that day, he felt as though he had found someone he could trust. He grabbed the stocky merchant's arm where a Mark would be, and held on like a drowning man. "What has happened to this city? This is Mepsila—isn't it?"

Zakar seemed faintly intimidated by John's desperation, but he responded with a mellow calm John was beginning to think habitual. "This is Mosul on the Tigris. Got burned by the Tartars twenty-eight years ago. They're serious men. Don't do things by halves."

Twenty-eight years? John turned, looked over the ruined basilica to the great mound of ancient Nineveh and the squinched dome of the shrine atop it.

Zakar tried to pull away, but John tightened his grip. "Wait. The great battle, when Emperor Heraclius defeated the Persians. When was that?"

"The *emperor* Heraclius? Wait, you mean the emperor of the Greeks?" Now Zakar looked distinctly unsettled. "He lived six hundred years ago, friend."

Chapter V.

"Nineveh." Rahel said numbly. "Well, that's a little further than we thought, but it shouldn't take you more than a week or two to get back."

John's voice shook. "There's more. I don't know how to tell you this."

Tonight, he had lain down to sleep at the foot of a tree growing amidst the ruins. Now, his dreamself faced Rahel in the tree's shadow, the night around them clear and full of stars. Not too far away, the camels of the caravan grumbled in their sleep.

Rahel darted him a worried look. "Are you hurt?"

His bruises were developing into large, purple blotches that speckled his body. Zakar—apparently unconcerned that John might be a dangerous madman—had loaned him a comfrey salve, but even in his dreams John could feel the persistent ache.

"No, I'm well." He swallowed. "Listen, Rahel. Things have changed so much. Mepsila is ruined—surely we would have heard *something*. Everyone speaks Arabic now and…" he took a deep breath. "They say they have heard of the great battle of Nineveh. They say it was six hundred years ago."

From Zakar's talk, John had gleaned something of the tale of the intervening centuries. He took a shaky breath, still trying to come to grips with all that had happened. The Arab invasion had not stopped with Syria; now heretics ruled from Spain to India. Some were barbarians from the remote plains of Asia: Turks, Tartars.

"I don't understand." Rahel was trying to hold back tears. "What are you trying to tell me? When are you coming home?"

He buried his face in his hands as his own tears spilled over. "I'm trying to tell you I can't; not without a miracle. Khalil performed magic in Oliveta that night, and I woke up in the Tigris river not just miles away, but centuries." He sniffed, looking up into her horrified face. "Even if I return to Syria, it's too late. I won't find you. No matter how long it takes, it will be hundreds of years too late."

Fear crumpled her face, disrupting her dream. Her ghostly form began to disintegrate. "It can't be…John! No!"

Desperately, John reached for her. "Rahel! Dear heart, don't leave me!"

She vanished, and John's racing heart jolted him awake, into a night darker and more dreary than his dream. She was gone. John fell back with a groan, haunted by the anguish on her face.

Determination swept through him. It didn't matter how many years it had been; if Khalil had sent him through time one way, he could be sent home again.

He got up and prowled out of the little ruined house where he'd bivouacked. A campfire burned in the forum; near it, a slow breath whistled through a piece of brass water-pipe. The breath hitched a little when he approached, and in the firelight John saw Butros' hands tighten on a peculiar weapon that resembled nothing so much as a small, light ballista, with a short thick bow mounted crosswise on a heavy shaft.

John stopped a spear's length away. "Butros? No hard feelings, I trust?"

The guard grunted. "You mind your business, and I'll mind mine, *Prester John.*"

John shrugged. "As you like it." The other man, understandably, still felt cool towards him. He didn't know why Butros seemed fixated on the way John had introduced himself. A chill went through him as he remembered Zakar's response to those words—*I'd keep that mark covered if I were you.*

He moved on, down towards the river, pondering the events of the afternoon. Zakar was just one of several small-time merchants with a single camel's-load worth of goods who'd joined the caravan for protection on his way home from Baghdad—a new capital built by the heretics not far from the ruins of Persian Ctesiphon. After the altercation with Butros in the marketplace, Zakar had suggested John join the caravan as a guard, and the other merchants had readily agreed. They would travel in an arc along the Euphrates and disband in Damascus. From there, Zakar meant to cross the Lebanon mountains to Tripoli. Despite the graciousness of Zakar's invitation, John still hadn't decided whether to accept. When it came down to it, he didn't *like* accepting help from these people. He was a Bessarion, damn it. He'd never had to accept charity in his life; certainly not from a poor crippled merchant. Surely there was another, quicker way home.

With a deep sigh John came to a halt on the riverbank, watching the moonlight on the water and still trying to absorb the enormity of what had happened. Six hundred years…

He hadn't stood there long when uneven footsteps crunched on the gravel behind him, bringing him warily on guard.

"It's me, friend," Zakar said quietly. "Heard you speaking to Butros."

John straightened. The afternoon's discussion had given him scant opportunity to be honest with Zakar. "Just the man I wanted to see. You're a Watcher yourself, aren't you?"

In answer, Zakar pushed back his sleeve. It was too dark to see much more than the dim blotch of a Watcher's Mark, but John felt instinctively that he could trust the man. "You're one of us, then." He sighed. "You realise Butros is some kind of spy, don't you?"

Zakar didn't seem surprised. "Certainly. He's some sort of Frankish noble, clearly. I'll lay you a copper to a silver groat his true name is Sir Peter of Somewhere-or-Other."

Zakar paused hopefully. John shook his head. "No, thanks."

"Anyway, I s'pose he was on some sort of mission to the Tartars in Baghdad."

"A Frank?" Unlike the Tartars, he'd actually heard of them; barbarians from the far west, beyond Rome. "What is a *Frank* doing out here?"

"Hm." Zakar watched him, his face unreadable in the dark. "Something tells me you aren't from around here either, John Bessarion."

John took a deep breath, unable to do anything but blurt it out. "Zakar, I don't know how to explain this to you, but I don't belong in this time. Last night I was in Antioch. It was late summer…and Heraclius was emperor."

"Well, stink," Zakar said meditatively. "That's…not what I expected to hear, friend."

John rushed on. "I have a wife and four children back there, and the heretics are about to overrun us. I have to find my way back. I have to…" His voice trailed away, replaced by slow certainty. "I have to *stop* all this. Will you help me?"

"Can do. What part do you want help with, exactly? Undoing time, or travelling back through it?" Zakar's voice was dryly amused.

He knew how mad he sounded, but it still stung to be made the butt of a merchant's jokes. "You don't believe me?"

"I don't know, friend. I believe you need help."

"That will do," John said grimly. "Let's start with getting me home. You don't happen to be a Messenger or Portentor, do you?"

"'Fraid not. But there's a Messenger back home in Tripoli."

Tripoli. A month's travel by the caravan's leisurely route. John gritted his teeth.

"Or you could go east. To Baghdad. The Watchers there have been protected since the Tartars came."

If he managed to find a way back through time from Baghdad, he'd still have to travel all that way home—through enemy territory of one sort or another. John shook his head. "Tripoli will do. I suppose that means I'm accepting your offer." He hesitated. "But—*Franks?* Here?"

Zakar gave the ghost of a laugh. "Sit down, friend. You have a great deal to catch up on."

Although John had no more curiosity about the history of this strange and inhospitable future beyond what would serve to bring him home again, Zakar seemed certain that the tale would hold his interest. As the story continued, perhaps he mistook John's appalled silence for absorption. The gist of it was that since its conquest six hundred years ago, his people had never been their own masters again.

The centuries his people had endured since he was torn from them in Oliveta were one long record of conquest, occupation, and the slow, steady descent of the once proud Roman empire into subjection. There was still an Emperor in Constantinople, but he ruled little more than the splintered rump of an empire and had little to do with the matters of Syria and Palestine. Two hundred years before, an army of Franks had come from the west to "liberate" Jerusalem and the rest of Palestine and Syria. Many of them had settled down to occupy and defend the land, but a hundred years ago they had lost Jerusalem and most of the kingdom to a counterattack by the sultan of Egypt.

Egypt was now the base of heretic power—or as Zakar called them, Saracens. Their sultan ruled all Egypt and much of inland Syria. Meanwhile, the Frankish holdings had dwindled to a few cities on the coast: Acre still styled itself the Kingdom of Jerusalem, but only Tyre, Beirut, and a handful of other fortresses remained in its control, and its king now ruled from Cyprus. The principality of Antioch was gone, destroyed in a ghastly cataclysm twenty years previously. The county of Tripoli still enjoyed a certain measure of independence, but in Zakar's opinion the peace was fragile.

"The Saracens don't fear us anymore," he finished. "But the Tartars in Baghdad—oh, them they fear. If Sultan Qalawun knew the Franks were sending ambassadors to the Tartars, he'd fall on us like a thunderbolt. Best not to meddle in Butros' affairs, friend."

And where were his people in all this? Had they all become small-time merchants, like Zakar? The thought appalled him. It was the loss of a whole future, and as John and Zakar returned to the camp, the awful weight of years pressed down on him with intolerable weight.

Towards morning, Rahel came to him again.

"I hoped to find answers with the Watchers here in Mep—in Mosul. But there are no Messengers closer than the Coast. I'll have to waste more time in travelling." He closed his eyes, trying to exhale his disappointment without breaking down entirely. "Rahel…I'm sorry."

She had regained her composure since their last conversation, but at that, she let out a little sigh that told him how much the news hurt. He reached out, wishing he could hold her hand. "I'll make my way back to you, dear heart. I only have to find it."

"It's all right, John." A deep breath. "I'm sorry if I panicked you, before. I should have known we'd be taken care of. The weapon is safe in Antioch, and so are we."

Relief burst over him. "What happened?"

"We managed to escape to the remaining Watchers here. They weren't particularly happy with your letter to the Syrian council, either." She swallowed. "I know you wanted me to work with them, John, but there's no hope of that. We're going back to Jerusalem."

"You're going *where?*"

"Back to Jerusalem."

"I heard you the first time. I assumed you were joking."

"I never joke."

The attempt at humour did little to lighten his mood. "Rahel, please. Jerusalem is about to be besieged. Go to Constantinople and be safe."

"I can't," Rahel said soberly. "Elisa's prophecy was true. I'm the only Watcher left now, and Palestine needs me."

"No." John dragged his hands down his face. "The *children* need you. And I—I need to know you're safe." *So that I'm not out of my mind with worry about you.*

She shook her head. "No, John. You need to know I'm doing the work. As for the children, they have their own gifts. We can't protect them forever. I'm beginning to realise we were never meant to."

She was right, of course—and yet.

"Have you seen anything of Lukas or Marta?" Rahel asked softly.

"No." John closed his eyes, his heart aching. "I have a theory, though. I think they survived Oliveta. Before the crisis, Paulus broke out of the sigil, but Lukas and Marta, like me, remained inside the lines. My guess is that they, too, have been displaced."

Rahel nodded, that carefully brave mask back on her face again. "We had our chance to prepare them."

"If I find news of them, I'll tell you. As for you, there's still a chance of saving Jerusalem. You still have the weapon. If you found someone with the training to wield it—"

"No. I'm not taking the weapon. Neither Paulus nor I can do anything with it, and you and I both know there are no Watchers in Jerusalem we'd trust to wield it."

"Then leave it in Antioch, and I'll collect it when I come home."

Rahel looked down at her fingers, where they lay knotted together in her lap. "What if you can't come home?" Her voice had almost disappeared, and her eyes were bright. She swallowed painfully. "John, don't be a wanderer. Wherever you are, I want you to find a home."

"But don't you see, dear heart? I can't. Before we left Jerusalem, I made a vow to return. I made vows to *you*." He took a deep breath. "I have to come home. For the same reason you are going back to Jerusalem: we're *Watchers*. We have to defend our people."

"I know." Rahel looked up, her dark eyes glowing with the embers of a distant dying campfire. "Just remember what Oliveta showed us—that when the Watchers are corrupted, fighting will do us no good at all. When the fire falls, no weapon forged will save us. Not even yours."

John put a hand over his mouth, trying to hide his emotion. "Be careful, dear heart. If the fire must fall, try not to get burned."

"I will." A half smile. "I have help, you know. Until you return, I'll be safe."

"Oh, Rahel." He couldn't stop himself, falling on his knees before her and reaching to pull her into his arms. "Who am I if I can't protect you? Who—"

He stopped as his hands passed through her. He braced himself on the stones each side of her, closing his eyes in frustration.

Rahel's voice was thick with tears. "Who are you?" she whispered. "Still the man I love best in the world. If you will wait for me, then I will wait for you."

"Always," he breathed.

She sighed, whispering his name.

"We know I can come home," he added doggedly. "If I could be sent here, I can be sent back."

"But at what cost? The slaughter of a town?"

The very idea should repel him; yet such was his desperation to return home that he might have embraced it with relief if not for the horror in Rahel's voice. John cleared his throat, resolutely putting the thought aside. "To gain that much power, Khalil had to make a sacrifice large enough to compel some wicked power to help him. But the spirits on our side are stronger. And while they cannot be commanded, they may be entreated or persuaded."

"A guardian…" Rahel's eyes shadowed over, unfocused. "Wait."

John sat back, his pulses quickening as he recognised the signs. She was having a vision. He wouldn't have to wait until Tripoli.

"I see a small, rocky island at night," she said after a moment. "There is a storm and…I think there's someone on the island."

"Who?"

"I can't tell." Rahel's eyes focused on him again. "That was all. I'm sorry. I haven't been having many visions lately, and this was only a glimpse."

John nodded, trying to conceal his disappointment.

"I think it means you go to the Coast," she said at length. "And…I think there's a guardian there for you to meet. On the island."

John nodded again. At least he had some sense of direction. "Tripoli, then."

Chapter VI.

Before venturing into the streets, Sir Gerard of Montreal checked his teeth in the small silver mirror that hung on the back of his door. If something went wrong and he died tonight, he thought ruefully, at least he would leave a handsome corpse.

Not that he meant to die if he could help it.

"Each man," he murmured to the reflection in the mirror, "is the architect of his own fate."

He was already dressed in the new suit of clothes he'd purchased in Acre before this mission to Tripoli—a long white tunic and a sleeved surcoat over it in dark blue with wide bands of gilt embroidery at the neck, hem and wrists. His shoes were fashionably pointed, but not frivolously long. Looks were everything on this mission. Gerard felt he'd achieved the precise balance of dignity and reliability that he needed for his official business, with the dashing good looks he needed for his own.

He shrouded the new clothes in a thick warm mantle, pulled on his gloves, and picked up the unsigned message that lay on the table.

There was no need for a seal or signature; Gerard would have recognised that round, comfortable minuscule anywhere, and done what it said if it had bade him throw himself from the highest tower in Tripoli. As it happened, the message asked for nothing more alarming than that he should present himself at a side door of the palace of Tripoli at Vigils, in the dead of night between the greater and lesser sleep.

That would, in itself, be enough of a challenge. Yet, *each man is the architect of his own fate.* He'd laid his plans hours ago and sent his servant ahead to help clear the way. Two hours after midnight, he left the Templar commandery.

As expected, he was followed.

Although Gerard was only a lay confrere of the Poor Fellow-Soldiers of Christ and the Temple of Solomon, rather than a full brother knight, he was not surprised to be shadowed. The Temple, like the Hospital, was a monastic order of knights owing allegiance only to the Pope. Nearly two hundred years ago they had begun escorting poor pilgrims through dangerous territory, to worship at the shrines in Jerusalem and other places. Now they manned a great many of the remaining fortresses in the Holy Land. They owned castles, knights, slaves, and spies; their wealth and influence reached from one end of the Mediterranean to another. As powerful independent entities operating within secular counties and kingdoms but answerable to no earthly powers, it was no wonder a close eye was kept on their comings and goings. Particularly in Tripoli. Countess Lucy was no fonder of the Templars than her father and brother had been, and as the personal envoy of its Master, William of Beaujeu, Gerard had been under close surveillance since he'd disembarked on the county's shores two days ago.

Whatever was afoot tonight, Gerard assumed that things would proceed more smoothly if he didn't have a spy on his tail. Maybe he was paranoid, but he hadn't become Master William's right-hand-man by taking chances. He continued through the cramped, winding streets of the great port city until he came to a public-house that glowed with light and music. The crowd within spilled out into the street, where a pair of lighted torches at either side of the open door provided enough light for a party of Genoese sailors to roll dice in the gutter. Gerard paused until he was sure the spy had seen him hesitating at the door, then slipped inside and elbowed his way through the crowd to the hot kitchen where his servant was sitting by the hearth with a beakerful of wine, gossiping with the publican. Gerard tossed a silver groat to the publican who barely spared a glance from the spitted pig he was basting over the roaring fire, unwound his mantle and handed it to his servant.

"Evening, Alessandro."

"Evening, sir." The young servant paused in the midst of his animated conversation to take the mantle and shove it casually behind him, to act as a cushion between his back and the rough stone of the fireplace. Gerard emerged into the narrow alleyway outside and stood for a moment, listening.

A crash sounded from the public-house, followed by uplifted voices. With a smile, Gerard set off briskly toward the palace. His servant's name was, in fact, Marco, *Alessandro* being a code word for *I'm being followed.* A foot thrust out at the right moment, loud recriminations, a threat to call the garrison, and he would leave the shadow far behind.

So far, his fate was obediently following the plan laid out for it; but this was the easy part. He wished he felt equally confident in his designs for the rest of the evening. Still, there must be hope for him. To hear from her again, after that last disastrous interview five years before—and in such affectionate terms, too.

He had to believe there was still hope for him. He had never loved anyone else; and he didn't mean to be a simple knight forever.

It was a short walk to the palace, where, although the side-door indicated by the message was locked, the sentry opened at a whispered word. Beyond, Gerard crossed a small service courtyard and ventured through a covered alleyway. He emerged in the shadows of a peristyle looking onto the small palace garden, with its well-kept hedges, its chuckling fountain and scented herbs. As the message directed, he settled in to wait. The February air was cold, and he paced the peristyle to keep warm.

Was she well? Had she changed? Was she ready to forgive him?

He had waited a quarter of an hour when a door opened nearby, and a gleam of light emerged from the palace. Quelling his eagerness, Gerard stepped into the shadow of a pillar, waiting for the shuttered lantern to come nearer.

"Gerard?" she called hesitantly. "Are you there?"

It was her voice—low, musical, beloved. It was her soft, rounded form. Five years and a lifetime's worth of regrets fell away, leaving both his shoulders and heart feeling lighter.

"My lady," he murmured, stepping into the light and falling to his knees. "It's so good to see you again."

"And you, dear." Margaret, the Lady of Tyre, held out a plump, beringed hand and Gerard kissed it affectionately. When Lady Margaret was a young princess of Cyprus, travelling to marry the Lord of Tyre, he had gone with her as a page. Then, if the eyes of youth and infatuation could be trusted, she'd been the most beautiful woman in the East. Twenty-one years later, she had fattened to the point of obesity, her fair hair had thinned a little, and there were crows-feet around the shrewd eyes.

Yet her beauty had always been beside the point to Gerard. It was her kind heart that had won from him a fierce and never-ending loyalty when they were young and homesick, early in her marriage. Time, it was clear, had made no alteration to *that*.

"Did you wait long?" she asked.

"It felt like forever," he said, getting up off the pavement.

"Flatterer," she said, turning slightly pink. His heart quickened half a beat; still, she had always liked to be flirted with.

He cleared his throat. "It's been a long five years, my lady."

She looked up at him with melting blue eyes. "Gerard, I never meant to hurt you. I hope you know that."

My feelings have not changed. He didn't speak the words. "I was wrong," he said instead. "The moment the words were out of my mouth, I would have cut off my right hand if it could have brought them back. You might have called me back to you the very next day, and I would have kissed your feet."

She looked away from him. "You needed time." Was there regret in her voice? He thought there was regret. "And perhaps I was afraid."

"Not of me?"

"No," she said, still not looking him in the eye. But her voice was very soft. "Not of you."

Of herself, then. That gave him hope.

He still didn't know why she had refused him, but he remembered what she had said as though it had been yesterday. *You and I are better off friends, Gerard.* His own words had been spoken in too much pain to be clearly remembered, but he knew their gist: Friendship wasn't enough for him; he didn't think it was enough for her, either. The Lord of Tyre was dead and she had been granted the rule of the city in his place; she had mourned a year and there was no reason in the world why a young and wealthy widow shouldn't marry a second time. He was young; he loved her; they knew and trusted each other. He had sworn to have her love, or nothing.

Nothing he had had—for five years. And yet he still meant to have her. He knew she cared for him; he had only to make her admit it.

Each man the architect of his own fate.

Lady Margaret drew the sort of breath that signals the death of one exchange, and the beginning of another. "I take it you managed to shake off Lucy's spies, then."

"Yes, but how—"

"Oh! Lucy has everyone watched. Poor dear, she had to fight hard enough for the inheritance; and you mustn't forget she was in Tripoli when the Templars laid siege to it. It's left her somewhat short on trust…even of me." Margaret took a breath, looking him in the eye with a level blue stare. "She's agreed to see you, but…"

This was the official part of his business. "She has? Tonight?"

"Yes, but I hope you know what you're doing, Gerard. Eschiva and I came to Tripoli to help her, if we could. If this turns out to be another of Beaujeu's little political games, she won't listen to us again."

Gerard glanced at the quiet garden, thought of the city beyond, slumbering in a rare moment of peace. A pang of foreboding went through him. "It's no game, my lady. God knows I wish it was."

She looked at him an instant longer. "That bad?"

"She should be the first to know."

Lady Margaret nodded, pursing her lips a little. Then at last, she beckoned him to follow her through the peristyle, circling the gardens toward the audience hall of the palace. In the pillared portico, a black-haired young woman about Gerard's own age waited, wearing heavy brocade the colour of lavender and a mantle lined in grey squirrel.

"Oh, *finally*," she said in a lazy drawl. "I thought the two of you must have got lost. I'm half dead of cold."

Lady Margaret looked repentant. "I'm so sorry, Eschiva; I forgot about you."

"What an unfamiliar experience for me. Hullo, Gerard; you look nice. What's the occasion? Are you going courting?"

Eschiva of Ibelin was the Lady of Beirut, and she and Lady Margaret had married brothers, though both were now dead. There had always been a disconcerting directness about Eschiva, and Gerard bowed to hide his confusion. "I'm here on Temple business, my lady."

"Oh! So you're still working for Beaujeu? Still just a secretary?"

"As a confrere, I'm naturally not eligible for higher rank," Gerard said stiffly as Eschiva led them towards the doors of the audience chamber, which were outlined in golden lamplight.

"Whyever don't you take vows? Beaujeu trusts you a great deal. You might rise to Commander."

Gerard cleared his throat. "I mean to marry."

He couldn't help glancing at Lady Margaret when he said it. Eschiva's demand to know the fortunate lady's name passed both of them by: Lady Margaret beamed gently at him and said, "I hope you do, some day."

Unlike Lady Eschiva, she didn't presume he already had a different lady picked out; and that, for some reason, seemed encouraging. There was no time to say more, for at that moment the doors to the audience-hall folded back to let them in.

Though lit only by a single wrought-iron candelabrum on the dais, the echoing room sparkled with muted splendour. Frescoes of curling vines and small animals decorated the walls above their marble panelling, making the place seem like a garden. On the dais, in front of a red and gold tapestry, were gathered a bishop, a lord, and a third young woman. Still in her twenties, and dressed in shimmering, expensive black silk, Gerard recognised her immediately as Lucy, titular princess of Antioch and actual countess of Tripoli. When Gerard entered the hall, she sank into her chair and sat with her hands clutching the armrests as though she was half afraid he would try to drag her off it.

It was time to put aside his private concerns, for if tonight's mission failed, all their lives were at stake. Gerard halted three paces from the dais, and bowed low.

"You are Gerard of Montreal, personal envoy of the Master of the Temple?" the countess asked.

"Yes, my lady. I believe you received my credentials."

"You were good enough to send them together with your request for an audience."

Two days ago. Gerard merely bowed again. It was only too clear that although the countess was finally admitting him to her presence, the audience was late, reluctant—and secret. At just under thirty, Countess Lucy would be unable to remember a time when Tripoli had been at peace, and in the civil wars that had racked the county, the Templars had played a prominent—and hostile—role. The truth was that if Lucy found it difficult to trust her vassals and allies, there were few who'd done more to deserve that distrust than Gerard's master, William of Beaujeu.

It was no easy task that lay ahead of him.

"I come in a spirit of good faith and Christian brotherhood, my lady," Gerard said. "I grieve to be the bearer of bad news. We have received word from Egypt that Sultan Qalawun means to lay siege to this city."

There was a long and strained silence. Gerard knew what must be going through their minds. Twenty years ago, the Egyptians had taken Antioch—and wellnigh obliterated it. Since then, their advance had been slow, inexorable and ruthless. By now, the Franks retained only a handful of cities along the Coast—the remnants of a once thriving kingdom. If Tripoli's turn had come, there was very little that could be done.

And yet resistance was vital. If Tripoli fell, would Acre stand much longer? Would all the prayers and blood and gold poured out for the kingdom of lost Jerusalem over two centuries be in vain?

Countess Lucy's knuckles were white on the arms of her chair and her answer, when it came, was hostile. "What's this? Are you trying to frighten me?"

"No, my lady."

Behind her, the bishop cleared his throat. "It's true that the sultan was preparing an army in the autumn," he said smoothly. "But it was our understanding that the campaign was called off, following the death of his heir—"

Gerard had never met Bartholomew, the bishop of Tortosa, but having been thoroughly briefed on the situation in Tripoli before he left Templar headquarters in Acre, he knew the bishop was a major figure in the ruling family's faction in Tripoli. By extension, that meant he was an old enemy of the rebel barons and their allies, the Templars—which explained why he was here tonight, watching Gerard with so much suspicion.

He bowed to the bishop. "The campaign was postponed, not called off, my lord. By now, the Egyptians are already marching north."

"Why presume that he's coming *here?*" Countess Lucy added. "The sultan rules all of Syria and most of Mesopotamia. He might have business anywhere."

"We haven't presumed, if my lady will permit me to say so." He drew a breath. "For his own safety, I can't tell you who our informant is. Suffice it to say that he's *very* highly placed in the sultan's government, and his information has always been good. I went to Cairo to meet with him in person."

Gerard paused, looking towards the second man on the dais. Still hanging back, waiting in the shadows, this weather-beaten warrior must be the Genoese admiral who had put Countess Lucy on the throne of Tripoli a few short months before. It had been a nine-days' wonder, for the leaders of the rebel barons had been the Embriacos of Gibelet, a family of Genoese extraction. Just seven years before, Lucy's brother had bricked the Embriaco leaders and their allies into a moat and left them to starve in their dark tomb. After the former count's death, the rebel lords had turned to Genoa to protect them from the countess' claim to the throne. Instead, Genoa and Lucy had joined forces and carved Tripoli up between them.

"Sir Benedetto Zaccaria may be interested to know what our informant told us." Gerard nodded toward the reticent admiral. "It seems that a pair of Venetian merchants went to Alexandria in the summer and asked to see the sultan. They warned Qalawun that if the Genoese were permitted to retain their influence in Tripoli, they would rule the sea and prey on all the other merchants coming and going from Egypt. As you know, the sultan depends on the slave trade to supply his mamluk warriors, so if Genoa should throttle the trade, he would lose a great deal of his manpower. Since it seemed to the sultan that the threat was real, he began to prepare men-at-arms, and way-stations along the road. We already have confirmation of supply depots in the Bacar valley."

The countess glanced over her shoulder, at the admiral, but he didn't move. She turned back to Gerard. "We were informed about the supply depots by our own agents. It was suggested the sultan meant to attack Nephin."

"Can you afford to take that risk?" Gerard asked, his patience wearing thin. "My lady, you have nothing to lose by preparing."

Next to Gerard, Lady Margaret shot him a warning look. Beyond her, the Lady of Beirut spoke for the first time, in a sleepy and relaxed voice. "He's right, Lucy. You fought hard for this county; 'twould be a shame to lose it on a wager."

The bishop scowled at her. "That's all very well for you to say, Eschiva of Ibelin. But your family's been in bed with the Templars for decades."

"One at a time, my lord, one at a time," Lady Eschiva replied with cold amusement. "We Ibelins are strictly monogamous."

The bishop recovered his composure with commendable rapidity. "I see what is going on here, Countess. The Master of the Temple knows he is hated in this county, so he pretends he has secret information, and sends his lackeys to alarm us. No doubt he expects us to appoint him as a go-between with the sultan, so that when no threat eventuates, he'll get the credit for staving off disaster."

Gerard tried not to gape. "With all respect, my lord, why would Master William do a thing like that?"

"It would be foolish to disbelieve such a report for merely a *lack* of evidence, dear," Lady Margaret said. Gerard knew her well enough to detect the genuine alarm in her affectionate words.

"What more evidence do I need?" Countess Lucy spoke in a quiet, concentrated fury. "My brother had to decimate the Embriacos of Gibelet and burn the Temple commandery in this city to the ground before he could sit at peace on his throne. What guarantee do I have that William of Beaujeu means any better by me? It is he who must prove his honesty, *not* me."

"Then *let* him," Lady Margaret pleaded. "Lucy, Lucy. You are not your brother. You need not prove your worth through vengeance and fury, my dear. No one will think the less of you for overlooking past wrongs, for taking counsel."

"I *have* counsellors, cousin." But Countess Lucy bit her lip, and then slewed around to peer into the shadows behind her chair. "Sir Benedetto? What do you think?"

The Genoese admiral stepped into the light. For a long moment he looked from face to face—the obstinate bishop, the intent countess, the Ladies of Tyre and Beirut, Gerard.

Gerard watched the admiral, trying not to let his relief show in his face. Zaccaria would never be fool enough to oppose him. Since the most recent war, Genoa owned a quarter of Tripoli. They were poised to rule the eastern Mediterranean.

All they had to do was hold onto Tripoli—which meant at least considering Gerard's news.

Zaccaria looked Gerard in the eye, his face shuttered. "I think the bishop is correct. We cannot put blind trust in the Temple."

This could not be. Surely he'd heard wrong—but beside him, Lady Margaret drew a sharp intake of breath, and Gerard realised she'd heard the same thing he had.

Countess Lucy lifted her chin with decision, and rose from her chair. "There. I have taken counsel. Thank the Master of the Temple for his message, Sir Gerard," she said, though there was not much gratitude in her manner as she stalked away. The bishop cast a supercilious smile at Gerard and followed her, leaving a heavy silence in the room.

Lady Eschiva tutted. "Margaret, dear, I am growing perilously short in patience with your protégé."

"Oh, don't be like that, Eschiva; she's a good girl, she's just frightened out of her wits, and doesn't know who to trust. Oh, Sir Benedetto! You seriously don't think the Egyptians are a threat?"

Zaccaria shrugged. "Well, naturally they may be."

Gerard was still struggling to understand. "Sir," he said deferentially, "do you have some more recent information that we don't know about?"

"I shouldn't think so. No."

"Then why…"

"The Genoese presence in Tripoli is hotly contested," Sir Benedetto said abruptly. "If the Egyptian sultan really does pose a threat, no doubt that will become clear in due course. In the meanwhile, I don't mean to make any enemies in this city. Good night."

He bowed to Lady Margaret, then to Lady Eschiva. For some time after he left, the echoes of his hurried footsteps rang in the big, empty room.

The two ladies looked at each other. "So," the Lady of Beirut said, "he will ignore a clear threat to curry favour with the bishop."

"I *counted* on him," Gerard said, yet to emerge from his shock. He'd seen some dreadful betrayals in his time, but this was plain idiocy. "How am I going to explain this to Beaujeu?"

"It's just Tripolitan politics, dear." Lady Margaret heaved a sigh. "By my holy dame! I begin to think it must be something in the water."

* * *

This time, Soraya was deeply dormant when the command came to drag her from her prison. She was still disoriented when her body took form; it staggered and fell before she managed to wake up long enough to struggle into it.

She groaned and dragged herself off the stone floor. It took a moment to get her bearings. Lamplight. Stone floor. Weapons racks. Ah, the sparring-room.

"What is it now?" she mumbled.

"I can't sleep." Saif spoke from somewhere above her.

She turned and glared up at him. "Odd. Neither can I, now." Not that the mental dormancy of bodiless confinement was comparable to real sleep, or the relaxed drowsiness that came with waking.

There was a feverish flicker in his spirit. "We have a new mission tomorrow."

"I'll try to contain my glee," she said wearily. "Whom do we poison next?"

"In the name of God, we're going to Tripoli."

"God help them."

"Amen." He tossed her a staff. "Now get up and fight. We both need to stay sharp."

Chapter VII.

"Awake, Prester?" Butros spoke hoarsely from beside John, making him jump.

Strife. He'd give himself away if he wasn't more careful, staring at the landscape with such speechless astonishment. The Frank had hovered over him like a bird of prey all the way from Mosul, and John would have felt better if he knew exactly what it was Butros suspected him of being. A rival spy? An exiled dignitary? John swallowed, pointing towards the bare hills of the Lebanon sloping away to the sea. "They're so barren. From the ancient texts I…I expected cedars."

Ranks upon ranks of them, the lordly trees, congregating in every fold of these mountains, green and prickly. Their number had been dwindling in John's day, but now, after two days in the mountains, he hadn't seen a single tree.

Butros hefted his crossbow over one shoulder, watching John with cold eyes that missed nothing. "The Cedars of God are further down."

John couldn't tell him that he'd travelled this road before, that he knew whole groves of the trees had vanished. In peacetime, Lebanon's cedars provided masts for ships, timbers for building. But such felling of timber did not denude whole hillsides without the planting of new timber to replace them. It was war that had done this; war that demanded fleets of new ships and towering siege engines by the dozen; war that destroyed and did not stop to rebuild.

With a sigh he turned away from the devastation, waiting for Zakar to catch up.

They had left Damascus a few days before, and John was grateful to be out of the overcrowded city, for the Egyptian sultan had been in residence and the whole place was filled to bursting with his soldiers. Upon leaving the city, he, Zakar, and to his disappointment, Butros, had split off from the main caravan and turned north up the Valley of Bacar to cross the mountains to Tripoli. The roads were good, recently mended. From time to time they passed small encampments of Saracen guards watching over farms or outbuildings that seemed already to be bursting at the seams with supplies, although harvest was not for another half a year.

The details nagged at his soldier's instincts, but he ignored what they told him. He was going home. He didn't mean to be embroiled in whatever was about to happen here.

The wind was cold in this high pass, and snowdrifts lingered among the rocks. John shivered in the threadbare cloak which was all he'd been able to buy with his wages from guarding the caravan, and thought of Rahel's journey through these same mountains towards Jerusalem. The young children would have made her journey a slow one, and she had only one guard to protect them from violence—a heretic, no less. He didn't trust the barbarian; but what choice did she have? The tribesmen of these mountains were unruly and independent, unlikely to respect a lonely woman even if she was the Praetorian Prefect's wife.

He spoke to her nearly every night, reassuring himself that she and the two youngest children were well. Still, it only took moments for something to go irretrievably wrong, and he knew he wouldn't sleep easy until he was with them again at last.

Zakar was a little further down the road, finishing an argument with the donkey he'd bought in Damascus—everything else, camel and stores, he'd sold along the way. Nearby, Butros allowed his skewbald pack pony to nose for grass, and watched John with calculating eyes.

"So, you're from the far East, hmm? Are many of your people Christians?"

Somehow, Butros had got the idea that John originated from Persia or Khorasan or some such place. John didn't want to lie, but he sensed he couldn't afford to set the other man straight, either. "I believe many of them are, yes," he hedged.

"So what happened when the Tartars came through?"

The Tartars. He'd heard them mentioned once or twice before, and now he sensed that he stood on shaky ground. Evidently, he was supposed to know who the Tartars were.

"I don't think I know them by that name," he said cautiously. "Describe them to me."

"The Tartars are a very warlike people from the far east, north of Cathay." Butros stroked the haft of his crossbow, his eyes narrow with distrust. "At first they lived in a great sandy plain where nothing good would grow; and they were kept in want and servitude by the great kings of the east, until a wise man arose who unified their tribes and gave them good laws. Then he led them against their oppressors and conquered them. This was a hundred years ago. Now they rule all Cathay, Khorasan, Persia, Georgia, and even parts of the Rus and Anatolia."

John kept a tight rein on his incredulity. Such an empire was unimaginably immense; larger than any the world had ever known. How could a single people rule such an immense swath of land? Was this a test? Was Butros spinning impossible stories, wanting to see if John would betray his ignorance by pretending to know of these people? After a moment, he rejected the thought. If Butros wanted to trap him into a falsehood, he would invent something more plausible than this.

"One of their kings now rules in Baghdad," Butros added quietly. "Sultan Qalawun's mortal foe."

No, Butros could not be lying. A cunning man might lie about something unimaginably distant, but not about lands so close.

"Ah," he said, taking refuge in ambiguity. So, Zakar was right: Butros must have been in Baghdad on some mission to this Tartar king.

When John failed to go on, Butros tried a different tactic. "You're a trained warrior," he said at length. "Are many of your people like you?"

John thought of the Roman cataphracts who had fought by his side during the Persian wars. Despite the cold wind, a glow of pride went through him. "I am only the least of them."

"And your king—does he seek allies?"

John froze a moment, then turned to look at Butros' face. Only the man's profile was visible as he stood looking down the looping road. From here, glimpses of the coast were visible: the broad sweep of green grass, orchard, pasture, and the grey sheen of water curving to the horizon. Yet it was the Frank who held his attention.

All the way from Mosul to Damascus to the Lebanon, the other man had watched him with a discomfiting blend of cold hostility and forced joviality. John had endured it in silence. After all, he'd nearly killed the man. But now...

That calculating look in his eyes. Those probing questions. That insistent habit of referring to him as a Prester. Who exactly did the man think he was?

"Look, I'm only passing through," John said at last. "I'm not looking for any entanglements here on the Coast."

A corner of the other man's mouth quirked, and the faintly jeering tone returned to his voice. "As you like it, *Prester*. But I think you'll find that in Tripoli, entanglements have a way of finding you."

"What's that supposed to mean?" John demanded, his patience wearing thin.

Butros only turned away with a smirk. "Ho, Zakar. How's the beast?"

Zakar grinned as he got underway again. "Good news, friends. Her Ladyship has deigned to continue the journey."

Despite whatever intrigues Butros had in mind, John was glad to press on with the journey. The sooner they reached the Coast, the sooner he could find the guardian from Rahel's vision and beg to be taken home.

After the pass, the road began to drop again into the green coastal plains. This side of the mountains, the fertile landscape was speckled with orchards, vineyards, farms, fortresses, villages, and churches. Fields stood full of wheat and cane-sugar. But amongst it all, the old scars of war were still visible: crumbling watchtowers, groves of felled trees, shells of burned houses.

It had been just so in his own time, all those centuries ago; John felt the dreamlike illusion that he had never left at all. Yet, illusion was all it was. Working many of the farms, or riding by road in steel armour were the Franks who ruled now, with their pale skin and imposing height.

Their small party was evidently too humble to attract the attention of bandits, and so they came safely to Tripoli early in March. The city was a familiar view on its small peninsula, surrounded by sea on three sides and approachable only by a narrow spit of land, along which ran the high aqueduct that carried water into the city. Radiating out from the walls, fruit orchards imparted a distinctive perfume to the air—fresh, zesty, and clean. Opposite the city, barely two miles inland at the landward end of the aqueduct, someone had built a massive fortress on a tall spur of the mountains. At its foot collected a new suburb—an unwalled jumble of houses, hospices, and churches.

As they passed beneath the aqueduct to enter the suburb, Butros halted. "Oi, Prester."

He winced. "John will do."

The narrow street was crowded, so Butros backed his pony into a quiet cul-de-sac between two houses. John and Zakar followed to find the other man unbuckling his great sword and strapping it to the pony's packs.

"Do me a favour?" Butros asked. He had swung back into his forced joviality. "I have a man to see here in Mount Pilgrim. If you'll take old Patch here into the city and have him lodged at the stables of Jacob of Gibelet, I'd be grateful."

Reluctantly, John agreed. Butros hesitated, then pulled off his thick wine-coloured cloak and handed it to John. "You can deposit this with the stable in earnest of payment. I don't mind if you wear it."

John wasn't quite sure he trusted the other man's smile, but the cloak was warm and the errand not out of his way. Besides, he'd been waiting for ten days to get Zakar to himself. "I'd be pleased to," he said, swinging the cloak over his shoulder. Butros grinned and strolled away, a spring in his step.

With a sigh, John turned to Zakar. "I thought he'd never leave."

"He was hanging around like a bad smell," Zakar acknowledged, hobbling back into the street to take the lead.

John followed, but as they wound their way through the streets of the suburb, the questions he'd nursed since their last private conversation in Damascus faded away. "Who built this place?"

"Mount Pilgrim? Oh, the Franks built it around the old citadel of Raymond Saint-Gilles."

John answered only with a short, delighted laugh. The tall sandstone tenements had flat or tiled roofs and round arches, but otherwise little ornamentation. As they emerged into a central forum, John found himself looking up at a massive basilica on his left and, atop a stone outcrop on his right, the even more massive fortress. He'd never seen such formidable defences, but it was the cathedral that captured his attention, with its square tower, pitched roof and polychromatic marble façade. There was no dome, but it was lit by a great round window above the door. The central nave was surmounted by a pediment and supported by two aisles with sloping rooflines. Blind arcades adorned the façade. It was symmetrical, strange, and severely beautiful.

"A pitched roof instead of a dome," he found himself saying softly.

Zakar's voice broke in on his thoughts. "They build them that way in the north to shed the snow and rain."

"It's not what I'm accustomed to," John confessed. "But it's beautiful."

"Do you want to see inside?"

John's fingers itched for paper and reed with which to sketch the basilica. He hesitated, tempted; then shook his head. "We both have families waiting for us." This wasn't his home. He couldn't let anything here steal his heart, not even the architecture.

On the far side of Mount Pilgrim, the road ran between orchards and the aqueduct. The trees were laden with yellow and golden globes, some already ripe for harvest. Oranges and lemons, John realised, breathing in the delicious scent. They must have been imported from India since his own time. In the golden light of a spring afternoon, farmers moved through the groves, tending their trees. Ahead, the walled city hummed quietly with business, ships lying at anchor in the harbour on the city's north shore.

Unbidden, a traitorous thought came to John: *there will be peace, even long after we are gone.*

Yet his own family would not be there to enjoy it. Where were the old Roman patricians in this Tripoli? They'd lost their birthright. Their fatherland was no longer theirs; this future belonged to others. Those who enjoyed this peace enjoyed it only because of the war, the death and brigandage that had torn it away from his own people. He glanced at the lame man beside him, a humble merchant content to look on as more powerful men determined his fate.

"Penny for your thoughts, friend," Zakar offered cheerfully as they approached the city's landward gate.

He could hardly tell the man that he pitied him for his low estate. "Oh, they're hardly worth so much."

He followed Zakar through the gate into the city. The wall was massive—wide enough for three horses to ride abreast, Zakar boasted. Beyond, the sandstone buildings were both familiar and strange, as though the memory of the city which had been new in his own time was still lurking in an old tenement here or the dome of a church there. Lost in the sights and sounds, John forgot to watch where he was going, and collided with a frail old body.

"I beg your pardon," he said, reaching out partly to steady the old beggar on his feet, partly to avoid being enfolded by the man's flyaway grey beard and repulsive smell. "Did I hurt you?"

The man simply stood and stared at him, his jaw dropping open slightly. He didn't look entirely sane. John reached into his purse for a copper—perilously slim though it was, he couldn't quite break the habit of bestowing largesse.

"Here, take this," he said, holding out the coin.

Instead of taking it, the old man came suddenly back to life and grasped John's wrist with surprising strength, his eyes suddenly full of sharp intelligence. The beggar breathed with a rasping voice, *"I know you, John Bessarion."*

Every hair stood upright on John's head. He was quite sure he'd never laid eyes on the old man before; why did the fellow look at him with such hungry delight?

Suddenly Zakar shoved between them, breaking the old man's grasp. "Get away, Katsaros, you old buzzard. If we want your help, we'll ask for it."

The old man backed away without another word, and John hurried after Zakar as the merchant turned abruptly into the street again. "A friend of yours?" John inquired, glancing back with an unpleasant prickling feeling on the back of his neck. Katsaros stood in an archway, watching them go with those keen malicious eyes.

"He's a sand diviner," Zakar said grimly, "and I *don't* think he's a charlatan. Come on; I'll take you to the stable Butros told us about."

John followed, his interest in the strange familiarity of the city quenched. Not five minutes in Tripoli, and he had already drawn the wrong kind of attention. He could only hope that it would be as easy to get the attention of the guardian he so fervently sought.

The stable was a humble stone building across the road from an imposing new fortress floating a red cross on a white banner. Having stabled the animals and deposited the cloak, John followed Zakar to a narrow street not far from the harbour, where a humble two-storey house stood overshadowed by tenements on either side. Two boys were playing on the step, and when they saw Zakar approaching, they shrieked a welcome and launched themselves at his midriff.

"Matthias! Hugh!" Zakar laughed, let his crutch fall, and pulled them into his arms. He'd explained that his children were adopted, a set of five siblings who had lost their mother to a plague and their father in an accident at the docks.

The delight of their welcome sent knives of agony through John. Perhaps Zakar was less to be pitied than he thought.

Zakar slapped his shoulder. "Don't hang back, John! Come up and eat!"

"I couldn't," he began awkwardly, assessing the poverty of the house and the carefully mended rents on the boys' tunics.

"Nonsense, friend. I won't have you going hungry."

Zakar ushered him and the boys into a dim lower room containing a pair of looms and bolts of pure white silk stacked in the shadows. A stairway led up to the living quarters above, and a babel of voices floated through the open door, the scent of a spiced lentil pottage lacing the air.

He could never have imagined how hard it would be to join a family for dinner.

Zakar led him on into a single cramped upstairs room. A girl of about ten was laying out mismatched wooden spoons for dinner, and two others were playing on a sleeping-platform near a window. Zakar's wife, like himself several years younger than John, bent over the hearth sweating as she snatched flatbread out of the ashes, beating them clean with a wooden spoon. When Zakar entered, she straightened, wiping hair out of her eyes with a smile.

"I'm home," Zakar shouted, holding his arms out for the three girls. "Don't worry, Sara," he said to his wife over their heads, "I've only brought the one extra mouth this time. This is John Bessarion, a Watcher from far away."

She nodded, planting a basket of fresh bread and a pot of lentils on the floor in the middle of the room, and leaning over to greet her husband with a kiss. "Welcome! Sit down and eat."

It was simple fare, but John was ravenous, his last meal having been a few mouthfuls taken at dawn. After the meal Sara produced four oranges to be halved among everyone, and John entertained the children by flicking almonds high into the air and then catching them in his mouth. Once a certain level of hilarity—and noise—had been reached, Sara sent the children into the street to play, allowing the men to stretch out their legs and talk while she washed the few dishes.

"You told me a tall story in Mosul, friend," Zakar said. "But I'll say this for you: you don't *seem* crazy."

"Very kind of you to say so." John suppressed his instinctive reaction. In his old life he would never have befriended a man like Zakar, but despite himself he was coming to like the man.

"All the same, I trust you." Zakar waved a segment of orange with half a grin. "Mostly because I can't otherwise explain why else a Watcher would be in Mosul, displaying his Mark to all and sundry. If there are any of us left in Saracen territory, they're keeping their heads down."

"Why are they disappearing?" John asked. "Is it the sultan?"

Sara shook her head. "I never heard of him having a grudge against the Watchers. But…there are stories about a killer they call *the Chosen*."

There was a moment's silence.

"Always thought it was a creative way to make children behave, myself." Zakar waved a dismissive hand. "I'm sure John doesn't want to hear about that. How can we help you, John?"

With a deep breath John leaned forward, wiping orange juice off his fingers. "I came to Tripoli because I was told there is a guardian spirit here. Saint, angel, whatever it is, I need to speak with it."

Sara hummed, uncertain. "There are stories, of course."

"It's said that there is one," Zakar agreed. "But to be honest, I've never believed the rumours. No Watchers have ever spoken with it."

Zakar and his wife exchanged looks, and Zakar heaved a sigh. "We do what we can, Bessarion, but the outlook isn't good. Tripoli has been rotten for a long time. When we aren't fighting our neighbours, we're fighting amongst ourselves."

"The Embriacos," Sara murmured.

Zakar nodded. "It's only seven years since our count walled up Guy of Jubail and his followers in their own moat and left them to die of hunger and thirst. Unfriendly of them, if you ask me." He shivered. "And then the count died, and the war started all over again—and his lady sister sold us to the Genoese. Sweet saints, my friend, times have been hard."

"And a guardian might have prevented some of that?"

Zakar shrugged, weary. "It might have helped."

John nodded, staring at his hands in his lap. Strong, capable hands, scarred by battle but somehow useless in this predicament. He only wanted to go *home*.

"Are there islands near the city?"

"Yes; there's Saint Thomas just outside the wall, and others further out."

Guardians could usually be expected to stay within their own territorial boundaries, which meant that if he was destined to meet Tripoli's guardian on an island outside the wall, it would be no ordinary occasion. Still, he would visit this Saint Thomas isle. "What about Gifts?" he added. Rahel's visions had been few and far between lately; perhaps someone else could help. "Do you have any Messengers in the city? Portentors?"

"There's Hubert the dyer," Sara said. "He's given Messages on occasion."

John glanced to the small window. Sunset colours bled across the sky. "Will you direct me to his house?"

"He was coming tomorrow anyway, to collect bolts for printing," Sara said.

And Zakar added, "You've had a long day's journey, John. Why don't you stay here for tonight?"

John looked around the small room, feeling suddenly trapped, almost suffocated. "I couldn't impose."

"No imposition at all."

He got to his aching feet. "Really, I should leave. The sooner I meet this Hubert, the sooner I can find my way home."

Zakar relented, deep sympathy in his eyes. He and Sara escorted John downstairs to the workshop, and whistled the children in from their games in the street. They clamoured at Zakar's waist for goodnight-kisses, and he complied cheerfully before sending them upstairs with good-natured cuffs.

John watched with his heart tearing to shreds. As Zakar turned, grinning, to face him, he cleared the lump out of his throat. "If I'm still here tomorrow, I'll come back and tell you how I fare."

Zakar nodded and held out a hand. "I'm sure Hubert will have some guidance for you."

John nodded, trying to hold onto hope. Rahel didn't make mistakes. There was a guardian here, maybe dormant—if spirits *could* lie dormant. He only had to find it.

Zakar's grip tightened. "We could use Watchers here in Tripoli, John Bessarion. There are orphans to foster, hospitals to staff, wars to clean up after."

He couldn't care for other people's children while his own went fatherless, but there was no gracious way to say that. Instead, John forced a smile and a smooth little lie. "I'll think about it."

He stepped out the door as Zakar latched it behind him and set off up the narrow street towards the harbour.

As soon as he was alone in the street, two men who had been loitering in a doorway straightened and stepped out onto the cobblestones, blocking his way. Swords hung by their sides. A glint of steel at their necks betrayed the armour beneath their tunics.

John turned to find two more men confronting him.

"You left a horse with Jacob of Gibelet this afternoon," one of them drawled in very bad Arabic.

John frowned. "I left a cloak as deposit."

"Oh, we're not here on behalf of the stable," the man said in his lazy, nasal voice. "We're here for Countess Lucy. You're wanted at the palace."

Chapter VIII.

John surfaced from a dreamless sleep expecting to find Rahel waiting for him. Instead, he looked up into the face of a woman so immaculately beautiful, so sharp and vivid and fleshless that the first instinct he felt was pure terror.

"Whom have we here?" she purred, bending over him from her vantage-point straddling his chest. Her lips were too red, her lashes too long, the black waves of her hair too buoyant to be quite real. John tried to move, to speak, but such was the oppression of her gaze that he could do neither. Only a strangled protest came from his throat, and died on his lips.

She laughed. "John Bessarion, at last! A little bird told me you had appeared."

"Get—off." John tried to shout the words, but they were barely a whisper. Helplessly, he glanced about him, but there was no escape from the tiny cell next to the countess' stables. Her sergeants had shoved him inside this small stone room and shot the bolt hours ago, leaving him to fret and wonder and eventually fall asleep on the lumpy straw pallet. Even if he could have moved, there was no escape.

It was only a dream, but he could have sworn he really felt the cold sweat beading his forehead as the creature on his chest ran her fingers across his lips. He certainly felt the numbing cold trail her touch left behind.

"Tell me your desires, mortal. Tell me what you want."

He gritted his teeth, gathering all his willpower. "I want my wife." His lips moved, but there were no words. He tried again, and this time there was a faint rasp to the words. "I don't want you—I want my wife. Rahel!"

The last word tore free from his lips, full and potent. As it did so, a glimmer of light illuminated his cell, and the weight on his chest lessened.

"Begone, spirit." It was Rahel's voice, blithe and unworried. No more was needed: with her words, the nightmare vanished and John sat up, shivering a little with the fading horror.

"Rahel!"

"You called?"

Dressed in a white tunic, she glowed slightly in the dark, the edges of her spirit slightly soft and fuzzy. He wished he could reach for her, gather her into his arms for comfort. Instead, he took refuge in shaky humour. "That…was not as much fun as it might have seemed."

"I find that people who are having fun don't usually scream for help. What was it?"

"I was hoping you might be able to tell me that." He shivered, feeling once again the helplessness with which the nightmare had assailed him, and the prickling on the back of his neck as the mad old sand diviner had watched him after their encounter at the gate. Was it his anxious brain that had summoned the nightmare after that unsettling encounter, or had Katsaros himself sent the spectre?

"I don't know what it was, but it felt real, and I'm not convinced we've seen the last of it." Rahel watched him with suppressed worry in her eyes.

He sighed, unsure. "It seems I have attracted all the wrong kinds of attention today." He waved his hand around his cell. "The garrison has me locked up, but I don't know why. For all the hurry, they don't seem terribly keen to see me."

Rahel inspected the cramped stone room with its sleeping mat and chamber pot. "Not quite what the Praetorian Prefect is accustomed to," she teased. "How on earth did you end up here?"

John rubbed his eyes. "Honestly, I have no idea. I don't even know who this countess is—and I've been racking my mind for any idea how I might have offended her."

"It isn't the happiest place I've seen." Rahel held out a bright hand to him. "Let's try something."

She backed away, melting through the door. John's dreamself followed before she quite vanished from sight, and a moment later he and Rahel stood in the courtyard beyond the locked door. The stars were clear overhead in a velvet sky, and John could hear the soft sound of crickets chirping in the distant garden.

"Let's find somewhere to sit," Rahel whispered, setting off across the empty courtyard. They floated weightlessly upstairs together and went through a dark hall that took them to a loggia overlooking a sheltered garden.

Rahel sighed happily and sank onto a low wooden settle that faced the garden. "This is a beautiful place."

Ordinarily, the loggia's beautiful stonework, with its round arches supported on foliate Corinthian capitals, would have captured his full attention. Tonight, however, John barely even noticed them. Rahel's wavy dark hair flowed loose down her back, and his gut twisted with the desire to touch it. "Any place with you in it would be beautiful."

She looked up at him with eyes softly glowing. "Flatterer."

She didn't seem particularly concerned, but John felt eaten up with worry. Something was dreadfully wrong here. What did that nightmare mean? It almost seemed as though someone had been expecting him. Perhaps there were things he needed to say, here and now, before he lost this last link with her.

Or perhaps, even if he survived the day, she would not—separated from him as she was by an ocean of time, stranded alone with only a barbarian heretic for company.

"Tell the children I love them," he said at last. "Tell them I'm sorry I can't be there."

"I will." She frowned a little. "At least, the ones I can reach. You haven't heard anything of Lukas or Marta?"

He shook his head. "You haven't seen them in your dreams? Like you see me?"

"I wouldn't even know how to try," she said, biting her lip.

John considered Lukas, prickly and hot-headed; Marta, impulsive and idealistic. "I hate to think what kind of trouble they must be getting into."

"In some ways it would be easier if they were dead, wouldn't it? At least then we would know; we wouldn't fear for them so."

"There isn't anything you can *do* to get through to them?"

"No. It's beyond my control; just like the Messages." She sent him one of her brave smiles. "And that may be a comforting thought. Someone evidently thinks you need me more than they do."

Doubt gnawed at his heart. "How can anyone survive in this world without a family? Will the birds in the air bring them food, or give them shelter?"

"Who says they will not? Stranger things have happened," Rahel countered. "We had them fifteen years or so, John. We did our best. They will never forget who they are."

She had such faith, such certainty. John envied her a little, but the worry still itched at him. "There's nothing we can do for them now. But you, Rahel—be careful, even once you are home in Jerusalem."

"Do you really think there's danger?"

He took a deep breath, trying not to let it shake. "There's always danger."

She looked down at the hands on her lap, then back up at him. "Today we arrived home in Jerusalem again. I had to tell Patriarch Sophronius that the emperor wasn't coming…and that you'd been unavoidably detained."

"And what did he say to that?"

"That nothing is certain in this life."

"Philosophy," John said, the word sour between his teeth.

"He doesn't blame you, my love."

"I made a promise."

She put out her hand with a little confiding gesture, a habit she didn't seem able to break, even though her fingers passed through his hand like a mist. "Let me keep it for you, John."

He kept a stubborn silence. Of course, Rahel couldn't keep his promises for him, whether it was the one he'd made to the people of Jerusalem to return and defend them, or the one he'd made earlier on the battlefield at Yarmouk.

What would happen if Rahel *did* keep his promise for him? What if, by some miracle, allied to cunning diplomacy, she was able to save Palestine and send the invaders to conquer new territory?

What if Rahel saved the future…and he, John, was not there to see it? How could he bear it if that happened?

At once the thought horrified him; he had not thought himself capable of such selfishness. "Have you had any visions?" he asked, his voice strained. "Or has Elisa?" After the night at Oliveta when Elisa had given the Message, the child had begun to manifest other powerful gifts.

Rahel sighed. "I'm afraid neither of us have seen anything since Antioch. Elisa still has Oratory and Interpretation, but her Messenger gift has lain dormant. I believe it isn't uncommon for the very young to manifest many gifts before settling on something less showy for their maturity. I suppose it keeps us wise old folks humble."

"You're neither old nor proud enough to need that," he said gloomily.

"Tell me about *your* day," she prompted, gesturing to the seat beside her. "Have you learned anything about the guardian?"

John sighed, forcing his incorporeal spirit to assume a sitting posture on the cushioned bench. Dreamwalking, he could neither feel, nor smell, nor taste. As he told his story, he watched the soul-light flicker across the smooth, pale surface of Rahel's cheek, the curve of her neck, the dark waves of her hair.

The life of the spirit, he thought, was so much less satisfactory than he'd imagined.

He finished his story and Rahel smiled wistfully. "You'll have to give them my thanks—these Tripoli Watchers. I had hoped you would find a home, family…"

"They aren't my family," he interrupted sharply.

"John…let them be. Even if only for a while."

A stab of something went through him—guilt, or anger, or weariness. He owed her an apology, and offered it up in the form of something he'd been hiding. "I never told you, their name is Zakar."

"But that was my name," she said, wonderingly.

"Yes." *Rahel Zakar:* it was a distinctively Jewish name, although her family had settled in Egypt and Hellenised long before the first-century destruction of Jerusalem. And so the Zakar family had survived that bloody holocaust, which had seen their people around the empire slaughtered by the million.

"In fact," Rahel added, more slowly, "as we were travelling south, we travelled as Zakars. There are so many rumours flying about Oliveta, John. I found using the Bessarion name…disruptive."

"What do you mean?"

Rahel sighed, reluctant. "They're blaming *us.*"

He might not be inhabiting his body, but he could have sworn his skin prickled with fear. "You mean they're blaming me."

"Yes." A pause. "I'm sorry."

"What about in Jerusalem?"

"Sophronius believed me, but I'm not sure how many others do."

"Strife," he whispered. He'd known, when he began to confront the Watchers, that he was going to make enemies. He'd never imagined he was setting fire to his own reputation and putting his family in danger from the very people who should have cared for them during his absence.

"It was easiest to call ourselves Zakars." Rahel hitched a shoulder. "Maybe, if you come home again…"

"Not *if.* Say *when.*"

"*When* you come home again," she murmured. There was silence for a moment, and then she said with a silvery shimmer of laughter in her voice: "You know, these people might be our descendants, John."

"They aren't," he growled. Because he was going to find his way home. Because they were going to be the Bessarions again.

This future needed undoing. Still, in this telling of the world's story, he hadn't yet gone home to Rahel, which meant that they very well might have descendants by the name of Zakar.

He thought of the small home with its sparse furnishings, the meal of bread and lentils, the careful division of oranges. Zakar must be better off than many in Tripoli, but still. John sighed and admitted what he'd been thinking. "I want better things for my grandchildren. I *will* find my way home, Rahel. I'll find the island you saw in your vision, and I'll find this Hubert and get a Message or a Portent or *something*. Just as soon as I get out of here…"

His voice faded away.

If he got out of here.

* * *

The young countess stood near his cell door with a clove orange held to her pointed nose, and spat words in a language John didn't know.

Before she entered, her guards had forced him to kneel, binding his hands tightly with cord to a ring set in the wall behind his back. The compression on his wrists was obviously intentional; John felt his hands swelling as the blood pooled in them.

So far, the pain was bearable, but he'd seen this form of torture employed in his own time, and it made an ominous beginning. Perhaps it was a matter of divine justice that he endured it now.

He took a careful breath and replied, "I speak Arabic, my lady."

Her brows knit together and she said something else in her own language, taking a while to do it. She watched his face closely as she spoke, and at last her words trailed away into a sharp question.

John shrugged, switching languages with each sentence. "I also speak Greek. And Latin. And Armenian. And Persian—"

For the first time, she looked confused. "You are the Templar, Peter of Alba," she said accusingly in Armenian. She spoke the language like a native, and John thought he detected a hint of that blood in her black hair and insistent nose. "Speak Frankish."

He was born and bred noble himself, and knew that as little as he might deserve this treatment, he would gain nothing by impertinence. Instead, he answered mildly. "I do not know the person you mean. My name is John Bessarion. I am a Greek from far away, a stranger in your city."

She looked him up and down, doubt flickering in her eyes. "Do not think that because I am a woman, I am soft and easy to cozen. The pain in your hands may be small now, but in another hour or two it will be far worse. You *will* tell me the truth."

Beads of sweat formed on his forehead as it occurred to him, not for the first time, just how much trouble he might be in. Why did the people in this time suspect him of being other than he was? "It will not change what I've already told you, my lady." A thought struck him. "The man you seek—is he Frankish?"

Her eyes narrowed. "Yes."

He hesitated a moment, the weeks of travel and the fact that he'd nearly killed the man holding him back. But it was foolish to feel a sense of loyalty to someone who had tried to kill him—and whose more recent actions suddenly took on a more sinister meaning. "I entered the city last night with a horse, sword, and cloak belonging to a fellow traveller. He said he had business in Mount Pilgrim and asked me to stable his horse."

The countess hummed suspiciously. "A convenient story."

"Then confront me with someone who knows this Peter by sight. He's head and shoulders taller than I am. It won't be—"

The door to his cell opened, letting the grey morning light flood in. The countess swung around with a gesture of irritation. "What is it?"

A slim woman stood in the open door, looking at John with cool grey eyes. About his own age, the lady wore heavy brocade the colour of lavender, her black hair caged in a silver net beneath a crisp white hat and coif. She was very tall, very pale, and like Countess Lucy, she looked at him like a commander sizing him up for his usefulness.

She spoke to the countess in Frankish, and Countess Lucy responded with clipped, hostile words. For a moment they argued like equals, the grey-eyed newcomer laughing and shaking her head. Finally, she folded her arms and stood, watching.

Countess Lucy turned to him, switching back to Armenian. "Last night you told my people you had come across the mountains from the Valley of Bacar. Why is the Temple sending spies to Syria?"

The Temple, and Butros was apparently a *Templar*. He had no idea what that was supposed to mean. "If I was who you think I am, I might be able to tell you."

"How long did you travel with this man?"

"Since Mosul."

"And what was your business in Mosul?"

"I was only passing through, trying to find my way home."

"And this man? Did he give his name and business?"

John didn't hesitate. Butros must have known that the stables were being watched, that he had a better chance of getting into the city if he hid his face and parted from his horse. Likely it was even his intention to have John arrested in his stead.

"He said his name was Butros, and that he was returning from Baghdad, lady."

The name struck the countess like a dart. Her lips paled. "Baghdad? What was he doing *there?*"

"I don't know."

She started forward, her hand clenching as though she would have liked to strike him. "Did he speak of me? Did he say he meant to unseat me in Tripoli?"

There was real fear in her eyes, and John tried to speak comfortably to her: "I assure you he did not."

The observer in the corner spoke in halting Armenian. "Did the man happen to say what he *did* in Baghdad?"

"No, my lady."

"Pardon me, Eschiva, but *I* am asking the questions here," Countess Lucy snapped. The grey-eyed lady smirked, but held her peace. Silence stretched out like the string on a lyre, tuned to breaking-point, until it was broken by some sort of disturbance in the courtyard beyond. Throughout, the countess kept her eyes fixed on John, pale lips pressed together.

"Perhaps you are telling the truth," she said at last. "Perhaps not. In another hour or two, we will know better."

"If you leave his hands bound like that, you'll maim him," Lady Eschiva objected. "Do you mean to tell me there are no men in this city who know

Alba by sight?"

"Am I lady here, or are you?"

There was a brief silence, during which the grey-eyed lady did not quite heave a sigh, nor raise her eyes to heaven. "You are, Countess."

"Then leave me to the ruling of my own city." The countess pointed to the door. "Leave us."

With a shrug, Lady Eschiva turned to go. For a moment John felt like a drowning man watching his ship sail away, but when as she reached the cell door, the grey-eyed lady stopped in her tracks, and called out in Frankish, beckoning to someone in the courtyard. Countess Lucy hissed in annoyance and made an angry gesture; but then Eschiva drew back from the door with a catlike smile, and John looked up to see a soldierly man in a white mantle that was decorated with a red cross.

Immediately behind him was Butros, now clad in a similar mantle.

Relief swept over him. John nodded toward the Frank and said, rather weakly in Armenian, "There he is. That's the man I met in Mosul."

"Ahhh, Pierre d'Alba," Lady Eschiva said with a glimmer of cool laughter. Pointing to John, she asked the countess a lilting question. Countess Lucy sent an angry glare at John, made a dismissive sound and stalked out of the cell to meet the stranger in the white mantle. Her guards followed her, leaving John alone with the grey-eyed lady, who was now laughing in triumph.

Immediately, she drew a small knife from a sheath at her belt and spoke in Armenian. "I am Eschiva of Ibelin, the Lord of Beirut."

The masculine title she claimed suggested that she herself was the ruler, and not merely the ruler's wife. Strange customs, for a strange future. "I am John Bessarion," he answered.

Her eyes widened in recognition. "What did you say?"

"That my name is John Bessarion?"

Eschiva took a deep breath. "Fortunate meeting, then."

She bent down and carefully sawed through the cords that had sunk deep into his flesh. The blood rushed back into his body with excruciating pain, and for a moment all John could do was breathe.

"Why do you help me, my lady?" he asked, when the agony receded.

She beckoned him toward the cell door. "I heard the countess was interrogating a spy of the Temple, and for the sake of old allegiances I thought I should attend."

John followed her into the daylight, blinking. The countess and her high-ranking visitor had gone, but Butros—or Peter of Alba—was still there, lounging against one of the pillars of the peristyle. He grinned nastily when he saw John.

"What cheer, Prester?" he rasped in Arabic. "Was all your boasting empty, that you could not save yourself from a little duress?"

Boasting? John simply shot the man an expressionless look. What had this been—some kind of test?

Evidently, Lady Eschiva understood the Frank's jeers. "Beware, Alba," she said icily in the same language. "If you mock this man, you mock me."

Instantly, the smirk vanished from the man's face. He straightened, bowed, and walked swiftly away. John stared after him, feeling little better than he had when the countess had mistaken him for a spy. Who *was* he to these people?

He didn't want to know. "Am I free to leave, my lady?"

Eschiva frowned. "You seem in a very great hurry, John Bessarion." There was still a note of steel in her lazy voice and John sensed that, now she had championed him, she meant to exact some kind of price.

"I beg your pardon," he said humbly. "I have urgent business in the city."

She glanced toward the palace entrance hall, with its magnificent carved and painted portal. "Very well." Dipping into the purse at her side, she extracted a small leaden seal, stamped on one side with a crude human figure and on the other with a cross and tiny letters which read, in Latin, *Sigillum Eschiva Domine.* "Wait on me at Sext at my lodgings on the Street of Fish. Do not be tardy."

She turned, snapping her fingers to a cluster of attendants and following Peter of Alba towards the entrance hall of the palace. Shaking his head, John slipped the small leaden token into his pouch next to Rahel's wax-sealed packet. This city was too full of people who wanted urgently to speak with him.

By now, the sun was getting high and the city buzzed with activity. Outside the palace gate, John stopped to survey the crowded street. Zakar had given him directions to the Messenger's silk-printing workshop, but apparently this Hubert had planned to visit the Zakars today anyway. He might as well go by way of the Zakar house and try to catch Hubert there.

At least he might allay the half-formed fear at the back of his mind that the countess might have wished to speak to Zakar as well. John set off briskly, pausing to admire a large new ship anchored in the harbour beyond the water gate before turning down the narrow street that led to the Zakar house.

Odd. For a house with five children, the place was very quiet.

As he approached, the door opened and a woman emerged. Not Sara Zakar: this woman was younger and dressed in crisp, fine clothing: blousy pants, a knee-length embroidered jacket, and a striped sash to outline her trim waist. There was a sombre look on her face, but as she caught John watching her, she summoned a smile and flashed him a wink. She was extraordinarily handsome, he thought absent-mindedly. The woman turned away and walked up the street, pausing once to look back at him through downcast lashes.

John stopped outside the Zakars' closed and silent door. Something was definitely wrong. He tried knocking, but as his hand touched the wood, the door swung open.

John stepped into the dim room, waiting for his eyes to adjust. "Zakar?"

No answer.

The house should be like a beating heart, the looms clacking, children's footsteps pounding overhead. Today—silence. Something else teased at his senses.

A smell.

These people could be our descendants.

"No," he groaned, flying for the stairs that led up to the second floor. "No, no, no, no, *no...*"

He burst through the door at the top of the stairs and stood motionless, staring at the scene inside.

Red. Wet. Stench. Death.

He recoiled a step, clapping a hand over his mouth to keep his stomach down. A moment later he fumbled for the door and closed it again.

The only sound in the house was his own quick breathing. All else was silent.

The red. The wet.

The smile. The wink.

"Strife," he said thickly, and dashed downstairs to the street.

Chapter IX.

Soraya had awoken to the taste of blood; drowning in the hot, sickly, coppery tang. Saif's hands—and the ring that formed her prison—must be drenched with the stuff. She howled a voiceless protest into the dark, rigidly ignored until at last the command came to force her into the open.

Once she had formed eyes, Soraya found herself crouching above a clean fireplace, the ashes having been swept up into her body. She groaned and spat, still unable to clear the taste of blood from her mouth.

Or the smell from her nostrils.

Or the weeping from her ears.

By the grey light struggling in at the windows, Soraya guessed that it must be somewhere around dawn. Illuminated by a single oil lamp, Saif stood cleaning his spear in the midst of slaughter. The battered body of a man was clenched around a sticky wound in his gut on the floor at Saif's feet, and a woman lay motionless nearby with her hands stretched out toward the man's body.

There were children, too. Huddled together on the sleeping-platform. Still alive. As Soraya approached, they burst into renewed tears. She backed away from the small mortals and gazed down at the broken bodies on the floor, the slowly thickening blood.

She wondered what she'd feel. She expected shock, disgust. What she actually felt was a dull loathing, and the bone deep exhaustion of a sight she'd seen too many times before.

She swallowed hard. "We've done this before, haven't we?"

It took an instant before Saif met her gaze. There was still blood on his hands, and they were shaking. For a moment, his eyes were vulnerable. "I don't remember."

Soraya stilled. *"You* don't remember?"

His eyes dropped to the floor. "I remember the first man I ever killed. One or two of the most recent ones. But that's all."

Soraya didn't know what to say. It had never occurred to her that she might not be the only one with missing memories.

Saif went on, mechanically cleaning his hands and weapon. "It's not like yours. I mean, there are only days missing, here and there. I remember going on the missions, just not what we did on them. Antioch. Damascus. Saphet. Jerusalem."

"Stop," Soraya choked. Too many places; and she must have been complicit in all of them. Too many memories like this would destroy her. "I don't want to know."

Saif swallowed hard, and blinked. In a heartbeat, he'd shuttered away his guilt, so quickly, it was frightening. "It's all right, Soraya. We did this for a reason, may God forgive us."

"What reason could possibly—" she caught herself and swallowed her anger, unsure if it was for the children's sake, or her own. "What reason?"

"There's something we had to find out, something the Watchers would know. They didn't."

"So we killed them."

"Watchers are our enemies, may God have mercy upon them. I've done no worse to them than they would do to us, if they caught us."

"You mean they're the enemies of this master of yours. If they ever did me any harm, I don't recall it. How could I, when my memories were stolen?"

Saif's voice hardened. "Are you going to help me, or shall I put you back in confinement?"

What did it matter? Her past was lost. Her future was damned. All she had was today, and today she wanted to enjoy a little freedom before she was forced back into her prison.

"I'll do whatever you want," she said dully.

The tension between his shoulders unstitched a little, as though her words came as a genuine relief. "Thank you."

His sincerity bothered her. When it came to Saif, she didn't want to have to deal with any feelings more complicated than adamant hatred.

He glanced at the children. "The sun is rising. I have business to deal with, but I want you to watch this house. Anyone else who visits, remember them and tell me when I come to relieve you. If there are any other Watchers in Tripoli, we'll root them out."

Saif must have been rattled by the night's events: it was the first time he had been so careless with his words. *I want you to watch this house* was not a binding command; merely a statement of desire which she was not compelled to obey. Eager to prevent him noticing his oversight, Soraya changed the subject. "What about the children?"

"Take them downstairs and turn them out onto the street. I'm done with them."

The command wrapped itself around her feet, marching her over to the sleeping-platform to pull them to their feet. Compelled to obey, she took refuge in sharp words: "Oh, so you aren't going to kill them too? What's wrong, Saif? Lost your taste for blood?"

"They were adopted," he said with perfect sincerity. "Had they been Zakars by blood, we would have had to kill them."

That took Soraya's breath away. But the command still compelled her, and she could neither disobey, nor delay obedience. She pulled the terrified children to their feet, shooed them down the stairs, and let them out the front door. She had to bolt it behind them before the force of the command was spent. Afterward, Soraya stood staring into the darkness, listening to the muffled wails on the other side of the door; hating herself and Saif and his master and everything in the world.

After a moment, she went back upstairs. "I'm already looking forward to our next mission, master. Should we set fire to a widow's house or just drown someone's pet kitten?"

"God knows best," he said in all sincerity, throwing down the bloody cloth he'd used to clean his hands. Opening the door leading upstairs to the flat roof, he took a breath of fresh air, glancing up at the clear stars above.

"Just remember what I told you," he added, leading the way onto the roof. "And take care; I don't want anyone catching sight of you."

Soraya felt the tug as he drew on the soul tether, absorbing more of her strength and speed. Taking a short run, he raced for the parapet, launched himself into the air, and sailed across the street to the house opposite. She heard him hit the distant roof and roll. Then he was gone.

Shivering, she retreated into the house—hot and stinking compared to the roof—and raided the room for a blanket, a leftover morsel of bread and a pot of honey. She took the lamp downstairs, where the smell wasn't so bad, and ate the honey there. Even after that, her mouth still tasted like blood. She knew how it would have gone; Saif bursting in to drag the father from his bed, the wife throwing herself forward to shield her man, the quick, brutal killings when they could not tell him what he wanted to know, while the children watched with wide-eyed horror. Her gut churned at the image.

Saif might speak like a sincere believer, but even she, hopelessly wicked as she was, knew his actions were evil. While she feared God too much even to invoke the Name, Saif used it to stamp piety upon his misdeeds. She might be destined for the abyss, but she didn't for a moment doubt she would be alone. He would be right there alongside her.

Oh, mercy. She was going to be stuck with him for eternity.

She wrapped herself in the blanket and lay down—sleep was one of her favourite earthly pleasures—but as the hours dragged by, the sleep didn't come. Eventually, bright light seeped through the crack beneath the door and the sound of traffic going to and fro in the city outside rose to a steady rumble.

She got up, ran her fingers through her hair and re-tied her sash. She agreed with Saif on one thing: she didn't want to be caught in this house. The sooner she got out of this cursed place, the better. Saif's carelessness meant she wouldn't be forced to obey him—and so, until he realised his mistake, for a few precious hours, she'd be *free.*

As usual, she had a veil with her, but after a moment's hesitation she tucked it into her bosom rather than wear it: she wasn't afraid of being accosted, her reputation was the last thing she needed to worry about, and she wanted to feel the sun on her face. She threw the blanket into a far corner behind the silent loom that stood there, and let herself out into a narrow street. Outside, the salty smell of the sea mingled with the sweetly sour perfume of the citrus orchards. Soraya breathed deeply, letting the scent cleanse away the stench of death that clung to her.

When she looked up, a man was walking down the street towards her. Pleasantly surprised, Soraya took a moment to drink him in: he carried no weapons but held himself like a soldier, wiry and well-built. His greying hair and beard glinted in the sunlight like iron, the same wintry colour as his eyes. His clothing was well-worn but clean, an embroidered white tunic beneath a shabby woollen cloak. Perhaps she had lived among mortals too long, but the sight made her feel better at once.

He met her gaze without slackening his pace, and Soraya shot him a smile and a wink. It was foolish to let herself be seen leaving a house full of dead bodies, but with any luck, by the time the slaughter was discovered she'd be far away and no passer-by in the streets would be able to find her again. Soraya hurried away in search of her escape, but when she glanced back, he was still staring after her with those wintry eyes.

He knocked at the door she'd just pulled shut behind her.

Energy burst through her body like a flame, the mysterious physical impulse to fight or flee. Soraya controlled it grimly, forcing herself to walk on at the same pace. A moment later she glanced back again. The street was empty, the door open.

Praying that the terrible scene within would catch the man off-guard long enough to let her escape, Soraya quickened her pace. A sun-washed intersection of streets ahead promised thicker traffic and a chance to escape. Beyond, she glimpsed a wall and the mast of a ship. The harbour.

Behind, footsteps slammed into the street. "You! Stop!"

Abandoning caution, Soraya leaped into a run. In ten steps she burst out onto the main road leading to the harbour gate. A flood of early-morning traffic slowed her to a walk and Soraya elbowed pedestrians out of her way, looking for another opening between the houses. She might draw on the soul-tether to scale the city wall, but that would certainly alert Saif. And besides, she wasn't supposed to be putting on an acrobatic display for the public. She was supposed to be lurking near the house, keeping discreet watch.

The iron-haired soldier burst out of the street on her trail. Through the crowd, their eyes met. "Stop that woman!" he shouted. "Thief!"

Strike her blind! He was quick.

"Here, what's this?" someone asked, and a hand reached out to grab her collar. Soraya aimed a precise jab at the man's gut and skipped past him, twisted like an eel to avoid another man's lunge, and slid into a small covered street. All she needed was a moment's privacy, but the iron-haired one was hot on her heels. These streets were a thin winding network, some dark and dripping and barely wide enough for one person to pass through, others decorated with graffiti in Arabic or something she instinctively recognised as Frankish.

Tripoli, no doubt. Soraya could not have guessed whether she had been here before, but something about the shapes of Frankish words and Frankish houses brought an instinctive sense of dread. Somewhere, buried deep, lurked bad memories.

Soraya flew through the dark narrow alleyways, trying not to pull on the soul tether as she poured all her strength into the chase. The man was too close; she could feel his hard breathing almost on her neck.

Enough of this.

She came to the end of an alley and whipped around the corner, once again in a populous street. Instead of running, she backed against the wall, hardly noticing the pain in heart and lungs. She felt wonderfully, gloriously alive. The iron-grey man burst out behind her and she stuck out a foot, sending him sprawling into the street. With a snarl, he grabbed for her ankle but she whisked it out of the way with a dancer's step, shimmied briefly and shot back into the alleyway. He scrambled to his feet, breathing hard, and came after her again, but Soraya had bought herself valuable time. She angled into another street and stopped, taking deep breaths, wrenching her body into a new shape, shedding limbs and cracking bones.

Had she not been enslaved to Saif, she could have simply dropped her body and returned to the spirit world—but if she did that now she'd be compelled to return to the ring, imprisoned once again.

Fortunately, other abilities were left to her. Within moments she was no more than a small, sleek grey cat standing daintily atop a slurry of damp ashes.

Her pursuer shot around the corner. Soraya hunched her back and hissed at him. He startled, then stood breathing hard, staring down the alley with a faint frown between his eyes. Two huge tenements rose to either side; the walls ran on, smooth and doorless, for fifty paces. Much too far for a mortal woman to run in the time it had taken for the man to pursue her.

"Damn it," he growled. He looked down at her again, and in the chill glare of those eyes, Soraya thought he must have guessed who was staring back at him from the small furred creature at his feet. Instead, he reached down and gave her a gentle scratch behind the ear. "Sorry to disturb you," he said, before continuing down the alleyway.

Soraya froze, staring after him.

Perhaps it was her more sensitive cat's hearing; perhaps it was that the words seemed familiar; perhaps it was the normal pitch at which he spoke, rather than his previous shouts. Whatever it was, it stole all rational thought.

She *knew* this man.

She had no idea when, where, or how. But she knew him, and a heady blend of emotion hit her: rage, impatience, frustration—and above all, *hope*.

Without thinking, she yowled and scampered after him, up the alley. Beyond was a chaotically busy street lined with stalls and the hot, tantalising scent of street food. People thronged to and fro in the marketplace. The iron-haired one had vanished and as a cat, Soraya was too small to see more than a hundred stomping feet crisscrossing the street before her.

She shrank back into the alley, shaking herself with a hiss. What had she been thinking? She should be glad she didn't remember how she knew this man—there was nothing in her past but evil. Most likely she had done him some terrible injury. She should stop thinking about yesterday and tomorrow. All that mattered was the fleeting present she had in which to enjoy herself.

Soraya withdrew into the alleyway and bent her body again, summoning the damp ashes from where they lay down the other end of the passage. Within moments she was up on two feet and out in the crowded street again, scanning the crowd for grey hair and wintry eyes.

Stop it! Even if you find him, he'll just want to throttle you for what you did to the poor people in that house.

An open door beckoned, and Soraya ducked through into the dim lower floor of a public house. The small room was furnished with low bench seats at a pair of tables, where men sat huddled together over glass beakers of wine.

A thin woman in an apron came forward, wiping her hands. "What'll you have, love?"

"Glass of wine and whatever else you've got."

"Today, hot bread."

"Perfect." In the street, Soraya's fingers had been busy. She glanced at the silver groat in her hand before passing it to the woman. On one side was a cross; on the other a fortress with three towers. *Civitas Tripolis Syrie.* It didn't take much Latin to understand that. Definitely Tripoli.

The public-house-keeper accepted the coin without giving any change, and quickly brought her a hot flatbread with two small bowls, one of oil, the other of pounded herbs and spices to dip it in, together with a beaker full of aniseed-flavoured wine. That was one of the few consolations to being an evil djinn: there was no point staying away from forbidden drink. Taking the food to the empty table at the back of the room, Soraya ripped a corner off the bread and dipped it first into the oil and then into the spice mixture.

The food melted in her mouth. Soraya let out a little sigh of pleasure and relaxed against the wall, savouring the taste. Crisp and tender, the bread must be fresh out of the oven, the spices freshly ground. Vivid sensations danced across Soraya's tongue: in her mind she saw spice caravans, wheat fields, stone mills.

There was so much these earth-bound creatures took for granted.

Soraya was only halfway through her meal when a shadow blocked the doorway, cutting off much of the light. She shrank back against the wall, but the wintry grey eyes fastened on her at once.

He crossed the room towards her and sat on the bench that faced her across the table. There was a crisp, pale fury in his eyes as he leaned forward and breathed, too soft for anyone else to hear: "Tell me who killed the Zakars."

Soraya would have given anything to say *Not me.* But it would have been false: she might be Saif's slave, but she endowed his body with strength and speed, protected him from swords and arrows. She took a drink, proud that her hands weren't shaking. Finally, setting the knobbly glass back on the table with a sharp *clack*, she met the man's eyes defiantly. "Trust me on this: you don't want to know."

"All right." He half rose, hands on the table. "You're coming with me."

She lifted an eyebrow, curious. "Who were they to you?"

For the space of a breath, he looked down at her in confusion. "What?"

She tilted her head towards him. "You aren't from around here. Your clothes, your voice—it's dead obvious."

He didn't take the bait; didn't give her any clues to his strange familiarity. "That's not relevant."

She shouldn't be trying to help him, but she seemed unable to stop herself. "Want some advice? Get out of this city while you still can."

She half expected him to laugh at her, but his grim face didn't change. "Are you threatening me?"

"I'm giving you some friendly advice, that's all."

His lips thinned. "Come on." He held out a hand to beckon her.

So, he thought she'd just come quietly, did he? Soraya smiled at him and got up slowly, bending a little too deep to give him a flash of cleavage, but his watchful eyes didn't get caught there. Well, it was worth the try. She slid past him and started for the door. Outside, the street was just as busy as it had been ten minutes ago. The man took her elbow gently but firmly to guide her into the street.

"Where are we going, then?"

"To the palace." As he steered her through the crowd, people shuffled out of their way, sensing the air of authority this man projected, despite his outlandish clothing. Who *was* he—and why did she know his voice?

As the street widened onto an open forum lined with shops, the crowd loosened a little, providing Soraya with her chance. She took a deep breath, pulling strength away from Saif and back to herself through the soul tether. As power flowed into her, Soraya yanked away from the grey-haired man, grabbed his wrist as it left her elbow, and threw him across the street.

Taken off guard, he landed on the stones with a grunt. Soraya dashed for another side street. Someone loomed up in front of her and she jabbed him below the breast-bone, doubling him in a knot of helpless agony.

People began to run to get out of her way. Soraya risked a glance behind. The grey-eyed man was already on his feet again, starting after her.

On the other end of the soul tether, surprisingly close, Saif yanked nearly hard enough to snatch her out of her body. Strength left her. Soraya tripped and ploughed into the cobblestones, coming to a halt at a man's feet.

Saif.

He stepped past her, not looking down. As the grey-haired man caught up to them, Saif whipped the butt of his spear around, cracking the other man across the side of his head just hard enough to lay him out in the street. He groaned once and lay still.

Still weakened from Saif's grip on the soul tether, Soraya climbed dizzily to her feet. Clearly, she'd had the ill fortune to stage her escape in the very square where Saif was conducting his business. "I can explain," she began.

"You'd better," he growled. Grabbing her wrist, he pulled her after him into the maze of streets. As he walked, Saif pulled his black turban from his clean-shaven head, shook out the folds of thin muslin and threw the cloth over Soraya, hiding her from sight and altering his own appearance. He moved in sharp angry jerks, keeping a tight grip on the soul tether, and Soraya hid a sigh. Of course, he was furious.

They came to a large tenement, and Saif dragged her up four flights of stairs to a small, spartan room in the topmost storey where a bedroll was unfurled in the corner well away from the single narrow window. He pulled her inside, slammed the door, and folded his arms.

"I can't trust you as far as I can spit. God have mercy, what were you *thinking?* Tell me the truth!"

"I was thinking I'd oil off and carouse while you weren't looking." It was the strict truth, but she leaned on the words sarcastically, leaving him staring at her in confusion until the compulsion of the command left her and she was able to lie to him. "Idiot! I was watching the house, of course, like you told me." She rubbed her aching wrist, glaring at him with a show of wounded virtue.

His eyes narrowed. "I smell wine and spices."

"This body requires sustenance, just as yours does!" She tilted her chin defiantly. "There I was watching the street, like you said, and that man came out of the Zakar house and gave chase. I shook him off and then bought some food, since there happened to be some nearby. Then he found me again."

He stared at her, evidently trying to figure out whether she was really as stupid as she pretended to be. "Why didn't you go straight back to the house?" he asked irritably.

"Because it stinks of *death.*"

With a puff of vexation he went to the window.

Soraya's fury built. Mortals! A race with every possible blessing, and the minds of donkeys. "You keep saying there's a reason for all this. What reason? I'm damned already; a creature like me has no hope of paradise—but *you do,* and you throw it away like this? *Why?*" Soraya spat on the floor. "I am compelled to obey; what's your excuse?"

"I do it for the good of the faithful." Saif turned from the window, his face set with utter certainty. "This is a just cause, and I must obey. It says so in the holy book."

"Oh. You read it in the holy book: al-Mukhtar Saif al-Din, in the month of Rabi al-Awal you shall go to Tripoli-in-Syria and slaughter a man and his wife, and turn his children out into the street—"

"No!"

"Have you even read this holy book?"

"Yes."

"And it told you…?"

"It tells me to obey those charged with authority over me. So I do, God willing. You don't understand! Soraya—we have the privilege of serving a master whose wisdom and insight is far beyond ours." The perfect sincerity in his voice took her breath away. "I only wish you could know him like I do. He took me in, you know. Bought me as a slave, endowed me with everything I have, made me strong and keen and sharp. I was nothing, and now I have a purpose in the house of faith. I would be a wretch if I was to give him anything but love and the utmost obedience."

As he spoke, her anger ebbed away. If what Saif said was true—and there was sincerity in every word—then the real evildoer was not this blind follower, but the one who had taken him and twisted him until he could ask no questions, make no protests.

"Did you enjoy it?" she asked, her voice low. Somehow, it seemed important to get an answer to that question. "Did you *like* killing them?"

"Of course not. The justice of God is very terrible." He jabbed a finger at her. "And I didn't turn the children into the street out of cruelty, either. They should have led me to the house of other Watchers."

"So that you could kill more of them before their children's eyes?"

His lips thinned. "That eldest boy was too clever for us. They went to the palace instead, to complain to the garrison."

"How dare he." Soraya shook her head. "So this is the justice of God, hm? Who are *you* to say you know the mind of God, Saif al-Din?"

He blinked, and seemed to remember that he was angry with her. "Since God is all-powerful, then if this was not his will, he would have stopped me. And if you can't accept that, then you'll have to be confined. I can't risk you subverting this mission."

"No!" Caught up in the argument, Soraya had forgotten just how much power he held over her. Her throat clenched as she remembered her last waking, the sensation of drowning in blood. She'd do anything to avoid another such awakening. "Please don't lock me up again. I know I fouled it up today, but truly, I'd rather be out here helping you than in there."

She meant it, too. Apart from the satisfaction of making her captor's life difficult, she knew she had nothing to gain from obstructing him.

But Saif's jaw bulged stubbornly. "I can't trust you."

She moved a little closer. Ran her tongue over her lips; a nervous gesture, but she took her time about it. Let her eyes get big and starry; willed a little more blood to her lips. "Please. I'd do anything to stay in this body."

As she put a hand on his arm, he froze.

"You didn't command me, last night," she whispered, letting her voice get low and husky. "You should have told me exactly what you wanted me to do. I *am* your slave. I have no choice but to obey. …Try me now. See what I would do for you."

His eyes dipped to her bosom, then back up again. He didn't breathe for a long moment. Then he reached up and took her hand in an iron grip, and threw it from him. "I have a wife," he snarled. "I don't want you."

"How is that relevant? Just think, I can take any shape you like. Don't tell me you've never thought about it."

He took a step back, more alarmed than she'd ever seen him.

"You *haven't?*" Six months ago she'd put a spear in him, and he'd shrugged it off. Now she'd actually frightened him, and all she had done was put a hand on his arm…

It was an intoxicating thought. "We've *never* done this before?"

He backed again. "We aren't doing it now." He took a convulsive swallow. "I seek refuge in God from the accursed devil! The master warned me you'd tempt me to my destruction."

He couldn't have been thinking straight, or he would have ordered her back into confinement. Soraya wanted to laugh. "And you *believed* him? Most men would kill for a slave girl like me."

"Soraya," he said tightly, "I don't want a slave."

That surprised her into stillness. Shattered the momentary illusion of power. "You could have fooled me."

"I want a comrade. Someone I can *trust,* someone I don't have to give orders that cover every waking moment." His carnelian ring glowed, and he clenched his grip on his spear.

"No! Please!" Soraya grabbed for his wrist, desperate now. What did it matter? She was already damned. Already today she'd killed, lied, stolen, drunk and tried to seduce two different men. This was who she was. What difference did it make if she helped him or not?

"Please," she said, breathlessly. "I mean it. I'll do anything. I'll be your comrade. I'll be your killer. Just don't confine me again."

For a moment, something in his eyes gave her hope. He believed her. He was going to agree.

And then he shook his head. "Impossible. I'm a man and a mortal. You're a woman and a djinn. We were never meant to be comrades, Soraya."

He firmed his grip on the soul tether, and yanked her out of her body.

Chapter X.

"And in this year of Christ 1264, John of Ibelin, Lord of Beirut, died, and left behind two daughters." Gerard paused with his pen poised above the parchment manuscript, trying to remember what else had happened in that year.

Here, behind his desk, was where Gerard felt most at home—among his translations, fair copies, memoranda, and in spare moments like this, the history he was writing. The Master, however, had other ideas.

A rap came at the door and a servant poked his head in. "Master William's greetings, Sir Gerard, and will you join him in his cabinet?"

With a sigh, Gerard got to his feet and grabbed a sheet of paper and a quill before emerging from his chilly office and walking the three doors down the loggia to the cabinet from which the Master of the Temple administered the Order and its vast properties across the sea.

Since the loss of Jerusalem to Saladin a century ago, the Templar headquarters had been relocated to the southwest corner of the small promontory where the bustling city of Acre had first been built. A vast, hexagonal fortress with unassailable walls, the Templar fortress boasted five massive towers along with stables, dormitories, warehouses, a chapel, a refectory, a treasury, and a very fine palace to house the Master and his many administrators.

Gerard himself was only an confrere of the Order, a secular associate rather than a fully committed knight-monk. Still, when Master William of Beaujeu gave orders, Gerard obeyed them without question. He knocked on the door to the Master's cabinet before venturing inside.

The Master himself sat at the head of his table; a grizzled, gaunt old man with aristocratic hawklike features which served to warn of the brilliant mind behind. He nodded as Gerard entered. "Montreal, thanks for coming. Now that we're all here, gentlemen, you may report."

At his right hand, two men nodded civilly to Gerard as he settled himself at the table and dipped his quill in an inkwell, ready to take a record of the meeting. He recognised the two other men instantly. Peter of Alba had been born in Tripoli and was now one of Beaujeu's trusted agents in the turbulent county. Brother Reddecoeur, a former Templar commander in Tripoli, was a tall, imposing Spanish knight of royal descent; one of the most respected Templars in the kingdom—even Gerard had to admit, more respected than Beaujeu himself. Both had just arrived via ship from Tripoli.

Alba's voice was unusually faint and rasping as he began his report. "My lord, I proceeded to Baghdad as ordered and received an audience with Arghun, king of the Tartars—the Il-Khan, as he calls himself. I told him we had information that Sultan Qalawun would be marching on the Coast this spring, and offered a significant financial gift if he would threaten Damascus, to be doubled if the sultan was forced to abandon his attack on Tripoli." Alba took a deep, rasping breath. "He said, *May you all have heart attacks.*"

No one laughed.

"He says the notice is too short. He has a great empire to rule, and other disputes require his attention." Alba shrugged. "So I returned to Tripoli and reported to Brother Peter of Moncada."

Gerard realised he was crushing the point of his quill into the paper. Quickly, he used his penknife to mend the nib, focusing hard to keep his hands steady. This tragedy was nightmarishly slow in unfolding. By now the Temple had known about the sultan's plans to destroy Tripoli for three months. For three months, Tripoli could have been fortifying her walls, calling on her allies, stocking her granaries, securing her future. Three months of ignored warnings, including his own. Three months of nothing. If each man was the architect of his own fate, then Countess Lucy was laying the foundations for her own destruction.

Beaujeu's thin lips disappeared as he pursed them. "Your report, Brother

Reddecoeur?"

Reddecoeur bent his head. "I arrived in Tripoli by merchant ship, incognito, and was welcomed by Brother Peter of Moncada. He confirmed that the countess keeps a close watch on the Templar commandery in Tripoli." The ghost of a smile danced across his face. "As it happens, on the morning we arrived, some poor devil was being interrogated on suspicion of being a Templar spy."

"Ah." Alba grinned. "Prester John."

Gerard's curiosity was whetted, but Reddecoeur continued with his story.

"I assured the countess of Sir Gerard's truthfulness. That the sultan's target for this campaign is in truth Tripoli itself." He cleared his throat delicately. "The countess stated her opinion that the Master intended to frighten her."

Beaujeu stared at his linked hands. To Gerard's surprise, there was defeat in his voice. "I knew they hated me in Tripoli. I did not think they would deny the obvious merely because it was I who warned them."

"Courage," Reddecoeur said. "Their own spies had just reported that the sultan had travelled up the valley of Bacar and entered the pass leading to Tripoli. I was able to convince her to take action."

"How much time do they have?" Beaujeu drummed his fingers restlessly on the table.

"Perhaps none," Alba put in. "When I was in Damascus, the Egyptian army was under orders to leave by the end of the week. If they followed the prepared road, Tripoli may be encircled already."

Beaujeu swore softly, and went into a cold, soft eruption. "Months ago, I warned them! And *now* they choose to believe me! The fools! I *knew* it."

Gerard put down his quill. "You did, my lord. And thanks to you, we are prepared even if they are not."

"Indeed." Beaujeu took a slow deep breath. "Tell me they'll accept help."

A nod. "She's sent for the king's brother at Tyre. Likewise a general call for help at Acre; there are messages for the French Regiment, the Hospital, the Genoese, the Venetians, and the Pisans. I even convinced her to accept our help."

"Miracle upon miracle," Beaujeu said dryly. "I have ships ready and waiting to leave by the next tide. Marshall Geoffrey is in charge of them, but I want you with them, Reddecoeur. So far you're the only Templar they'll listen to. Can you leave with the next tide?"

"Within the next hour, my lord, if necessary. I'm already packed."

"Good." Beaujeu turned to Gerard. "What do you think, Montreal?"

Gerard grimaced. "She's called on the Genoese, the Venetians, *and* the Pisans?" The Italian trading cities had been at war with each other for most of the last thirty years. To say there was bad blood between them would be a gross understatement. "And don't forget the Hospital was at war with the Tripoli rebels last year, before they accepted Lady Lucy as countess. I don't like it, my lord."

"Have you anything to suggest?"

Gerard shook his head gloomily. "I was there last month; I've seen for myself how much cachet the Temple carries up there. None of them are going to trust us."

Brother Reddecoeur nodded. "As Templars, any influence we exercise will need to be gentle, diplomatic, invisible. We'll have to guide without seeming to guide."

Another drum of Beaujeu's fingers on the tabletop. "Is there anyone who *will* listen to us?"

Gerard swallowed, oddly shy to speak her name before these men. "There's the Lady Margaret, but no doubt once the siege begins, she'll be returning to her fortress in Tyre."

"The Lady of Tyre," Beaujeu's fingers stilled. "She's a kinswoman of Lady Lucy's, isn't she? Didn't she help you gain audience with the countess?"

"Yes, yes, and she acted as bailli during the interregnum, but…"

"Then she's our mouthpiece. It's vital she stays in Tripoli throughout the siege."

Anxiety gripped him. "My lord, what good—"

"If you want her out of danger, you'll have every opportunity to watch over her in person." Beaujeu nodded tightly, as though coming to a decision. "Gerard, I'm sending you to Tripoli to liaise with Lady Margaret during the siege. You'll work with her to keep the defence running smoothly and to head off any factional strife. Your ship leaves with the tide at Nones. Be on it." Beaujeu flicked his left hand at them. "You may leave, gentlemen."

Gerard found himself standing outside the Master's cabinet, his head in a whirl. Well, perhaps all was not lost. If Lady Margaret was to endure the hardship and danger of a siege, at least he would be there to protect her. He thought of her soft sympathetic words at their last meeting, and felt emboldened. Working in close partnership with her, amidst the danger and heightened emotion of a siege—he would never again have such a chance to win the woman he loved.

Reddecoeur had departed with a condescending nod, but Alba still lingered, watching him. "Why the frown, Montreal? The rest of us could do with a few more of those plum diplomatic missions."

Gerard glared at him, resentful that the man had interrupted his thoughts. "You'd be welcome to take my place, if you like."

Alba laughed. "I wouldn't dream of depriving you. But you won't be alone. I'm being recalled to Tripoli for the siege, of course."

He turned to descend the stairs to the courtyard, but Gerard stopped him with a question. "What was that about Prester John, Sir Peter?"

"Pardon?"

"Before. In the meeting. You said something about Prester John."

"Oh, that!" Alba leaned against the railing, folding his arms. "Some sort of renegade who travelled with us from Mosul. He claimed to be Prester John."

"You didn't mention that in your report," Gerard said sharply. "With Qalawun on the prowl, we need all the allies we can get."

Alba snorted. "Come, now! The man's more likely a myth than not. What are the odds of Prester John turning up alone in Tripoli? After all these years? Prester John's kingdom was destroyed by the Tartars years ago—if it ever existed at all, which is doubtful. All the same, I took the fellow seriously. I tested him, but he didn't claim nobility even to get himself out of prison."

Gerard frowned. Travellers told tales of Prester John's kingdom far in the east, beyond Persia, south of the Tartars' desert homeland. A Christian king of the east, paying homage neither to the Pope at Rome nor the Emperor in Constantinople, Prester John was said to boast fabulous wealth and military power.

For decades, the Franks still clinging to the coast of Palestine and Syria—a narrow strip of land reaching as far south as Jaffa and north to Alexandretta, encompassing Acre, Tyre, Beirut and Tripoli—had sent envoys east seeking alliances with the Christian kings of the vast Orient. At first the fierce Tartars, with their Nestorian allies and their hostility to the Mohametan caliph, had seemed like the answer to all their prayers. But the Tartars proved unwilling to enter an equal partnership: though they worshipped one God, they believed themselves divinely appointed to rule all lesser men, and that included the Franks.

If a traveller from the far East had arrived in Tripoli—if he really *was* connected to the fabled Presters—if he really commanded the treasuries and armies the travellers spoke of—if there was the slightest chance he could help—

Gerard cleared his throat. "This Prester John. What was he like?"

Slowly, the mockery faded from Alba's grin. "To tell the truth, I didn't know what to think. He was very strange. His dialect of Arabic was archaic. He knew nothing of this place…and he had the clothes and bearing of a prince."

"So there's a possibility he might have been telling the truth?"

Alba looked uncomfortable. "The Lady of Beirut vouched for him."

Eschiva of Ibelin. Rumour said the Ibelins had had something to do with Prester John years ago, in the Old Lord's time.

"I see," Gerard said thoughtfully. "Thank you, Sir Peter."

He walked back to his own cabinet, deep in thought. *Each man the architect of his own fate*—he lived his life according to the words of the philosopher. Wise men took firm action to secure their own future, and so would Gerard. That was how he'd managed to deliver Beaujeu's message to Countess Lucy when others had failed. That was why he would ultimately win the woman he loved. And that was why Beaujeu was sending him to Tripoli: to secure the future.

It was the incurious, the inactive, who lost their grip on the present and who were erased from the future. If the Coast would be saved—and he believed it would be—then it would be because men like himself hoped everything, did everything, risked everything.

"Montreal." As Gerard reached for the latch of his door, the Master strode down the loggia towards him, mantle billowing in the chill spring wind. "A word with you."

Mystified, Gerard nodded and beckoned the Master into his own small cabinet, chaotic with rolls of paper and stacks of folded parchment, seals, quills, and empty cups. Beaujeu didn't seem to notice, seating himself behind Gerard's desk and folding his arms with a scowl.

"Did you know what the Marshal said when I told him he was sailing on the next tide?"

"No, my lord."

Beaujeu wrinkled his aristocratic nose. "He said, *Are you sure of the threat, my lord?*"

"Saints," Gerard murmured. There was a silence. "That reminds me of a Greek story, my lord, about one Lady Cassandra, a prophetess, who—"

"Thank you, I know the story." Beaujeu's voice was cutting. He scowled at his linked hands. "Gerard, it's true that I'm sending you to Tripoli to liaise with Lady Margaret. But that won't be the most important part of your mission."

Another mission. Gerard swallowed.

Beaujeu's eyes narrowed. "A problem, Montreal?"

"No, my lord." The Master looked sceptical, and Gerard sighed. "I am a very good scribe, my lord, and I can acquit myself tolerably well on the battlefield, with a sword in my hand and a steel coat on my back. But I have no love for this business of skulking and spying."

Beaujeu stared at him through narrowed eyes. "I know," he said abruptly.

Gerard lifted his hands. "Then why—"

"That's why I'm sending you. You're the most careful man I have. Always on your guard—to a degree which, I admit, sounds exhausting. But it's what I need right now—it's what this kingdom needs." Beaujeu leaned forward, drumming his fingers on the desk in front of him, as he did when he was very focused. "If I didn't trust you, I'd hardly be sending you. As it is I don't know how I shall do without my right hand for the next month, or however long it takes. So, listen carefully, because you won't be getting written orders for this. In Tripoli, I want you to locate an old Greek diviner named Stephen Katsaros. Find this man, put him on a ship, and send him to me."

"Katsaros," Gerard repeated. "I understand."

"I'm not sure you do." The Master pinned Gerard with a fierce glare. "Katsaros might be our last chance to protect this kingdom, Montreal. I'm sending you because you're the only man I can trust. You aren't to speak of this mission outside this room, not even to Templar brothers. Find Katsaros. Bring him to me."

Gerard touched his tongue to his lips. "Our *last* chance, my lord? Surely things aren't that bad."

"Not you too," Beaujeu said wearily. "Has no one been paying attention?"

Antioch was gone, Tripoli was trembling. And the kingdom which had once reached from Beirut to Gaza, from Transjordan to the sea, was now little more than a fragmented handful of lordships which paid only nominal homage to the seat of government at Acre. Acre herself remained fabulously wealthy from the trade which flowed through her ports, her revenues worth more than whole kingdoms in the West. But beyond her own city walls, her authority was weak, choked by the Egyptian sultans who had inexorably swallowed city after city. Protected only by walls and a veteran garrison contributed by various western kings, Acre could not even put an army in the field. Yet it was difficult to believe that the end might really be in sight. Acre was not like Tripoli—improvident, riven by conflict.

"We have allies," Gerard said. "Cyprus. The Tartars. Our brothers across the sea in France and England. And Sir Peter says that Prester John himself has come to the Coast—"

"Prester John's power was broken long ago, if he ever existed at all." Beaujeu's voice was low, a rumble. "The Tartars have their own affairs to mind. And no army is coming across the sea. It cannot be done. Times have changed. No one will come to save us."

Gerard stared.

Beaujeu gave a bittersweet smile. "You are young, Montreal. But I have been Master nearly as long as you have been alive. That whole time, I have known that the end was coming. I have only tried to ensure that it did not come during my lifetime; but if Tripoli falls, the end is upon us indeed."

Of course Gerard had always known that things were bad. Yet he'd never really expected the worst. "With the right preparation, my lord, we can master our own fate."

"Perhaps, yes. And Stephen Katsaros is how I plan to do that. I owe the man a favour from my days as the commander in Tripoli. All you must do is find him and convince him to come to Acre."

Gerard nodded. If Beaujeu was right—if the situation was so dire, and if Katsaros could help them, then he needed to make sure the man got to Acre safely. Meanwhile, perhaps he could find this Prester John and find out for himself what help the man could offer. If Beaujeu was right, if the situation was so dire that the loss of Tripoli would doom Acre…Gerard sighed. What would it profit a man to wed a wealthy lady and lose her estates?

"I can do this for you, my lord. What about Lady Margaret? If I find Katsaros quickly, do I abandon my mission to her? Will the Marshal permit me to leave?"

"I'll give you a sealed order permitting your return to Acre at any time." Beaujeu stilled his jumping fingers. "I do not think it will be such a quick or easy job, Montreal. Make sure you listen to whatever Katsaros has to say. Moving such people over running water can be…ticklish, without the right precautions. Try to make sure that you satisfy his demands, as outlandish as they may be. But when you find him…" Beaujeu stood up. "When you find him, and when you convince him to come, leave Tripoli, leave the Lady Margaret. They don't matter. Only Acre matters…and Godspeed, Montreal."

Chapter XI.

John came to in a fire-burst of pain that unfurled its tendrils through the whole left side of his face. He tried to elbow himself up from the street, only to be shoved down again by a big, meaty hand.

"Lie still, son," said an equally big, meaty voice. "No need to get up; we'll carry you to the Hospital."

Colours swarmed in his vision and John blinked up into a broad, grizzled face. A burly man with a tonsure loomed over him in dusty black robes, marked with a white cross stitched onto the shoulder. A ring of passers-by peered down at him. Beyond them stood the tall parapets of tenements and warehouses.

It took him a moment to realise what had happened. He'd barely seen the attack coming; one moment he was running after the young woman from the Zakars' house. The next, something had slammed into his jaw.

That woman.

"Let me up," he growled, and staggered to his feet, ignoring the pounding in his head. A steadying hand caught his elbow as a warm trickle wound its way down his cheek.. There was no sign of the woman in the crowd that flooded the square.

"Easy, easy, now," one of the brothers was saying.

John blinked. "Is my head broken?"

"I don't think so," one of them admitted. "But now we've been called out, we'd like to carry you to the Hospital and probe your jaw—"

John opened and closed his mouth. Painful, but all in working order. "Jaw's fine."

"You likely have a commotion of the brain."

A hand plucked at his other elbow and John looked around to see a scowling labourer. "Don't trust anything they say, friend."

"Hospitallers, go home!" someone else yelled, and a clod of dirt smacked against the meaty man's habit.

The crowd jostled close, restive; some crying out for the monks, others against them. John blinked at the faces surrounding him. He didn't have time for this. "Commotion of the brain, right. Rest, no food or drink, stick with a friend and come back if I worsen."

He shrugged away from the clutching hands and slid through the crowd in the direction he'd last seem the woman running. Behind him, the crowd didn't seem inclined to forget whatever dispute they'd cooked up amongst themselves. Ignoring the growing uproar, John put a hand to his tender jaw and tried to focus on his next move.

Zakar—dead. Sara—dead. No sign of the children. John closed his eyes, breathing hard. It made no sense. Who would slaughter such humble Watchers? They could have had nothing worth stealing, no great power with which to provoke enmity or vengeance.

And it couldn't have been his own visit that did it, either. Had the Zakars died for sheltering him, the woman would scarcely have tried to frighten him away, and his attacker just now would have killed him at once.

No, the reason for the Zakars' deaths was here in Tripoli, among the people and things they already knew.

John swallowed painfully. Each moment he spent doing something other than finding his way home was a moment robbed from his own wife and children. But the Zakars—maybe they *were* his children's children, and as desperately as he tried to tell himself that they weren't his concern, he couldn't quite convince himself. They had taken him in; they had offered him hospitality, and he had endured it proudly, telling himself that it was his place to do *them* good, not to receive charity at their hands.

Damn it! The local Watchers would track down the killer and find justice, surely—but then, the Watchers didn't know about the handsome woman with the dancer's feet. And the Watchers might not have what he had. John dug into his pouch, extracting the lead seal he'd been given in the palace courtyard.

The Lady of Beirut had told him to wait on her today. She might not have much authority here in Tripoli, but she almost certainly had the power and connections to bring the Zakars' murderer to justice. The longer he looked at the seal, the more attractive the thought became. Petitioning a powerful lady on behalf of the Zakars would discharge his responsibility to them, and free him to focus on his own quest.

A young boy went running past him toward the disturbance he'd left behind. John snapped his fingers in summons. "You, boy. What is Sext?"

The boy gave him a suspicious look. "Noon, sir."

It was reaching midday now. Time he kept his appointment.

The Street of Fish, as its name suggested, began near the harbour, but the house where the Lady of Beirut was lodged was at its far end, on the wall looking out to open sea and comfortably far from the oily aroma of the fish markets. It seemed that someone was making preparations to depart, as John, once admitted to the inner courtyard of the house, noted a cart piled high with chests and furniture, and servants busy saddling a lovely grey horse.

He was ushered into an upper room of the house, where he found the Lady of Beirut in grey brocade and a fat older woman in wine-coloured silk standing with their heads together at a triple lancet window looking onto a sea blue as cobalt. There, just beyond the city wall, the pendentive dome of a small basilica rose from a very tiny rocky island barely a bowshot from the shore.

Could that be the island of Saint Thomas, of which the Zakars had spoken? John made a silent resolution to visit the island as soon as he had done his duty by the Zakars. If all went well, there would be a guardian there—he might be kissing his own children within a day or two, please God.

The two ladies by the window were lost in some intense conversation: Lady Eschiva gripped the other woman's plump arms with white fingertips, her voice a low, insistent plea at odds with her usual lazy manner.

The fat woman shook her head with a smile. Lady Eschiva swallowed and kissed the other woman's cheek, before turning to face John and switching to Arabic.

Her first words astonished him. "In honour of your name, John Bessarion, there is a berth for you on my ship. We leave within the hour."

John blinked. "I beg your pardon?"

"I am returning to Beirut. You will have the honour of attending me." She pulled on white riding-gloves with a flourish. "Whatever happened to your face, man?"

He didn't know where to begin, so he answered the question. "I was attacked in the street."

"I swear there's something in the water of this city," the fat woman put in, shaking her head.

"This won't do, Bessarion. I can't have my followers getting into brawls."

"It was no brawl, my lady. I believe it had something to do with a terrible crime." John hurried on with his story before they could interrupt. "Last night a poor man and his wife, Thomas and Sara Zakar, were murdered. They were kin. I wish to beg justice for them."

The Lady of Beirut lifted a mocking eyebrow. "You cannot be serious."

"Of course he wishes to see justice done," the fat woman said quickly. "Leave it to me, my good man. You must go with Lady Eschiva."

Lady Eschiva gave a soft snort of laughter, and gestured to the other woman. "This is Margaret of Tyre, my kinswoman. She has the softest heart in Christendom, so you may trust her to do what she can. Now come along—the tide waits for no one."

John took a deep breath. So this was how it felt to be at the beck and call of the powerful. When he got home, he would take care to speak to his own servants with more consideration.

"My lady, I thank you, but I'm not looking to enter anyone's service. I only want justice for my kinsman."

Eschiva looked at him with a faint frown. "Don't you know who I am?"

He opened his mouth, then closed it again. "I have prior loyalties, my lady."

"Oh! Very well, if you *wish* to perish with this city—"

John took a sharp breath. "Perish?"

"In the siege, of course." She watched his face with her catlike smile. "Saints. You didn't *know*? Sultan Qalawun is coming with an army from Damascus. Within the last hour his envoy arrived to say that he'd burn Tripoli to the ground if she resisted him. That's why I'm leaving, and so is everyone else who can afford to."

But he did know, though he had tried his best not to see. The army quartered at Damascus; the supply depots; the newly repaired road; the young woman's warning to leave Tripoli. All the signs were there, and his soldier's instincts had known it even if his conscious mind had repressed the thought.

Was that why the Zakars were dead? After all, they were Watchers. Perhaps someone knew that a city without Watchers was vulnerable to the divine wrath. Could the Zakars have been slaughtered by Egyptian spies?

Someone rapped on the door, and an attendant put her head in. "Half an hour, my lady."

"I'm perfectly aware." Eschiva buttoned her gloves at the wrist and picked up a grey cloak. She pinned John with an imperious gaze. "There is no relief army coming, Bessarion. When Tripoli falls—and it will—the same things will happen here as happened in Antioch twenty years ago. With good fortune, you and I can stop that happening to Beirut as well."

John's chest felt tight, the tender side of his head throbbing with every heartbeat. Antioch? What had happened to Antioch? And why should he concern himself with Beirut?

He swallowed, clearing his throat. His family needed him. Jerusalem needed him. He had no call to be throwing away his life while that was true—but if what Eschiva said was true, only Watchers could save this city. Watchers like the Zakars, who were dead and must be avenged.

Watchers like himself.

He thrust it all down. What kind of husband and father would he be if he stayed here when he had no call to? The siege was not his business; he must find the guardian on the island in the storm, and then he must go home.

Watching his face, Eschiva frowned. "Ibelin has need of your service, John Bessarion."

There was haughty displeasure in her voice, but John took a deep breath, forcing the words out quickly before he could take them back.

"Thank you, my lady, but I'll take my chances here."

* * *

By the time John returned to the Zakar house, his head was pounding like a hammer and only the emptiness of his stomach prevented him from vomiting his guts out. As he made his shaky way past the gate that divided the city from its harbour, he caught a glimpse of the Lady of Beirut boarding her ship. Momentarily, he wished he'd asked her what connection the Bessarions had with her family. Perhaps she could have given him news of Lukas or Marta. But time had been short, and she had been too imperious to make him trust her. As it was, he suspected she had allowed him to leave only because she was in such a hurry to catch the tide.

Lady Margaret had assured him she'd speak to the countess about the Zakars' death, but John knew it was an empty gesture. If a siege was imminent, every able-bodied man would be needed to man the walls; and if the situation was as dire as Eschiva thought, then what use was it to prosecute the murders of a family that might shortly have died anyway?

If justice would be done, he would have to do it himself. That meant finding—and warning—the other Watchers in Tripoli. The best way to do that would be to return to the house of death in hopes of meeting Zakar's friend, the Messenger Hubert.

When he reached the Zakar house, it was dark and silent. John entered warily, letting his eyes adjust to the darkness within and checking that the downstairs room was empty. At the foot of the stairs he hesitated, wanting nothing more than to rest his aching head. But the Zakars were still lying upstairs, and they deserved better respect than they had been given. Taking a deep breath, he went upstairs and opened the door.

Zakar lay nearest, hunched over a puncture wound that had crushed his breastbone, his eyes wide and staring. Sara was near him, face down with her arms extended as though she'd been trying to protect or help him.

John retched, reaching for the wall to hold himself up. He closed his eyes, but it was no good; he could see their final moments playing out, the terror, the pleas, the weeping children.

The children.

He forced his eyes open again and made himself look more closely. Except for the thickened pools beneath each body, there was no other blood in the room. They must have survived, then. The Watchers would have to find and provide for them.

John bent over the bodies. Each bore one precisely-targeted wound. Whether sword or spear, the weapon seemed to have been wielded by a giant: calm, dispassionate, and strong enough to shatter bone.

On the far wall, a window looking onto the street hung open, creaking idly in the wind. John wiped a hand over the sill, coming away with little but dust. When he tried to close the window, he found that the wooden latch had been broken.

That must be how the killer had got in—but how? The wall beneath was sheer, offering very few handholds. Putting the mystery aside, John tried the door leading to the roof: unlocked, showing no signs of having been forced. He climbed to the roof and found himself in the shadow of the taller buildings on either side. Again, nothing seemed to have been disturbed. A washing-line was set up here, with clothing fluttering in the wind, and there was a little clutter of children's toys – shards of a broken pot with the sharp edges smoothed off, a doll made of gorgeously dyed silk offcuts, an upturned basket on which someone had been serving dry scraps of bread.

John looked at the things a long time without seeing them, thinking of his own children.

Below, in the street, the door rattled as someone shook the latch. "Hullo, there! Anyone home?"

John hastened to the parapet and leaned over. His heart jerked as he recognised the small knot of children in the street below, clinging to each other with tearstained faces. They congregated behind a man in the garb of a well-to-do tradesman.

"One moment," he called. "I'll come down and let you in."

The man stepped backwards in alarm, looking up. "Who's that?"

John swallowed, suddenly protective of his true name. Apparently, it had brought last night's nightmare and had given Lady Eschiva the idea that she owned him. He was beginning to feel nervous about sharing it with anyone else.

"Call me John Zakar," he said, picking the first thing that came to mind. "A terrible thing has happened here."

In the upper room, he covered the bodies with a sheet. Downstairs, he opened the door to admit the sombre procession. The man, as it happened, was Hubert the Messenger, and despite his Frankish blood it was clear from his black hair and warm skin that a great deal of Syrian blood must flow in his veins.

"Zakar?" Hubert said, with a slight frown. "I thought I knew all Thomas' family."

"You had a different name yesterday," the eldest Zakar boy said accusingly.

John looked at the young boy's angry, tear-tracked face. Kneeling down so that he was on a level with the boy's eyes, he said gently: "I come from far away. My real name is not important, so I have borrowed your father's name, as a sign, until I have brought justice for his death."

The boy glared at him.

Nearby, Hubert was stiff and watchful. "Matthias? You've seen this man before?"

"He's not the one that did it," one of the other children piped up; the eldest girl, who had picked up the youngest, a solid toddler, and balanced him on her hip.

"No," Matthias said grudgingly. "That one had a turban and a spear and there was a pretty lady with him."

"You saw it happen?" Although he was grimly glad to have the boy's information, John felt heartbroken. It wasn't right that these children should have had to witness such a thing.

The children fell silent, avoiding his eyes.

Hubert cleared his throat and said, "Stay down here, children. I'll go upstairs and find you the things you'll need."

He beckoned John, who followed him upstairs. Once the door closed behind them, Hubert crossed himself at the sight of the shrouded bodies, and then turned to John. "I apologise for my suspicion just now, but from what the children said… If the rumours are true, I fear the Chosen has come to Tripoli."

The Chosen. A shiver ran down John's spine, but he put out his arm to display the Watcher's Mark. "I'm a friend of Zakar's, and I came with him to Tripoli to speak to a Messenger. He gave me your name."

Hubert looked at the shrouded bodies; a little blood was seeping through the sheet. A deep breath. "Thomas and Sara were friends to anyone who needed it. True Watchers. We've never needed them more."

They could be his descendants. John swallowed the lump in his throat, ashamed of the contempt with which he had viewed them—their poverty, humility, and contentment. In Zakar's place, would he have extended such hospitality to a wandering madman?

"Is there someone to care for the children?" he asked, with a vague feeling that he ought to do some sort of penance for his sins.

"I'll take them in," Hubert said. "Best if they go to people they know. I gather they were released by the murderer, and since they were frightened of leading him to me, they went to the palace and asked to speak to the garrison."

John felt a flicker of hope. "The garrison? Do you suppose they'll bring the killer to justice?"

"Not likely. None of Countess Lucy's property was harmed, so they washed their hands of the matter and summoned me to collect the children. I only came by for their spare clothes."

John followed him onto the roof, where Hubert unpegged the children's spare tunics from the washing-line. "Will you take them out of the city?"

Hubert glanced at him with a faint frown. "Why would I do that?"

Strife. "There's going to be a siege, Hubert. Anyone who can afford it is already leaving."

"I've heard the rumours. But surely, if the sultan was coming for us—"

"I saw the supply depots all the way up the Bacar valley. And now someone is in Tripoli killing Watchers?" John took a deep breath. The Watchers of this place must stand or fall by their own decisions, of course; and yet he could not simply watch and keep his mouth shut. "You should collect all the Watchers and leave—today—while you still can."

Hubert shook his head, unruffled. "We aren't rich people, John. We can't afford to leave the city; we'd starve. Best we take our chances."

He led the way downstairs again, and paused over the bodies. "I'll send someone to help prepare them for burial."

"Thanks." John bit the word rather short, thinking he ought to be glad that the children would be cared for by someone else, that someone else would prepare the bodies for burial. Yet still he could not help worrying.

Hubert's voice broke into his thoughts. "You said you came to Tripoli to find a Messenger?"

"Yes—I'm trying to find my way home. I need to find a guardian and I thought you might help me."

"I see." Hubert shifted the clean laundry to his left arm and touched two fingers to John's forehead. John tensed—he'd never met a Messenger who did this before—and then waited as Hubert closed his eyes and began to whisper in a language he didn't know.

At length, Hubert changed to Arabic. "I don't know how helpful this will be, friend. But I see the isle of Saint Thomas, beyond the wall."

John gave a sharp intake of breath. "Saint Thomas?"

Hubert dropped his hand and smiled faintly. "It *is* helpful?"

"Very." Rahel had seen an island in a storm. Zakar had suggested it was the island of Saint Thomas—and now Hubert had confirmed it.

More and more promising. He had identified the place now; the only thing lacking was the time and date. Clearly, he must wait, and in the meantime, there was the Zakar killer to find.

John followed Hubert downstairs, where the children waited. Once again, he knelt down before them, and held out the small, bright object he'd collected from the roof while Hubert was taking down the laundry:

the doll of silk offcuts. "Does this belong to you?"

"That's Elisa's," said Matthias. The familiar name cut through John like a knife as the younger of the two girls edged forward and took the doll shyly from his hands.

He swallowed a jagged lump in his throat and stood before they could say anything else. Hubert put out his hands gently to shepherd the children towards the door. "We'll come back for more of your things later," he said. "Godspeed, John Zakar."

* * *

There was only one cemetery within the walls of Tripoli, the others being in the suburbs beyond. Right now, a burial beyond the walls was out of the question. By the time Thomas and Sara's bodies had been prepared, two days had passed. The Mamluk army had entrenched itself amidst the orange-orchards, the sultan's banner fluttering from the Mount Pilgrim citadel, hammers ringing as the siege-engines were constructed.

John stood in the walled graveyard as the Zakars were lowered into the charnel-house where they would be left while their flesh rotted from their bones. Around him stood the Watchers of Tripoli: perhaps six or seven families, no more than forty souls, all of them rather poor and shabby. Hubert and his wife stood near John with bent heads, their arms around the Zakar children. Some of them, Hubert said, had suffered terribly from nightmares.

The graveyard was small, its ground pocked with weathered headstones and shaded by ancient olive trees. The priest of the neighbouring church, St Mary's, was reading the liturgy in Latin. The words washed over John, eternal and comforting. *I am the resurrection and the life; he who believes in me will live even if he dies.*

The Zakars had justice already. It was their killer who did not; and while that killer was loose, John would be uneasy about the safety of the remaining Watchers. The best thing he could do for them now was try to find the killer. Rahel had agreed, when he had seen her the previous night.

But how? Whoever the murderer was, he might not even be in Tripoli anymore—and even if he was, the city was full to bursting with fugitives from Mount Pilgrim and the other surrounding villages.

It would be like looking for a needle in a haystack, but his hackles were up now and he didn't mean to fail.

Help me find this son of a bitch.

There came a tug on his hand and John looked down into Matthias' brown eyes. The boy gave a subtle jerk of his head. When John followed his gaze, his eyes met those of a woman standing beneath the shadow of an olive tree not far from the cemetery gate. A black veil was pinned to her headdress, hiding her entire face except for her eyes. Beside her stood a turbaned man, also in black.

The woman dropped her eyes at once, moving away, behind the tree. Beneath her black veil came a flash of a green embroidered jacket.

Matthias didn't have to say anything. John's entire world narrowed to the two watching figures. The words of the liturgy faded as he wove through the crowd, trying to keep pace with the couple as they turned and headed for the gate, their business done.

They had come to see and remember the faces of all who attended the Zakar funeral: all the Watchers in Tripoli.

The woman was the one he'd chased from the Zakars' house two days ago; the man in the turban could only be the Zakar killer. It wasn't until John broke free of the crowd, with his quarry no longer concealed by the trees, that he got a clear look at the turbaned man. The Zakar killer glanced over his shoulder and met John's gaze. Tall, dark, and lithe with grey-green eyes that shone like jewels in his pale face. But it was not his eyes that arrested John's attention. He carried a spear in his right fist, a spear like the one that had to have killed the Zakars.

And not just any spear.

Dark old wood, gleaming with oil. A narrow, razor-sharp blade rippling with the patterns that were made only in Damascus.

John's gut clenched and turned inside-out. He'd broken promises, watched a town die, doomed his family and blighted his future in a bid to keep this weapon safe.

And now his spear was in the hands of a heretic murderer.

Chapter XII.

The man and woman turned away from him and went on out the gate as though nothing was amiss. John gave a hoarse yell and raced after them. "Stop!"

Instantly the two broke into a run, taking the first opportunity to cut down a side-street. John followed, only to be confronted with a cul-de-sac hemmed in with tall sheer walls, the doors locked with heavy padlocks. Ahead of him, the man threw off his black robe, revealing a closer-fitting tunic and trousers. John skidded to a stop and fumbled instinctively at his hip, but he was weaponless.

Saint George, protect me. He really needed a way to defend himself.

The killer didn't attack. Instead, he slung the spear across his shoulders and took an impossible leap from the ground to an upper window, crouching on the sill with one hand hooked inside the protective bars.

If the presence of the spear explained the Zakars' shattered bones, this impossible agility likely explained how their window had been forced.

"Don't pull so hard," the woman hissed at her friend, throwing off her own cloak. Agile as a cat, she threw herself at the wall, fingers and slippered toes clinging to the tooled margins of the rough ashlars. Above, the man scaled the apparently sheer wall, then threw himself upwards to catch hold of the parapet. For an instant he hung there before his feet scrabbled on the nebule moulding and he lifted himself over with a straining grunt.

At the same moment, the woman shrieked and fell.

John pounced as she lay groaning on the stones. With a snarl, she reached for a knife under her jacket, but he captured her wrist and threw the blade at the opposite wall.

She seemed to yield, falling back with a bitter laugh. "Well, I suppose you've got me where you want me. I hate it when this happens."

Beneath her husky voice, John detected a hint of real dread. He realised he was straddling her body, and got off quickly. "I'm not going to hurt you," he said gently. "I know you didn't kill the Zakars. I know it was him."

She blinked at him, distrustful.

"Can you stand?" John reached down and helped her to her feet. "What's your name?"

She looked at him in confusion, and said it like she was unveiling some terrible secret. "Soraya."

"Soraya," he repeated. An old Arabic name. He'd once broken a promise to a heretic woman by that name; a twinge of guilt made him all the more determined to treat her gently. "Your friend killed a lame man and his wife, and turned five children out into the street, Soraya. Help me bring him to justice."

"He is not my friend," she spat. Then it was as though the full meaning of his words caught up with her, and once again she blinked at him in confusion. "You want him…*you want him dead?*"

"If that's what justice demands—yes."

Something flared in her eyes, and John felt suddenly small before a towering and thunderous rage. She reached up and clasped his neck in her hands, printing a burning kiss on his lips. It was brief and hard, and there was neither lust nor affection in it. John knew instinctively that it was something like the clasp of hands with which merchants might seal a bargain, but so much the more forceful as it was the more intimate.

She pulled back, staring at him with those fiery, terrifying eyes. "Only I can help you. This man is very difficult to kill."

John nodded, somewhat dazed. Her hands were still tight on the back of his neck.

"What do I call you?"

"John Zakar."

A tight nod. "I will help you find justice, John Za—"

Abruptly, her eyes went dead. The words in her throat died, her grip on his neck slackening as she collapsed.

With a sound of alarm, John caught her in his arms, a dead weight. "Soraya!"

He had no time to check her pulse, or search her body for wounds. She lay there for an instant unmoving—and then the fibres of her clothing, her very skin, began to flake away. Before he could call her name again, she crumbled through his arms.

John stood alone in the cul-de-sac with his heart pounding like an anvil, staring down at a little heap of dust.

* * *

For fear of disrupting the funeral further, John didn't return to the graveyard, but instead turned in the opposite direction, back towards the harbour and the Zakar house. The whole way, he kept his eyes on the rooftops, on the people around him, looking for a black turban and a spear.

I need a weapon. The caravan from Mosul had allowed him to hire weapons, taking the money from his wages, but he'd had to leave the sword and spear behind in Damascus. Now he barely had the money to buy food, let alone a new sword. He'd have to build or improvise, rather than buy. Something that could deal with a magic lance wielded by…

By what, exactly?

What had *happened* in the cul-de-sac? Soraya herself was either dead—killed from a distance by some deadly magic—or she was inhuman, subject to commands she couldn't refuse. John shivered. Presumably the latter, or the Zakars would not have been murdered by spear. As for the killer himself, his strength and agility was prodigious. It had to be more than the spear. John had wielded it before, knew that it granted the bearer strength and speed and luck. But even with its help, he didn't think he would have been able to leap so high, to scale such a wall.

Wonderful. The killer who wielded the spear was supernaturally gifted in other ways as well. No wonder Soraya said he was difficult to kill. No wonder the orthodox were quickly losing their grip on the Coast. No wonder Eschiva had warned him that to stay in Tripoli was to perish.

Fear crawled through his veins like ice. What had he done? Why had he stayed?

For the Zakars, he reminded himself as he turned into the narrow street that led to the small stone house. To seek justice, and to find his way home. Yet, what now? Soraya was gone, and he couldn't even count on seeing her again, let alone having her help. As for the killer, he'd seen the faces of every Watcher in Tripoli now. He would work his way through them all, slaughtering them at his leisure, and there wouldn't be a thing John could do about it.

Or was there?

Unlocking the door of the house, John stood on the threshold, letting his eyes adjust to the darkness within. A pale glimmer caught his eye from the loom. Before her death, Sara had been working on the length of fine, supple white silk that was rolled into a heavy bolt at the loom's foot.

It was easy to solve problems with a sword, but a sword would never prevail against a man armed with a magical spear. He needed something more. John smoothed a hand over the cloth, frowning as an idea sprang to his mind.

He had seen the man's face, and that knowledge would cut deeper than any weapon. John would make sure of it.

∗ ∗ ∗

Three nights later, John groaned as Rahel's voice drifted into his dreams. "You've been busy," she said brightly from the centre of the Zakars' upper room.

On the sleeping platform, John pushed himself into a sitting position. "I'm so tired I even feel sleepy in my *sleep.*"

Rahel knelt, throwing a silvery glow on the last few scraps of silk littering the floor. John's hand-carved wooden printing block and the remnants of cheap brown dye made from bark lay discarded nearby, along with the shears he'd used to slice the silk into rectangles.

Now each scrap bore a print showing the face of a young man in a turban, along with a blurred but tolerably readable set of words: *The Zakar killer. Justice!*

"This is the man who did it?" Rahel's voice was soft.

John nodded. "The other Watchers helped distribute the posters. They're hanging on nearly every wall in Tripoli, and by this afternoon I was seeing graffiti as well. Everyone's talking about it, despite the siege. If the killer shows his face, he'll be recognised at once."

"What do you hope to achieve?" Rahel sounded dubious. "I mean, you said he has the spear; he must be nigh invincible. What happens if someone *does* catch sight of him?"

John rubbed his eyes. "It's always risky calling a man-hunt. I worried that someone might start the hue and cry, and set on an innocent man. But all the Saracens who could left Tripoli long before the siege began—the only ones left are slaves and unlikely to be roaming the city alone. As for the real killer—if I'm correct in thinking him an Egyptian spy, I'm counting on him going into hiding for a while. Whatever he's up to, he won't be able to do it with a whole town breathing down his neck, and that gives me time to work." He leaned back against the wall, silently appreciating the way Rahel's tunic of white silk flowed over her ghostly body like water, hinting at curves each time she moved. "What about you? What has been happening at home?"

She came to sit opposite him on the platform, knees drawn up to her chest. "Paulus and Elisa miss their siblings." Her eyes were shadowed. "No sign of Lukas or Marta?"

He shook his head. "I'm sorry. I should have asked the Lady Eschiva."

"No. You don't know what price she would have demanded." She looked down at her linked fingers, and her next words froze him to the bone. "The heretic army has crossed the Jordan. They are coming to besiege Jerusalem."

"Already?"

She nodded.

He squeezed his eyes shut. "I should be there. I *promised.*"

"We don't control the future, John."

True as that was, it didn't absolve him from trying. "I have debts to pay. I did terrible things to the people I ought to have been protecting. What good is repentance, if I never have the chance to make amends?"

"Perhaps you were never meant to make amends to *them,*" Rahel said thoughtfully.

"To whom, then?"

"Are there no heretics in Tripoli for you to do good to?"

John scowled. "Besides the one who is going around slaughtering Watchers, you mean? Or the ones camped outside the walls, throwing javelins at us?"

"What about that woman—Soraya?"

"Oh, her! I haven't seen her again. I almost wonder if I dreamed her."

"Oh! So you're dreaming of *another* woman?" Rahel teased.

"You know my dreams belong to you, dear heart."

"In all earnest, though." Rahel became serious again. "Do you remember what you told the Jerusalem council, when they objected to reconciliation with the Monophysite heretics?"

John sighed. "That God sent not his Son into the world to condemn the world; but that the world through him might be saved."

"Indeed," Rahel said. "The ancient law condemned heretics to death; but grace and truth came by Christ. Are men so wise, in your time, that they no longer need these things?"

"No, but is it *my* place to provide for them? My children are with you, Rahel. *If any provide not for his own, he hath denied the faith, and is worse than an infidel.*"

"*Yet the dogs under the table eat of the children's crumbs,*" she rejoined, "as a woman of *your* people said to Our Lord, in the days when *you* were heretics looking for crumbs on the ground."

"Rahel," he cried, stung beyond bearing, "what are you trying to say? Do you not want me home?"

"Of course I do, but—"

"I am not able to forget my own children, dear heart. Don't ask it of me."

She sighed, and looked down at her linked hands. "I cannot argue with that."

"I *will* return. I promise. I only have to find this guardian." He sighed. "I know which island you saw in your vision now. It's a small islet within a bowshot of the shore here. I visited it yesterday."

"And?"

"There was a priest at the small basilica there, but he couldn't help me. It was the wrong moment." It seemed there was no hurrying this: if there was a guardian in the city, he would meet it on Saint Thomas during a storm, and not before. He forced a smile, not wanting to spend all his time with Rahel agonising over their parting. "You ought to have seen the basilica, Rahel. So much has changed. The icons, for example! Everyone is so *serious* about icons these days. I asked Hubert about it and he told me to read up about the Second Council of Nicaea."

"The *what?* A *second* Nicaea?"

"I swear I'm in earnest. They had another one!"

"Do tell me what you learn." Rahel bit her lip, thoughtful. "It's rather sobering, isn't it, to think of doctrine…*growing,* and *changing,* for hundreds of years after you're gone. It makes one wonder what one might have got wrong."

"I suppose it does. By the way, Hubert made me a list of things he says I need to catch up on. There's the Second Council of Nicaea, and then there's the Norman Conquests of Sicily *and* Britain, only they're calling it England now."

"What are the Normans?"

"A sort of Varangian, I'm told. Still, what a nerve! Sicily belongs to *us.*"

"So did Jerusalem, lately. What's next on the list?"

"Let's see. There's Cluny and Clairveaux, monasteries in Francia that everyone's very proud of. Oh, there's a new Church of the Holy Sepulchre, which is supposed to be very fine; the Saracens burned it down about three hundred years ago and the Franks only finished rebuilding it last century. Then there's something called cockentrice."

"Bless you."

"No, it's a real thing. You take a capon and a suckling pig, and you sew them together so that the juices mix."

Rahel let out a snort of delighted laughter. "I can see how that might appeal...to a rather peculiar mind."

"Let's see...ah! King Arthur and Charlemagne. They are the Frankish heroes, I gather, like Aeneas and Odysseus. Then there's someone called Elias Fonsalada, a...*jongleur*. That's a sort of popular singer. And finally, apparently I need to read a treatise by one Thomas Aquinas. The Latins are terribly taken with him."

"It strikes me as a very Frankish-centred list."

"I know. I didn't tell anyone I haven't even read Augustine. I think they'd be shocked."

He and Rahel were still laughing when there came a sound at the window overlooking the street. A scrape and then a moment later, a knock.

John leaped from the sleeping platform, all senses instantly alert. The window—that was how the Zakar killer had got in the first time.

It was the one possibility he hadn't considered—that the killer would find his way back here and his revenge on the man who'd compromised his mission.

He had no weapon yet. Just the sharp knife Sara Zakar had used to cut meat. In three steps he crossed the room and grabbed for it, but his fingers trickled through the handle like sand.

"John, wait," Rahel whispered.

He was still asleep.

And the window was opening.

Chapter XIII.

Gerard held a clove-orange to his nose as he preceded his servant Marco and a heavily-laden Saracen slave down the gangplank to the Tripoli docks. The population of the city had doubled with the arrival of the Egyptian army, and its sewers were struggling to cope with the increased load. Certainly the harbour itself stank, a ring of filth already visible at the ship's waterline.

Despite the danger from the Mamluk siege engines—visible less than a mile away, ringing the city's landward wall—multiple ships were crammed into the tiny harbour. Most of them were waiting to unload fighting men, before selling passage to anyone wealthy enough to flee. More galleys rode at anchor further out, just within signalling distance, four of which flew the St George's flag that marked them as Genoese vessels.

In the recent struggle over Lady Lucy's accession to the county, the Genoese had paid dearly in men and ships to get a whole trading quarter and various other privileges in Tripoli—an investment they now clearly planned to defend. It was the least they could do, Gerard thought bitterly. If not for Genoese greed and Venetian envy, Tripoli would not be facing extinction today.

He strode down the quayside and onto the road leading through the sea gate into Tripoli proper. Marshal Geoffrey of Vendac was already at the gate, receiving official permission for the Templar knights to enter the city. "Montreal," he called sharply as Gerard passed, and pulled him aside. "I know the Master has sent you on your own little business, and I won't interfere. Just be discreet. The countess doesn't trust us as far as she can spit."

Gerard hid a wry smile. Like most of the Temple's career soldiers, Vendac knew him only as a secretary, not as a spy. "I'll see to it, Marshal. And I'll be staying in the Temple commandery, for now at any rate. Otherwise you'll hardly know I'm here."

Vendac gave a tight nod and waved him on. Beyond the gate, the street seethed with people. Gerard stopped, curious, to inspect a poster someone had pasted to a wall: it showed a man in a Saracen-style turban. *The Zakar killer,* it read.

Marco and the slave caught up to him, bent under Gerard's valises and puffing slightly. "Doesn't look much like a killer, sir."

Gerard knew what Marco meant: even as a crude print, the face was handsome and aristocratic. "What divides a knight from a common killer, Marco, is faith in the justice of what we're doing. That's a man who believes in himself." He took a deep breath of orange-and-clove. "The Temple commandery's that way, along the wall. Why don't you and Usama take my luggage there? There's a spot of business I need to handle before I settle in."

With a nod and a bow, Marco and the slave headed towards the commandery. Left alone, Gerard took another deep breath of cloves before shoving the orange into his purse. Quickly he stepped into the thick stream of passers-by heading down the main thoroughfare to the central market, not far from the palace.

He hadn't gone far before it became apparent that he was being followed. Ten minutes ago, the man skulking behind him had been bent over a pouch, laboriously counting coins in the shadow of the water gate. Now he made his way through the street behind Gerard at a brisk walk that never got too close.

Gerard stepped abruptly into a recessed doorway and hummed quietly to himself as the man behind hastened his pace, assuming that Gerard had taken a sudden turning. The sun glared off his clothing—a striped, full-skirted tunic with a white coif for headgear. The clothing marked him out as a newcomer from across the sea, unlike the inconspicuous turbaned or straw-hatted Syrians Countess Lucy had sent to shadow him last time.

So, someone else was having him followed. But who?

That kind of information was worth a risk. Gerard counted ten heartbeats, and swung out of the doorway again, face-to-face with his shadow. "Why are you following me?"

The other man pulled to a stop, alarm flaring in his eyes. "Sir? I beg your pardon?"

"You were following me." Gerard's accent changed shape to take on the cadences of Tripolitan Occitan. "What's your excuse, hey?"

"Sir, please! I'm an honest man on honest business. I'm not trying to harass you."

It was enough of a speech to let him pinpoint the man's accent. Gerard narrowed his eyes. "You're a Genoese spy." Their altercation had attracted attention from passers-by in the street. Still mimicking the Tripolitan language, Gerard raised his voice. "Anyone want to keep this Genoese rat occupied while I go about my business?"

A burly, grinning sailor and his companion advanced on the Genoese. "We'll douse him in the harbour for you. Our pleasure." Venetians, by their accent.

"How dare you? My lord Zaccaria will hear of this!" the Genoese protested, as they seized him.

"Stop squealing, or we might slit your gizzard first," the Venetian threatened. It didn't sound as though they'd make it to the harbour, however; as Gerard retreated, he heard another Genoese accent raised in strident protest of his countryman's treatment. Gerard hoped he hadn't gone too far; the last thing Tripoli needed right now was a resurgence of the Italian merchants' war. Still, he'd learned that Zaccaria, too, was now having him watched—and he'd loosed a warning shot across the admiral's bow. The Genoese would think twice before having him shadowed again.

Within another five minutes, Gerard reached Lady Margaret's lodgings and knocked on the door. The porter appeared behind a sliding grate. "Her Ladyship's at the palace."

Gerard frowned, weighing his options. "Did she say when she'd be back?"

"No, sir."

"Then tell her I'll wait on her tomorrow at Terce."

"I didn't catch your name, sir."

"Tell her it's Gerard. She'll understand." As the porter went to slam the grille shut, a thought struck him. "One moment, my man. I'm looking for someone, a sand diviner named Katsaros. Have you ever come across him?"

"Oh, that old charlatan." The porter chuckled. "Don't expect too much, sir. He squats in the courtyard behind a block of tenements in the Chicken Market."

"Thanks," Gerard said, somewhat surprised by the ease with which he'd learned the information. As the grille slammed shut, he glanced at the sky. If all went well he could have his main mission in Tripoli completed in time for the next tide.

He had no trouble locating the chicken market, or the block of once-elegant tenements that housed the sand diviner. Both were near enough the city wall that people scuttled along the street nervously, watching the sky for Saracen missiles. A passage led through the overcrowded tenement into a little bare courtyard beyond, unpaved and dusty with the smell of sewage emanating from beneath a small outhouse in the corner. The courtyard itself was partially roofed by what had once been a peristyle, and beneath the crumbling roof, an old man sat cross-legged atop a mess of rags, smoking a water-pipe.

Gerard was standing directly in front of the man before his watery eyes blinked and focused.

"Stephen Katsaros?"

"Oh," the diviner said vaguely. "Come for a reading, have you?"

"No." Gerard got out his clove orange again and squatted down to face the old man. "This city is under siege. I've been sent to transport you to Acre."

The man's watery gaze fell to the ground before him and he picked up an old stick, making aimless dots in the bare earth. He began mumbling to himself.

"I don't hear you," Gerard said.

The old man seemed to have forgotten that he had a visitor at all, and Gerard sighed. *This* halfwit was Beaujeu's last hope of saving Acre?

"Are you Katsaros?" he tried again.

No answer.

He glanced around the courtyard and stood. "Get up. I'm putting you on a ship to Acre."

That got a reaction: the old man stared up at him in alarm. "No! …No ships."

"I have orders from William of Beaujeu, the Master of the Temple."

The old man's watery gaze returned to the sand. For a moment, he sat utterly still and did not breathe.

When he looked up again, and his eyes were precisely focused on Gerard, his voice crisp and a little sullen. "I do not cross water."

The hairs rose on the back of Gerard's neck as though a cold finger was tracing his spine. He cleared his throat, trying to fight back an instinctive fear. "All the knights of Egypt and Damascus are camped outside the walls of this city. Do you really want to be here when they break in?"

"If I leave they certainly will break in. Within days, maybe hours."

Everyone knew what fate Tripoli faced if her defences were breached. Gerard was only a boy when Antioch fell to the former Egyptian sultan, but well he knew that those who survived were broken by what they'd seen, waking in the night to scream with terror.

Part of him wanted to know why the old man was so sure his departure would be quickly followed by defeat. Another part of him warned not to ask.

"I have my orders. There must be a safe way for you to cross the sea—"

"There is none. If you put me on a ship, you'll destroy me and Tripoli together." The old man leaned forwards, and Gerard numbly realised that Katsaros, too, was afraid. "This city has a chance, but only as long as I stay."

Gerard ran his tongue over his lower lip, forcing his fear back long enough to think. Tripoli might weather this storm. With access to the harbour, the city would never run out of men or supplies. So long as morale held and the walls endured, the siege was a waiting-game in which the city held all the cards.

"All right," he said at last. "But I want you lodged safely at the Temple commandery."

"No."

"You'd be much more comfortable there."

"Comfortable, and *trapped*." Katsaros glared at him. "No."

Gerard hesitated. Beaujeu had warned him not to force the diviner aboard ship, but he'd said nothing about taking him into protective custody.

"Do not test me," Katsaros said harshly, as though he could read Gerard's thoughts. "Send your men to capture me, and you will feel my wrath."

"*Your* wrath?" Ridiculous as the boast was, the hair prickled on Gerard's neck once more.

The other man levelled a terrifyingly remote gaze on him, and Gerard flinched.

"For eighty years I have ruled this city. *Do not presume to give me orders.*"

For a moment, he found it hard to breathe. The air in the little courtyard was thick, like the air before a thunderstorm. "No, sir," Gerard gasped, using the honorific before he realised what he was doing.

"Leave me," Katsaros said.

"Yes, sir."

The sense of oppression didn't lift until Gerard was outside, catching his breath in the chicken market.

What *was* Katsaros? What was the Master mixed up in?

He shook the thought hastily out of mind. Best not to ask too many questions. This was Beaujeu's responsibility. He was only the secretary, only following orders. If he didn't ask questions, he couldn't be held responsible.

Gerard sniffed his orange and started back towards the Templar commandery on the town's northern wall by the sea. It was slow going: the streets of Tripoli were packed with people. Every spare courtyard and corner was taken up by makeshift shelters as those who could not find sanctuary within the bursting tenements laid claim to a few feet of space on the cobble-stones.

Thankfully the spring weather was still cool, the nights fresh with a nip of frost, and the rain enough to flush the septic pits beneath the public latrines. Otherwise they might have a plague on their hands, as well as the Egyptians. Gerard paused, listening, but there was no sound of assault from the orange-groves beyond the walls. Just thin hammer-blows as more siege-engines came together.

Qalawun was doing this properly. Taking his time.

Gerard pressed on into the main thoroughfare leading from the palace to the harbour, and a litter carried by eight sweating slaves jerked to a halt as it squeezed past him. "Gerard of Montreal!" called a delighted feminine voice. "I didn't know *you* were here again!"

He glanced up, alarm threatening to choke his joy. "Lady Margaret!"

"Set me down," she called to the slaves, and beckoned to Gerard. Within a heartbeat he stepped into the litter, kneeling at her feet, and she dropped the curtains around him, sealing him within a brightly-coloured, perfumed tent.

"I *am* sorry, dear. You're here on business, aren't you?"

Her welcome had gone to his head, and he decided to be bold. "I came partly for you, my lady."

"You're not going to try to send me home, are you?" Perhaps she intentionally misunderstood him. "I had enough of that with Eschiva, and besides, Lucy needs me. Poor child, she's no experience with ruling."

"So you stayed to help her?" he put in admiringly.

She sighed tragically. "Oh, Gerard, I *do* want to see her triumph. You'll laugh at me, I know, but for so long I couldn't help thinking that if only Tripoli was ruled by a *woman,* all those old wounds might be healed. We're different to men, you know. It isn't so important to us to avenge slights and wreak vengeance. Tripoli needs a ruler who can be diplomatic—conciliatory—and when I look at Lucy, I see *hope.*"

Gerard sighed, thinking of the countess—a peculiarly adamant woman, he would have said. "I wish you might have remained *bailli,* my lady."

"Lucy means well," Margaret added. "Only, she is lonely and afraid. If I can only set her feet on the right path, Gerard, all might yet be well. Now, what's Beaujeu thinking of, sending you back at a time like this?"

The sudden change of subject and tone was somewhat destabilising, and choked him off just as he was about to return to his personal hopes. "Beaujeu? Oh. He's worried about Tripoli."

"Aren't we all?" Margaret sat back in her chair, lacing her pudgy fingers together. She didn't seem particularly worried. "Lucy panicked and called *everyone*—Genoese, Venetians, Pisans, Hospitallers. Given the history of this county, if we make it to Tuesday without a civil war it'll be a miracle."

"The Temple agrees with you," Gerard confessed. "That's why I came to see you, my lady. We hoped there was something we could do to keep things civil. Together."

"Together, eh?" Her eyes turned to crescent moons of laughter. "You mean, since Lucy doesn't trust a word the Temple says, you want me to be your mouthpiece in the council."

Gerard felt his face redden. "Well, my lady, we both want to keep the peace. And although Beaujeu doubts, I've always believed in the power of prudence and forethought. This city is strong and well garrisoned; so long as we remain united, there is no reason it should fall."

"Certainly not." She fetched a deep sigh. "Well, I have ideas of my own, I warn you. I've ruled Tyre for five years now, and I'm used to dealing with the Egyptians. I won't promote the Templar line at the cost of my own common sense."

"I understand," he said. "We only want the privilege of hearing your thoughts and advising you. The thing is, if we suggest anything, it will be dismissed out of hand, merely because of who we are."

She looked down at him with affection. "Very well, Gerard of Montreal. I shall agree on one condition. I like the Order well enough, but I don't much fancy the idea of being their puppet. I'll deal with *you*, Gerard, and only with you."

"You do me too much honour." Alight with hope, Gerard kissed her hand. "My lady, you don't know how I suffered, away from your presence all these years."

In answer, she was still and silent. "Gerard," she said at last in a very serious voice.

"Please don't," he pleaded. "For the first time in years I see your face, I have hope. Don't take it away from me."

She watched him with troubled blue eyes. "I hoped your feelings had changed."

"Never."

"I have changed," she said wistfully. Her hand still lay within his, and she did not try to remove it. "I was a beauty once."

"Your purest beauty is in your soul," he said, "and the years have done nothing to dim that."

She gave a decided nod, and took her hand back. "We will love one another as souls, then. In that I have not changed, Gerard. Call on me this evening and we will talk of the siege."

So neatly did she turn his words back on him and win their skirmish. Defeated, Gerard could do nothing but thank her and withdraw, pulling a fold of his mantle over his head to hide his face as he slipped from the litter.

A quick scan of the street revealed no familiar faces, suggesting that his meeting with the Lady of Tyre had gone unnoticed. The last thing he needed was to have Countess Lucy learn of the Templars' alliance with Lady Margaret. Still, the street was so crowded that he couldn't afford to relax his vigilance. Gerard kept his head down and took a circuitous route back to the commandery, where he sent Marco hastening to the harbour to tell his shipmaster to heave off the coast and wait for further signal.

As Beaujeu had foreseen, this was no in-and-out mission. Now he must ensure Tripoli survived, for the diviner's sake as well as Lady Margaret's.

His plans laid, Gerard kicked off his boots and stretched himself out on the narrow bed in the small room he had been allotted in the commandery, smiling at the ceiling above.

I was a beauty once. He remembered the wistful sigh Lady Margaret had given as she spoke the words, the way her soft hand trembled in his. Perhaps he had lost the skirmish, but he may yet win the war.

Chapter XIV.

Trapped in her prison, Soraya had no way to measure the time. Reduced to little more than a feverish consciousness, she found herself unable to sink into the deep trance that made the time slip by more bearably.

He had called himself John Zakar. Who *was* he? His name and face jogged no memories, but his voice had triggered recognition and hope. *John Zakar, John Zakar,* she repeated to herself—but nothing came.

That implacable man, who had hunted her through Tripoli with such cunning and determination, was on her side now—if only she could escape this prison long enough to give him the information he so desperately needed. Fretfully, Soraya strained against the commands that bound her. Whoever he was, she'd promised to help him. Once Saif was finally dead, she could find freedom at last, if not her memories. That chance was passing her by.

Some indeterminate time passed before she was called into physical existence once more. Soraya formed her body in febrile impatience, half hopeful and half afraid of what she would find.

She found Saif sitting on a bed-platform with his spear across his knees and a silver scrying-bowl beside him, etched with spells and full of water. At her appearance, he held out a scrap of white cloth. "I need your help."

Soraya studied the face printed on the fabric, and let out a delighted bark of laughter. "Well! This is much better-looking than you really are."

"It's all over the city." He picked up a whetstone and began sharpening the blade of his spear with quick, angry strokes. "If I show my face out there, I'll be mobbed."

Instinct told her this had to be John Zakar's work. Soraya stifled another cackle. "Does this happen to you often, al-Mukhtar Saif al-Din?"

Saif didn't seem to hear. "The Master is ready to skin me alive, and for good reason. We were to keep in the shadows, not draw attention to ourselves. I *told* you not to let yourself be seen."

He must be in communication with this master; doubtless through the silver bowl.

"*I* let myself be seen? *You* are the one who murdered the Zakars."

"How was I to know that such insignificant people would turn out to have connections?" Saif shook his head. "It doesn't matter. God knows best. The point is, I can't finish my mission like this. If I covered my face, it would arouse suspicion. So. I need your help."

Hope stabbed her to the heart.

"If God wills, I'll have to stay here until the hue and cry dies down," Saif went on, looking distastefully around the small, shabby room. "Forget about the Watchers for now; they'll be on their guard. I need you to visit every astrologer, fortune-teller, diviner, and faith healer in this city. Make up some excuse as to why you need their services."

"What are you looking for?"

Saif grunted. "Anything out of the ordinary. Territorial reactions. Possessiveness. Anyone who seems spiritually sensitive enough to know who you are."

"And what would that be?" Soraya regretted the words as soon as they slipped off her tongue. She should know better than to hope that there was anything good in her past.

Saif levelled an incredulous look at her. "You're a djinn."

That was the beginning and end of her story as far as Saif was concerned. Evidently it never occurred to him that she might be asking more; whether, for instance, she was the kind of djinn that did good, or one who had followed Shaitan into evil. Soraya sighed. "What a shock."

"I should have thought you knew," he said, straight-faced and apparently sincere. He really didn't understand sarcasm. "The Master says you can't be trusted, but the Watchers have left me no choice. I need you to swear to perform this task without fail and without subversion."

There had to be a reason for this strange task, but Soraya didn't have the time to sit down and consider it. It was enough to know that thanks to John Zakar, she now had the chance to escape her prison. Yet—Saif simply meant to hand her the chance? Impossible.

"What's the catch?"

He didn't meet her eyes; he just swallowed, hard. "You offered to be my comrade. Did you mean it?"

Soraya stared at him in blank shock.

As she hesitated, his eyebrows drew together. "Will you promise, or must I compel you?"

"One moment." She needed time to think about this in detail, it was all so new and strange; but he didn't mean to wait. She clutched at one fact she knew, instinctively, to be true: that he meant what he said. This was no elaborate deception, for the simple fact that he was incapable of such a thing. Let her meet honesty with honesty: "Don't you know why I have always found a way to subvert your orders? It's because *they were orders, Saif.* You never left me a choice."

"If I had, would you have done as I wished?"

Murderer. Fanatic. Fool. "Of course not."

"Then why should I give you freedom?"

"Because you said you didn't want a slave. Did *you* mean it?"

He didn't answer.

"There needs to be something in it for me," she went on. "The truth is, we will never be comrades, and for the love of you I wouldn't suffer so much as a gadfly's bite. And yet, where love fails, there's still self-interest." She hesitated, thinking. She needed a way to see John, without Saif's leave. "Let's make an agreement: I'll promise to do as you want, and I won't look for loopholes. But only if you promise to leave me free in my body. I don't want to be locked away, and I don't want to have to account for every moment of my time."

Saif's green eyes narrowed. "No loopholes?"

"No loopholes, as I live."

He stared at her for a long time, eyes narrowed in suspicion. With every moment that passed, Soraya lost hope. Surely there was no chance he'd trust her so far.

He cleared his throat. "I can't let you run free while I sleep."

Disappointment was bitter on her tongue. "Then don't be surprised if I find loopholes."

"Wait." He glanced down at his hands, the veined fingers and the glint of the carnelian ring against the rich brown wood of the spear. "God willing, I'll release you the moment I wake each morning. You'll have all day, so long as I'm awake."

She'd been so sure he would refuse that it took a moment for his meaning to sink in. "I will?"

He took a deep breath, apprehensive but resolved. "All day, as God wills."

He would trust her. He would give her freedom. A fire-burst of elation coursed through her veins, and Soraya reined in the sudden wild impulse to kiss him. She wouldn't forget his crimes so quickly—and yet her voice was husky with emotion as she replied.

"Done," she said. "I swear to do my best to help you, and I won't look for loopholes."

A faint smile touched his lips, reined in as quickly as her own excitement. "It's nearly noon. You'd better start at once."

Lightheaded and dizzy with hope, Soraya started for the door.

"Soraya," he added, as her fingers brushed the latch.

"Yes?"

"You might bring me a book or two, if you can find any." He sounded casual, almost friendly. "Please. I should very much like something to read."

* * *

Nine hours later Soraya stood outside the Zakar house, plucking up the courage to enter. After an afternoon of visiting charlatans who pretended to read her palm or divine her future, using wily guesses and purposefully vague words rather than any real knowledge, she'd rewarded herself with a meal. At first, she'd meant to steal enough to buy herself all the most costly delicacies in the Tripoli marketplace—meat, wine, sherbet.

But when the time came, she couldn't bring herself to do it. The fine things would be there tomorrow, and so, God willing, would she. Moreover, the thought of stealing from the harried, anxious people hurrying past her in the street had become strangely unpalatable. It wasn't just that she couldn't afford to get in trouble for pickpocketing if she meant to keep Saif's confidence; with a chance for real freedom in her grasp, she was unexpectedly having to ask herself what kind of life she meant to build for herself in the future.

She had no idea how long it had been since she'd had to make decisions that went beyond the bare moment, but she sensed it had been a while. It was an effort, like looking up at a distant horizon after years of close work with small and nearby things.

She had warned Saif that she planned to make discreet use of her strength, but she stood there with her heart in her mouth for a moment before she could bring herself to pull on the soul tether. At first it snapped taut as Saif tightened his grip reflexively on the far end. But then, true to his word, he let go and the power flowed smoothly into her.

It was like drawing breath in the moment after a strangling. Better, for she had never known what it was to breathe freely. A bitter freedom, for it ought to be hers by right, and yet she could not avoid an instinctive thrill of gratitude.

She reached the upper window in two bounds, then let go of the soul tether to reassure Saif that she didn't mean to exploit the opportunity. Instead, she tapped on the wooden shutters.

There was no answer, and Soraya's heart fell. Not all her investigations today had been on behalf of Saif: a Watcher she spotted at a fish stall in the marketplace had betrayed that John was living here, in the old Zakar house.

Perhaps she had misunderstood the woman, and the house was empty after all.

Or perhaps John had fallen asleep with the dark, and her rapping on the window was not enough to wake him. Soraya got her fingernails between the shutters and pried the broken lattice open.

"Come in, my dear," said a silvery voice from within.

Soraya hesitated, squinting into the dark interior. The clay of which her eyes were made responded to her will, becoming more sensitive to the dim light within. The room had been cleaned since she was last here, the scent of blood almost, but not quite, eradicated from the stones. On the other side of the orderly room, another window stood open above a sleeping-platform, letting in a little starlight. John Zakar lay there alone, inert and breathing steadily. Even with eyes adapted to the darkness, Soraya could have sworn there was no one else in the room.

"Come in," the voice said again. "If you sit on the windowsill all night, *someone* is bound to notice."

Soraya squeezed through and stepped down, staring around the room. "Who's there?"

At first, the apparition was blinding. It formed quite suddenly in a vaguely human shape, white-hot with light. Soraya gave an exclamation and staggered back, shielding her eyes.

When her vision recovered, a being of light in the shape of a woman sat smiling beside the sleeping man.

"Look at this, John. I can make her see me." There was a moment's silence. "Yes, I know. But here she is, all the same." Her eyes, which had fastened on a place somewhere in the kitchen, returned to Soraya. "One moment, Soraya—yes, well, why don't you ask her yourself? No, it's not difficult. Just *focus*."

After a moment, another ghostly shape flickered into view. The man who called himself John Zakar stood near her in the kitchen, staring as though it was she, not the dreamer, who was the ghost.

"I thought you died," he said dazedly.

"It's a long story." Soraya glanced at the woman. "You're a dreamwalker."

"I'm Rahel, John's wife."

"A *mortal* dreamwalker?"

Rahel shrugged. "I'm not sure how, either."

"But *you* aren't, are you?" John was still staring at her. "A mortal, I mean."

"No."

"Are you Tripoli's guardian?"

"No," she repeated, startled. "I came from Cairo." *Besides, I'm no angel. I couldn't guard a blade of grass.*

"But you're a—" he swallowed, glancing towards his wife and back again. "You're a spirit, and a powerful one. If you wished, you could send me home."

If there was something he wanted, there was no harm in knowing. "Where's home for you, then, John Zakar?"

"It's not *where*, it's *when*." He took a deep breath. "It's six hundred years ago."

Soraya stared at him, and his shoulders slumped. "I thought you might be able to undo it."

But it wasn't confusion that kept her silent; it was the unbearable, teasing feeling that she already knew something about this man. She waited, but it didn't come back to her. Whatever it was, it was buried deep in the mirk of her past—a past she had no intention of ever unearthing. The sound of this man's voice might fill her with a sense of hope, but that could only be illusory. Learning why she knew him would mean finding out what ghastly thing she'd been doing when they had met.

"I have no memories of that time. I'm sorry."

He rallied quickly. "But you must have, once?"

Rahel glided nearer, her eyes pleading. "Please. Try to remember. We aren't used to being apart."

Her hand slid through John's as, for a brief moment, she forgot their incorporeal form. Despite herself, Soraya felt a twinge of sympathy, for she knew what it was like to be without a body. With the feeling came something more startling: longing for something she dimly perceived between these two. Not their physical bond; that was now snapped, and Soraya was either too jaded or too unlike them truly to comprehend mortal desire. No, it was something in the way they spoke to each other; something in the way John Zakar looked at his wife, his stern face softening into something extraordinarily tender and vulnerable.

He turned to Soraya and repeated, very softly, "Please."

Soraya took a deep breath. "I can't. I wouldn't know where to return you."

"Syria, in the year of Our Lord six hundred and thirty-six," John said promptly. "The month of August, in the—"

"No, that's not what I mean." Soraya sighed. "At the very least I would have to *remember* that day, where I was and what I was doing. And I can't. I have no memory beyond the last few months."

"Why not? Can it be repaired?"

"No." To her surprise, the lie left a sour feeling in her gut, but she repressed the guilt. It was possible she might recover her memories; anything done by magic could be undone by stronger magic. Recovering them would entail figuring out how they had been stolen from her in the first place, and by whom. Then it would just be a matter of finding a greater spirit to overrule that magic. Still, she never wanted to recover those memories. All the blood Saif had spilled and she had consumed, all the fallen cities and slaughtered people.

"Besides," she added, "even if my memories could be restored—and it would take something immeasurably powerful to do that—I think I would have to have *met* you, before the moment of your departure, in order to send you back. Think of it as though I were building a bridge between two points in time. I'd need anchor points, and you would be those anchors. I...I would had to have *known* you."

The words only escaped her out of guilt, and she held her breath, watching John's face with close attention. Waiting to confirm if he knew her.

Instead, he looked as though he'd been punched in the gut. "Then we have no chance at all."

"I'm sorry," Soraya whispered. "It's possible I'm wrong—I'm only relying on instinct here. As I said, I have only a few months' worth of memories."

Rahel's hand hovered on John's shoulder, and Soraya felt another twinge of guilt. They weren't created to be bodiless, these two. Their history was one of flesh and blood and bone, the woman's body apple-shaped from childbearing.

Rahel said softly, "There will be others to ask. Others more powerful."

"Angels," Soraya put in, letting a bitter twist into her voice. "The followers of Shaitan have lost all but the dregs of their power. You want an angel."

"How do we find one?" John asked.

Soraya shrugged. "You can't. Strictly speaking, there ought to be a couple in this room with us at the moment. But they weren't made to be perceived by mortals, and if you ever did catch a glimpse of one without its knowledge, the sight would likely drive you mad—if you survived the first moments, that is. In revealing themselves to mortals, they usually exert considerable effort in making themselves safe."

Rahel looked around the room, forehead puckering as though she expected to bring an angel into visibility through willpower alone. Eventually she let out a sigh and shook her head.

Watching her, John let out a similar sigh.

They didn't even need words to communicate; that longing ached even more fiercely in Soraya's heart.

Rahel said softly, "I do sense them, our own guardians. They must know what we want. They just don't see fit to give it."

Soraya shrugged. "Or they haven't permission."

"John," Rahel said softly, "maybe we should consider the possibility that—"

"No." John had been staring into nothing, his ghostly brows knitted. Now he looked up sharply. "I made promises. There *must* be a way I can keep them." His scowl deepened. "I'm going to act on the assumption that there's something I'm meant to do here first, before I find my way home. All this *has* to have a reason."

"I think I know what that reason is." Soraya took a deep breath. "Al-Mukhtar Saif al-Din. The Chosen."

"So it's true? That's the man who killed the Zakars?" John nodded towards one of the scraps of white silk she'd seen decorating nearly every street in the city.

"That's his name. I am his slave, and…" in this, she must be honest with him. "It was through me that he was able to commit his crimes."

"Then we must free you," he said. "Tell us how."

That was all. No blame. No shock. She could have kissed his feet for that. "Maybe you shouldn't do that. I'm not…I'm not an angel."

"No?" Rahel said. "But you mourn your sins, and would mend your ways?"

Did she? Soraya hesitated, staring at her. Even today she'd lied and stolen. But that was because she thought there was no hope for her, no future. Not in terms of eternity. Even freed from Saif, she would always have been destined for the abyss, surely?

Rahel nodded at her. "I just can't help noticing you're in a body. I thought the Fallen had lost that power."

The Fallen—Rahel must mean devils, afrits, evil djinn. "You must be mistaken. Most djinn don't create their own bodies, it's true, but we can be either good or evil."

John and Rahel looked at each other. "A djinn?" John said in evident confusion.

"Maybe she means a nephilim," Rahel suggested. "As the offspring of demons and mortals, those would have free will, to be good or evil."

"At any rate, we needn't worry about that," John said brusquely. "Rahel can deal with a loose demon, if that's what you are. Humans are much trickier. Tell us about this master of yours."

"Right." Soraya pulled her attention back to the problem at hand. Saif would be wanting to sleep soon, dragging her back into the ring via the soul tether. She'd delivered a book of Avicenna to him that afternoon, together with enough candles to keep him reading all night if he wished, but she couldn't expect him to sit up forever. "With his face plastered all over the city, my master has gone into hiding at his lodgings."

"Where is he staying?"

"No, no. You need to stay away from him. If he ever decides you're a threat to him, your life isn't worth a copper."

"But—"

"You don't happen to be immortal, do you?"

"No."

"Just making sure." Soraya sighed. "You see, *he* is; probably because of me." She circled her index fingers around each other, looking for the best explanation. "Saif and I are linked. Through the ring that is my prison, he is able to use my strength, my immortality. It's a constant tug-of-war between us over a finite amount of power. But owing to the nature of the spell, he always has the upper hand. He's able to command me at any moment and I am forced to obey." She hesitated. "I should warn you that at any time he can command me to tell him exactly what I've done and to whom I've spoken, and to recite any conversation word-for-word. I'm very good at subverting those commands, and I've made him promise not to do that while we're in Tripoli, but if he chooses to break his word there's not much I can do."

John nodded. "We'll be sure not to arouse his suspicions."

"There are three ways to deal with such a person," Soraya went on. "First: destroy the item—ring, lamp, jar, or so on—that binds the djinn to its master."

"Or steal it?" John suggested.

"That might work if the djinn was the only one bound to the item, which is the usual procedure. But whoever made this bond chose to bind Saif to the ring as well. Even if it could be stolen—and good luck stealing a ring from the hand of an invincibly strong and immortal man—even then he could still access my strength and power, though he could no longer verbally command me. The second option would be to locate a spirit that's stronger than the djinn of the ring. A man or weapon possessed by a stronger spirit would be able to overpower Saif, and could either kill him or take his ring long enough to destroy it."

John grunted. "So again, we'd need an angel."

"The third option?" Rahel prompted.

"The third option would be to attack the master using the item. Craft a weapon from the lamp, sharpen a shard of the pot." Soraya shrugged. "That's why rings are so popular. It's impossible to use one as a weapon. I did think of making him choke on it, but we'd have to stuff it down his throat somehow, and—"

"And even if you did," Rahel put in, "the air would just whistle through the band." At Soraya's surprised look, she smiled. "Small children. Don't ask."

"What about the spear?" John put in suddenly.

Soraya blinked, confused. "What spear?"

"The spear he was carrying that day at the funeral. The magic lance. Could that kill him?"

"The *spear?* You're mistaken. There's nothing magic about that old thing."

"I've…" John shifted uncomfortably. "I've seen it before."

Soraya shook her head. "No, you're mistaken. It's I who make Saif invincible, through the ring."

"Maybe you were mistaken," Rahel said to John.

John frowned, but didn't respond. Instead, he said, "It's clear we need to find an angel, then." He stared at Soraya without seeing her. "Of course, if you were a demon Rahel could simply exorcise you. But I'm inclined to agree with her: I don't think you're one of the Fallen."

"If I thought so, I already would have exorcised you." Rahel smiled impishly, and then covered her mouth with her hand, smothering a giggle.

John glanced sideling at her, his ghostly face glowing with affection. "I love how you do that."

"Do what?"

"Scandalise yourself and then laugh about it."

"Oh."

The ache had been building in Soraya's gut ever since she ventured in the window, but by now the pain was almost unbearable. *Comrades,* she thought. *This is what it looks like.*

She wanted nothing more than to be part of a bond like that; to trust the two of them as they trusted each other. But they were wrong about her: she *was* evil, and if they ever glimpsed what was in her past, they'd perform their exorcism and send her straight to the abyss where she belonged.

Rahel turned to her. "I have to ask," she added apologetically. "But since you're under this man's commands, isn't it at least possible that he could command you to be free? That you could escape him that way?"

"Ha." Soraya shook her head. "I suppose it's possible in theory. But Saif would never do such a thing. Think of all he'd be giving up—endless life, youth, and strength; and worst of all, he'd be risking the wrath of his precious master. No, John is right. You need an angel to help you."

John looked hopeful. "Could you help us with that?"

She spread her hands with a shrug. "My friend, I may be a djinn, but not even *I* could survive that kind of encounter. It's not just to do with mortality; it's also to do with quality. Trust me, I think you're far better prepared for it than I am."

John and Rahel looked at each other. "We might fast and pray," Rahel suggested.

"There's nothing else we *can* do, apart from waiting for the storm." John sighed. "That's the difference between sorcerers and Watchers. A sorcerer commands. A Watcher can only hope."

"There's more you can do," Soraya said. "Keep in touch with other Watchers, see if you receive a message or portent. And if I were you, I'd try the alms-houses. It doesn't always happen, but sometimes a place of worship, or a hospital, or an orphanage, can become holy ground—I mean *really* holy, with an associated guardian."

"If you went and slept on the doorstep of such places," Rahel suggested, "then we could explore them together in our sleep. A lot of my Messages used to come in dreams."

John grunted. "All right. We'll start with the island again, since Rahel dreamed of it." He grimaced. "Sleeping in the street on an empty stomach. It's all right for you, but it will be pretty grim for me."

Rahel swatted at him playfully, her hand passing through his head without impact.

"You missed," he said, straight-faced.

"I'll make you pay for it when you get home."

"Is that a threat or a promise?"

Feeling as though she was intruding, Soraya cleared her throat. "Saif will be wanting me back in confinement soon. I had best return to him. But I'll come again tomorrow, God willing." The Name slipped through her lips unexpectedly. Was she a fool to seek to curry favour with one she knew she had offended a thousand times over? Was hope even possible for someone like her?

Banter forgotten, Rahel looked at her with sympathy glimmering in her eyes. "Oh, Soraya. We'll do our best for you, I promise."

"Thanks," Soraya said huskily. She didn't quite believe they really wished to do her a good turn. Surely they were only doing this to get justice for the Zakars; all the same, it was good to have them on her side. "If the angels will reveal themselves to anyone, I'm sure it will be to you."

John escorted her downstairs to let her out at the door on the street. Since he was still dreamwalking, Soraya had to unlatch the door herself; but before she left, she cleared her throat. "I didn't know you were married." *Not like this.*

He looked surprised. "Well, I didn't tell you."

"I meant to seduce you. I didn't know…"

"Ah." He frowned slightly. "You wouldn't have seduced me."

Having seen him with Rahel, she believed it…and yet.

"But I *meant* to do it."

"It's all right, Soraya. You only did what you thought you had to. I forgive you."

He couldn't understand. He didn't look shocked enough, or disgusted enough to have understood. "But you can't."

"Why not?"

"I don't deserve it."

"None of us *deserve* forgiveness Soraya; that's why we need it." His smile was swift and bright, not at all what she would have expected from such a forbidding-looking man. "Off with you, and sin no more."

Chapter XV.

"Do you feel anything? Are there any other spirits here?" John scanned the small basilica looming over his and Rahel's dreamselves where they stood on the tumbled rocks of the tiny isle of Saint Thomas. It was only a barren fleck in the sea, about the size of a polo field, separated from the mainland and the city by a narrow channel less than a hundred paces across. There wasn't even room for a presbytery, and the basilica itself was locked and dark.

Beside him, Rahel shook her head readily. "None on the island, save myself."

"We might as well move around and make sure," he said with a huff of disappointment. It was the first night of their search, and already the effort seemed pointless. "Who knows? We might find Tripoli's angel hiding like a crab beneath a rock."

Rahel didn't laugh, but she did follow as he began his circuit. "You saw me meeting the guardian here in a storm," he said, trying to keep his spirits up. "Even if we have to wait for the next storm, it can't be too far away. The winds are strong on the coast in March."

"Oh, yes," she said. "I'm sure Qalawun will be kind enough to hold off his sack until we get a decent storm. How will you convince the guardian to help you once you find it?"

The sarcasm was unlike her. "I was hoping you might help with that," he said mildly. "There isn't much we can do but ask."

"A long shot, even if we find the creature." He heard her mouth twist in a smile. "It makes one wish the Unfallen were at least a *little* corruptible, doesn't it?"

John had to laugh at that. "If you have any idea how I could bribe an angel, go ahead. I can just imagine it now. *Please, my lord, take me home to my family and I'll...make you a citizen of Jerusalem.* How could he resist?"

Rahel was silent for a while. "Most creatures want something," she said at last. "It's only a matter of finding out what."

John watched her thoughtfully. "Is something the matter?"

She looked up at him with suddenly wide eyes. "No...wait. Oh, I can feel something beyond the city walls. A powerful spirit, battering the guardian's defences."

"The Egyptians have a demon with them?" John shook his head. "Of course they have. But surely it isn't a problem so long as Tripoli has a guardian."

"It would take a very strong guardian to resist this spirit," she told him. The light of her image faded a little, and her voice, when it came again, was faint. "I'll see what I can find out about it. I want my husband back, John."

With that she was gone. John shivered a little in the cold spring wind and turned to survey the island. He completed the circuit without further revelation, thinking about Rahel's words. Was this a fool's errand, after all? Rahel was hopeful, but if only he *knew* that the guardian would help him—

Suddenly, Rahel was beside him again. "Back again," he said in surprise. "What news?"

"Have you waited long?" She blew him a kiss, their usual greeting in the intangible world of dreams. "I had trouble getting through—almost as though something was trying to hold me back. Shall we begin our search?"

John blinked at her. "But you were just..." His voice trailed away, for a troubling possibility had occurred to him. Were his dreams playing tricks on him, or had he been visited by two different Rahels? "At least you're here now," he said slowly.

She turned to look out across the island, frowning slightly. "I don't see or feel a thing on this island."

"What about beyond?" he asked. "In the city, or beyond it?"

"I'm not quite powerful enough for that, dear." She looked across the narrow straight with its small purling waves, to the small postern leading through the massive city wall. "We might go into the city and see what we find there."

Out into the city, and leave his mortal body lying helpless by the church? "No," John said at once, too sharply.

Rahel—if it *was* Rahel—turned to him in surprise. "Is something the matter?"

Feeling the pull of his mortal body as his heart began to race, John tried to calm himself. Doubtless Rahel's first visit had been a dream. He'd had vivid dreams before, waking up the morning before a battle or a visit to the surgeon convinced that he'd already gone through with the unpleasantness. Or perhaps this part was the dream. Either way, it was foolish to worry.

"It's nothing. Talk to me. Tell me about your day." It had become a litany, of sorts.

Rahel sighed. "Jerusalem is under siege. So far there has been no great hardship for us; but do you remember Zahir?"

"I remember him." A young heretic who had chosen to help Rahel in the dangerous days after Oliveta's fall, and had guarded her on her long overland journey home from Antioch to Jerusalem. John was grateful to the boy for what he had done, but a part of him would always be curled up in resentment at the thought that he must rely on a barbarian stranger to protect his wife when he could not.

"He ran an errand for me to the marketplace this morning," Rahel said sombrely. "Someone threw pig's guts at him. I'm afraid he won't be safe if this siege goes on much longer."

"What did he expect? His people started this war."

"And he's a lonely, frightened boy caught in the midst of it." Rahel's words hung in the air, an unspoken reproach echoing in the silence. "From now on, he must stay inside the house."

"What, keep him with you? In the house? With the children?" John felt his heart begin to race again. "Those people aren't just heretics; they're dangerous barbarians. If you won't think of your own safety, think of the children. Please promise me you won't put this barbarian's safety above theirs. If you won't hand the boy to the authorities for safekeeping, you should at least send him back to his people."

Rahel sounded incredulous. "Zahir has done me no wrong, and you want me to send him to prison?"

The heretics committed no crime, and we had murdered them. His own words to the council at Oliveta came back to him like a dash of cold water to the face; and John jolted awake on the hard ground beneath the basilica eaves. Tiny, cold flecks of rain flew through the wind, spattering his face; but it was his agitation that had dragged him from his sleep.

What would the council at Oliveta say if they could see him now? Had he not condemned them for their hard hearts? John pulled his hands down his face, wrestling with his own fear. Perhaps Zahir could be trusted; after all he had protected Rahel and the children all the way south from Antioch. Rahel, though tender-hearted, was no fool—yet his heart rebelled. One must love one's enemies, but did that mean sheltering them in a time of war?

Groaning, John rose and took his hired rowboat back to the city. He was shivering by the time he reached the Zakar house again and kindled a fire for warmth. He spent the rest of the night hunched over the small blaze, avoiding sleep—and Rahel.

Chapter XVI.

"How many did you see yesterday?"

"Just the one; a sand diviner. It took me all day to track him down."

"And?"

Soraya shrugged. "Nothing whatsoever. He was just an old imbecile squatting in a corner of a courtyard. Unless you're after a lunatic, I don't think he's your man."

Saif slammed his book down and jumped to his feet, full of pent-up energy. "This was a mistake. I ought to be doing this myself."

"Yes, because it worked so well last time you tried," Soraya pointed out.

Saif scowled, then danced toward her with jabbing fists. Evidently, it was time for their morning sparring-match.

By now, the siege had dragged on for five weeks. Many of the wealthier burgesses of Tripoli had left, but the city was still overcrowded with the poor who could not afford to leave. At first, Tripolitan hopes had been high—with the harbour open, supplies of food and new defenders could keep the city going indefinitely.

So long as the walls held.

Outside the city, Sultan Qalawun's archers kept up a fierce barrage of arrows, forcing the defenders to abandon the parapets along the wall and the aqueduct. Meanwhile, his siege engines never rested as they bombarded the wall with a constant stream of stone missiles. Little by little, they took their toll. Little by little, the wall crumbled.

As the city's hope ebbed away, Soraya's impatience mounted. Over five weeks, John Zakar had spent a night sleeping in the porch of every basilica, hospital, alms-house, convent, and orphanage in the city. When none of them had brought a result, John had doggedly begun making the rounds again, and the last of Soraya's patience had left her. She knew that this arrangement could not go on forever. Sooner or later, she would either find whatever it was Saif had her looking for, or he would realise she was going as slowly as she could and take over himself.

Meanwhile, Saif himself had grown restless. Soraya always knew when he'd had to make a report to his master, for afterwards he always found more faults with her work, and their morning sparring sessions were longer and more tiring. Thankfully, owing to the siege, Soraya had plenty of excuses to hand: there were a great many people packed into the city, she had not been provided with a list of diviners to consult, people were difficult to find and rumours must be weeded out.

Yet she hadn't lied to Saif: from Countess Lucy's own court astrologer down to the hedge prophets and gutter healers, she'd never seen such a pack of charlatans in her life. The only exception to the rule had been a Watcher named Hubert.

"Are you a friend of John Zakar's?" he had asked, when she waylaid him one day in the marketplace.

"How did you—"

"There seems to be something you haven't told him," Hubert had said. "No, it's between you and John. Not my place to intervene. Good day, mademoiselle."

Naturally she hadn't told Saif about Hubert. Nor had she told John, if it came to that.

Saif had waited all of three weeks before deciding to take matters back into his own hands. Unfortunately, the people of Tripoli were bored and fond of making trouble, and Soraya had taken care to spread rumours of a sizeable reward should the Zakar killer be found. A mob had descended upon Saif before he had made it more than a bowshot from the tenement. If he'd been mortal, it would have been the end of him.

Now, he scowled in concentration as he danced around her, looking for an opening to strike. "It worked *well?* For whom? For you?"

"It was sarcasm, Saif." She ducked swiftly, evading his jab.

"I wish you'd say what you mean," he said. "This is dragging on too long. The sultan expected to be inside the city by now. I'm failing all of them."

"You've been talking to that master of yours again." Taking advantage of Saif's momentary inattention, Soraya pressed forward with a flurry of blows. Left. "If he really is as kind as you say, why are you so terrified of failing him?" Right. "Surely he'd understand." Left.

"Don't presume to speak as though you know him." With a grunt of effort he caught her wrist and twisted, forcing her effortlessly to her knees. "You need to work faster."

"I'm down to my last fortune-teller." Her next words bubbled out before she could stop them: "I could be more help if I knew exactly what it was you're looking for." They sounded exactly like something Rahel would say, and she regretted them the moment they were uttered. The slight widening of Saif's eyes that told her he was surprised.

And distracted.

She swept a leg, dancer-like, in a wide circle, toppling him to the floor. She got up, breathing hard, telling herself not to make the same mistake again. What John and Rahel had—she and Saif would never have that. She shouldn't be trying to help him; she was conspiring to *kill* him, God forgive her. How could she possibly succeed if she forgot all the ways he still treated her as a slave, or worse, began to see him as a friend?

He got up, his eyes now narrowed and suspicious. "Just do as you're asked, Soraya. There's a limit to my trust, and the Master will be unhappy enough if he finds out I've been letting a djinn do all my work."

So he hadn't told his master of their arrangement. Interesting.

Gingerly, he rubbed the corner of his elbow where it had slammed on the stone floor. "You have only one fortune-teller left to visit, yes? Once you've seen her, bring me a list of the names and addresses of the Watchers we saw at the Zakar funeral." He looked at the floor, scowling. "The Master will no longer tolerate our inactivity. Either we find the fortune-teller we seek, or we must go back to weeding out the Watchers."

* * *

Before going in search of the last fortune-teller in Tripoli, Soraya found a quiet garden in which to perform morning prayers. She didn't know if it did her any good to pray, but since meeting John and Rahel, she'd made an effort to begin the habit. This morning, she felt the need all the more keenly.

Her alliance with Saif was fraying. If she didn't get results today, he would kill more Watchers—and he'd use her strength, her power, to do it.

The fortune-teller she sought lived in a small single-room apartment beneath an overcrowded tenement, damp and musty. Soraya found the building and followed her directions downstairs to the dark apartments carved into the earth below. At the end of the stairwell was a dark passage lined with doors. When Soraya knocked, the door inched open to show the pale, lined face of a woman who might have been anywhere between forty and seventy.

Their eyes met. The woman's nostrils flared, and a look of suspicion crawled across her face. "Not open for business today."

She went to slam the door, but Soraya thrust her elbow against it. With her other hand, she slipped a gold piece from her pouch. It was not stolen; she'd raised some money from a forgotten, unsalvaged shipwreck. "Please, good mother. I'll pay you well."

The woman stared at the coin, touched her tongue to her lips, and shuffled back to let her enter. Soraya followed the woman into a small, cave-like room lit only by a small grille high up on the wall. It was almost impossible to see into the shadows with ordinary human eyes, and after a moment's thought Soraya left them the way they were. She wasn't sure she wanted to see whatever was evidently festering away in the dark corners of this cellar.

The woman dragged a small table into the ray of light and cleared dirty dishes off it, then slammed down a small dish containing needles and shards of metal. *Aichmomancy,* Soraya thought. Thrown onto the tabletop, the diviner would read her fortune from the pattern the shards made as they fell.

"I'll need your name."

"Soraya," she said. It was always a risk giving out her name, but she was trying to provoke a reaction.

This time, she got one. The woman halted, looking at her with eyes that glittered. There was a long, stifling silence.

"What do you want with me?" she demanded in voice subtly different to the one she had used a moment ago. "Why are you here? This is *my* place."

Bound to a mortal body, Soraya had only the prickling on the back of her neck to warn her. "What does my name mean to you, then?"

The woman responded with a wrathful scream. Her hands flicked out towards Soraya as if she was throwing something. On the table, the dish of needles overturned, sending a cloud of shards into the air. The shaft of sunlight glittered with sharp steel.

Stumbling backwards, Soraya raised her hands to shield herself. A futile gesture. Tiny metal shards ripped through her body from all directions, and in her mortal form there was nothing she could do to stop them. For a blinding instant, she could only scream as they tore her body to shreds, unseating her spirit.

Soraya's spirit rose from the crumbling body, glad just for a moment to leave its torment behind. In the fortune-teller's place before her, a black demon shape coiled and seethed, lashing out a tentacle to hold her. Soraya felt it fasten around her, black and tarry like burnt oil as its serrated maw opened to feed—

—and then the soul tether whisked her out of the room, out of the grip of the afrit, across the burning soul-lights of the city and back into her prison.

Soraya arrived screaming Saif's name along the soul tether. Unless he was asleep and dreaming there was little chance of being heard, yet he ought to sense the soul-tether go slack once she was no longer exerting her power to maintain a body. Sure enough, moments later, his command plucked her back out into the physical world.

Without the disintegrated materials of a former body in the room to draw from, Soraya contented herself with a smaller, feline body. Saif stood opposite her, gripping his spear with white knuckles and eyes like coals. "What happened?"

She answered as soon as she had a mouth and lungs, modifying them slightly to produce a human language. "I visited the final fortune-teller. She had an afrit."

Saif gave a grunt of triumph. "God is great. That's what I want. Where?"

"Under a tenement near the pig market."

He grabbed a satchel and pulled the hood of his cloak deep over his head to conceal his face. "Take me. Now. We don't want her getting away."

Still in the form of a cat, Soraya mewed at him to follow and bounded downstairs. Saif's feet pounded behind her, his breath sounding like a bellows to her sensitive hearing as she wove through the streets towards the fortune-teller's house.

She hoped that this discovery had bought John and the other Watchers some time to find the guardian. Still, the encounter had left her shaken, nervous. Somehow, the woman's demon had scented her true nature; worse, her name had frightened it enough to shred her body and attempt to consume her.

Why? What did her name mean? Who was she, that even an afrit feared her?

As they reached the door to the tenement, Soraya put her paws against it and looked back to Saif with an expressive yowl. Saif threw the door open. Within, the house was quiet.

Once more, Soraya gave her cat-mouth some more human characteristics. "Downstairs, on the right."

Saif grunted, groping in his satchel. "Good. Back into confinement with you."

Soraya yowled indignantly. "You promi—"

Before she could finish the words, the command snatched her back into her prison for the second time in the quarter-hour. Sightless, soundless—it was like being smothered, and a sickening realisation hit her. Her agreement with Saif had been for the duration of his mission here in Tripoli. Now that mission was completed, he had no reason to leave her free.

It hadn't taken long to forget what captivity was like, to forget that an end would come to her freedom. For a brief time, confinement had meant nothing more than a welcome rest at the end of a busy day. Now she could kiss goodbye to purpose, to friends, to hope. She might never even have the chance to tell John and Rahel how her freedom had come to an end.

Then it came: the hot, sticky, metallic taste of blood. Once again, she was drowning in the unbearable sensation.

How much more of this did she have to endure?

What if John and Rahel *never* found the guardian they sought?

She was still reeling from the sickening glut when Saif ordered her out of her prison again. The remnants of the body which the woman's demon had destroyed were still in the room, providing her with the raw material she needed. As it formed around her, her lungs drew in foul air and she doubled over, retching.

A moment later she had recovered sufficiently to see the woman's remains sprawled on the floor at Saif's feet, utterly still.

"Did you have to kill her?" Soraya asked faintly, wiping bile from her mouth.

Saif shrugged. "Likely the thing had consumed her mind, God have mercy on her."

Violently unseated from its host body, the demon must be angry; but in her embodied form, Soraya could do little to prevent it taking whatever revenge it wished. She recoiled, all her senses at alert. "The afrit—where is it?"

On the table was a heap of personal belongings half wrapped in a tablecloth, as though the woman had been interrupted partway through packing to flee the apartment. Saif swept them aside and in their place set down a sealed earthenware jar about the size of a medicine-jar, tall and thin. "Safe in here."

The jar jumped, as though something was fighting to get out. Saif steadied it with a grunt of surprise.

Soraya took a deep, cautious breath. *"This* is what you've been looking for?"

"Yes." He looked at the jar with a glow of pride. "The guardian of this city."

Soraya stared at him incredulously. "But…this is an afrit," she said faintly.

"And now it's been captured, it can't go on protecting the city. Tripoli will fall, God willing." He straightened, looking at Soraya with a surprisingly genuine smile. "You've done well. The Master will be pleased."

God have mercy, what had she done?

"It can't be," she said, dazed. The afrit had attacked her, but it had relied on the element of surprise. In absolute terms, she would have been stronger. "I doubt this one is strong enough to protect an entire city. You'd need something else for that; a genuine prince of the afrit, or an angel."

Saif's smile faded, replaced by suspicion again. "What are you playing at?"

"I'm not playing at anything! I'm only telling you, this is not what you think it is."

A few short weeks ago Saif would have brushed her comments aside—but perhaps she wasn't the only one letting her guard down. At any rate, he paid her the compliment of believing her. Tilting his head consideringly, Saif rapped on the jar's seal. "I seek refuge in God from the cursed devil… Speak, creature. What's your name?"

A small and angry voice within the jar snarled, and Soraya recognised the attempts of a spirit to disobey the command put upon it by a greater. Whoever had spelled the container must have been invoking a far stronger spirit; probably not herself, Soraya guessed. More likely the same afrit that had bound her to Saif's ring.

The spirit quickly lost its battle. "My name is Envy-By-Night."

If Saif was here to capture the city's guardian using a spelled jar, he must not be expecting an angel. Such devices would only work on lesser beings—like herself, or whatever *this* was. Since there was no chance of the real guardian being captured, perhaps it was worth helping Saif to glean some information from the creature. "Ask its rank," she suggested.

He relayed the question, and the afrit said, "Twenty-eighth rank."

Saif lifted an eyebrow at Soraya, and she shrugged. "*Someone* took my memories, so I don't know what that means, but it doesn't sound impressive, does it?" Likely the force and desperation of the creature's malevolence had fooled her into thinking it was even stronger than it really was.

Saif rapped on the jar again. "Is there a higher-ranking guardian in this city, then?"

Another snarl, longer this time, before the smothered voice in the jar shouted, "Yes, damn you!"

Saif scowled. "Where?"

"Set me free, and I'll tell you where to find her."

Saif glanced up at her. Soraya swallowed, hard. So. She was about to find John's angel. "Go ahead, but set commands on it before it emerges. We don't want a fight on our hands."

"Give us the name first," Saif commanded the afrit. "And by the name on this seal, you will tell the truth."

This time the resistance was only momentary. "You'll find the guardian possessing a sand diviner named Stephen Katsaros. Now let me go!"

The voice rose to a high-pitched howl, and the jar on the table jumped. Saif grabbed it and said, "You will depart to the opposite side of the world and not return. Be released."

Soraya couldn't help flinching as she sensed, rather than saw, the creature flow through the walls of the jar. There was an awful, oppressive silence. For an instant, the room was full of malice. Then Soraya took a deep breath and knew it was gone.

Wait.

John's guardian, possessing a sand diviner? But then—

Soraya stood rooted to the spot, her stomach slowly clenching. Angels did not possess mortals. There was no angel. There was only another devil, a djinn or afrit.

"Katsaros," Saif repeated, thoughtfully. "Praise and thanks to God. Isn't that the sand diviner *you* said was an imbecile?"

Soraya blinked. Cleared her throat. "It lied to us," she said desperately. "Katsaros was empty, I'd swear it." Or if there was something…inhabiting him…it must have been hiding. Dormant, deep down inside.

Saif shoved the jar back into his satchel, and snatched his spear from where it leaned against the table. "Still, I mean to see him. Lead me to Katsaros."

He may not have meant the words as a command, but the terms of her enslavement picked up her feet and marched her out of the room, incapable of disobedience.

There was no angel, there was only another afrit, and Saif was going to enslave Tripoli's only guardian.

She had to warn John…and she couldn't. Her feet carried her inexorably towards the shabby tenement where Stephen Katsaros and his afrit waited, and Saif followed with Tripoli's destruction in his satchel.

Chapter XVII.

Dinner at the Templar commandery was always a silent affair, for the Rule of the Order commanded a dish of cooked meats eaten in reverent silence while the chaplain read aloud from Scripture.

"If any man will come after me, let him deny himself, and take up his cross, and follow me. For whosoever will save his life shall lose it: and whosoever will lose his life for my sake shall find it. For what is a man profited, if he shall gain the whole world, and lose his own soul? Or what shall a man give in exchange for his soul? For the Son of man shall come in the glory of his Father with his angels; and then he shall reward every man according to his works."

Under the table, Gerard's knee jumped. The reading was doing little to calm his nerves—all this talk of losing souls, and he couldn't quite muzzle the voice in his ear, whispering that Beaujeu's plan to save Acre came with infinite risks for the mortals involved.

Gerard glanced sidelong at the commander of Tripoli, Brother Peter of Moncada, flanked at the high table by Reddecoeur and Vendac. The three of them kept their attention on the reading. Brother Reddecoeur had his eyes closed, his lips moving in time with the words. Marshal Geoffrey stared into the distance, stolidly picking his teeth with a silver implement.

Next to Gerard, Peter of Alba and another brother had abandoned all pretence of listening. "I'm telling you, it's not breached, it's *gone.* Looks like a landslide."

Despite its massive fortifications, under the Saracen bombardment, the Bishop's Tower had finally collapsed into the city moat in a scree of rubble. The Tower of the Hospitallers seemed close to joining it. Unable to stifle his worries any longer, Gerard leaned towards the brothers on his left and muttered, "We can hold it. The rest of the wall is still strong." *We won't have to bring Katsaros to Acre.*

"They'll demolish it sooner or later," Alba hissed. "We're helpless. The Egyptians are here to stay this time."

Gerard didn't reply, clinging to the truth that cities had weathered far worse, and survived. You never knew. Say the Tartars took it into their heads to attack Damascus—or the sultan died of some campaign-related illness—or a mamluk emir in Cairo took the opportunity to snatch the throne. A siege was never over until it was over. At Antioch two hundred years ago under Godfrey of Bouillon, Raymond of Saint-Gilles and Bohemond of Taranto, had there been similar conversations among those men? Had they, too, sat silent at table under the dark and lowering certainty that the city would fall? Did they, too, despair of mastering their own fate?

The reading ended, the chaplain said grace, and the brothers rose in silence. Some went out to begin a long dark watch along what was left of the city wall, but most of the others headed towards the dormitories. Many would sleep in their armour, a sword close to their hands. At this point in a siege, it didn't pay to be caught unawares.

Gerard headed out towards his own quarters in the guest-house. He'd set up a small cabinet in a corner of the humble room, and there were still a stack of dispatches on his desk to look over. During the last five weeks, he had immersed himself in the problem of bringing sufficient food and reinforcements to the city, managing the constant flow of passengers away from the beleaguered city to the Frankish kingdoms in Acre and Cyprus, and planning for a possible breach of the wall.

At least, insofar as the Temple was involved in these activities. The other factions in the city were presumably running similar operations, and none of them were talking to each other or coordinating their efforts. As usual.

Approaching his quarters, Gerard found Marco waiting outside the door, hat in hand. With Katsaros located, Gerard had been occupying his servant's spare time with a search for Peter of Alba's Eastern prince. At a nod, Marco followed him into the small room. Gerard dragged a chair away from a small writing-desk against one wall and sat down heavily, kicking off his pointed shoes. From the look on his servant's face, the news was not good. "All right, then. Let's have it, Marco."

The young servant cleared his throat. "I've asked at every noble house, sir. There's no rumour of the man you described."

Marco was good at his job; he could always talk his way into a kitchen and get the servants gossiping. If he said there were no rumours, there were none. Gerard pulled his chin, thinking hard. "Perhaps the Prester already left the city. Perhaps I should send you to Acre or Cyprus."

Marco cleared his throat, and Gerard shot him a surprised look.

"You disagree?"

"Sir, from your description, this Prester John was not travelling in any particular state. He could still be anywhere in Tripoli, among the common sorts of people."

"Be serious, Marco. I'm looking for the prince of a great kingdom. Would such a man adopt the guise of a common labourer?"

"Well, Our Lord did, sir."

Gerard stared at him. "I don't appreciate it when you do that, Marco."

"Do what, sir?"

"Bring theology into a completely unrelated conversation."

"I do apologise."

Gerard scowled at his cluttered desk, trying to figure out his next move. Marco cleared his throat again.

"Oh, what is it?"

Marco seemed hesitant. "Sir, are you familiar with the organisation known as the Watchers?"

"The group that was so influential in the kingdom's politics about a century back? Weren't the Ibelins involved in that?" Gerard frowned. "I don't see how they're relevant."

"It's a hunch I have. Their officers are also known as Presters, and I couldn't help wondering—what if this man you're looking for is actually a *Watcher* Prester, not a king from the ends of the earth?"

Gerard's gut churned. "In that case, our last hope of an effective foreign alliance is gone."

Marco rubbed his chin. "If you'll give me leave, I could visit the local Watchers and ask them. There's a meeting tonight, and I've been invited."

"I didn't know there *were* still Watchers around."

In answer, Marco touched his left forearm. "Still plenty of us left, sir."

Gerard didn't much like the thought of his servant having loyalties beyond himself, but so far Marco had always been faithful. Besides, the boy had a point: he'd forgotten about the Ibelin connection with the Watchers. Possibly the Lady Eschiva had taken an interest in the traveller not because he was a king, but because he was a Watcher. Gerard threw himself back in his chair with an annoyed gesture. "Well then, go to the Watchers and rule it out. We don't have time for a wild-goose chase."

With Marco gone, Gerard dragged his chair back to the desk and tried to focus on his work. Repeatedly, however, he found himself staring past the words on the parchment toward the broken city wall beyond.

What was he *doing* here? He should be getting Katsaros and Lady Margaret out of this city, but both of them refused to leave, and now it seemed that his hunt for Prester John was futile as well.

There came a timid knock on the door. "What is it?" Gerard snarled.

Usama, the slave assigned to him by the Temple, cracked the door open. "My lord, are you ready for me to sweep your room?"

He'd been sitting here all day, working. "Why didn't you do it when I was at dinner?" he asked disagreeably. The old Saracen began a stammering apology, but Gerard cut him off. "Never mind, you might as well do it now. I'll leave."

Lady Margaret, as ever, was able to restore him to a good humour. "The Watchers, if I remember correctly, are a layman's order with councils all over the world," she said equably, admiring her needlework in the light of the many lamps blazing in her bower. "Isn't it possible that a man might be both a king of the east, and a Prester of the Watchers?"

"I suppose he might."

"In which case he might prefer to ask his fellow Watchers for help, rather than the nobles of the Coast, whose hands are full with their own affairs." Lady Margaret planted her needle in the fabric and set it aside. "But you didn't come to me because you wanted to discuss the Watchers."

"No." Gerard blinked, pushing his thoughts aside, and smiled up at her warmly. "How did you fare at the palace today?"

Lady Margaret folded thoughtful hands over her belly. "Sir Benedetto Zaccaria suggested a surrender."

"He wanted to give up the city?" Gerard put a fist to his mouth. "Devil take it."

"I didn't reply in quite those words, but yes."

"Tripoli can be held. All we need is for the defence to stand firm."

"Hmm." She looked into the fire thoughtfully. "Is it the Temple who advises thus, or you?"

"Both of us. We'd hardly be here, otherwise."

"Yes, I suppose that's evident. But advice changes." She tapped her lip with a forefinger. "In any case, I concur; and that's the advice I gave Lucy. She promised Zaccaria additional land in the city once the siege was concluded, and he agreed to stay."

Gerard let out a sigh. So far, Beaujeu's gambit was working: although Countess Lucy pointedly did not solicit the Temple's advice in council meetings, she was getting it anyway through Lady Margaret. Better yet, she was following it. "That buys us some more time, at least."

"Does it?" she asked, looking up at him with candid blue eyes. "How much time, Gerard? The wall is crumbling. This can't go on forever."

She was right; but that didn't mean all was lost. He swallowed. "I believe we are the architects of our own fate, my lady."

She looked thoughtfully at her embroidery. "Dear me! I devoutly hope not."

"What do you mean?"

"What fate have the people of this city built, Gerard? Backbiting, envy, discord, revenge—you have no idea how desperately I pray the fate of this city is better than it deserves."

The conversation had cut suddenly deeper, and in quite a different direction than he intended. Gerard shuffled his feet uncomfortably. "If we believed that, we might as well give up—we might as well play the lute until Tripoli burns."

"We might try casting ourselves on the Mercy," Lady Margaret said. She looked up at him, and his discomfort must have showed on his face, for she softened a little. "Forgive me. You didn't come to be preached at."

He forced a smile, and dragged his seat a little nearer. "You may preach to me as much as you like. Never fell fairer words from sweeter lips."

A delicate flush touched her cheeks, but her voice was playful. "You say that to all the ladies, I'm sure."

Since their meeting in the street, Gerard had offered her the friendship she asked for, spiced with a little harmless flirtation, and had found a measure of contentment therein. When it made him so happy just to be in her presence, what good did it do to demand more? Yet, as she had pointed out, time grew short, and tonight he was in no mood to retreat.

"Only you," he said in a low voice. "Only and always you."

She looked at him reproachfully, but the blood was still high in her cheeks. "Must you say such things?"

He fell on his knees at the arm of her chair. "Tell me it doesn't please you, and you will never be vexed with me again. I told you my feelings had not changed—"

The pink in her cheeks only deepened. "Nor have mine."

"I don't understand," he burst out. "You are your own mistress, you are young, you have a heart. Why turn your back on me? You made the political alliance that was expected for you; but that is over, and you can please yourself as other ladies do."

"And I *do* please myself."

"Time grows short—you said it yourself." He captured her hand and pressed it to his lips. "Why, my lady? If we loved each other less, I might understand it. Do I disgust you?"

She turned her head, and looked him up and down. The blush was no longer a delicate affair—and yet, she looked. "Oh, no," she said.

"Is it a religious vocation, then?"

"Perhaps it is."

He closed his eyes, remembering all the years he'd known her. "You were never meant for a convent," he urged. "With me, you might have children."

"I was married for fifteen years, Gerard. If I had been capable of that, don't you think it would already have happened?"

He had struck a nerve there; her voice was sharp.

"Then marry me for your own sake," he pled. "For companionship, for delight. I trust—I believe your heart is with me. Listen to it. Listen to me."

"No, dear, listen to *me*." She sighed. "I cannot say it kindly, Gerard, and I am sorry. You come to me each day with flattery and badinage, with such arrangements of hair, and in clothes I know for a fact you cannot afford; and now you offer me children and delight. I don't mean to accuse you either of vanity or fatuousness, but I wonder if you really know me. Do you think me such a slave of my appetites? I am the Lady of Tyre. I am not accustomed to making such weighty decisions so very lightly."

Now it was Gerard's turn to redden. It was true; without thinking, he had appealed to Margaret, not as a reasonable being, but as one driven by mere appetite. For a moment he wished that he'd had the good sense to love a lady less perceptive, who had not known him since childhood.

"It makes me wonder," she continued sadly, "whether you know me at all. Whether it's myself you love, or my position as lady."

It might have been easier if she had burned him alive, but he couldn't turn tail now. "In that last accusation you wrong me," he protested. "Perhaps I have slighted your judgement, but it was unthinking. I would love you if you had not a copper to your name."

"But you wouldn't marry me. You've always been ambitious, Gerard."

He opened his mouth to protest, but her words hit too close to home. It was true. He had always known he couldn't afford to marry a penniless woman, and he'd be lying to himself if he said her wealth meant nothing to him whatsoever. For a moment he didn't know how to answer. Then he plucked up his courage again. "And you have always found it hard to believe you could be loved for anything but your beauty, my lady. Don't turn me away only because you think it is lost and cannot imagine why else

I might long to be near you."

She reddened, and tried to pass it off with a laugh. "You're too clever for comfort, my friend."

"I might say the same of you." He smiled up at her. "Tell me how I shall prove myself worthy of you."

"Tell you? Oh, no." She patted his hand. "You're a man of great sagacity, Gerard, and you know me better than anyone else in the world. It will come to you."

More than that she would not give him—and yet, she had encouraged him to try. It almost wiped away the sting of her words, and he got up with a painful smile. "I'll do as you ask, my lady. And now I had better take my leave—there's a stack of dispatches on my desk that I should answer before I sleep."

He returned to the Temple commandery through steadily rising winds and the first flecks of a rainstorm. Usama had finished his sweeping and disappeared. Still aglow with determination, Gerard sat down in the tidied room and worked steadily through his dispatches. Another hour passed before Marco returned.

The servant burst in without waiting for an answer to his knock. "I found him! I found Prester John!"

All doubt vanished in the face of Marco's excitement. Tonight was his night. Gerard swallowed the rebuke he'd been about to utter, and jumped to his feet. "Take me to him. Now. You can explain on the way."

He followed Marco into the shadowed streets with pulses thrumming in anticipation. He had to shout to make himself heard above the rising wind. "So, I take it you did find him at the Watchers' meeting."

"Yes, and he told me I had a Gift." Marco's excitement glowed in his eyes. "I'm a Healer."

"Oh?"

Marco waved his hands vaguely. "Sometimes Watchers have gifts. He said his wife had had a vision about me. She's a Messenger. I'm a Healer, apparently."

"Marvellous." Privately, Gerard thought it sounded as though his servant had been treated with rather unkingly familiarity. "Don't forget you're also an excellent manservant, Marco. Did he say anything about where he came from? What military capabilities are we looking at, if any?"

"I don't know, sir, but he did say something about the siege."

"Which was?"

"He hopes to save us."

"Well *done*, my boy." Gerard slapped Marco on the shoulder, then crossed himself as he recalled Lady Margaret's words earlier tonight. "God and his saints are ever merciful!"

Marco led him towards the sea gate, then doubled back into a narrow, dark alley. A light shone from the downstairs window of a small house, and as they approached the door opened, allowing two men and a woman out into the street. Huddling into their mantles, they hurried away, leaving a fourth man standing on the threshold, peering up into the stormy night sky.

Marco picked up speed. "Prester! It's me, Marco!"

The man beckoned them into the lamplight. Gerard had to duck to avoid hitting his forehead against the low door. Upon entering, he found himself in a downstairs room with one lamp hanging from the centre of the ceiling, face to face at last with the legendary Prester John.

He was a man of medium height and middle age, with a straight nose, a neatly-trimmed beard, and hair that had gone prematurely grey. His eyes were as sharp and bright as steel, his arms corded with sinew, and he held himself upright like a king and a warrior. Gerard swallowed, no longer doubting that he stood in the presence of the saviour he'd been seeking.

"Are you Prester John?"

"I am," the man said.

Gerard fell to his knees, took the man's hand, and kissed it. "My lord. We've been waiting for you."

The Prester stilled, as though surprised by Gerard's recognition. Before he could reply, however, the door flew open with a bang.

Gerard turned as a ragged scarecrow burst into the room. Marco's sword flashed as it was drawn, and the Prester reached for something lying on a bench just out of sight, but Gerard, on his knees, glimpsed the newcomer's face and shouted, "No! Stand down!"

The newcomer put up a gnarled hand and yanked the tattered blanket from his head, revealing a gaunt and wrinkled old face. Stephen Katsaros.

"Prester," he croaked in Greek. "I am the guardian of this city. Take me under your protection, I beg you."

Chapter XVIII.

For a moment, the small lower room was silent, motionless. John stared into the face of the old beggar who had accosted him on his first day in Tripoli. How could *this* be the guardian he was seeking?

Sidestepping the noble Frank, who was apparently about to pass out from some mixture of reverence and elation, John inched nearer to the bench where his weapons lay—weapons he'd spent much of the last month scrounging and constructing.

"Who are you," he asked the scarecrow, "and from whom do you seek protection?"

"My name is Lilith." The old man straightened and John's flesh prickled as he sensed a stronger, darker will beating against his own. "For eighty years I have watched over this city."

Lilith. He knew the name from every frightening childhood story: the queen of the night, the spirit of pestilence, the dark mother who suckled children with poison, the dark lover who fed on the lust of the lonely.

His gut churned as he remembered the nightmare that had come to him five weeks ago. *Lilith.*

"*You* are the guardian?" His voice sounded strange in his own ears.

"You have been seeking me for weeks," the old man replied. "Here I am."

"Impossible."

"Are you a fool, or blind? Have you not seen my hand at work in this place?"

The tale of Tripoli was one of envy, strife, and civil war—her hand had indeed been busy. Piece by piece, John's hopes crumbled about his ears. He had not found an angel guardian because there was none. There was only Lilith. He had been roaming the city in his dreams for five weeks for *this.*

His throat was dry, and there seemed to be a terrible weight on his chest, but he managed a harsh laugh. "You make a strange choice of champion in me, my lady."

"You don't understand." The demon curled the old man's lips in contempt. "You've been seeking a killer, haven't you, Prester? The one who spilled blood in this house was hunting *me.* Trying to capture and enslave *me.* Save me, and you foil him."

"Wait." The rich young Frank had been staring at the demonised man in utter befuddlement, but now he seemed to latch onto something that made sense to him. "You have an enemy, Katsaros? Someone *inside* the city?"

Lilith nodded. "If he succeeds, I will no longer be able to protect you. Qeteb will descend on this city in a storm of fire and blood, just as he did at Antioch twenty years ago. Do you really want the Terror-By-Day to be loosed on this city? Ordinary men don't delight in such savagery. It takes our kind to do that."

"Tommaso," the Frank said. For an instant there was silence. *"Tommaso,"* he snarled, turning towards the young Healer, who stood by the door with his sword drawn.

"Sir, yes, sir," the young man stammered, and slipped out into the darkness.

"Well?" Katsaros was still focused on John. "What do you say, Prester?"

Doubt clawed at John's throat, preventing him from replying. How could he offer the protection she asked? Lilith was a demon—a *queen* of demons.

Strong enough to undo Oliveta and send him home.

The treacherous thought slipped into his mind before he could stop it. Others followed. Who was the real threat here—the demon who had been protecting the city, or the Saracens outside, waiting to destroy it? Lilith, or the Chosen who lurked within, plotting to betray it, whose hands were slick with the blood of Watchers?

Most creatures want something, Rahel had told him.

"Who is trying to enslave you?" John asked, his voice husky. Soraya had shared what she knew, but that was too little. "Who is this Chosen?"

"The Chosen is only a servant himself. When he has captured me, he will turn me over to his master: Khalil ibn Hassan."

At first John was sure he'd misheard. "Who?"

"Khalil ibn Hassan, whom you know of."

"Yes, but…six hundred years ago!" Protest as he might, John was bitterly certain the demon was not lying.

The Chosen had the spear. *Khalil* had the spear. The realisation jolted through him like lightning. Despair followed like a thunderclap, and John took a slow, deep breath. *No. For this, Oliveta burned. To keep it out of his hands.*

"Of course I can't just leave it," Lilith snapped in response to a question from the Frankish knight. "This body is my hiding-place. The moment I abandon it, Qeteb will pounce. That's why I need your help, Prester."

"Whatever's happening, the Temple can protect you," the Frank said stiffly.

Lilith only sneered at him. "You aren't equipped for this, Frank. Not like the Prester is."

"What *is* Qeteb?" asked John. Lilith's voice was full of dread when she spoke the name, but there was more. The name was somehow familiar, but how?

There was a note of desperation in Katsaros' voice. "Qeteb is my brother, and he has always hated me. Now he has allied with Khalil, and is using him to build an empire. Tripoli is only the beginning. He will take first the Coast, and then the world. He will possess Khalil entirely, and destroy every soul that resists him. Fail me, and you deliver the world into his hands."

John stood transfixed. Hadn't Rahel *told* him there was a powerful demon with the Egyptian army? He'd never imagined what it might mean. He opened his mouth to ask more, but Lilith turned the sand diviner's head toward the door with a sudden snarl of awareness. A moment later the door jumped and rattled as fists beat against it.

John reached for his weapons. The Frankish knight seemed to be expecting his servant's return, for he threw the door open with an exclamation of satisfaction before catching himself in surprise.

"John! It's me!" Soraya stumbled through into the lamp-light. It must have been raining hard outside, for she was soaking wet and shivering. She didn't seem to notice the old scarecrow, nor the Frankish knight. "He plans to destroy the guardian. But it's not who you thought. It's—"

Lilith moved, scuttling away from Soraya and baring the old man's crooked teeth in a snarl. His hands rose in claws, and for the first time John realised how long and sharp the fingernails were. Formidable weapons, and with Lilith possessing him, the man would wield remarkable strength.

"Soraya." The demon hissed the name like a curse. *"You."*

Soraya registered the demon's presence for the first time. For an instant she froze in place; then she said very softly, "You have the advantage of my name, my lady."

For an instant the room was very still as the two spirits faced each other. In that silence, John thought he might have heard a sound from upstairs; but he'd left the casement open, and most likely it was the wind getting in amongst the dishes.

Lilith's teeth flashed in a predatory grin. "You don't remember me."

"Should I?"

"Should a child remember its own mother?"

Soraya paled to the lips. For a moment, she seemed to be muttering something under her breath—a prayer or recitation. "Don't pretend to know me. I won't believe a word you say."

Lilith lowered her claws, coming off guard with a smirk. "How fascinating. I beg your pardon; you were saying?"

"Soraya, where is the Chosen?" John asked.

Soraya turned to him, hands on her hips. "Someone told us where to find the city's guardian. We went, but the guardian was gone when we got there." She shot Lilith another narrow-eyed glare. "Saif wanted me to stand guard, watch for the old bat to return while he tried to find out where it had flown. So I ran at once to warn you."

"If I tell you how to unmake the Chosen," Lilith interrupted, "will you leave me in peaceful possession of this city?"

John forgot what he had been about to say. "Unmake him? You mean kill him?"

"It's not about killing him, it's about breaking his connection with the djinn." Lilith nodded at Soraya. "And then, yes, you'll be able to kill him."

"Tell us," John said.

"What kind of djinn am I?" Soraya said at the same time.

But Lilith shook her head. "A bargain first, then answers."

There was an agonised silence. John dragged a hand down his face. *Would it be so wrong?* he thought wearily. He hadn't sought her out. He hadn't forced her to obey him. She would offer this freely.

Even Rahel would agree this was the only way. He could get justice for the Zakars, thwart the barbarian army surrounding Tripoli, and make his way home.

Soraya turned with an abrupt pleading gesture. "Don't risk it, John! I don't know exactly who this creature is, but we both know it will lead us to the Abyss if it can."

John managed a smile, tried to shrug her off. "For someone who says she's damned, you're terribly worried about your soul."

"For good reason," Lilith drawled in the old man's creaking voice.

"Stop using that man as a puppet, damn you," Soraya said furiously. "John? What would Rahel say?"

The Frankish knight had been watching them all in utter bewilderment, but now he spoke. "You have a duty to protect the city, Prester."

"Yes." John refused to meet Soraya's eyes. Rahel would agree with him. The more he thought about it, the more obvious the decision seemed. It was almost a stroke of luck that the guardian had turned out to be someone who needed him so desperately. The Frank was right: he must protect the city. He must protect the Watchers. He must find his way home.

He turned to Lilith. "When all this is done, I want to be sent back to Oliveta. Can you do that?"

"I can send you back in time, yes."

"And the other children? Lukas and Marta?"

"Of course. So long as the Chosen dies, and I am left in peaceful possession of this city."

"John," Soraya protested again. "Rahel would never agree to this."

John opened his mouth to agree, but the words stuck in his throat. After all, his dreams of Rahel had been confused lately. Sometimes he knew he was really talking to his real wife. Sometimes he woke up sure that all he had heard was the unspoken urges of his own heart.

What would his true wife say?

Did it matter what she thought, so long as he made his way home? He was awake, separated from Rahel by half a dozen centuries; he *ought* to be able to say the words.

Before he had the chance to draw breath, a strangled sound came from Soraya. Suddenly her eyes were wide, her chest heaving as she struggled to draw breath. She put one hand to her throat and reached out toward the stairs behind him—

Footsteps echoed down the stairway.

Upstairs—that sound. John pivoted on one heel, his heart climbing up his throat.

"Don't move," the Chosen said crisply. The spear was poised in one hand, ready to throw; a leathern thong fastened it to one wrist for quick retrieval. "Not a word from any of you."

As he stepped into the light, Lilith inched back a step towards the Frankish knight. "Oh, it's the failure," she muttered in something like resignation, but no one paid any heed to her.

Spasms raced across Soraya's body as she fought for breath. Al-Mukhtar paused in front of her.

"It was a test, Soraya." His scorn was withering. "You've spent a great deal of time sneaking off on your own lately. Now I know where."

"You—followed me?" she gasped.

"Khalil warned me never to trust a woman or a djinn." His eyes shifted to John. But as al-Mukhtar stepped towards him, Soraya moved quickly to keep pace, one shaking hand going to the small knife at her belt.

The Chosen looked down at her with cold amusement. "Glory to God, are you trying to fight me?"

Soraya gasped again. "Can't—let you—"

"What I do is not up to you." He lifted the spear, and rapped it against the flagstones.

"Soraya, no!" John shouted.

Too late; Soraya was crumbling apart, her body returning to dust and water. John froze, telling himself the girl wasn't dead, that he'd seen this before and that she had come back.

Al-Mukhtar turned to John with murderous eyes. "Who are you?"

There was no way to win this fight, so John did not reach for the weapons behind him. Instead, he slowly lifted empty hands and watched the spear levelled at his breastbone.

"You killed two Watchers in this house, al-Mukhtar Saif al-Din. They were *my* family. What blood-price will you pay to satisfy justice?"

"Ah. You are the one who has kept me mewed up in a tenement for weeks while you seduced my slave away from my service." The Chosen reached into his satchel, coming out with a sealed jar. John glimpsed sigils stamped in the wax that sealed the jar's neck, and a chill ran down his spine. Soraya had said it was his intention to capture and enslave Lilith—this must be the vessel he meant to use.

What could Khalil do if Lilith was his slave, as Soraya was al-Mukhtar's?

The Chosen went on. "The blood-price I will pay you is this, Watcher: I will spare your life. Leave the diviner to me, and God willing, no one else need suffer."

The Frankish knight stepped in front of Katsaros, hand on hilt and nose in air. "This man is under Templar protection," he announced. "I do not recommend—"

With one hand, the old sand diviner swept the knight out of the way, his mouth opening in an eldritch scream. A hurricane of hot air swept forth with the howl, striking al-Mukhtar and throwing him bodily against the wall.

The Chosen rebounded at once, still grasping the spear in one hand and the jar in the other. But Lilith had bought them a precious few heartbeats.

John reached for the bench behind him and came up with the weapons he'd fashioned for himself over the last few weeks: a pair of small crossbows. His first shot shattered the sealed jar and nailed the Chosen's hand to the wall behind. His second caught the man precisely in the throat.

The Frankish knight thrust open the door into the street. "Marco," he bellowed. "Where are you?"

Through the rain and wind, the distant tramp of armoured feet.

Al-Mukhtar should have been a dead man. Instead, he snarled at John, then reached for the bolt in his throat, plucked it out and threw it back with lethal strength. John ducked, barely missing the thick, bladed dart as it flashed through the air towards his head. The Chosen ripped the second dart from his hand with a feral cry.

"Surrender," the Frankish knight said, but the command carried little conviction.

The Chosen bent down, coming up with a handful of pottery shards and the seal from the top of the jar. He stared at it for an instant, shock quickly turning to rage.

"Don't sleep, if you wish to live," he whispered, his voice hoarse with fury. "Do not let your guard down; do not relax your vigilance even for a moment, for I strike from the shadows, and I will show no mercy."

He turned and slammed his fist into the wall behind him. Rock tumbled; the house shook. With a second blow, the wall burst under the impact, and the Chosen shouldered through and was gone.

"Did—did he—" The Frank's voice was breathy, incredulous.

More rocks fell from the gaping hole where the back wall had once been. The Zakar house trembled. John turned and bolted for the open door, reaching it a moment after the old sand diviner did.

"You—Frank!" John yelled as the knight stood motionless, still staring.

The knight turned and staggered across the threshold as the house fell in on itself. Stones rained around John, and a blinding cloud of dust belched from the ruins. He couldn't see anything—not the knight, not the sand diviner a few paces away. Through the streets came the rolling tramp of marching feet, closer now. The Templars, summoned by the young servant.

Katsaros heard them too; and with a whimper, he turned to flee in the opposite direction, tripping over fallen stones as he went.

"Wait!" John raced after him and caught the old man's skinny wrist. "Lilith!"

Doors and windows slammed up and down the street as people leaned out, shouting to each other, pointing to the dust cloud brooding over the ruins of the house. Illuminated by the pale light from a window, the old man looked up at John with empty, glazed eyes.

If Lilith was there she lay dormant, deep within.

"Must hide," Katsaros whimpered.

The Chosen was out somewhere in these streets, the Templars were coming, and people were venturing out of their houses.

"Can't help but agree," John muttered. He hooked both his crossbows to his belt and took the old diviner by the elbow, hurrying him into the dark alleyways of Tripoli.

Chapter XIX.

He had been called Reshep, Rudra, Apollyon; but in all his manifestations, Qeteb was a noonday spirit. At night, his power waned, and so all he could do was float blindly in the wind and rain far above Tripoli, beyond the borders of Lilith's influence.

Yes, it was certainly her influence; until now he had never been quite sure. If Qeteb was a creature of treacherous foresight and iron-fisted order, Lilith was a being of blind chaos, consumed by her own appetites. Nearly a hundred years ago, having grown impatient with his plans to build an empire, Lilith's hunger had led her to seek a more immediate satisfaction through an alliance with the Franks. Until now, he'd half suspected she was in the wealthier city of Acre. But tonight's exertion—the summoning of a wind—bore her signature. Amidst the myriad soul-sparks in Tripoli, her spirit had lit up with unmistakeable power. Her presence was beyond doubt now.

Once Lilith fell, the whole of the Coast would be easy pickings. Qeteb licked his jaws in anticipation. This place was holy to all mortals, and it pleased him to think of the desecration he meant to wreak upon it.

The memory of the blood he spilled here would drive his other enemies into a panic. By the time he was done with the Coast, his foes, from the kings of Nubia to the il-Khans of Baghdad, would sue for peace. Then, when Khalil had taken possession of the throne, he would take possession of Khalil and conquer whatever was left.

The time was long gone when he might have masqueraded as a god. Instead, he would crown himself emperor.

There was no sign of Lilith now. She had coiled back in on herself, damping her power to hide behind the light of another, and Qeteb couldn't pick her out from among the sparks below. Still, he didn't need to see her to know she was there. Khalil's pet mamluk must have come close to capturing her.

Qeteb scanned the city for other soul-lights. Near to where Lilith's light had glowed minutes before, a smaller soul-light flickered, lending its warmth to another. Small as the light was, it was pure and intense; Qeteb winced. Tripoli still had Watchers, then; Gifted ones even. He would recognise a Healer's light anywhere. He ought to have had Khalil command the mamluk to eliminate them all, for the damage they might do to his plans, even now, was immense.

Ah, there it was—Soraya's soul light, different again from either the mortal Watchers or the blaze of Lilith's power. Qeteb focused on the pinpoint of light, checking that the bonds he'd put in place might had not come loose. It was a risk, letting an ignorant meat-creature like the mamluk have access to such a spirit, but from what Qeteb could tell her bonds remained firm, her light slumbering as though dormant.

Tripoli would not fall tonight. The mamluk was moving more slowly than usual, but tonight had evidently witnessed...developments.

Patience, Qeteb thought, had never served him ill in all the endless years of his life. Once Lilith was captured, he'd be waiting.

Chapter XX.

The rain had stopped, but it was still a miserable night—wet and stormy with the rumble of nearby waves gnawing the city's walls. Instinctively, John steered the old sand diviner towards the most comfortable of the nooks he'd slept in these last few weeks: the porch of the church adjoining the graveyard where the Zakars were buried.

Few of the city's beggars liked to sleep between a graveyard and a locked door, and no one had taken shelter here tonight. John led Katsaros in out of the rain and helped him find a dry corner to curl up in. Apparently worn out after the confrontation in the Zakars' house, the old diviner fell asleep at once.

John had more trouble. For a long time he lay hugging himself, shivering too hard to get warm. At the Zakar house that evening, his only goal had been survival. Now, too late, he remembered Soraya's warning: if the Chosen ever decided John was a threat to him, his life wouldn't be worth a copper. With shaking hands, he reloaded his crossbows, placing them within easy reach on the ground. The Chosen had seen his face, might even have followed him here.

John waited, listening vainly to the wind. As the minutes whiled away and no intruder appeared, he forced himself to relax. Al-Mukhtar would have attacked by now, had he managed to track them down. No, the arrival of the Templar reinforcements must have convinced him to return to hiding; that, or the breaking of the sealed jar had made it useless for him to pursue Lilith.

That was another reason not to sleep: the demon slumbering opposite.

After a moment, however, John ruled her out as a threat. Lilith had had the opportunity to attack him; instead she had begged for help. Now she must be lying dormant, hoping to evade notice after her confrontation with the Chosen. He should take the opportunity to sleep while he could. Besides, he wanted to speak to his wife.

John got up and went through a few knee bends and jumps to get his blood flowing. So warmed, he fell asleep within minutes. The next thing he knew, Rahel was sitting with him in the porch.

"We already searched this place twice," she said, looking around them. "Did you hear something new?"

She seemed dispirited. "How was your day?" John asked. It had become a litany, of sorts.

"Tiring," Rahel admitted. "I had to send Zahir away. People were beginning to talk. I…you know how far we travelled together, and how we came to depend on each other. But he's better off with people who understand him, and I'm better off without the malicious rumours." A sigh. "Friendship is hard enough to find in this world, without it being evil thought of."

"I can't say I'm sorry you have him at a safer distance." The words sounded cruel in his own ears, and he hastily added: "Will you still be able to see him?"

"Well, he hasn't gone far. He's joined the garrison, and moved to the barracks."

A bitter reminder that Jerusalem was now occupied by heretics. The siege had ended with a surrender. John fell silent for a moment before moving on with the litany. "And the children?"

"I passed on the story you told for them. They don't understand why you aren't here—but I think it helps them to hear from you, to know you love them."

John nodded. As a spirit, he couldn't weep; yet he still found himself blinking hard, a tight feeling at the back of what seemed to be his throat. "Lukas and Marta?"

"No word."

But Lilith was confident she could find them; which suggested they were somewhere in John's past. The words stuck in his throat. He didn't want to admit who had given him news of them.

And that was the end of his side of the litany. *Strife.*

Rahel didn't take up her side of it. Instead, she looked about them, uneasy. "Is someone else here?"

"What do you mean?"

She shivered. "It feels as though we're being watched." Her light intensified a little, revealing the sleeping man on the other side of the porch. Katsaros shifted, mumbling in his sleep. "Who's that?"

There was no hiding it from her. He ran his tongue over ghostly lips. "It's been an eventful day, but the short of it is…I found our guardian."

Her face lit up. "This is him?"

"Hush," John warned her. He didn't want to rouse Lilith; something told him he didn't want to see what happened if she was brought face to face with Rahel's spirit form. Instead, he got to his feet and beckoned Rahel out into the graveyard. As dreamwalkers, the wind shaking the olives and gaunt rose bushes didn't bother them. John glanced towards the porch where the old man slept in the shadows. "It's the guardian, Rahel, but the guardian isn't…precisely who we thought."

Rahel only looked puzzled. "But will he send you home?"

"Yes, I think so."

Her face slackened in delighted relief. "Oh, John."

"She can send me home," he repeated. "She can help me bring justice for the Zakars, and she can protect Tripoli from the Saracens. There's one catch."

"She?"

John bit his lower lip. *Here goes.* "She is one of the Fallen."

The delight froze on Rahel's face and her voice swung into high incredulity. "She's a demon?"

"Yes, but she wants to help."

"Demons *never* help!"

She was reacting more strongly than he had anticipated. John shook his head. "You object to *this* demon, but not Soraya?"

"I've never believed Soraya was a demon, John! If I'd thought she was, I would have exorcised her already!"

"All right, but still—I know it sounds mad—but Rahel, this city would have fallen to the Saracens long ago if this guardian hadn't been protecting it. Meanwhile, I'm being hunted by a bloodthirsty mamluk. And did I mention that *Khalil is here*—in this time? He's allied himself with a terrible demon, a creature they call Qeteb."

Strife! How *did* he know that name?

He cleared his throat and went on. "I don't know if I have much of a choice here, dear heart. Right now, Lilith is the lesser evil."

"The *lesser* evil? John, she is literally a demon. You *know* what that means."

"I..." He put a fist to his mouth. Superstitious people believed that so long as they didn't actually pledge their souls to damnation, it was safe to deal with demons. John knew better; knew how crafty the creatures might be, knew the infinite variations of torment and corruption that the Fallen might use, once given the slightest foothold in a mortal's life. And yet—*and yet.* "She's promised to send me home. And Lukas. And Marta. If I don't help her, Qeteb will enslave her and make himself emperor."

"John." Rahel's voice softened. "We can still save our future—but not like this. Wasn't that what you went to Oliveta to say? We're Watchers. We don't compromise."

"I said that, yes." His voice had gone husky. "And what good did it do me? What good did it do any of us? The Watchers denied us, labelled us heretics. We took our stand at Oliveta, and not a single one of them listened."

For a long moment, Rahel looked at him with tears dancing in her eyes. "John," she said at last, very softly. "*I* listened. The children listened."

"Lukas and Marta. Where are they now?"

"I don't know—"

"But Lilith *does.*"

She shook her head. "Listen to me John. Wherever they are now, their last memory of their father is of him doing something brave, not because it worked, but because *it was right.*"

He had always had a deep loyalty to his own conscience, but somehow, choosing to face the Watchers at Oliveta had been easy by comparison to this—this throwing away of his only chance of ever seeing his children again. John groaned. *"You* were the one who told me there was a guardian in Tripoli."

"And you were the one who thought the angels were only silent because they meant you to complete a task here."

"What task, though?" He dragged his hand down his face. "I can't let Khalil get control of Lilith. He'd use her as a weapon."

"No. You'll have to exorcise her. If nothing else, that poor old man she's possessing deserves freedom."

The thought of an exorcism was no more appealing than letting Khalil get control of another demon. John took a ragged breath. "And Tripoli? If I send Lilith packing, the city will fall, and the rest of the Coast after."

"Will it? Who told you that?"

There was a silence. *She did,* John thought. He shook his head. "But I've never performed an exorcism before. That's why I married you."

"Believe me, I know." Rahel sighed. "I married *you* so I wouldn't have to fight off heretic raiders, and yet…"

"Well, that's nice to know. I thought you only married me for my looks."

She swiped a hand through his head, but her eyes remained serious. "We always knew marriage wasn't an end in itself. What if it wasn't just meant to make us stronger together? What if it was meant to make us stronger alone as well?"

He still didn't like it. "Strong enough to defeat *Lilith?*"

"There is nothing I have that you lack," she said softly. "We're both Watchers. Remember that. What is in us is greater than what is in there—"

Abruptly Rahel's voice faltered, and she began to fade. "John!" she called out to him, her voice sounding very faint and far. Then she was gone.

Had something woken her in her own time? John barely had time to worry before her voice sounded behind him. "John?"

He turned. Rahel blew him a kiss and said, as though it was the most ordinary thing in the world, "How was your day?"

"Tiring," he said, feeling rather dizzy. He'd met Rahel so often over the last five weeks, some of them certainly dreams, and some of them certainly real. Yet this Rahel felt every bit as real to him as the one who had just departed. "Rahel, you were…"

"What is it?" she asked, a little pucker between her brows as she observed his agitation.

"Nothing," he said after a moment. "Tell me the news."

She let out a soft sigh. "I had to send Zahir away. People were beginning to talk."

He must be dreaming, John thought as she told him the very same story he had just heard. She stopped at the end of it and watched him, heaving a soft little sigh before asking wistfully, "I don't suppose you had any luck finding the guardian?"

"He's in the porch," John said without ceremony.

"John!" Her face lit up, just like his wife's. "I thought I felt something powerful nearby. Did you speak to him? Will he send you home?"

"For a price." He watched her face closely. "We thought the guardian was an angel; but it's one of the Fallen. Her name is Lilith, and she asked for my protection."

A mask of horror descended across Rahel's face. "Oh, *John.*"

"The problem is, she's the only thing protecting this city from worse things," he said, pleading his case to this new Rahel with sudden energy, as though she might change her mind and give him leave this time. "There's a demon named Qeteb out there with the Egyptians. He plans to enslave Lilith and slaughter everyone in the city."

Rahel ran the tip of her tongue across her lips. "So…Lilith wants you to expel this Qeteb?"

John blinked at her. "She *said* she wanted me to kill the Chosen."

"There's a way?"

"There *has* to be a way. I'd swear the spear can do it. I used that weapon at Yarmouk. No matter what Soraya thinks, I *know* it's no ordinary weapon."

"You're sure the Chosen's spear is the same weapon you used at Yarmouk?"

"Dear heart, I saw it up close tonight. There's no doubt at all." He frowned. "Do you think I should exorcise Qeteb instead? Is it even possible? I would have to get outside the wall and into the Egyptian camp somehow. Even then…" His voice trailed away. Was he ready for that kind of battle? Qeteb was even greater than Lilith, and such powerful spirits did not easily concede defeat.

"To fight your way into the camp, you would need the spear," Rahel agreed.

"Which would mean dealing with al-Mukhtar first." John watched his wife. "Doesn't it bother you? Doing what Lilith wants?"

"Just because she wants it doesn't mean it's the wrong thing," Rahel said practically. "What is she asking, after all? First, justice for the Zakar killer. Second, the spear back in your rightful possession. Third, destruction of the Egyptian army waiting to slaughter everyone in Tripoli. Fourth, the exorcism of a demon even more powerful and dangerous than herself." She sent him a glimmer of laughter. "John, she only wants you to do your job as a Watcher—and she's offering you a way *home*."

"*Thank* you," he said triumphantly, before recalling, with another dizzy feeling of confusion, who it was that had urged him otherwise. Chastened, he added: "But she wants me to leave her in possession of Tripoli."

"Is it *your* place to stop her?" She looked at him with swimming eyes. "Jerusalem is occupied by the enemy. More cities surrender every day. The emperor has given us up for lost. You're the only one who could possibly save us."

"I know," he said, torn. "But we're Watchers. We don't compromise."

"This isn't about compromise, John." Her voice shook. "This is about doing what we must. Haven't we prayed so long for a way home? This could be our only chance to be together again, and you'll throw it away on a scruple?"

Her pain was unbearable, and he reached out, desperate to wipe her tears.

She said softly: "Other good Watchers have done worse things to protect their people."

John stilled and drew his hand back slowly. A feeling of disquiet had been growing on him for some time now. Rahel had been with him a moment ago. Rahel was with him now. Both equally vivid, equally like his wife—except that one wanted him to ally with a demon.

Not just any demon, but Lilith, who preyed on dreams. John felt his distant pulse begin to race, but found he couldn't wake. Something held him in the dream, muting his terror, flooding him with weary lethargy.

"Who are you?" he whispered.

She watched him with a look of innocent puzzlement. "I'm your wife, John."

He opened and shut his mouth, finding it difficult to form thoughts. Perhaps by some great exertion of willpower he might break through the confusion holding his mind in thrall—but how could he, when every fibre of his being begged him to believe her?

"I should wake," he said dizzily. He sped through the air into the shadowed porch where his body lay huddled in a corner. By now he'd figured out how to wake himself from a dreamwalk, but as he bent to converge with his sleeping form, sick dread engulfed him.

His spirit would not bond with his flesh.

In a blink, Rahel was beside him. She didn't look at him, but instead gave a hiss of surprise. "He's gone!"

She could only mean one person. In speechless dismay John turned to see that the sand diviner was no longer there. Katsaros must have wandered away unseen while he and Rahel were speaking.

Rahel swept back into the graveyard and John followed her—perhaps of his own volition, or perhaps not. For a moment there was stillness as the two of them waited, listening. The night was full of the sounds of water; the song of rain hammering on rooftops and trickling through sewers, the crash of waves, the sigh of wind. There was no sound of running footsteps in the street beyond the gate, and the cloudy darkness hid all else.

Beside him, Rahel stiffened. "Something's coming."

John turned. The night was too dark to see much beyond their immediate surroundings, but after a moment his eyes adjusted sufficiently to see a dark shape gliding through the garden, silhouetted against the wall.

Heading for the porch.

The Chosen, John thought with a new jolt of terror.

Rahel was suddenly in front of him. "You've had a bad dream, John Bessarion," she told him urgently. "Wake and forget."

Her ghostly fingers passed through John's forehead and his sleeping body lurched into consciousness, heart racing, sweating, terrified. John sat, running shaking hands through his hair. What could have woken him in such a pother? Had it been a nightmare? One moment he had been speaking to his wife, and the next—

Wait. There was an intruder in the churchyard.

His crossbows lay before him, ready to hand. John rolled up onto one knee, lifting one bow just as a dark silhouette appeared on the steps, outlined against the clouds.

"John?" It was a woman's voice.

"Soraya?" Heart thudding, he lowered the weapon. "How did you find me?"

"I knew you had been sleeping in churchyards." She moved into the porch. No longer silhouetted against the sky outside, she faded to little more than a voice in the shadows. "Where is Lilith?"

As his tension ebbed away, John felt drained and exhausted, his body craving sleep after too brief a taste. He slumped back against the wall with a sigh. "I don't know. She disappeared while I was asleep. How did you get free again? Did al-Mukhtar let you out?"

She didn't answer, instead countering with another question. "Did Lilith say how to destroy him?"

Maybe he wouldn't have noticed it if he'd been able to see her. But all he had of her was her voice, and something about the persistent way she asked the question made his scalp prickle. *Something is wrong.* John lifted his crossbows softly from the pavement and stood up. "No. Lilith hasn't spoken to me since the house fell."

"Who was the Frank? How much does he know about Lilith?"

"I don't know. He walked into the house a moment before she did. I'd never seen him before in my life."

"Where is he now?"

This was certainly an interrogation. "Why did al-Mukhtar let you out?" he countered. "Soraya?"

No answer. Just a soft whisper of sound as she moved.

John threw himself sideways, staggering down the porch steps just as the moon emerged from between dark clouds. He twisted as the lithe figure leaped after him, the pale blade of her knife glinting in the moonlight.

John lifted his bows.

"I'm sorry," he whispered, unloading both bolts into her heart.

Instantly, her attack lost focus. Before her blade reached him, it clattered to the stones amid a cloud of dust.

John fell back a step, coughing as some of the fragments drifted into his face. His bows were shaking in his hands, the *thunk* of his bolts sinking into her body still echoing in his ears. A cold anger trickled through his veins. Soraya was his *friend,* and he'd been forced to tear her apart with cold steel. He was *her* friend, and she'd just been forced to track him down, interrogate him, and attempt his murder.

It was a desecration.

It was a warning. When they'd first made their alliance, Soraya had warned that the Chosen might command her to repeat every word they'd spoken. Doubtless, that's exactly what he would be doing now.

Breathing hard, he stopped only long enough to retrieve his bolts and reload his bows, before fleeing into the streets, seeking a new hiding-place.

Chapter XXI.

"I thought you didn't want a mindless slave," Soraya spat. This was the second time she'd been violently killed today. The experience was never pleasant, but that wasn't what made her furious enough to tear Saif's head off. "How *dare* you force me to do that?"

Saif's voice was hard as ice. "To do what, Soraya?"

"To betray him! To kill him! My…" Her chest was full of remembered pain. "My only friend."

Saif grunted. "Then maybe you'll think twice before betraying *me* again."

Soraya's mouth opened, incredulous. He was furious, she realised. *He,* who sent her lurching out into the streets, a horrified prisoner inside her own body. *He,* who had used her as a weapon against the only person in the world who wanted to help her.

Oh, God. John would never trust her now; the worst part was that she couldn't blame him in the least.

"God have mercy, I thought I could trust you," Saif growled. On the floor at his feet were a handful of shards bearing a seal still decorated with the sigil of power. Useless, once the jar itself was broken. His face reddened, and he sank onto his bedroll, burying his head in his hands.

"The more fool you, for trusting a djinn."

He paid no attention to her. "What will I say to the Master? Everything was riding on this mission, and now it's in ruins."

Soraya looked down on him contemptuously. "You're afraid of him, but you still serve him. You fool."

"Silence," he snarled, and her mouth locked shut. "Why, Soraya? What has that Watcher ever done for you? I did everything you asked. I *trusted* you." He looked up at her, his eyes full of painful betrayal. "Speak."

"It doesn't take much to earn my loyalty. All you have to do is not use me to kill."

"I *told* you there was a reason for it. Besides, if it wasn't God's will—"

"Then he'd have stopped you; I know." Soraya planted her hands on her hips. "You want to talk about God's will? *Whoever purchases the magic shall not have in the Hereafter any share.* Whoever your master is, don't try to tell me he acts for God when he's neck deep in the blackest possible magic. Just as *you* are."

He flinched, then jabbed a finger at her. "Listen—"

"Yes?" Soraya said, when the silence threatened to lengthen.

"It's a superseded verse," he said, but his voice lacked conviction.

"It's no such thing, and you know it." The words surprised her; she must have studied theology at some point. "How can this Khalil speak for God when his actions are so disobedient?"

Saif stared at her. "I don't know," he said at last. He sounded drained. Defenceless. "But I know there's an explanation. I've probably just… forgotten it."

Soraya frowned, unsure of herself. "Have we had this conversation already?"

"I don't know. Maybe."

There was something strangely disarming in his weary honesty. His memories had been meddled with, too. Who was al-Mukhtar Saif al-Din, really? Did he even know, himself? Soraya watched the light of their tiny oil-lamp play on his smooth face, casting shadows in the faint line etched between his brows. There was so much she didn't understand about this man.

"How can you trust someone who expects you to kill for him, and won't even leave you with the memory to explain why?"

The silence stretched out. Saif didn't meet her eyes. Soraya tried a different question.

"You know what Qalawun has promised to do to this city if it falls. Why are you helping him? Why do you hate them so much?"

Once more, she thought he meant not to answer. Then, softly, he said: "I don't remember my father, but I have one memory of my mother…she was soft. She didn't speak much, but when she held me, I always knew I was safe.

"The Franks stole her. I don't remember it; the Master says the memory was too painful for me to bear. Apparently we had gone towards Aleppo when a Frankish bandit took her, and I never saw her again. With both my parents gone, there was no one to give me a home. Khalil bought me and made me his mamluk—his heir, if anything should happen to him. I owe him everything. But to the Franks who stole my mother from me, I owe nothing but pain."

Soraya swallowed hard. "Have you ever tried to find her?"

He looked at his hands for a long, tormented moment before replying. "She's dead."

"You can't know that for sure."

"She's *dead*," Saif repeated fiercely. He shook his anger away, let his voice drop into ominous softness. "It's not only my mother. The Franks stole this entire land from us, along with the lives of thousands of my people. The past makes heavy demands of the present, Soraya, and I will dishonour neither my ancestors nor my Master. In God's name, I *will* set things right."

Soraya shook her head wearily. Doubtless Saif was right, and the Frankish invasion *had* trampled thousands of his people into their graves. Still, most of the people in Tripoli were Christians, eager to resist the sultan's invasion; she didn't see what claim Qalawun could possibly lay to the county now. There would be no use debating that with Saif, however. Her next question surprised even herself.

"You could have killed John and that Frank last night. If you hate them so much, then why did you let them go?"

Saif shrugged. "There was no point. The jar was broken and they had reinforcements on the way. I would have had to slaughter half the city."

"Then why didn't you? You're capable of it."

"Perhaps I am not as invulnerable as you think."

"So you left them alive—with Lilith, who might help them destroy you?"

"But she hasn't. Not yet. God is merciful."

Soraya didn't know why she kept pushing; she tried to convince herself it was to find the weak points in his defence. "You were mobbed in the street two weeks ago. Rather than fight back, you let them beat you."

"Killing someone would only have made it harder to carry out the mission."

"After you saw them at the funeral, you could have been going out every night slaughtering Watchers. You could have been killing people every night for weeks; and instead you sat reading."

"Enough—"

"And what about the Zakar children? Does Khalil know you let them live, or didn't you tell him that?"

"Enough," he shouted. There was a silence like an open wound; and then he took a deep breath and said, in a voice that shook, "God forgive me! Is it so hard for you to believe that I loathe the killing as you do?"

It was the last thing she had expected to hear from him. He offered her a look, as a man flayed open might offer his tormentor a bloody heart. For a moment Soraya stared at him in speechless confusion. For a moment, she nearly believed him.

Then, blind fury took her.

"Yes. For if you loathed it as I did you would do anything, *anything,* to stop it. How dare you? How *dare* you claim to know the depths of my torment?"

His throat worked, but Soraya gave him no chance to speak.

"You dog! You make me sick. You're not man enough to stand up to your master. You're not man enough to bear the consequences of your actions."

"Silence," he said between his teeth. His voice was dangerously quiet, and Soraya had no choice but to obey. "I *am* bearing them," he went on at last. "So far, my judgement has been rewarded: John Zakar lost Lilith before she could tell him how to kill me, and the Frankish knight will pose no threat, half-dead as he is." Evidently, while Soraya was marching through the streets to attack John, Saif had been spying on the Temple. "The only question is, what to do now? I don't have the skill to make a new jar. The only man who can do that is in Cairo. With this siege, there's no getting back there. God forgive me. I'll be lucky if the master doesn't have me strangled."

He stared at the broken shards in something close to despair. "Say something," he murmured at last, unsealing her lips.

"He sounds like a kind and just master, indeed." Soraya smiled crookedly, but again, her sarcasm passed him by. She sighed, compressing her anger deep down to the place it had always occupied, in a small hard knot behind her breastbone. "It's a shame you can't just kidnap the old sand diviner and send him to Cairo."

"Why not?"

She shrugged. "Well, Lilith's not bound to Katsaros, so at great need she could just abandon him and slip through your fingers. And even then—as we saw tonight—she still has some fight left in her."

He scowled, with something like a return of his anger. "Glory to God! If you aren't going to help, you can go back into confinement."

"No. Please." The word burned her lips coming up, but if she was locked away again, there was nothing she could do—for herself, for John, for anyone. "I *am* trying to help."

He grunted, suspicious, and Soraya swallowed more bile. In order to do anything at all she must first creep and genuflect before this idol of fragile glass. Well. She would do so gladly if it ended by letting her smash him to pieces.

"I may have betrayed you," she pointed out, "but I faithfully did what I promised to do; and without that you would never have found Lilith in the first place. We are neither friends nor even allies. But I'll tell you what we *are.*"

"Oh?"

"Chained," she said simply. "So long as we are bound together, we must make allowances for each other."

"Allowances?" His eyes narrowed. "You were plotting to *kill* me."

"I was trying to get *free.* If you don't like being chained to me, you could always *give* me my freedom."

His lip curled. "You wouldn't be satisfied with freedom. You'd put me down like a dog."

She thought of the Zakars and acknowledged silently that he was right. Still. "Is that a risk you can afford *not* to take?"

"I haven't the right to make that choice," Saif said after a long silence. "To free you, I mean."

"Don't give me that. You could do it with a word."

"I haven't the right," he repeated, doggedly. "But once this is over, God willing, I'll ask him. Bargain?"

He must be terribly naïve to think that such a promise meant anything to her at all. Soraya suppressed her contempt. It didn't matter: the important thing was to stay free, find John, salvage something from the disaster that had befallen their plans. "Bargain."

"This time, you *will* be accounting for your every moment and every word."

"Understood." Soraya wiped sweaty palms on her jacket. "So. The important thing is to get Lilith out of the city, right? So that the sultan's army can break in."

Saif looked wary. "Yes."

Soraya nodded. "I know exactly who can do that."

Chapter XXII.

Gerard came to with a groan. His head ached as though it had been split open, and the piercing morning sunlight in his room was only partly to blame.

"Sir!" Marco's voice was soft, but it sent a stab of agony through his head. "How do you feel?"

He focused slowly on his surroundings. He was lying in his narrow bed at the Temple commandery, and mid-morning sunlight trickled through the shuttered windows. Gerard groaned. "What happened?"

"The—er—the Zakar house collapsed," Marco said. "You were struck by a falling beam. We found you just as the dust was settling."

"Is my head broken?" Gerard muttered.

"No broken bones, but the surgeon wants to watch you for a few days."

Reassured, he put up fingers and probed his own skull. The pain had already receded since his waking, and although the spot was tender he could feel neither swelling not indentation. Not even the skin was damaged. "Feels like it *should* be broken."

"I…" Marco swallowed. "I laid hands on it. Might have done something."

That's right. Last night, Marco had claimed to be a Healer.

Last night. Fuzzily, his memory returned. Prester John; he found Prester John. Katsaros, the sand diviner, was there. They called him Lilith, and spoke as though he was possessed by a demon.

Beaujeu meant to ally himself with a demon.

A demon who needed help and protection, as though it couldn't even protect itself.

Because a man who could punch his way through walls was hunting it.

"Devil take it," Gerard breathed, the profanity escaping before he could stop himself. What had Beaujeu embroiled him in? Hurriedly, he crossed himself. "Marco."

"Sir?"

"Has anyone been here asking for me?"

"No, sir."

"No disturbances of any kind?"

"No, sir."

Good. He pushed back the covers and swung his legs out of bed. Pain shot through his temples; when his head floated back to its proper place, he grabbed Marco's arm, halting the manservant's objections. "Stop. Marco, you have no idea…"

Silence fell. Gerard breathed heavily, still trying to gather his wits. Devil take it, the man had gone through *a stone wall.* What had Zakar called him? The Chosen?

God only knew where Katsaros was at this moment, whether he was still alive, whether this Lilith creature had been captured already.

If she *was* still in play, then somewhere, a Saracen spy who could break through walls was hunting her. A spy who knew that Gerard had seen his face—the same face that had been written on the walls at the start of the siege; the Zakar killer.

They were all linked together—Prester John, Katsaros, the Chosen—but how? What did it all mean?

"Something happened last night, sir?" Marco probed, as the silence lengthened. "Do you remember?"

"It was a man who knocked the house down," Gerard said.

"I beg your pardon?"

"It was a man," he repeated. "One single man with his bare hands, and he knows we were there. So now we're both in a spot of trouble, Marco."

"Saint Mark, pray for us."

"Amen." Gerard stared at the opposite wall, breathing slow to strangle his worry. *Each man the architect of his own fate.* Usually the words made him feel calm, confident—the master of himself and his surroundings. This morning they sounded rather hollow.

"What now, sir?"

It was a good question. "We need to leave this place and disappear. Pack for a few days, and find your way to Lady Margaret's house on the Fish Street. As you value your life and hers, do not be followed. We must leave by Terce."

"Terce was half an hour ago, sir."

"By halfway to Sext, then!"

"Sir, you're still very sick. Are you sure—"

"I will *be* there. Make sure you are too." Gerard got up, checked his reflection in the mirror behind the door—he was still in yesterday's clothes, but it was too late to change now—took a cloak, and limped out into the courtyard. Marshal Geoffrey's cabinet was empty, the marshal himself at the palace, according to the secretary.

"Should I ask him to call on you when he returns, sir?" The other man was looking at him apprehensively, as though afraid he was about to keel over.

Gerard gave a sickly smile. His head felt better by the moment. It was his thoughts that troubled him. "Thanks, but no. I'll go find him at the palace."

He shrouded himself in a cloak, pulling the hood deep over his head, and eased into the flow of traffic through the street outside. Despite the strong wind and intermittent rain, he immediately glimpsed a young loiterer peel away from the wall and begin to follow him. This time, Gerard did nothing to evade the shadow. He was going straight to the countess anyway, and following the previous night's events, if anything he was glad of the company.

Not that it would help if a man like the Chosen wanted to kill him. Saints, there had been a woman last night too; a young beauty with the skin of a child and eyes dark and old enough to make him shiver. What the blazes had happened to her? Turned into a pillar of salt? Crumbled into dust? The Prester and Katsaros had both taken it in their stride.

He wasn't dealing with familiar, aboveboard things here. He was dealing with demons and magic; and despite the hot sun, his hands felt cold and clammy with fearful sweat. Would he be damned for speaking to the creature? Had he already lost his soul?

When Gerard arrived at the palace, he found that the marshal was meeting with the countess and the other commanders. He collapsed into a chair in the marble-lined antechamber and sent in a false name; a code-word that should have brought the marshal hastening out at once to see him.

Instead, the chamberlain threw open the door to the countess' cabinet. "Sir Gerard? You're summoned to attend the countess."

It wasn't what he expected, but Marshal Geoffrey must have his reasons; and the sooner he delivered his message and went into hiding, the better. Gerard trudged into the cabinet, where Countess Lucy glared up at him from the canopied oaken chair at the head of the table. Lady Margaret, at her right, watched him with concern—how strange to think that yesterday evening his most pressing concern had been the matter of her heart. The occupants of the room were all straining to look at him: the commander of the Hospital, the Venetian and Pisan admirals, the representative of the county's barons, the Genoese admiral Zaccaria—and Marshal Geoffrey himself.

"Shouldn't you be in bed, Montreal?" the marshal inquired.

He *should* be in Acre, sitting behind a desk making translations. Gerard didn't say it aloud. "I would be, sir, but..." He stopped. His head had settled somewhat, but it was still difficult to come up with a strategy for this meeting he'd unexpectedly found himself in.

"You indicated that you have news of grave importance." The Marshal looked at Countess Lucy challengingly. "The Temple has nothing to hide. You may deliver your message now."

Gerard took a deep breath, rapidly sorting through plans of attack. "I've come as soon as I could. Last night I learned that there's an Egyptian spy in the city. You know the face: it's the Zakar killer."

The room froze into silent stillness for a moment. Countess Lucy paled slightly, but her voice was haughty. "Do you mean to say this spy has been here the whole time?"

"Apparently so." Gerard took another breath. "He's known as *the Chosen,* or Al-Mukhtar in the Saracen tongue. But the important thing is that if he's seen, he must not be challenged. He is dangerous; do not seek him out."

Marshal Geoffrey nodded, his eyes narrowing; but the admirals looked at each other and bristled. "You speak peremptorily," Sir Benedetto said.

Gerard hesitated, then lied. "Rest assured, I have him under observation. It's necessary not to startle him until we've had a chance to learn whether he's in communication with the sultan, and how."

If he admitted there was a problem in the city he couldn't address, then the Marshal and the other commanders would insist on arresting the Chosen. The battle would be uneven, the cost immense. The garrison would be weakened. Morale, shattered.

The thought surprised Gerard even as it occurred to him. Last night's confrontation must have terrified him more than he knew. He was operating purely on instinct now; everything warned him to keep out of al-Mukhtar's way. A man like that couldn't be fought. A man like that could do anything he wanted. Such a man could be the architect, not only of his own fate—but that of thousands of others.

A cold certainty crawled over him, and he looked up, seeking out Lady Margaret. "I fear this city will fall. I would advise the noble council to consider an immediate evacuation."

Countess Lucy seemed to turn to stone. Her voice was flat, soft. "What."

There was a deep silence in the cabinet after the countess' whisper. After a moment, the Venetian admiral set down his glass and spoke in a cheerful, booming voice. "As I was saying a moment ago, the city is on the point of falling. I beg leave to inform the countess on behalf of the city of Venice that I will be withdrawing my men and ships."

"No." Countess Lucy started up from her chair. "Admiral, I beg you."

The Venetian got to his feet ponderously and bowed. "My ladies, gentlemen, good day. No doubt, if you think you can yet hold the city, the loss of two galleys will make little difference. Unfortunately, the risk now outweighs whatever benefit my city might have hoped to gain in

Tripoli."

Countess Lucy looked away for an instant, as though making mental calculations. "That can be remedied," she said in a remote, faraway voice.

"I am afraid not," the Venetian said jovially. A load seemed to have rolled off his broad shoulders. "I believe you have already made more promises to my Genoese friend than you can easily keep. Godspeed, my lady."

The door closed behind him, leaving Countess Lucy gripping the edge of the table with white fingertips.

A baron at the table scowled. "My lady? *What* promises have you made to the Genoese?"

"That is no concern of yours, Embriaco."

"I beg to differ!" The baron's voice boomed through the room. "You cannot hand over *our* property to anyone you choose!"

Lady Lucy reddened. "I am your *lady.* The city is mine; the decision is mine."

A babel of voices broke out. "Not in Tripoli," one of the barons shouted.

Embriaco jumped to his feet, red-faced. "Have you learned *nothing* from your brother's mistakes?"

Lady Lucy's spine stiffened. "I have learned from his example how to deal with *traitors.*"

Another awful, echoing silence followed her words. From the look on Lady Margaret's face, Gerard knew she was mortified. The previous count had quelled the Embriacos' last insurrection by burying the head of the family and his brothers alive in the Nephin moat.

Embriaco's face turned almost purple. Wheeling around, he jabbed an angry finger at Zaccaria. "Take warning, my lord. Whatever she's promised you, the council will never ratify it."

He stalked from the room, followed by his supporters and attendants, and the door slammed behind him, sending a thunderclap of echoes rolling from one marble wall to another.

"This meeting is dismissed. Leave, all of you." The countess' face was pale with suppressed anger. Suddenly she lifted a finger, pinning Gerard where he stood. "Except *you,* Templar."

He'd been wrong about his headache. It had returned, and now throbbed with each beat of his pulse. Gerard swallowed, trying to feel grateful that Marshal Geoffrey and Lady Margaret remained in their seats as the other commanders filed past him. When the door closed moments later, the countess stood back and folded her arms.

"Was this your plan?" She spoke with compressed fury. "You have just torn this city's defences apart. Are you satisfied?"

Gerard stood stiff and attentive, not daring to speak or look her in the eye. His head beat a little faster. Beaujeu had sent him to Tripoli with two missions to carry out—and he'd just managed to foul up both of them.

Even Lady Margaret was now witnessing his humiliation.

He had always believed that fate was something determined men forged for themselves, but devil take it, he couldn't see how he could possibly have foreseen or prepared for this. Last night, faced by an immortal warrior, not even the supernatural power inhabiting Katsaros had known what to do.

"Answer me! Was this your plan?" the countess repeated, and Marshal Geoffrey shifted, clearing his throat.

Here it comes, Gerard thought in a frozen, detached sort of helplessness. The only sensible thing for the marshal to do now would be to disown him. And then he would be left to fend for himself in besieged Tripoli, with an immortal warrior on his trail.

Instead, the marshal bowed and said, "The Temple is ready to withdraw its men and ships from Tripoli if you wish it, my lady."

Gerard blinked. Well. Of course the marshal could always just threaten to leave.

In response, Countess Lucy stiffened slightly. "No," she blurted. "You can't do that—what of your mission to protect the holy places?"

"My lady, we wouldn't for the world force our help on anyone." The marshal got up, bowing to her. "A short while since, you accused the Temple of concealing information from you. I trust I have set your mind at rest on that account."

For a moment, Gerard though the countess might be about to erupt again. Her face reddened; yet it seemed that the marshal's words had restored her to a sense of caution. With a visible effort, she swallowed her anger and gathered her dignity, but she spoke through her teeth. "Thank you, sir marshal."

With another murderous look at Gerard, the countess walked to the door and opened it. In the antechamber on the other side, a voice was speaking in hurried Italian. "—the galleys, and have the men board immediately."

Zaccaria. Gerard looked at Lady Margaret; she didn't know Italian, and could not have understood. Countess Lucy, on the other hand, did. Standing in the doorway, she had gone very still.

The Genoese flowed easily back into French Occitan. "Countess?"

"Stop that messenger at once! Close the palace gate! Sir Benedetto, what do you mean by ordering your men aboard their ships?"

She advanced into the antechamber, the Marshal and an aghast Lady Margaret following after her. By the door, Countess Lucy's guards had seized a Genoese messenger—Gerard recognised his shadow from several weeks ago. Beneath a traceried window, Sir Benedetto Zaccaria stood alone with a tight knot of Genoese knights, turning toward the countess with the kind of smile that sensed an approaching storm.

"Answer me," the countess repeated, her voice beginning to betray her. "Do you mean to abandon me?"

"Not at all, my lady." The admiral smiled blandly. "Since the Venetians are going aboard their ships, and our galleys are anchored offshore unprotected, we simply mean to go aboard until…"

"But I need you." The countess was whispering now, begging. "I cannot hold this city with half a garrison."

Zaccaria's voice hardened a trifle. "And I cannot risk the lives of my men by allowing them to be stranded here, should our enemies commandeer our ships."

"Stop," Lady Lucy cried as he turned to go. A deep breath. "If you go now, I shall consider myself free of every promise I have made you."

"I see." Zaccaria tilted his head, considering. Then he gave a tight nod. "Yes, my lady—perhaps that would be best."

Beckoning to his knights, he strode from the antechamber, leaving the countess staring after him with trembling fists.

At length she drew a long, trembling breath. "Margaret," she almost sobbed.

"Go, dear. I'll be with you in a moment."

The young countess nodded. Without looking back, as though she meant to hide her face, she hastened from the room.

Lady Margaret turned to Marshal Geoffrey. "How many have we lost? A quarter of our men? A third?"

"Something like that." The marshal looked at Gerard with a faint frown. "And you say there's an Egyptian spy in the city? Tell me you have this under control, Montreal."

"I have. I will." He rubbed his temples. Then he blinked at Margaret. "My lady, have you some intelligent men to spare? Somewhere in this city are two men, and it's imperative we find them at once."

Prester John. Stephen Katsaros.

Lady Margaret agreed at once, but Marshal Geoffrey frowned. "Why not use the Temple's men?"

"Because the Chosen knows who I am. He saw my face. We have to assume he will be watching the Temple." Gerard took another long, deep, steadying breath. "I'll have to disappear."

Lady Margaret nodded. "You'll use my house, of course."

It was what he had hoped, but so much more than he deserved; especially after their conversation last night. "You are generosity itself, my lady. I must ask for one more thing."

Her blue eyes were serious. "Anything, if it will save Tripoli."

He wasn't trying to save Tripoli. He was just trying to save her, himself, and what was left of Beaujeu's mission. The future was not yet so far beyond his control that he could not do *something.*

"I presume you have a ship, my lady? Will you make it ready to leave? Tonight, if possible."

Her eyes widened. "Tonight?"

"He's right," the Marshal rumbled. "The die is cast. Tripoli will fall. It would take a miracle to save it now."

Chapter XXIII.

Wedged among a group of other unfortunates sleeping in an abandoned courtyard, John found shelter but little peace of mind.

Al-Mukhtar was controlling Soraya. Tripoli's guardian had put a terrible choice before him. And Rahel…

With a stifled groan, John pulled a hand down his face. His dreams had been confused of late, and now he couldn't recall exactly what Rahel had said to him. She had wanted him to take Lilith's part in the battle against Qeteb—no, that couldn't be right. But what if he didn't? He might as well throw open the gates and wave the enemy inside. That couldn't be right either. They had certainly spoken, but dream and reality were hopelessly mixed up in his mind. He took a deep breath, trying to focus on what he *did* remember of their previous conversations. That didn't help, either. For every word that might have encouraged him to make no concessions to Lilith he could think of half a dozen more begging him to come home at any cost.

Someone evidently thinks you need me, she had told him once. Until now, Rahel had always been his guiding light, the voice of Wisdom herself. Now he felt crippled, cut off from his own conscience. If he refused Lilith's offer, he doomed Tripoli; and if he took it, he left the city to the tender mercies of a demon who had already half destroyed it through envy and strife.

We're Watchers. We don't compromise.

That sounded like something the Rahel he knew would say, but it couldn't be right to abandon his own people like that, nor to hand Tripoli over to the sultan. He gave another sound of stifled frustration. He had been sent here, to *this* time and to *this* city, for a purpose. He had been given help and guidance in the form of his wife. Why was it so difficult to know what he should do?

We're Watchers. We don't compromise.

Why could he not go home, leaving Lilith in possession of her city? Must he destroy these people, and himself with them?

He hurled the questions at the heavens, but no answer came. Towards dawn John fell into fitful sleep and dreamed of Rahel standing outside the courtyard, waving at him and trying to shout warnings he didn't understand. He woke too early, with a sore head and bleary eyes, but not before an answer had come to him.

If it was not clear what he must do, and if Rahel could not help him, he must go to the Watchers.

Having employed the morning in a clandestine visit to one of the guardrooms on the wall, John cautiously made his way to the house of a Watcher named Maryam. She gave him breakfast, a basin to wash in, and a mantle to hide his features. Then she asked a neighbour to watch her children, and accompanied him to Hubert's dyehouse.

Tripoli was full of people today. A steady stream of the wealthier sort headed towards the harbour in little cavalcades of household belongings, eager to flee the city before it fell. To either side, others simply went about an ordinary day's business, aware that the storm was about to break, but incapable of doing anything to stop it.

Maryam led him down a crowded street and into the courtyard of a comfortably-sized warehouse rich with the scent of hot dyes—pomegranate rinds, indigo leaves, madder root. John glanced anxiously behind as he followed her in at the gate, looking for a flash of green silk. There was no sign of Soraya or her master. God willing, his mantle and Maryam's company would have been enough to put any hunters off the scent.

Still, he wouldn't rest easy until the Chosen was dealt with.

The ground floor of the warehouse was full of the clack of wooden printing-blocks stamping intricate patterns on once-white silk. As Maryam went to find Hubert, a joyous shout rent the air and a little girl clutching a bright silk doll launched herself at his knees. "Uncle John!"

"Little Elisa!" he greeted her, and threw her in the air till she shrieked with laughter. In the five weeks since the siege began, the Zakar children seemed to have adopted him into the family—or he had adopted them; he wasn't sure. At any rate, the other four children gathered around him, and Elisa Zakar drummed her toes into his stomach in excitement. "Did you bring us dates?"

He pulled a long face. "I only had a few dates left and I ate them last night."

Her face fell. "Ohhhh."

"But I have a hug if you want one."

She considered this for a moment, before nodding magnanimously and locking her arms around his neck. For one brief, guilty moment, John was perfectly contented.

Someone tugged at the bulging bag he wore on a strap over his shoulder, and John looked down at Matthias. "Don't," he said quickly, "there's something in there you definitely don't want to break."

"Sorry," Matthias said. "I just wanted to ask if you caught the Chosen yet?"

John's breath caught as he saw flashes of memory; smelled stone dust in the air, heard the rumble as the house fell. "Not yet," he said, trying to keep his voice easy, "but soon, I hope."

Matthias' mouth slanted sideways and he nodded. Thankfully, at that moment Hubert and Maryam emerged from the small room the merchant used as a cabinet and beckoned John towards the stairs leading to the warehouse's upper storey.

"All right, friends." John bent down to set Elisa on the ground, ruffled Matthias' hair and followed the two Watchers upstairs to the cramped room where Hubert lived with his wife Anna—and now, five children. The rest of the floor was taken up with lodgings for other workers; some of these were already sitting on the sleeping-platform, passing around cups of watered wine. Not all the Watchers in Tripoli worked for Hubert, but unless he wanted to wait for the next meeting, this was the easiest way to speak to a few of them.

In the corner, one stocky, fair-haired man stood alone, twisting a white coif in his hands. John nodded to the westerner. "Marco?"

The young Healer nodded, and after a moment bobbed a nervous bow. "Prester."

"All right," Hubert said, swinging his hands in a businesslike clap. "I think we're all here. Maryam said you had learned something important, John."

John took a deep breath. "The good news is that I found Tripoli's guardian. The bad news is that it's not an angel, friends." Quickly, he relayed the story of the previous night's events.

His tale was greeted with appalled silence. The Watchers glanced at each other, and John had the feeling that silent messages flew around the room. Quickly, cups were replaced on the table and sticky fingers wiped. Distaffs, leatherwork, and whittling appeared. Although their heads bent over their work, John had the feeling none of them were distracted from his words in the least.

Marco cleared his throat and raised his hand. "I was there for some of it. It's all quite true."

"If Lilith has been in Tripoli these last eighty years, it would explain a great many things," Maryam said slowly. "You've heard what they say about politics in this county."

"Thomas Zakar said the spiritual atmosphere wasn't good," John admitted.

"First she was stirring up the raids against the hill tribes, and then as the Egyptians tightened the noose, she had to make do with factional strife." Hubert rubbed his chin. "It wouldn't matter to a creature like Lilith, so long as she was able to feed."

"With friends like these, who needs enemies?" Maryam said with the shiver of a laugh. "If not for her meddling, all these great lords might have had a chance to defend this city, instead of biting each others' throats."

"The question is, what are we going to do about it?" John put in.

Hubert frowned slightly. "She will have to be cast out, of course."

It wasn't quite the answer he'd been hoping for. "The problem is, Lilith claimed to be protecting the city. If she goes, the city falls."

Silence fell once more as they all considered just what that might mean for them.

"Can we trust her word on that?" Hubert's wife Anna asked after a moment.

"Can you take that risk?" John countered.

Hubert grimaced. "It's possible that an exorcism might be the only thing that *can* save the city now."

"Or it might not," Maryam put in. "Her kind feeds on and colludes in mortal sin, but she cannot create it. Even if Lilith was gone, it might not be enough to save us."

"She said she was protecting the city from a demon among the Egyptians," John said, feeling desperate. "His name is Qeteb."

"All the more reason to expel Lilith," Anna said quietly, "or we surely will do no good against Qeteb."

"Yes." Hubert turned decisively to John. "I say do it. Exorcise Lilith. I don't know if it will help us, but we can at least send this demon to her reward."

The other Watchers were nodding. John opened his mouth to protest, then stopped himself. Rahel had been of their opinion, surely. Yes; that part of the night's wanderings had come back to him now. She had been sure it was right; she had promised him he could do it even without her help.

Yet his whole soul choked on the idea. Lilith was his only way home, the miracle he had sought for so long, and they wanted him to cast her out?

Presently, he became aware that the Watchers were looking at him, waiting for an answer. He saw puzzlement creep into their eyes as he hesitated.

"All right." He tried to put some determination into his voice. "I went down to the wall and spoke to one of the men on guard this morning. He says there are now two breaches in the wall, one at the Bishop's Tower and another at the Hospitallers' Tower. Moreover, the Saracens will know that we've lost seven galleys' worth of men; they would have seen the ships coming and going. Barring a miracle, there's bound to be an assault sometime in the next forty-eight hours, so if any of you can afford passage to Acre or Cyprus, now is the time to buy it."

All of them knew the sultan had promised to burn Tripoli if she resisted. "I think it would be better to plan how to survive the sack," Hubert said, after a strained silence. "Most of us can barely afford food."

"Hubert, perhaps *we* can't afford it, but you should take care of yourself," Maryam said.

Hubert looked at his wife, and she shook her head with a laugh. "Don't look at me like that, Hubert. I won't be sent away. I'd rather you paid for someone else."

Hubert reached out and took her hand. "In any case, this is a stout building and it would be easy to conceal the door to one of the underground storage rooms. If the worst happens and there is a sack, I'll pass word for all the Watchers in Tripoli to gather here. If we cannot flee, then perhaps we can hide."

And then what? John asked himself. *Perish as the city burns?*

But already Hubert was signalling the end of the meeting. "Best we get back to work. We don't want to draw anything's attention. Godspeed, John. Tell us if you need anything."

The Watchers filed past him, shaking his hand and thanking him for his information. John, feeling like a fraud, wished only to be away so that he could have room to think.

Marco paused in front of him, still twisting the white coif in his hands. "My lord, my master is searching for you, and also for Katsaros. If you wish, I will send word if he finds the demon."

John focused on the young man. Marco seemed nervous, his movements jerky. "The Frank is your master?"

"Yes, my lord."

John sighed and put a hand on his shoulder. "I can find Lilith. If it grieves your spirit, don't betray your master."

Marco looked up at him gratefully. "Thank you, but—I want to help. I love my master. I don't want him to lose his soul."

The young Italian departed, leaving John to follow more slowly with Hubert. He descended the stairs set within the thick wall and emerged into the courtyard, but it felt as though he was walking into a prison. There was no other way; he would have to exorcise Lilith.

John hesitated before taking his leave. "Do you think it's true, Hubert? That a man might lose his soul in any alliance with a demon, no matter how trifling?"

Hubert gave half a smile. "Perhaps not at once. But it's a path no man can afford to walk, for its walls are steep, and its natural end is death."

This wasn't his miracle; he should know that. Surely, he was being tempted. The thought made no impression upon his aching heart.

"Pray for me," he said with an effort, turning toward the gate.

"Godspeed, friend."

He emerged into the street, barely aware of his surroundings. Perhaps Tripoli was truly doomed. Even if Lilith was cast out, its people would likely continue to backbite and squabble—treachery seemed to be a way of life with them now. If the city burned, would it be Lilith's fault, or their own arrows falling back upon their heads?

What of himself? Would Oliveta have burned, had he not stolen treasures and broken promises? This hopeless exile he suffered, was it not the natural consequence of his own actions?

Was he not just as compromised than the Watchers he had upbraided at Oliveta?

He was lost in his thoughts, his feet carrying him of their own accord, when a flash of green silk brought back to his surroundings. Suddenly on guard, John looked up to see Soraya ahead of him, blocking the way.

Chapter XXIV.

Soraya had first glimpsed John from her vantage-point on the parapet of a run-down warehouse as she sunned herself in the shape of a large black cat. She was bored, and looking at every passer-by, or she would have missed him—muffled up and escorting a middle-aged burgess woman.

The woman led him into the courtyard of the warehouse below, where the clack of wooden printing-blocks could be heard. The dyehouse was owned by a Watcher named Hubert, and Soraya wasn't surprised to find John arriving here for a meeting with the Messenger. Places like this had certain advantages, if you wanted to escape the attention of spirits.

It was useless trying to breach the dyehouse to eavesdrop on their conversation, and besides, Soraya did not mean to put herself in the possession of any information which Saif might be able to extract from her later. Pleasantly liquid and relaxed after an hour's sun, she flowed into a stretch, then scampered towards the exterior stairs that led down into a back alley. By the time John exited the warehouse half an hour later, she was once more in human form, keeping watch from a doorstep some way off.

Seeing him, Soraya stepped into the traffic and waited for him to notice her. As he did, his stride hesitated and his hands went to the crossbows at his belt.

Of course, after last night, he couldn't afford to trust her. Still, the little motion made her heart twist with sadness.

She was well within bowshot, but much too far to do anything about it. Instead, she swept her jacket back to show that the sheath at her side was empty, and lifted defenceless hands.

John's distant figure glanced to his left, where a double row of columns opened onto a forum. He gestured towards it with his head before walking up the steps, beneath the shadowed round arches supporting the forum's upper galleries and into the wide empty space beyond. Keeping her distance, Soraya followed suit.

In more prosperous times, this paved area would have been lined with booths below and above. Horses, sheep, and oxen would drink from the large cistern pool that opened at the forum's centre. Today, the place was deserted, only a few bits of debris drifting in the cool wind to hint at a human presence. The morning's sunlight had vanished behind thickening clouds, and the place was grey and lifeless.

Soraya turned to face John, keeping her hands where he could see them, palms up. After a moment he approached, but he had both his crossbows aimed at her heart and there was a stern line etched between his brows.

His first words were not what she expected. "Soraya—are you well?"

Now that he was nearer, she found his eyes watchful, but not angry. Soraya ran a tongue over her lips. "It's really me this time. I convinced Saif to let me approach you as myself."

The crease between his eyebrows deepened into a scowl. "Al-Mukhtar? Who is he? Where did he come from?"

"He is the Chosen." It felt as though something jagged was crawling up her throat; a novel and perplexing thing that made her voice higher and faster as she spoke. "I know nothing more. I don't even know who *I* am—when I *am* myself, that is, and not some damned puppet on a stri—"

"Soraya." John lowered the crossbows, and she flinched. Yet the emotion on his face surprised her; if there was anger, it was not for her. "Soraya, I know exactly what happened last night. He gave you so many orders, you could only move and speak like an automaton. You don't have to blame yourself."

It was all she could do to keep her breath steady. He had gone oddly blurry, and her eyes were hot. "I want to be better," was all she could manage to say before the hot tears spilled down her cheeks.

She couldn't remember weeping before; she'd never inhabited a body long enough to succumb to an illness like this.

"I can't stop thinking about what Lilith said last night," she sobbed. "What if that vile creature really *is* my mother?"

"If I were you, I shouldn't trust the word of a demon." John reached into his pouch and produced a clean, white kerchief, which he shook from its crisp folds and offered to her. "Here."

Soraya looked at it through a sticky veil of tears and mucus. "I—I'd spoil it."

"And I'd wash it. In the army, I came to enjoy doing my own laundry." Come to think of it, he was always as well-groomed as a cat; she had presumed he hired servants. Perhaps he even cleaned his own house, before Saif knocked it down. "There's something satisfying about making things clean and new again."

"I expect this will be beyond saving," Soraya said, but she blew her nose, and felt much better. As she expected, the kerchief was a wreck, but he folded it back into his purse without seeming to notice.

Perhaps he was used to having women cry on his shoulder. He had a wife and daughters, after all. Soraya's heart cracked open again with sorrow. Was love and friendship something that only mortals enjoyed? Was that, like heaven, denied to a djinn like herself?

With an effort, she wrenched her thoughts away from that dangerous topic. "I'm a free agent today, but once I return Saif will have me repeat every word of this conversation back to him."

"All right." John settled back into his habitual frown. "What does al-Mukhtar want with me?"

"Help. You shattered his soul-jar and now you're his last hope to complete the mission. He needs Lilith out of Tripoli. You can do exorcisms, right?"

John's eyebrows climbed, and he took a sharp breath. "Rahel is the one with experience. Why does he want her out of Tripoli?"

"Because he believes she's keeping the Saracens out."

For a moment John was silent, his grey eyes losing a little of their ice. "Ah."

Soraya knew what he was thinking. With the wall broken and the garrison depleted, it was a miracle the assault hadn't already started. The sultan still bided his time in Mount Pilgrim beyond the orange-groves, his drums silent, his men whetting their steel around their campfires.

At length, he said, "Some of the Watchers think an exorcism could save the city."

An unspoken *but* hung in the air.

Soraya swallowed. "Lilith has been controlling this city for decades, creating war and drinking blood. If she's the only thing keeping Tripoli alive, then maybe Tripoli deserves to die."

John focused on her again. "But not all these people, these…*children.*" The word seemed to cost him something.

"So you'd leave Lilith free to prey on them?"

"No, but…now you tell me that it would play into the Chosen's hands." He shook his head. "Al-Mukhtar may be the enemy of my enemy, but he isn't my friend. I've sworn to bring him to justice."

"All the more reason to keep him near. That's why he wants *you* close." Soraya lifted her thumb, drawing it across her throat in an unmistakeable gesture. It was all the hint she could give; whatever she said aloud, Saif would make her repeat to him.

John looked from her eyes to her fist and back again, and she willed him to understand. As long as he and Saif circled each other like cat and mouse, John would have little opportunity to find a way to hurt him. Working with the Chosen was a risk, but it would enable both of them to concentrate on finding Lilith, and it would give John the best opportunity he'd ever have to steal the ring and deal with Saif.

Soraya hoped he had understood, but John's face was always difficult to read. "An alliance?"

"Yes, of a sort." A knife-in-the-back sort, but he understood that.

He glanced around the forum, then buried his face in both hands with a defeated sigh. After a moment he looked up. "There will be conditions."

"You'll have to come and discuss them with him. He's waiting for you now."

That line was back between his eyebrows, and his fingers caressed the stock of his crossbow. "All right," he said at last. Then, with a shake of his head: "What am I doing? This could be a disaster."

"Try not to worry," Soraya said dryly. "A disaster will likely happen no matter what you do. Coming?"

"All right," he repeated.

Wanting to keep his real living-quarters a secret, Saif had instructed her to bring John to meet him at an empty palace, rather than the small upper room in the tenement. As Soraya led the way, fresh doubt assailed her. John was a mortal—fragile and vulnerable. If Saif *did* mean to lay a trap, what could she do to protect him?

Surely she was worrying for nothing. John had managed to survive one confrontation with Saif already; and if such doubts had occurred to her, then certainly they had also occurred to him.

Before she could say anything, the soul-tether jerked taut and began to pull. With a little hiccup of surprise, Soraya tightened her grip, fighting the undertow that threatened to yank her from her body.

Saif must be under attack.

She found John's arms around her, steadying her on her feet. He didn't waste words; by now he knew exactly what was happening. *"Where?"*

"The House of Botron," she whispered, before her grasp failed and the last of her spirit rushed away to be swallowed up in Saif's battle.

Chapter XXV.

The House of Botron stood at the southern corner of the city, deserted by the noble family that had once occupied it. John skidded to a halt as he took in the damage: its great double gate stood half open, one door tilted off its hinges, with broken links of chain and fresh splinters scattered across the courtyard.

Beyond, the sound of hard breathing and the crash of weapons quickened his pulse. John took a deep breath, fighting back the fear that suddenly gripped him. The Zakar killer was beyond that door; and as far as he knew, the only other being in Tripoli strong enough to break open a pair of gates was the demon he was supposed to exorcise.

He wasn't ready. He'd never be ready.

Lifting a crossbow in his left hand, and reaching into his satchel with his right, John peered between the half-open doors.

The Chosen moved with fluid grace, dodging each blow as his assailant attacked. As John expected, it was the old sand diviner. Katsaros' white hair flew as he pressed forward, wielding a mace in each hand. The weapons boasted knobs of heavy iron atop stout wooden staves. The frail old man shouldn't have been able to lift even one of them, yet he wielded the two with eye-watering speed, blocking each counterthrust of the Chosen's spear as he advanced, and forcing the other man back across the courtyard.

Apparently Lilith had taken matters into her own hands, and it was the most beautiful thing he'd ever seen. She must have ambushed the Chosen, hoping that a surprise attack would render him vulnerable. As they fought, the warrior in John drew him a step further into the courtyard, then another, his own weapons forgotten in the depths of his wonder.

Such ferocity. Such skill. Such power.

And if he allied with Lilith, all this might be his.

It was the voice of temptation, and it chilled him to the bone—for he'd heard it before, or something very like it, at the battle of Yarmouk when he first beheld that enchanted spear. Was that what had brought him to this moment? Was it the bloodlust, the delight in violent power that he flattered himself he'd conquered long ago?

He had no time to follow the thought further. Across the courtyard, Al-Mukhtar caught sight of him and his eyes widened. The distraction lasted a bare heartbeat, but it was enough: in that brief moment, Lilith swept the spear aside with one mace, swung the other in a tight vicious circle, and released it. The weapon flew true, catching the Chosen square in the chest and hurling him across the courtyard.

Saif dropped the spear.

As the weapon fell, Lilith lunged towards it, withered hands grasping, eyes alight with desire.

In a flash, every shred of self-restraint burned away. The years of regret rolled back, and John was once again Bessarion, the blood-drinker, the death-dealer, the demigod.

The spear belonged to him. Lilith must not have it.

John stepped forward, raised his bow, and shot a bolt with pinpoint accuracy through Katsaros' temple. The old sand diviner stumbled. John drew one of the fire-jars he'd filched from the guard-room this morning from his satchel and hurled it down at the old man's feet. The clay pot smashed and the mixture within ignited upon contact with the air, erupting into a sheet of flame. Katsaros was wrapped in fire, his grotesque screams enough to move any civilised heart to pity.

But John felt nothing.

In one fluid motion the Chosen regained his feet. The spear had been tethered to his wrist with a leathern strap, and with a practiced snap of his arm, the strap coiled in on itself—but only a charred and broken end of it, for the spear itself lay on the cobbles in the midst of the blackened shards of the fire-pot.

John Bessarion, demigod, death-dealer, dipped into his satchel for the second fire-pot, loosed his second crossbow into Al-Mukhtar's eye-socket, and planted his foot against Katsaros' chest, propelling the burning sand diviner further away from the spear. Still screaming, the old man collapsed onto the cobbles and rolled. Some of the flames snuffed out, and in their wake, the melted flesh began to knit over, receiving a new layer of pink skin.

In another moment Lilith would be on her feet again, ready for battle. John cast the second fire-pot, and again Katsaros screamed.

The spear lay between his feet—the weapon for which so much more than Katsaros had burned. John crouched to retrieve it—and his hands closed on nothing. Only a burn of wood against his palms as the weapon was snatched away.

He looked up into the Chosen's bloodied face as the other man reeled back with the spear in his hands. Al-Mukhtar slumped against a pillar like a drunk man; he had not yet bothered to remove the crossbow-bolt from his eye.

If he'd had any fire-pots left, he might have used them, as he originally intended, on the Chosen. But he'd thrown both of them at Lilith, and his crossbows were spent.

Al-Mukhtar reached up and yanked John's bolt from his head. Instantly the crater it had made filled out, and the bleeding stopped. At the same moment Lilith quenched the flames on her host's body, and lifted the smoking, bleeding, rapidly-healing Katsaros to his feet.

Both of them turned to face John.

Lilith screamed, an animalistic howl of rage as Katsaros' flesh shifted from black and scorched to white and unmarked. She snatched a discarded mace from the ground and flung it towards him. The missile whined through the air as though shot from a ballista. John saw it coming an instant too late, the sluggishness of his own body holding him in place a fraction of a heartbeat too long. Twisting his body in the air, he managed to get out of the way—or nearly. The knob caught in the folds of his tunic and the wooden handle whipped around, delivering a punishing blow to his ribs before clattering to the pavement.

John collapsed to his hands and knees with a groan of pain.

Lilith leaped at him.

In the same moment, al-Mukhtar lurched away from his pillar and flung the spear. Its point burst through Katsaros' breast just below the collarbone and the Chosen followed a moment later, snatching the weapon back out of the wound. Katsaros howled again; then Lilith pressed a hand to the wound to stem the flow of blood, and charged towards John.

Still wheezing with pain, he staggered to his feet and prepared to sell his life dearly, but Lilith didn't attack. Instead, she circled him and raced through the gate and into the street. John staggered after her, fumbling for another crossbow bolt in the small quiver at his right hip. A useless gesture. Long before he could get either bow loaded, the sand diviner's diminutive form vanished into an alleyway.

Moving quickly, John reloaded his crossbows. His hands were shaking, but his mind was clear and detached. The hot clarity of battle was a blissful relief after the torment of the last twelve hours. Lifting the weapons, he turned back to the courtyard, half expecting to see his death standing behind him with an enchanted spear and furious green eyes. Instead, the Chosen stood within the courtyard facing a pillar of whirling dust, which coalesced rapidly into a human shape.

Soraya.

She groaned and shivered and spat. "So you forced blood down my throat, and you don't even have a corpse to show for it?"

"It was Lilith. Follow her to earth, and come back," the Chosen growled, wiping blood from the eye John's bolt had pierced.

"She went down the first street on the right," John volunteered as Soraya marched toward him. "And that wound she got from the Spear—I don't think she was able to heal it."

Soraya nodded and passed him in a flurry of dust. He would have been glad to see her stay, but evidently she was under a compulsion, and there was nothing he could do to break that.

So he faced al-Mukhtar, and as her feet went down the street behind him, he spat on the ground. "Does she have any choice?" he asked the Chosen. "Or are you using her to get to Lilith the same way you used her to get to me?"

Al-Mukhtar snarled, lowering the spear in John's direction.

If it had been anyone else, John would have pointed his crossbow right back. He'd spent so much time collecting the materials for these weapons, lovingly crafting them from odds and ends he'd scrounged in garbage heaps and abandoned warehouses, only to find that they were almost useless for fighting this kind of battle.

Instead he said, "I was told you wanted to bargain."

The Chosen scowled. "You shot me in the face."

A reasonable objection, but John shrugged it off. The blood still hummed through his veins, hot from the fight. Deep down he felt the dark, bloody horror of what he'd just done—yet in this moment he would do it all again if he must. "I was busy with Lilith. I knew you'd live."

Al-Mukhtar's lips thinned, angry. "What is Soraya to you?"

"I beg your pardon?"

"Her loyalty was mine once. Now, if I allowed it, she'd serve only you. So, what is she to you?"

John ground his teeth. "No. No, that's a question her family would ask. How dare you assume that role?"

"So, what—you're her family now?"

He wasn't going to concede an inch to this man. "I'm all she has."

Al-Mukhtar's teeth showed. "Who are *you*, then?"

"You have no right to that answer, either."

"Lilith recognised you."

"We aren't the best of friends, if you noticed. Is that all?"

There was a long, distrustful silence. For an instant, John wondered if he should just walk away. If al-Mukhtar would let him.

Then the Chosen straightened a little, frowning. "Soraya said you could force Lilith out of Tripoli, God willing."

"Perhaps."

"Excellent." A smile flashed across al-Mukhtar's face, transforming it. "In return, please God, I will guarantee your safe departure from the city and a generous payment of not less than—"

"The lives of these people," John interrupted.

"I beg your pardon?"

Did he truly wish to save lives, or was he only trying to wreck this embryonic alliance? With the heat of battle singing in his veins, John truly couldn't tell. "If Tripoli falls, you must promise me there will be no slaughter."

The other man's face was unreadable. "That is the sultan's decision. I cannot alter it."

"Tripe," John retorted. "If he wants my help, he must meet my terms."

The Chosen's mouth tightened. "I'm not in the sultan's service."

"No, you serve a sorcerer." The Chosen flinched, and John was grimly glad to see it, still riding that wave of reckless wrath. "I presume that master of yours can arrange it."

The other man swallowed. "Impossible. He's in Cairo."

So that was were Khalil was hiding. John very carefully kept his satisfaction from showing. If he did get trapped in this time, at least he'd have the pleasure of hunting down the bastard responsible. "But you're in communication with him."

To John's amazement, al-Mukhtar looked slightly guilty. "Not presently," he said after a moment.

"I see," John said. From what Soraya had told him of the Chosen, he thought he could guess why. Ashamed of having failed last night at the Zakar house, al-Mukhtar must be keeping clear of his master until he could present him with more concrete results.

Well. John had no intention of making this path any easier, for either of them. "Those are my terms. Send Soraya when you can give me the sultan's guarantee." He turned towards the gate.

"Twenty souls," the Chosen said, before John had taken two steps.

"That's contemptible."

"Listen." Al-Mukhtar took a step forward, lowering the lance-point to the ground. "Sultan Qalawun has sworn to burn this city and slaughter the inhabitants. Not even to please his own son would he go back on his word. The only thing I *can* promise you is the lives of a few. Take them."

John hesitated. There was truth in the young Saracen's face, and given that he'd promised Rahel he'd exorcise Lilith anyway, he had scant room to bargain. "Give me fifty." There were fifty Watchers in Tripoli, more or less.

The Chosen's eyes narrowed. "No fat ransoms or valuable slaves. No nobles, knights, or skilled craftsmen."

Mentally, John surveyed the Watchers he'd met in the city. "About a dozen skilled craftsmen, but no one more valuable."

"That, God willing, I can do for you." A weight seemed to roll off the Chosen's shoulders. "And for this, you will exorcise the demon, leave Soraya to me, and depart in peace?"

"I will exorcise Lilith, and I will take my fifty souls out of this city," John said. "But Soraya is her own, not yours, and you are my enemy. I won't swear peace to you."

A flicker of amusement shone in the Chosen's eyes. "An honest man," he said, extending his hand. "Done."

"Done." The word fell on John like a stone and settled, cold and foreboding, in his gut. With it, the last embers of his anger went out. What had he done? He'd sworn to bring the Chosen to justice—Matthias Zakar was counting on him. Instead, he'd made a covenant with his parents' murderer. Worse, he'd let the blood-drinker out of its cage and brutally tormented a helpless old man.

His mind reeled, that deep-down horror rising over him like a storm wave. What would Rahel have said, if she'd seen what he did this afternoon? God pardon him, what was wrong with him? How could he deal out so much violence and feel so little?

He knew the difference between right and wrong, just as he knew deep down which was the true Rahel. Only his heart seemed barren and hard, a dry and thirsty land.

"Give me some token for my fifty," he said heavily.

"We deal with the demon first." Al-Mukhtar's mouth thinned as he glanced towards the gate. "As soon as Soraya gets back with the information we need."

John nodded, too weary to speak. Regardless of the state of his heart, there was now nothing left to do but exorcise Lilith and resign himself to a life in exile, never to see his home again.

He could feel sorrow for *that,* if not for others. John left out a soft breath and fastened his gaze on the spear. Unless this gave him the chance to repossess the weapon and get vengeance for the Zakars, this was hardly a bargain worth making.

Chapter XXVI.

"What do you mean, no sign of them?" Gerard knew it was unfair to berate Marco. Tripoli was a maze, full of holes where a crazy old sand diviner and a cunning warrior could hide. Still, time was rapidly running out. "The ship leaves at sunrise. I need those men *now.*"

"Y—yes, sir." Marco stared at a point on the wall just beyond Gerard's right ear, his body stiff with discomfort. "That is…"

"Well?"

"I might have some idea of where to find the Prester, sir. But if so, he isn't with Katsaros anymore."

Gerard yanked angrily at his blankets. After the gruelling meeting at the palace, Lady Margaret had packed him off to bed for a few hours' rest. For a while, the steady plash of waves from the other side of the city wall had lulled him into calm. He'd even spent some time thinking about her words last night. How did she mean him to court her? Should he present her with an illuminated book of hours, or offer his services as a strategist to plan victories and territorial expansions?

Now, Marco's news had banished every shred of composure.

"Don't weary me with the details—find them. Search every house if you must."

"We only have a limited number of men, sir." Marco kept his eyes fixed on the tapestry behind Gerard. "Everyone else is needed on the wall. And are you sure the countess will be happy with our disturbing her subjects?"

He ought to have thought of that himself. Countess Lucy would go into fits if Templars started rummaging through her people's homes. "All right.

Go back to your Watchers, then. If anyone knows where the Prester is, I presume they will."

Marco's throat worked nervously, but before he could say whatever was on his mind, there was a knock at the door and it inched open, letting in an indistinct feminine murmur.

"What the blazes do you want?" Gerard snarled at the unseen intruder. "Did no one teach you to wait before barging in?"

At that, the door snapped decisively open and Lady Margaret swept in. "They did not," she said. There was a faint edge of steel in her voice. "I see you're feeling better, dear. I thought you might be asleep."

Hot embarrassment poured into his face. *Devil take it!* "I thought you were a servant," he muttered.

"Remember that they are *my* servants, and it is not so long since you were among them." She held his gaze for a long moment, an oddly wistful look in her eyes, and cold understanding gripped him.

This was what she meant when she told him to recommend himself to her in a way that went deeper than flattery. What a fool he was! Above devotion, far above ambition, Margaret of Tyre was known for her gentleness and compassion. Gerard thought he would be consumed with shame, but she spared him further humiliation by adding quickly: "There's someone here to see you."

He sat up a little straighter in bed, embarrassment fleeing before more urgent worries. "Saints. I was followed?"

"Yes. He seems rather the worse for wear, but he was adamant that you'd want to see him."

"His name?"

"Stephen Katsaros."

Gerard almost sobbed with relief. "I'll see him."

"No, stay where you are," Lady Margaret added gently. "He's right here."

She beckoned, and Katsaros appeared in the doorway.

No, not Katsaros; Lilith was in control at present, her spirit glittering hotly in the old man's eyes, moving him with the feline grace of a predator despite both his age and the great wet crater in his shoulder where a piercing wound had spilled a long streamer of blood down his tunic.

"Gerard of Montreal," Lilith said in the old man's reedy voice. The words were clipped short and hard. Brusquely, she turned to Lady Margaret. "Woman, you may bring the healing things now."

There was something horrible in that bloodstained figure, as though the old man was dead and yet walking. Gerard swallowed. "What happened to you? How did you find me?"

"I was attacked by a greater spirit, and a lesser spirit led me here. I may have bound myself into this body, but I still have servants of my own kind."

Behind the old sand diviner, Marco crossed himself. Lilith seemed to sense it, for she turned to snarl at him. "Send this one away. I won't have him near me."

"Go and find the Prester, Marco."

The servant hesitated with a troubled glance at Lilith. "Sir, do you think that's wise?"

Gerard nearly snapped at him, but caught his breath before the hasty words toppled out. Instead, he spoke gently as a lamb. "Thank you, Marco, but I can handle this."

An emotion Gerard couldn't identify flitted across the servant's face—worry, or shame perhaps—but as Marco left, it was Lady Margaret he looked towards, hoping she had marked his effort. Instead, Lady Margaret reached out towards Lilith. "Sit," she said gently. "Your body won't take much more."

For a moment, Lilith resisted. There was something like desperation in the old man's eyes, in the reedy voice. "You must send me out of this city. I can no longer stay here."

Gerard let out a sigh of relief. Finally, things seemed to be going his way: he had been anticipating a wearisome argument. "Lady Margaret has a ship waiting in the harbour. It leaves at sunrise tomorrow and I want nothing more than to send you with it."

The old man swallowed. Nodded.

Gerard glanced at Lady Margaret, remembering Lilith's previous objections to leaving Tripoli. "What will happen when you leave this city?"

Slumped into a chair facing Gerard's bed, Lilith shook the old man's head. "We shall see wonders in the deep."

Gerard frowned, confused. "What?"

"Likely we will all drown, and I will be forced out of this body and out of this sphere," Lilith snarled.

"But it's spring—the waters are calm this time of year."

"The waters are *always* treacherous for such as me. Do you understand? They *know* me."

Gerard thought he began to understand why Lilith had been so loath to leave the city, why creatures such as herself feared running water. He turned to Margaret. "Perhaps you should ready a different ship for yourself, my lady."

She was uncharacteristically serious, staring at Lilith with pursed lips. "Perhaps I will."

Gerard fervently wished to cross himself, but he didn't want to offend Lilith. "And the city? What will happen to Tripoli?"

"At present, the battle is between mortal and mortal, flesh and flesh." Lilith touched the bloodstain on Katsaros' tunic, looked at the red wetness with fascination. "Beings such as me, we are territorial. Because Tripoli is under my protection, Qeteb cannot trespass without drawing...attention."

"What kind of attention? Who is Qeteb?"

"Let us only say he would be visited by something too powerful even for him. As for Qeteb, he has many names and many shapes. He is the blazing midday, the desert heat, the fire among the orchards, the pestilence that festers on battlegrounds. When the sun is at its highest he is strongest, and—"

"I see," Gerard interrupted. Every hair on his body was standing on end, and he wasn't sure he wanted to hear more. "So when you leave..."

"When I leave, he will be free to enter. Do you remember the fall of Antioch, twenty years ago?"

Gerard's skin crawled. Child though he'd been at the time, he remembered the stories. He nodded.

"Well," Lilith said wearily, "now you know."

"Is there a chance to save the city if you remain?" Lady Margaret had been listening, the shuttered blankness of her face eloquent witness to her worry.

Lilith shook the old man's head. "I can't. I must leave."

"Why?"

"The Watcher. I overheard his plans while he was dreaming." Lilith bared her teeth. "He means to banish me altogether from this sphere—and I think he's in league with al-Mukhtar. I'm certain I was followed here."

"The Watcher? You don't mean Prester John?"

"That's exactly who I mean."

Dazed, Gerard recalled the events of last night. "But that's impossible! He was there last night—he *foiled* the Chosen."

"He's a *Prester,* meat creature," Lilith said testily. "I'm a demon. What do you think he'll do if I fail to entice him? Serve me the Eucharist?"

Gerard buried his face in his hands. Just once in his life, he'd like to work with people who *weren't* constantly trying to stab each other in the back. "Tripoli," he murmured. "You were right, my lady; it must be something in the water."

Just then a knock at the door announced that the surgeon had arrived. Gerard nodded to Lilith. "They'll patch up your shoulder. And then we'll put you directly on the ship."

"No," Lilith instantly countermanded. "Not on the ship. Not until the last possible moment. I stay on land."

Gerard ran a hand through his hair in desperation, his head aching again. "But if you've been followed to this house, you can't possibly stay."

"Don't worry, dear," Lady Margaret said to the ancient being of malice that inhabited Katsaros' body. "I know just the place for you. Now, off you go and get that seen to."

She opened the door and handed Katsaros out to the servants beyond. After that, she closed the door firmly and faced Gerard with horrified furrows in her brow.

"Gerard! My dear! What have you got yourself mixed up in?"

He barely heard her. "Saints." He stared at the windows and the tempestuous sea below. "Saints, why would he do a thing like that? Why would Prester John, of all people, betray a Christian city?"

The bedstead creaked as Margaret sat heavily on the edge of it, gripping Gerard's hand. The touch pierced him like lightning. "That man said he had a *demon*, Gerard. Does Beaujeu know what you're doing?"

"Beaujeu?" He came back to the moment with a jolt. Margaret lifted an eyebrow at him. "This was what Beaujeu charged me to do in Tripoli. Everything else was secondary."

"But why is Beaujeu importing a *demon* to Acre?"

Gerard ran the tip of his tongue over his lips. "He said it would save us."

"And you believe him?"

He stared at the quilted damask on the bed. It was the question he had been dreading, and not because he had no answer. Because he did. "Each man is the architect of his own fate…through foresight, determination, and decisive action. My lady, if there's even a possibility that any of this could save Acre, I *have* to try."

Lady Margaret shook her head. "We can't control the future, Gerard. Certainly not like this."

He looked away, unwilling to contradict her, but incapable of anything else. "I have Beaujeu's orders. I *must* obey." He swallowed hard. "He will bear the guilt for this; not me."

"Gerard, no. Don't do this. Leave Beaujeu's service, if you must."

He looked up at her, wrapping his fingers more tightly around her soft hand. "And enter yours, my lady?"

"If you wish."

It was a way out of it all. He might leave the Temple, leave Tripoli, sail back to Tyre with Lady Margaret. As her servant, not her equal; to sun himself in her presence, but never to enjoy it as lord; and perhaps to lose all anyway, and go into exile at her heels should the Saracens triumph.

It might be good enough for some, but it was not good enough for him. He had been her servant once. He was her partner now in the defence of Tripoli, and he did not think he could go back to the silence and obedience of a servant.

Gerard lifted their linked hands with a wistful smile. "I will enter your service on one condition only."

Her gaze fell, sorrowful; as though something in his words had hurt her. "I only wish to do you all the good that lies in my power, dear."

"Then help me hide Katsaros. You said you knew the place."

She extracted her hand from his, and stood with a deep sigh. "I think so. I won't promise he'll be comfortable there, but it's not the sea, and it's not Tripoli either."

"Then sh—then he should go there." Gerard nodded. "And send someone to recall Marco. If Prester John has turned against us, we need to respond accordingly."

Chapter XXVII.

"Even locked into a mortal body, Lilith is strongest at night," Soraya warned Saif and John as they held council of war over lunch. She had returned to the House of Botron with Lilith's location, a stack of flatbread, a jar of olives, and a massive block of goat's cheese still dripping from the brine in which it had been stored. "The house is well guarded, and attacking it will be risky by night and foolhardy by day. So which should it be?"

"Night," John said decisively. "It will be easier to bypass the guards, and Lilith herself will not have any power that matters."

"With me, you won't need to bother avoiding any guards," Saif pointed out, but even he agreed that Lilith could not be attacked until the all-concealing dark of night had fallen.

Having laid their plans, the three of them split up. Saif returned to the tenement and locked Soraya back into the stifling oblivion of her prison so that he could snatch some sleep, while John no doubt followed suit in some hiding-place of his own. When Saif commanded her back to life that evening, thick clouds covered the sky and last night's wind had picked up again. The sunset was an angry stripe of red over the sea, and the great purple heads of the Lebanon mountains were lost from sight in the cloudy east.

Soraya shivered and tilted her head towards the storm-clouds in the window. "When did that happen?"

"While I was asleep." Saif unwrapped the bread and cheese left over from their lunch. "Come. Eat with me."

Soraya shook her head. "This is a new body. I should have enough to go on for a few hours."

He set a flatbread aside, topping it with cheese and olives, and then motioned toward it. "This could take us a few hours. I need you strong and active."

He smiled at her invitingly, but Soraya was in no mood to humour him. John would have invited her to eat for companionship's sake. Saif just wanted his weapons in good condition. "By your leave, I'll go to the meeting-place early. John said he'd be eating there."

The smile vanished. For a moment he looked disappointed, but then his eyes hardened to chips of grey-green ice. "All right, then. Go." The word was an order, picking up her feet and moving her towards the door, but Saif had another command. "Don't eat with him. He's no friend of mine, or yours either for that matter."

"What?" Soraya yelped in outrage, but the two commands were at work on her, marching her out the door and down the stairs before she could protest any further.

* * *

Outside, rain lashed the streets. Inside, the small public-house was warm and quiet, redolent with the rich scent of pork and fennel stew. On any other occasion, John would have enjoyed filling a stomach which was too often empty these days—but tonight, for a whole host of reasons, the meat tasted like dust and sat like a brick on his stomach.

Perhaps he ought to be fasting; but that depended on whether he wanted to succeed tonight, or to fail. And that, despite everything, was the one thing he couldn't decide.

The door opened to a flash of green, and John got to his feet. "Soraya."

She pulled a mantle from her dark hair and snapped her fingers to distract him from his watch on the door. "Saif isn't here yet. He's sulking at home."

"Ah." John leaned across his table to kiss her cheek in welcome. "Will you eat?"

Soraya laughed bitterly, sliding onto the bench beside him and stretching out her sandalled feet toward the fire. "Saif has forbidden it. Besides, that smells like pork, and I'm trying to turn over a new leaf."

"Everyone's eating like kings because they've stopped trying to conserve the livestock," John said sombrely, forcing himself to take another spoonful. "I don't think anyone expects the city to last much longer. What's bothering al-Mukhtar? Doesn't he know I'm loyally married?"

Soraya snorted. "Apparently so is he. He just about bit my head off when—" She caught herself, wincing. Perhaps some bad old memory. "Never mind. I have no idea what goes on in Saif's head."

The door opened, letting in another gust of wind. At the sight of the spear clenched in the hooded newcomer's left hand, John stiffened and reached for his crossbows. Al-Mukhtar, however, only readjusted a loop of concealing fabric around his face, before approaching their corner with his head bowed.

"Just so long as we can trust him tonight," John muttered to Soraya, before standing up to face the young mamluk.

"You're early," Soraya needled as al-Mukhtar sat down facing them. "Does this mean I can have some stew? It smells wonderful."

She'd barely been here two minutes. John hid a wry smile—clearly the Chosen was jealous to some extent, or he would not have rushed to follow her.

Al-Mukhtar shot her a look. "It's pork."

"Oh, is it? I hadn't noticed."

Sarcasm dripped from her voice, but al-Mukhtar was apparently impervious to her mockery. John sat down and took another mouthful, trying not to stare hungrily at the spear.

He would need to convince the Chosen to let his guard down if he were to have any chance of reclaiming it. John cleared his throat, seeking a topic of conversation. "So, al-Mukhtar. Do you have family in Cairo?"

Al-Mukhtar looked at him suspiciously for a moment, then seemed to relax a fraction. "A wife." Another silence. "You?"

"A wife, back home. And four children."

"Glory to God." He sounded wistful. "Ghaliyah and I...we never had children."

"Probably just as well," Soraya muttered under her breath.

John pretended not to hear. "You're still young. Give it time."

The Chosen grunted, shifting his grip on the spear. "Any sons?"

"Two."

A respectful nod. "Not bad." Al-Mukhtar's comment seemed disparaging somehow.

"Wait till you have daughters. They'll surprise you. My youngest is a prophetess."

"Sounds risky." The Chosen chuckled, then became serious. "You are a rich man, John Zakar."

"Thanks." Casually, John nodded at the weapon al-Mukhtar cradled in the crook of his elbow. "Nice spear. Mind if I have a look?"

Al-Mukhtar's sinewy hands tightened on the shaft, almost as though he expected John to grab for the weapon. "Yes, I do mind."

There was an awkward silence. John took another mouthful, conscious of Soraya's wound-up tension beside him, and the watchfulness back in al-Mukhtar's eyes. "Where did you get the weapon, if you don't mind my asking?"

"It belongs to my master."

John decided to take a risk. "Khalil ibn Hassan."

Al-Mukhtar's eyes locked on John. His knuckles whitened on the spear's shaft. All the air seemed to be sucked out of the room, and Soraya, it seemed, had stopped breathing altogether. John made an effort to go on eating as though entirely unaware of the tension in the room.

"Where did you hear that patronym?" al-Mukhtar growled at last.

John swallowed a last spoonful of gravy and set the bowl down on the table. In the shadows, his left hand drifted to his crossbow. Useless as such a weapon was against a man like al-Mukhtar, the bow gave him at least the illusion of security. "Our paths have crossed."

It wasn't an answer, and John knew that didn't escape the Chosen for a moment. His eyes narrowed. "You've been misinformed. Ibn Hassan is dead."

A denial too specific to be taken seriously. John replied agreeably. "If you say so. Is it dark yet?"

"Dark enough." Al-Mukhtar stood up. "Keep on my left, Soraya, and don't drag on me."

So casually he issued his command, and instantly, Soraya got up and moved to the position al-Mukhtar had indicated. Her movements were jerky, as though she was not quite in command of herself. John had to swallow his outrage, but Soraya shot him a quick sad smile to let him know she had seen the disgust on his face. He hoped it comforted her to know that he saw her servitude; to know, from his face, that his promise to help her went deeper than mere words.

John followed the two of them into the street, savagely bitter.

He was supposed to be making this man pay for his crimes. Instead, he was helping him destroy Tripoli. There was an ache in his heart as he thought of the Zakar children—the eagerness in Matthias' eyes this morning when he'd spoken of catching al-Mukhtar. Not only the children, but also Hubert, Maryam, Marco—what would happen to *them* when Lilith was gone?

Despite the turmoil of his thoughts, it was comforting to find that he was not entirely devoid of compassion.

Outside, with every shutter firmly bolted and the clouds thickening above, the streets of Tripoli were dark as soot. Soraya had told them she could modify her eyes to a more catlike shape, widening pupils to drink in the dim light. Now, in the gathering gloom, she took the lead.

Lilith had gone to ground at the Lady of Tyre's house on the Fish Street, where John had met the Lady Eschiva some weeks before. As he followed Soraya's pale shape, John felt for his crossbows, checking for the hundredth time that they were loaded and ready, coated in beeswax to protect them from the weather. Yet he was not sure he wanted to use them. The sand diviner's thin, desperate screams, that had failed to make an impression on him this morning, now rang in his ears, and John shuddered inwardly at the thought of causing the old man more pain.

There was an alternative. He might simply leave Lilith in full possession of the sand diviner—and of Tripoli. Rahel, the Watchers, Soraya—all of them wanted him to exorcise Lilith. Wanted him to doom Tripoli, ally himself with a murderer, and throw away his one chance of finding his way home. Obedient to their counsel, his feet were taking him towards a confrontation; but his heart still rebelled. All their reasons were good ones, yet he felt as though he moved through molten glass, rather than wind and rain. Every step was agony.

Still, he followed Soraya and al-Mukhtar with blind trust toward the great house on the north wall, to which Lilith had flown. A little lamplight escaped from the shuttered windows, faintly illuminating the courtyard and its gate.

Out of the dark, a hand latched onto John's elbow. He turned with a sound of surprise, clutching at one of his bows. Sensing the motion, al-Mukhtar brought his spear to a blind guard.

"Who goes there?"

"My lord Prester? Is that you?" The man spoke just loud enough to reach them over the sound of the wind. "It's me, sir; Marco."

Al-Mukhtar swore under his breath, but John felt a moment's unburdening, like a prisoner facing a reprieve. "What is it, Marco? Have they moved Katsaros?"

"Yes, sir. He—she isn't far, but the Templars have her strongly guarded."

Beside him, al-Mukhtar grunted. "We can deal with them."

"No! You mustn't hurt them!" Marco's voice shook at the soft menace in the mamluk's voice. "I'll tell you nothing, otherwise."

The Chosen pounced on the young servant, grabbing him by the tunic. "Shall I peel the flesh from his bones?" His voice was conversational and utterly chilling, but John cut in before the mamluk could take his threats any further.

"Don't be afraid, Marco. We swear it: no killing." The air crackled with tension. "Let the boy go, al-Mukhtar." John put all the soft authority into his voice that he could; and perhaps that reminded the Chosen that without his help, there was no point in finding Lilith at all.

Al-Mukhtar lowered the spear, grumbling. "This is going to be enough trouble without trying to spare lives."

"We discussed this already," John said repressively.

Soraya moved forward. "Don't be afraid," she said softly to the young Healer. "Show us the way."

Marco didn't answer, only melted into the shadows. Soraya followed, and John and al-Mukhtar fell into step behind her as Marco led them along the front wall of Lady Margaret's house; then down a narrow passage that opened to the right, leading directly towards the city wall. Above them was a narrow strip of pale sky, and ahead, pierced through the great black bulk of the sea wall, was a small patch of faint grey light, and the sound of waves from the sea beyond.

John took a long, slow breath as he realised where they were going. Just beyond this gate, across a narrow strait barely a bowshot wide, lay the isle of Saint Thomas.

It was a stormy night, and he was going to the island of Saint Thomas to confront the guardian of Tripoli, just as Rahel had foreseen.

His feet carried him towards the gate. To what end? He could hardly turn back; not with al-Mukhtar and Soraya watching him. But with each step forward, the impossibility of what he was about to do rose up to confront him.

The moment had come. He was about to face Lilith.

Chapter XXVIII.

Thanks to her catlike eyes, Soraya saw her way ahead in ghostly shades of white and grey as Marco led John, Saif and herself to the bars of an iron gate, outlined against the foaming white turbulence of the sea beyond.

Marco stopped, fumbled for moment, then turned a key in a lock. With a muffled creak, he pulled open the postern-gate, letting them out onto a narrow wooden jetty that jutted out beyond the tumbled rock of the shoreline.

Here, beyond the city wall, there was no protection from the scouring wind, but at least there was a little light. The water was shallow here, abating the waves' fury somewhat. Within a bowshot of the wall stood the small rocky island. A small basilica was built atop it, a faint light shining in its narrow arched windows.

"Saint Thomas," John said beside her. He'd told her about Rahel's vision, but Soraya had nearly given up hope. Now, cautiously, she picked it up again. She wasn't sure exactly how this was going to help John find his way home and free her from Saif's ring, but if Rahel had had a vision of this place, surely they were where they were meant to be.

Beside them, Marco nearly had to shout to be heard. "They took the sand diviner across this afternoon. That's when the storm returned."

At his words, instinct knotted her gut and knowledge bubbled to the surface: death by water was deadly to her kind.

Now she also must cross that turbulent strait.

"How many guards?" John asked, his voice a low rumble.

"Sir Peter of Alba, my lord, and four Templar sergeants."

"Peter of Alba, you say?"

"Yes, sir."

"How the wheel turns," John said grimly. "Thanks, Marco. Will you leave the gate open for us?"

"Yes, my lord." He paused a moment. "I'll go tell the Watchers what you're attempting tonight. We'll keep watch for you."

"Thanks," John said, but there was an odd hesitation in his voice as Marco vanished into the passage.

Saif crouched on the jetty, staring at the sea. "We didn't plan for this." His voice was rough with displeasure; Marco's information had upended all their plans. "Just how far is this island?"

"There's no boat," Soraya observed. She flexed her fingers, feeling the wind's strength "If Saif allowed me the power, I might try carrying us across by air, but it would warn Lilith."

Saif got up with a gesture of disgust. "Can't you exorcise her from here, Watcher?"

"No," John said. "The water seems shallow enough; I noted it on my last visit. Will it hurt you to cross, Soraya?"

"Only if I drown," she said slowly. "For my kind, death by running water means being hurled out of this world. So long as Saif lets me have my strength, that shouldn't be a problem."

John nodded. "We will all cross. Al-Mukhtar will go first. Once you reach the shore, wait for Soraya and me to follow."

He seemed to have stepped naturally into leadership, and Soraya was surprised when Saif didn't object to the arrangement. Instead, he gave a curt nod and said, "And after?"

"Reconnoitre, I suppose. Try to isolate Lilith, and…"

His voice trailed away, but Saif was eager to go. "Sounds good." He got to his feet, stepped off the quay and plunged into the water.

Soraya's eyes adjusted to track his progress through the waves. "I don't like it. He sounded too happy by half."

"You think he might betray us?"

"I'm certain of it. I only wish I could predict when." A wave slapped the shore, flinging salty foam into their faces, and she shrank against his side. "Hold my hand?"

John's grip was reassuringly firm. "Do you still think you're wicked, Soraya?"

"I'm surely no angel," she replied, reflexively. The soul tether slackened, allowing her to gather strength. "Now."

They stepped off the jetty, chest-deep into the water. A cold wave hit Soraya instantly in the face and she reeled, more with instinctive fear than anything else. Yet John steadied her, and after a moment they moved off together, half swimming, half walking; to her surprise, there seemed to be a lull in the storm, as though it paused to let them pass. Presently they made it to shore somewhat north of where Saif had landed, closer to the basilica. Saif must have heard them crawl, shivering, up the rocks, for when they made it into the shadow of the basilica's wall, he was there to meet them.

"They have four guards in the porch." Saif had to raise his voice to make himself heard over the wind. "That leaves one, if that Frank was telling the truth. I haven't seen any patrols."

John nodded. "Most likely they'll be keeping Lilith in the church."

"The church! Isn't that supposed to be holy ground?" Saif needled.

"A place is only as holy as the people inhabiting it," John said levelly. "But we should leave nothing to chance. Saif, you search the rest of the island. Soraya, I take it you can get past the guards and search inside the church."

"I can deal with the guards," Saif said.

"Absolutely not. Soraya?" John repeated.

"Easily."

"Then do it. I'll keep watch from the rocks here; report back to me when you're done, and we'll make a plan."

Saif dissolved into the darkness. Soraya shed her limbs, melting into the shape of a small bat. Instantly, the wind swept her up in the storm, and for a few terrifying moments she was at the mercy of the elements. It took a moment to figure out how to control the small unfamiliar body—and then she spiralled through the wind on the edge of control and swept through the church porch into the dim lamplight beyond. Pillared arcades ran down each side of the nave; Soraya flittered into the welcome shadows and clung to one of the foliate capitals there, her tiny body pulsing with the exhilaration of flight.

Beyond, in the storm, thunder growled long and low. With only one of the lanterns lit over the altar in the crossing, the basilica was cold and dark. There was no sign of Lilith, nor of the fifth guard of whom Marco had spoken.

Shadows collected in the arcaded aisles. Having caught her breath, Soraya left the comfort of her column and wheeled across the nave to the columns on the other side. A dark shape the size of a man lay in the aisle beyond—Lilith, or something else?

Before she could decide, something moved in the dark.

A human shape hurtled from the shadows and a clawlike hand fastened around her tiny body, dragging her from her perch. In the dim light Soraya looked up to see the old sand diviner's face, the eyes bright with madness.

Lilith.

She struggled, reluctant to abandon her disguise. A knife found the furry angle beneath her chin and she abruptly stopped fighting.

"Soraya." Lilith half snarled, half whispered the word, backing deeper into the shadows. "If you want to go undetected, you shouldn't use your power. Who's with you? Speak, or I'll cut you open."

Something about the demon's proximity grated on her senses, like a scream too high and faint to hear. Soraya pulled on the soul tether, drawing matter from the baptismal font, the tapers, the sand they stood in, and the blanket on the ground at the sand diviner's feet, which she had mistaken for Katsaros himself. In a few moments she had knitted the materials into her body, returning to human form; but Lilith kept her grip on her throat, and the knife still tickled her jaw.

Soraya let out a soft breath of laughter. "What? You threaten *me* with a blade? Don't you know that I have died more times than I can count?"

Lilith hesitated, then let go of her throat. Fierce with desperation, Soraya took the moment to think. How could she let herself be caught like this? Now they had lost the element of surprise. Yet even limited to mortal senses, Soraya could feel the other creature's desperation thick in the air.

"They're going to put me on a ship at sunrise." Katsaros' battered old body shivered as thunder rolled overhead. "It will destroy me. The sea is hungry. It tried to swallow me on the way over. Not even the wind will obey me now."

"Why, you're frightened." Soraya was grimly humorous. "Just like a mortal."

Lilith grabbed her throat again, jagged fingernails scoring her skin. "Killing you may not help," she hissed in the old man's cracked voice, "but it would give me great pleasure to break every bone in your body. Your masters—tell me where they are."

Pain was nothing new, either. When she didn't reply, Lilith hissed with displeasure. "We could work together, Soraya."

Her only chance of getting away unseen to warn John and Saif was to goad Lilith into killing her. Soraya gave a soft huff of laughter. "It's true. You've inhabited this mortal so long, you've begun to think like one of them. Once, the great Lilith would have commanded rather than begged."

"I know you're on a soul tether." Lilith ignored her taunts. "I know you're enslaved to Khalil's young bloodhound; but don't you realise you can resist him? The power is yours; you only have to hold it for long enough that I can take the soul-anchor from him. Then he dies, and you are free…but only if we work together."

All thought of goading Lilith fled. She was right, Soraya realised in surprise. She wrestled Saif for control of the soul tether every day; in theory, she might take him by surprise, deny him the use of her strength long enough to let someone else destroy him.

So far, John's efforts to free her and defeat Saif had come to nothing. He was only mortal, after all, with a mortal's strength. But Lilith could wield strength comparable to Saif, enough to tear the anchoring ring from his hand. If they worked together—if Soraya could take him by surprise—

If.

It made no sense; it was not in Lilith's interest to help her. They might share a common enemy in Saif, but the real threat to Lilith was John. Soraya wasn't fool enough to believe that Lilith *really* intended to destroy Saif; not when John was outside waiting to expel her from the world.

And that made the question perfectly clear, of course. John was her friend, and she would never trade his life away for a doubtful chance at freedom. Soraya felt a little dizzy at the realisation. Once, she would have given anything for a chance like this.

Not that she could afford to let *that* cat out of the bag. She cleared her throat. "How do I know you'll keep your word?"

"Every bargain has an element of trust, little djinn."

"How do you know me?"

Lilith smiled unpleasantly. "You don't remember *anything,* do you? Not even meeting the Bessarion at Yarmouk? Fascinating. Six hundred years on, and you still can't keep away from him."

Yarmouk. Bessarion. Her heart leaped into her throat. Those names—they were some of the few shards of memory she retained, small precious illusions of hope; the sound of John's voice had been another. Could it be true? Were they connected?

"Tell me," she said in a stifled voice.

"First, the bargain."

That brought her spirit crashing back down to the ground like a wingless bird. Fool that she was, to give Lilith a moment's credence! There was no truth in the creature; only lies, and temptation, and a cruel will to dominate. Soraya took a long, steadying breath. "And if I refuse?"

"It won't save your masters." Lilith smiled coldly. "I'll send my guards out to search for them—and as for you, you make a pretty slave. Perhaps I'll keep you."

If Lilith sent her guards in search of John and Saif, there would be a fight, and one of those fragile mortals would die. Perhaps even John. Best if Lilith thought she meant to comply. "Could we leave this place by a second door?"

"Yes, over there." Lilith jerked a thumb in the direction of the south transept.

"All right." Soraya pretended to give in. "They're outside waiting for me to return with news. Come now and we'll get the better of them in the dark."

Lilith's eyes narrowed. "If you betray me, it's the mortal I'll kill first."

"Don't bother," she said wearily. "I know the usual terms."

Soraya took the lead up the shadowed aisle, pausing at the corner of the crossing to peer into the transept. Sure enough, the fifth sentry stood there with his back against a small door.

She didn't give Lilith the time to take the lead.

Only a thin stream of lamplight struggled into the transept, but it was enough. As Soraya rounded the corner, the Templar's armour whispered as he stiffened to attention. One leap took her down the length of the transept and she had her hands on his throat before he'd managed to draw his sword. A rumble of thunder masked his grunt of surprise as she found the pulse points on each side of his neck and pressed. Within moments, she was lowering him softly to the floor.

Lilith strolled down the transept towards her. "He'll come to and give us away, you realise."

"So we'll move fast."

"Not that fast." The old sand diviner's eyes unfocused for a moment, his mouth moving soundlessly. A moment later, Lilith refocused on Soraya and smiled. "There. A nightmare or two should keep him occupied for a while."

Repressing a shudder, Soraya lifted the latch and led the way out into the storm.

Again, her eyes altered to admit more light. Beside her, Lilith must have done the same, for she stilled, scanning the shoreline. A harmony of greys showed the church looming over them and a barren landscape of tumbled rock stretching towards the foaming sea. Soraya calculated that the whole island was a little smaller than a polo field, the basilica situated towards its eastern end.

"Where are they?" Lilith hissed. "If you betray me—"

"I haven't. Saif is *here.*" But where? Her heart stopped. Had he and John come to blows? Had Saif chosen this moment to betray them?

Before the fear could consume her, a dim shape approached from the darkness to the west. Saif. At the same moment, something she had taken to be a rock moved. John, waiting for their return.

Beside Soraya, Lilith gave a sound of triumph, then leaped, flying through the air with the sand diviner's tattered robes fluttering behind.

"No!" Soraya threw herself after Lilith, but she moved too late, and the mortals could not manipulate their human eyes to see what was coming out of the dark.

John turned at her warning cry, his crossbow lifted as he peered into the shadows. A slash of lightning split the sky, burning white-hot in Soraya's sensitive vision; somewhere in the dazzle, a bowstring thrummed and Katsaros shrieked.

Blinded, Soraya fumbled her own landing and hit the rocks with a crunch and snap. Pain shot up her right arm as the bone cracked. Somewhere nearby, Saif grunted in surprise, and the soul tether went slack. A shout from John was suddenly choked off.

The agony of her broken arm made it hard to think, to move. Soraya gasped as Saif lost hold and pure power rushed into her along the soul tether. Instinctively she channelled it into her arm, knitting the bone and dulling the pain. Vision returned as she struggled to her feet.

Saif was sprawled to her left, fumbling among the rocks for his dropped spear. To the right, Lilith straddled John. She had both her hands fastened around his neck, as he reached up, blindly, to grab the crossbow-bolt that protruded from the sand diviner's belly.

John. Not Saif. Just as she had expected; little as her foresight had done to save him. John was mortal, and right now Lilith's pain was the only thing keeping him alive.

Katsaros let out an awful groan as John twisted the bolt in the sand diviner's belly. The agony distracted Lilith just long enough. Soraya pulled power around her like a cloak and tore the old sand diviner off him by the scruff of the neck. Instantly Lilith twisted in her grip, teeth bared in a feral snarl, and whipped the old man's head forward in a vicious headbutt. Soraya's vision exploded in a fire-burst, but she locked her arms around

Katsaros and slammed him onto the rocks.

An involuntary groan escaped the frail body beneath her. *Strike me blind,* Soraya thought in momentary panic, *what am I doing to this poor old man?*

Instinctively she pulled back, giving the other djinn her chance.

Lilith rolled, toppling Soraya and pinning her to the ground with a hand at her throat. The sand diviner's other fist coiled back to strike; a blade glittered in his hand.

Somewhere beyond this moment, beyond the tiny grey-and-white rain-soaked world in which a demon was about to split her skull open between rock and fist and knife, Soraya felt the soul tether tighten and pull.

Saif meant to steal her strength.

She reached up and caught Lilith's striking hand. The shock as hand met palm was jarring, sending a flare of pain up the same arm she'd just broken and mended, but it awoke a desperation and ferocity Soraya had long forgotten.

She was stronger than this.

She could resist Saif.

Saif was still pulling, but Soraya ignored him, refusing him an inch of the soul tether. Atop her, teeth bared, Lilith leaned all Katsaros' weight on the knife, grinding it closer and closer to Soraya's chest.

Summoning every ounce of strength, Soraya bucked, rolling the sand diviner beneath her again. As they moved, the knife pierced her breast and a hot trickle of blood ran down her skin beneath her jacket. Lilith's nostrils flared at the scent, and with another snarl, she pushed up in an attempt to drive the blade home again.

Her grasp slipped on the soul tether, allowing Saif a little more power.

She was losing.

Feet crunched on the stones beside her. The point of Saif's spear came between Soraya and Lilith, halting a hair's-breadth from the sand diviner's throat. Abruptly Lilith stilled, Katsaros' eyes wide and staring with fear.

"Watcher," Saif gasped, "quick."

Soraya risked a glance at John. Her struggle with Lilith had taken a bare few heartbeats; he was sitting on the rocks, feeling his ribs with a shaking hand. At Saif's cry, he winced and hastily began, "O Eternal God, Who has redeemed the race of men from the captivity of the devil—"

Beneath Soraya, the sand diviner's body went suddenly limp, his eyes unfocusing. Soraya screamed. "Get to the *point!*"

The knife fell from the sand-diviner's hand. Soraya grabbed it, threw it into the waves. Katsaros let out a deep, rasping breath, then lay still.

It took her a moment to realise what had happened.

"He's *dead,*" she said in shock.

* * *

The full meaning of Soraya's words didn't immediately penetrate John's mind. Lilith's headlong attack had forced him against the island's sharp tumbled rock, and now a shooting pain lanced his chest each time he took a breath. Something inside him was torn or broken.

Al-Mukhtar recoiled from Katsaros' still form. "She's abandoned the body! Quick!"

John took a quick, stabbing breath and spoke into the storm—spoke the words he had been told to speak, without thought, too wrapped up in pain and urgency to say anything else: "Hear me, Lilith! Your time in this city is over. Depart to the place that has been prepared for you."

Above them, a red glow broke through the darkness of the storm. Unearthly fire outlined Lilith's true shape, visible at last; a woman with vast black wings and a feathered body. Her hands and feet were claws, and lightning played around her talons as she laid an arrow to her bow.

"This is my time of power, you fool," she said as she took aim. "If it were this easy, it would have been done long ago."

Exhausted and aching, John knew he could not escape that dart. Yet as Lilith loosed the arrow, and he braced himself for the blow, Soraya threw herself between them. The arrow passed through her and vanished. Soraya fell to the ground, both hands clutching at her breast, shivering and weeping. Without thinking John scrambled across the rocks to her and pulled her hands away from her chest, feeling frantically for blood on her clothing. "Soraya! Are you hurt?"

Her words were a panicked flood. "I'm going to die. I'm going to hell. Oh, God…"

It wasn't her body that suffered; it was her spirit. He laid a hand on her forehead. "Soraya. Look at me. Breathe."

"No," she sobbed. "Run! Save yourself!"

Above, as Lilith drew her bow again, al-Mukhtar hurled his spear. It passed through her with no effect, clattering to the rocks. The next moment Lilith's bow sang and al-Mukhtar sank to the ground with a wail of something that might have been pain but more likely was despair.

Lilith looked at John, and to his dread, she smiled. Lowered her bow. Looked down at Soraya and al-Mukhtar lying upon the rocks in mindless terror, and said, "Well, John Bessarion. It's you and me now."

"I command you to depart," he said, through a dry throat.

"You don't really mean that." She drifted closer; her smile was shaky, but terribly sweet. "You say one thing, but your heart says another. Does it not?"

It was hard to breathe, hard to swallow. The doubts that had felt so distant a moment ago came flocking back like birds of prey. "I…" he began.

Lilith was close, too close, filling up the entire field of his vision. "All you have to do," she said, "is say the word."

She thrust out her hand, piercing through his chest and into his heart. The pain in his ribs flared into blinding agony, then faded away again.

John looked up, blinking. Instead of Lilith, a soft, rounded little woman with a sweet face and dark waving hair stood before him.

Rahel.

Her eyes filled with tears. "John…you've come home."

Was he dreaming? Rahel reached out slowly, her hand glowing faintly in the dark. Numbly, John reached out his fingertips to hers—and felt them touch. A *real* touch; the soft texture of her fingertips brushed against his. He gripped her hand with an agonised gasp, and she pulled at him with eager eyes. Behind her was a cool blue light. He took one, two, three steps forward and found himself in the atrium of his villa in Jerusalem. The night was warm and still around them; soft moonlight fell from the opening in the ceiling, reflecting from the pool at the centre.

"John," Rahel sobbed, her arms wrapping around his waist.

He was home. His arms tightened reflexively around her soft hair, the scent of crisp linen and rose water filling his head. He could touch her—he could feel her—he was *home.*

"John," she sobbed again, lacing her fingers into the hair at the back of his head and lifting her mouth to be kissed. But he stiffened a moment. Before he lost himself in Rahel, he must satisfy himself of one thing.

"The children?"

"Upstairs."

"Show me. Please."

She kissed his fingers swiftly and pulled him upstairs, nearly at a run. Here, on the loggia surrounding the courtyard, were the rooms occupied by the children. Paulus and Elisa were in bed, asleep. Lukas and Marta sat in his room with their heads together over a game of chess.

John watched them from the doorway as all the pent-up frustration of the last weeks trickled out of him again. He closed his eyes, resting his forehead against the lintel of the door.

All you have to do...

Rahel's whisper was in his ear, her fingers sliding across his back. "Are you happy, John Bessarion?"

He was unsure whether to laugh or cry. Instead, he turned and pulled her into his arms.

...is say the word.

"Yes," he whispered, "oh, yes..."

"There's something else you should see," she said, nestling against him like a bird and pointing. "Look up."

He did as she said, raising his eyes to the courtyard wall, and the shape of the skyline beyond. The moonlight was strong enough to illuminate a dome toward the east, covered in gold and shining like a pale beacon in the light of the moon from above, in the glow of braziers that surrounded its blue-tiled walls.

It was as beautiful as a dream. "A new basilica?"

"It's *our* basilica," she whispered to him, "Do you like it? It's to be consecrated tomorrow."

"Like it!" he whispered. It felt as though a hand had fastened around his heart, wringing. "It's more beautiful than I imagined—but how—"

"The war is over, John." She put her arms around his neck, and there was endless promise and hope in her eyes. "Jerusalem is ours again. The heretics are conquered; our children's patrimony is secure; and the future is in *your* hands."

His heart was too full for more. He was home, and everything was perfect, too perfect to be true.

He let out a sigh and twined his fingers into the silken masses of her hair, scattering kisses across her eyes, cheek, lips. He went in search of the familiar little brown mole at the nape of her neck where the fine black hairs began, longing to kiss the place.

In the moonlight and shadow he was having trouble finding it; and in the stillness of the night as he bent over her, he thought he felt an ache in his ribs.

From a distance came a sound of mourning.

"Who is that, weeping, below?" he murmured, brushing her hair aside.

She raked her fingernails gently across the back of his neck, making each hair stand on end. "That is only the heretic captives, love."

He straightened, frowning slightly. There was no sign of the mole; and the crying and wailing was pulling at him. He thought perhaps he knew those voices. "Why are they weeping?"

"They will not weep for long. Soon they will grow accustomed to being our slaves, and then they will be happy again." She stood up on her toes to kiss him. "Come to bed, my sweet. You shall see them in the morning on the way to the basilica."

Something was wrong; everything was wrong. If only he could remember what. There was a ghost of pain in his ribs; and John shook himself free of her suddenly, and rammed a fist against the ache.

Agony unfurled within him, the pain like a cleansing flame. When he came to himself he was on his hands and knees at her feet, each breath a knife in his lungs.

"John!" She fluttered over him, touching him gently. "You're hurt? What's wrong?"

He reached for her hands and helped himself up again, swaying a little. "I want to see them now," he said, "the prisoners."

"Why? You haven't even gone in to kiss your children."

She sounded hurt, as though she thought him heartless. John almost gave in to her request, but the cries from the courtyard forestalled him. He *knew* those voices. They took hold on his heart like verdant shoots in hard desert ground, flaying him open to the bloody core.

John took another deep, cleansing breath. "But how they weep, Rahel! Has no one done anything to comfort them?"

In her eyes, a flash of unaccustomed anger. "You ought not to heed them, John. A man who does not care for his own children is worse than an infidel."

If he was the kind of man to put his children's comfort above matters of right and wrong, he would never have confronted the council at Oliveta. All his arguments came back to him now, the ardent words he had spoken in defence of the heretics of the Empire. How he had ached for their persecutions. How he had breathed curses against the Watchers for their hard, dispassionate hearts, wondering how they could fail to feel as he did.

How blind could he have been, to feel this way about the heretics of the Empire, but not the heretics beyond? Were not they all made in God's own image?

John took another breath. He saw everything now with perfect, painful clarity. Rahel strained closer to him, and a chill of terror ran down his neck. Disengaging her clinging hands, he stepped backwards until he came up against the rail of the loggia.

"You are not my wife," he whispered. God help him! She was not even the creation of his own dreams.

"*They* are not your children."

"Yet the dogs under the table eat of the children's crumbs," he said, "and who am I to deny them that?"

She saw the intention in his eyes before he moved. "You've had a bad dream, John Bessarion," she said urgently, lunging forward with hands that suddenly looked too much like talons. But he was too quick for her. He threw himself over the baluster, and fell—and—fell—

—back into his waking body, on a dark rocky island in Tripoli in a storm. John staggered backwards, away from Lilith's grasping hands. Everything from his vision was gone; everything but the terrified sobs and gasps that came from Soraya and al-Mukhtar on the ground at his feet.

It was to the Chosen that Lilith pointed an angry talon. "You fool! Will you really turn your back on your own children for the sake of *that?*"

He was weary, he was in pain, he had not even the spirit to be angry with the demon for taking his wife's form, although he knew he would be angry with himself, later. He ought to have known—what blindness was upon him that he did not know it was Lilith haunting his dreams and befuddling his mind?

"No," he said with an effort.

A flicker of desperation passed through Lilith's eyes, and she extended a hand suddenly soft and white and inviting. "Then take my hand. I can send you home, and you shall have your heart's desire."

A hand wrapped around his ankle; and John looked down into Soraya's eyes. Wide open, sick with fear. "D-don't leave me."

He bent down, stroked her hair. The ghosts of his desire flocked around him with mournful whispers, but his heart was cracked open and green shoots were bursting from the dry ground. Lilith had tried to kill him, and failed. She had tried to seduce him, and failed. Now, in desperation, she was finally willing to present him with a free bargain. She would send him home and be glad to do it. But he could not accept it.

They are not my children, he'd told himself. Yet he had made promises to Soraya. Once, long ago, he'd made promises to another Soraya, and broken them. Was he truly any better than the Watchers he had confronted at Oliveta?

His fate lay before him like an open parchment waiting for the pen. And in the end, by the grace of that overheard weeping in the fool's paradise of Lilith's dream, the choice was an easy one. If he went home the easy way, he would no longer be the man Rahel—the *true* Rahel—loved. So he would stay, and remain himself.

Gently, he smoothed Soraya's hair from her forehead as though calming a frightened child. "Look up, Soraya," he whispered, "Look up and face your fears."

Her eyes rolled, white in the gloom and the red gleam of Lilith's wrath. John bent and kissed her forehead; then he stood and turned to face the demon.

"He who by death put death to death and by his rising granted life to all men: may the Lord rebuke thee, Lilith!"

She shrieked, drew her bow, and loosed an arrow towards him. But it shredded into nothingness before it reached him.

"I have no need of your help," John said softly. "Your reign is ended here; depart to the place that has been prepared for you. So be it."

Black wings unfurled and red fire flamed from Lilith's body. That monstrous, birdlike figure bent over them with sharp menacing talons, and at his feet, Soraya whimpered. With a growl of thunder, a gust of wind raced from the south and Lilith seemed to lose her footing. She staggered, writhed in vain.

Screaming, she lifted from the ground and scudded out across the water. White flame flickered on the waves as she went, and then a great wave plucked her from the sky and dragged her beneath the surface.

The sea boiled with white and red fire, building to a foaming upheaval before stilling itself again. The wind died. Silence and darkness fell upon the world.

Soraya gasped; a panicked, whooping sound that was loud in the sudden stillness. John took a long, painful breath, then stooped to his knees again and took her hand. "Breathe," he murmured. "Breathe. I have you, child. I'm here."

Little by little her breathing slowed. Nearby, rocks scraped as al-Mukhtar pulled himself up with shuddering gasps. At length Soraya sat up suddenly.

"You *refused* her?"

What could he say? He put a hand over his mouth, and found that it was shaking a little.

"Strike me blind, she could have sent you home! John, why?"

"And she might have sent me anywhere else." He took a deep breath, dragged a hand down his face, and repeated the words like a litany. "No. Rahel wanted this. Rahel *wanted* this."

Gradually, the storm was calming. In the new silence, a lantern came bobbing around the corner of the church, five Templars shouting and gesticulating. In the glare of the lantern-light, one of them looked familiar. John got wearily to his feet. "We have callers."

Al-Mukhtar jumped up, lowering his spear in their direction.

"No fighting!" John winced at the pain that shot through his ribs. "It's done. Lilith is gone. We're done."

A heartbeat passed; then another. After a moment, still shaken from the confrontation with Lilith, al-Mukhtar lowered his spear. "All praise to God." The Chosen turned towards the shore. "Soraya, leave the Watcher and come."

"What?" Soraya shrieked as her feet marched her after the mamluk.

"Al-Mukhtar!" John bellowed. "You made me a promise!"

The Chosen appeared not to hear. Instead he rapped his spear against the rocks, and Soraya collapsed into the shallows as he dragged her from her body. Al-Mukhtar plunged into the waves. John staggered after them a step or two, but a rock caught his toe, and he fell to his knees before the still, barely-cold corpse of Stephen Katsaros.

He was still looking down at the face of the dead man when lantern-light blazed into his eyes. A familiar voice gave vent to an explosive curse, and John looked up into the face of Sir Peter of Alba, whom he had first known as Butros, the caravan-guard.

The Frankish knight spat on the rocks. "Prester John. I ought to have known."

Chapter XXIX.

"Sir? Sir?" A hand descended onto Gerard's shoulder and shook. Fuzzily, he awoke.

"Is it dawn yet, Marco?"

"No, sir." The servant's voice was nervous. "It's…uh, it's news from Saint Thomas, sir."

Gerard snapped awake. "Devil take it, Marco, don't tell me something happened to her."

By the time Marco had got him dressed and led him down to the postern gate, dawn was showing in the sky. The storm that had raged for so much of the night seemed to have blown itself out, and Lady Margaret's ship waited in the harbour to leave with the tide at sunrise.

But its most precious cargo would not be aboard.

In the island basilica of Saint Thomas, the sand diviner's body lay before the altar, shrouded in an old cloak. Silently, Gerard examined the corpse. Apart from the patched gash in the old man's shoulder, there was nothing to explain his sudden death. A bloody tear in the man's tunic suggested a wound to the abdomen, but when Gerard ripped the tattered fabric a little further to examine the skin beneath, he found only a freshly-healed scar.

Mystified, he turned to face his captive.

Prester John sat with his back against a column, his arms wrapped protectively around his ribs. One of his exhausted grey eyes was developing a ring of deep purple bruising. Sir Peter of Alba stood over him with a grim smile, the Prester's twin crossbows hanging from his belt.

Yesterday, Lilith had said this man was a threat to her. Gerard had only half believed her then; he wasn't about to repeat the mistake now, for all the good it would do him.

"What happened here, precisely?"

The Prester looked at the corpse with haunted eyes. His voice was rasping, as though his throat had been damaged—evidently, Alba had indulged his sense of fun with this prisoner. "I tormented him to death."

"What?" Gerard asked blankly.

The Prester glanced up at him. "He was possessed by a demon. You see for yourself that he was weak, sick, malnourished—and she was driving him like a slave, making him fight." He swallowed, hard. "He was burned, pierced, God knows what else. He died very quickly when Lilith abandoned him."

"She abandoned him," Gerard repeated. "Where is she now, then?"

"The sea took her." On registering Gerard's puzzled look, the Prester put it more plainly. "She has gone from this world."

Gerard took a step towards the prisoner, his fists clenching. "Stand up," he said softly.

Though half a head shorter than Gerard and obviously in pain, the Prester held himself erect and looked the Frankish knight in the eye. In most men, that would be insolence, but this man...Gerard swallowed, struggling with the instinctive fear that he might be facing someone of far greater rank and power than himself.

"She has gone from the world," he repeated softly. "Not of her own free will, I think."

"No," the Prester agreed in a hoarse whisper.

There was no guilt, no anger, no trepidation in his eyes. Nothing but watchfulness. "Who *are* you?"

"I am John Zakar, a Prester of the Watchers."

There was truth in his voice and no information at all in his words.

"You're lying to me. That's not your real name."

"It is the one I use."

Gerard tried something different. "Tell me you can mend this. Tell me you will take this city under your protection, now that you have destroyed its guardian."

The Prester stared back at him with those blanched-grey eyes and that forbidding scowl. "I *exorcised* its *demon*."

"To what end? So that a legion worse than the first might swarm in?"

Before the Prester could reply, the door of the church slammed open, startling them both. Marco stood on the threshold, silhouetted against the growing morning light.

"Sir! Something is happening in the city."

Instantly Gerard hushed, hearing for the first time drums beating—thousands of drums. The sound wormed its way into his veins and boomed in his ears. "Saints," he breathed, hastening to the door.

Outside the church, the world was grey like iron and granite, from the tossing sea to the lowering sky and the gigantic sweep of the mountains beyond the city. Across the narrow strait, pale yellow flame leaped from the braziers on the city wall. Signals, calling for help from the ships waiting at anchor beyond the harbour—Templar vessels, Hospitallers, royal galleys of Cyprus—and far off on the edge of the horizon, the Genoese fleet.

The signal-fires only confirmed what he already knew: that Lilith's warning was about to come true. "They're storming the walls," he breathed.

Empty walls, now held by a fraction of the men that were needed. Broken walls, ground to dust after a month's constant bombardment. He'd known it was coming, he just never believed it.

It was too soon; Lady Margaret was still in the city.

He whipped around and found Peter of Alba standing behind him in the porch. Just behind, two of the Templar sergeants held John Zakar between them.

"We'll be wanted in the city, Montreal," said Alba calmly.

"Devil take it." Gerard stepped toward the Prester. "Did you know this would happen?

The man's eyes were bleak, devoid of triumph. He didn't answer; but it was as good as confirmation. Gerard turned to Alba. "Go, but see that the prisoner is confined in the Temple."

"Didn't you want him aboard the ship for Acre?"

Gerard hesitated for a bare heartbeat, a triple stroke of the hectic drums. Prester John, the saviour he'd sought so diligently, had damned Tripoli. He couldn't allow the man to do the same for Acre. "No," he said curtly. "If the city falls, better men will need the space. You can leave him to rot for all I care."

Snapping his fingers at Marco, Gerard headed for the shoreline where Usama waited to row them back to the postern gate. As the small vessel made its short trip, Gerard sat in the prow nursing his anger.

Only a handful of people had known where he had hidden the sand diviner yesterday, and only one of them was likely to have given such information to the Prester. Gerard pulled his cloak around his ears, glared through the dim morning light at his servant. "So much for your Prester John, Marco."

Marco gulped and glanced away, at the steadily approaching wall. His voice was unnaturally high. "Sir?"

The servant's awkward posture screamed his guilt, and Gerard's heart, which had been hot with anger, chilled with a sick sense of betrayal. So this John Zakar had stolen his servant as well as his last hope for saving Acre. He cleared his throat and spoke a little too harshly to be sincere. "Don't apologise; you couldn't possibly have foreseen his betrayal."

Marco looked at him again, almost agonised, but he said nothing, though Gerard waited. And so, as the boat worked its way across the strait, he held his hurt as close as a ball of cool glass in summer.

Between himself and Marco, Usama worked the oars, his head bent as usual. Once, his eyes flicked up, looking Gerard in the face for a brief moment before dropping again.

There was some elusive emotion in that glance. Hope, perhaps. Usama was a slave; if the Egyptians got into the city, he would be freed. Gerard shivered, deciding to have Usama confined too as soon as they reached the Temple.

His mission, his very future was unravelling around him. No matter. He was still going to fight. *Each man the architect—*

The boat bumped the quay outside the postern, interrupting the thought.

Shaking a little with nervous tension, Gerard climbed out. Tide was high; Lady Margaret's ship must leave shortly or risk being becalmed within engine-shot of the Saracen army as they pounded their way through the defences. One large enough stone missile, one fire-jar, and defeat would quickly transmute into death.

"Don't lock the postern," Gerard directed, as he led the way through the tunnel that pierced the wall.

Marco pocketed the key and jogged after him as Gerard lengthened his stride. The drums were still pounding, the streets scoured empty as the remaining people of Tripoli took refuge in homes and cellars. At Lady Margaret's house the gate stood open, fresh horse-droppings in the courtyard hinting at a mass exodus.

"Ho!" Gerard called, banging a fist on the open gate. "Porter! Anyone!"

No answer. Already at the harbour, then. Gerard quickened to a jog down the deserted Fish Street towards the water gate, Marco and Usama on his heels. Halfway down the street, as he passed the Templar commandery, he was hailed by Marshal Geoffrey of Vendac. The high-ranking knight emerged from the gate leading a small band of ten Syrian mercenaries with crosses stitched to their gambesons.

"Montreal! I need Alba!" he called as Gerard stopped to order Usama back to his quarters.

Gerard turned. "Alba's on his way with the sergeants, sir."

Vendac's eyes narrowed as Gerard made to continue down the Fish Street. "Where are you going? You're needed at the breach."

"I know, sir. I'll be there in a moment." Gerard bowed and hurried on before the marshal could issue an order. As a confrere of the Temple, he was not part of the strict hierarchy that governed its brother knights. Still, he couldn't risk antagonising the highest ranking brother-knight in the city. To his relief, the footsteps behind him marched away in the direction of the wall, the drums, and the sounds of battle.

The screams of men, the crash of steel—it was a sound that made all his blood run hot and cold with terror and the will to fight. On an empty stomach, it made him queasy. Devil take it! For all the good he'd done in

Tripoli, he would have been better off fortifying himself behind his desk in Acre, working on his history.

As he'd feared, the water gate was a solid mass of people, their arms filled with bundled possessions, shoving and yelling in an attempt to get through and buy passage on whatever ships might be willing to take them. Bypassing the worst of the crush, Gerard fought through the crowd to the gatehouse. "Has the Lady of Tyre embarked? Has anyone seen her?"

The harassed guard barely spared a glance for him. "Friend, I wouldn't have seen the Queen of Sheba if she'd been doing a veil dance on the battlements."

That gave him an idea—the battlements, not the veil dance—and Gerard dashed for the stairs leading up to the parapet. Beyond, the quay was chaotic with people pushing and shoving. A handcart had upended into the water, strewing some poor family's goods across the rocks below. As distant galleys made their stately way towards the city, Lady Margaret's ship drew away from the quay to make room for them, its deck crowded with people and belongings.

At its mast fluttered the arms of Tyre, but if Lady Margaret was aboard, her personal standard should be flying: the arms of Antioch-Lusignan. Gerard's hand clenched on the parapet. Perhaps in the chaos of boarding so many fugitives, her personal standard had simply been forgotten.

Perhaps, but he didn't think so.

Gerard whisked around, coming face to face with Marco who stood catching his breath at the head of the stairs. For an instant, that ache of betrayal bubbled to the surface. *You did this.*

Marco paled. "Sir, please..."

Beyond the servant, thin and faint in the turbulent air came the blast of one horn and then a thousand others. The drumbeat paused, then thundered on with a new, more hectic note.

Gerard found he was waiting with a dry throat, watching the city's far wall and the silent siege engines beyond. Of course there was nothing to see: the battle would be fought on the ground, at the level of the breaches in the wall. The tenements, warehouses, churches and palaces of Tripoli blocked his view. Beyond, on the hillside of Mount Pilgrim, the captured fortress of Saint-Gilles was a black threat that gave no sign of the sultan's intent.

That fortress, with its conqueror's flag drifting above it, was built a hundred and ninety years ago to take this very city. From it, nearly two centuries later, the city would be taken again.

Marco grabbed Gerard's arm in a pincer grip and pointed towards the mountains. "Sir! *Do you see that?*"

The morning sun had lifted its head above the Lebanon mountains, flooding the coast with a slow tide of gold through a distant gap in the eastern clouds. Gerard blinked three times, straining his eyes to make out a black silhouette against that dazzling sunrise. It flew nearer, a monstrous shape riding a wolf that raced through the air toward the encircled city. A bow was in his hand, a full quiver on his back. One eye stared from his forehead, and the other from the centre of his chest. Covered in hair, like the wolf he rode, his body glowed in the sunlight.

The demon alighted on the roof of the palace, lifted his hands to his mouth and uttered a terrifying howl. Every hair on Gerard's neck rose as the Saracen horns sounded in reply. A moment later it began: the shrieks and screams of a city's death.

Lilith was gone. And in her place, *this* had come.

The Saracens were inside the walls.

"To the palace," Gerard said shakily. He bolted downstairs.

Between them, Marco and his Prester had doomed the city. All Gerard could do now was get Lady Margaret to safety.

Chapter XXX.

Soraya was left to chafe and worry, blind and helpless, for only a short time before Saif's command once more propelled her from confinement. Perhaps he had grown accustomed to her presence.

"You made a *promise*," she spat as soon as she was capable of speech.

He didn't answer at once, and as Soraya's surroundings came into view, she fell silent in surprise—and dread.

Early morning light streamed in at the window of an empty house that stood just inside the city's great south gate. Like most of Tripoli's fine houses, this one seemed to have been hastily abandoned. Heavy cabinets and chests stood empty, ajar. A thin linen veil lay across the great canopied bed, which was otherwise stripped of its blankets. A smashed lamp had rolled to one corner, scattering shards of terracotta and pools of hardened oil underfoot. Perhaps the place had been looted, or perhaps its owners had rifled through it before taking ship; it was impossible to tell.

A window was open. Next to it, atop a carved wooden chest, stood Saif's silver scrying-bowl. Today it was full of water, casting a splash of shimmering light on the plastered ceiling, and Saif bent over it speaking quietly with his master. Through the window, too loud, too close, flowed the sound of drums pounding the assault, the streets echoing with shouts and the clash of steel.

Outside, the tumult rose to a peak as war-cries and wailing mounted—and suddenly swept nearer. Saif stiffened like a dog at point, turning to look out the window.

"Glory to God, the wall is breached!" he cried, in a voice too loud for that small upper room. Immediately he threw a bundled cloth out the window. Folds of rich emerald green drifted lazily on the morning wind. A signal.

Soraya stood transfixed, listening to the noise of hard battle that now filled the streets. No doubt the city's defenders were rallying in a desperate attempt to force a retreat or else provide time for those who remained in the city to make their escape. The dreadful cacophony of shouting, screaming, pounding, and crashing steel continued; it went through her like a knife. She had no particular stake in this battle, but instinctively she recognised the sounds. They filled her mouth with blood, her gut with bile, her heart with despair.

Oh John, she thought desperately, *where are you? Was this what you feared?*

The sound retreated a little and Saif slammed first the shutters, then the glass casement. It was to the scrying-bowl that he spoke as he turned, revealing a face taut with stress. "She's here, my lord."

"Have the djinn approach," a man's voice replied.

That voice was muffled and indistinct, yet Soraya's gut slithered with cold dread. Again, instinct told her she knew that voice intimately. Knew it. Feared it. Hated it.

"Come," Saif said, and she had no choice. Her feet marched her over to the bowl of glowing water.

The face in the water was blurred a little, its outlines different somehow to what she had expected, in a way that filled her with formless alarm. Yet the voice was the same, and now that she knew there was magic in the room, something in her spirit recognised his.

Khalil ibn Hassan. The name John had spoken last night at the public-house resurfaced from the shadows of memory. Saif's master; the sorcerer who had trapped and bound her within the narrow circumference of a carnelian ring.

"This one has always tried to betray me," the hateful voice said. "Command her to tell the truth."

"Our master has questions for you, Soraya," Saif said quietly. "You will speak honestly."

A little more panic unfolded in her gut. Saif must have told Khalil about her alliance with John Zakar, and this was the reckoning. Lilith might be gone—but the spectre of last night's fear raised its head, and Soraya's body responded instinctively with a racing heart and the certainty of doom.

She was a djinn, she was damned. She, like Lilith, was only one misstep away from the fires of hell.

"Please, please don't cast me out," she whispered. "I'll do whatever you ask."

"Stop snivelling," Khalil ordered. "Is it true that the soul jar was broken by a Watcher two nights ago?"

The question caught her by surprise. "Yes, my lord."

"Is it true that al-Mukhtar then had the Greek sand diviner exorcised?"

Soraya looked up at Saif in astonishment. He didn't meet her eyes, let alone Khalil's. Sweat sheened his forehead as he stared at his feet.

Well, strike me blind. This interrogation was for *him,* not her.

"Well?"

Her fear retreated. "Yes, my lord. That happened last night."

"Who performed this exorcism?"

Soraya didn't know what Saif might already have told Khalil, but she wasn't going to volunteer any more information than was strictly necessary. "A Watcher, my lord."

Too late, Saif was looking at her with blank terror in his eyes. Khalil spoke in a soft, menacing voice that sent fear skittering up and down her spine.

"Saif."

The mamluk swallowed hard, came to peer into the bowl beside her. "Yes, my lord?"

"Let us be perfectly clear." The sorcerer enunciated each word hard and sharp like cut glass. "You failed to carry out my instructions in trapping Lilith. You kept that failure a secret from me. Then, rather than report for new instructions, you took matters into your own hands. You allied with a *Watcher* and *lied* about it."

Lied—Soraya nearly choked on her own astonishment.

Saif had omitted to tell Khalil about John at all.

She had just unwittingly betrayed John's existence.

Damn it—damn *her!*

"With the result," Khalil finished, "that Lilith, the objective of your mission, is now entirely beyond my reach."

This close, Soraya could smell Saif's sweat. He swallowed hard before replying. "God forgive me! I made a mistake, but it was an honest one. I truly thought the purpose of Lilith's capture was the capture of Tripoli."

"I didn't raise you to *think,* boy," Khalil snarled. "I raised you to follow orders. I don't give a damn about Tripoli; I wanted Lilith."

There was a strained silence.

"Well?"

"Forgive me," Saif whispered.

"You're straying from the right path." Khalil paused. "Perhaps it's time your memories were purged."

Saif looked up from the bowl and for one startling, vertiginous moment, his eyes met Soraya's. There was fear in them; horror layered beneath dark resignation.

He knows what it's like.

How often has this been done to him? Does he, too, yearn for what he has lost?

In that unguarded, unspoken moment there was nothing to feel but compassion. Soraya was relieved when Saif looked back down, at Khalil. "Please. No. I'll obey without question; try me. I don't want to forget anything else."

Khalil scowled. "The sultan has sworn to destroy Tripoli. Help him. Kill them all. If I hear a good report of you, perhaps we shall discuss your memories."

The sorcerer's hand lifted, scattering a white powder across the surface of the water. Soraya and Saif found themselves staring into a simple silver bowl as grains of salt obscured the fading image.

Saif turned away, running trembling hands through his hair. Soraya collapsed onto the bedframe, still shaken by that one, brief moment of compassion she'd felt for him.

Perhaps they weren't so different, after all. Yet the thought brought little comfort. In this world's vicious hierarchies, those who exploited others would be exploited in turn by those above them, and so on, in an unbreakable chain that stretched down to the worms and up to God himself. She and Saif might share one scant moment of fellow-feeling, but deep down he would always put his faith in that bloody chain, for it gave him some measure of power. He might be subservient to Khalil; but he had the consolation of being ruler over her. And so the chain held, and so it bound the world.

Perhaps, to see how cruel it really was, you had to be at the very bottom of it all, without even command of yourself. Without a voice; without hope.

A mute and bitter wisdom.

Across the room, Saif let out a deep breath, and Soraya felt the soul tether pull taut as he turned to face her. She looked up, feeling oddly deflated. "What is it?"

He scowled. "Last night, when we were fighting Lilith…" The soul tether pulled harder, shredding her grip on her body. "You tried to fight me."

For a few moments, she'd resisted his pull on the soul tether. "I was *helping* you."

"Your duty is to *obey* me."

Soraya smiled bitterly. "You sound just like him; do you realise that?"

"Is that meant to be an insult?"

"That depends on whether you *want* to be like him. Do you?"

"Of course."

"Then why did you lie to him? Why didn't you tell him about John?"

Saif swallowed, hard. "I'm in enough trouble as it is. If he knew I'd promised safe-conduct…to a Watcher, and a Zakar, he…I…" He looked away and said very softly, "Someone I love will die…and if he takes away my memories, I might not even remember."

A raw, bloody silence followed his words.

Saif was behaving strangely today: he'd been off-kilter, *terrified,* ever since he called her into life. Now these words flew to her like a bird seeking a place to rest and Soraya recoiled a step. "What is that supposed to mean?"

Everything was riding on this mission, he'd said yesterday.

What did he mean, someone he loved? Saif loved no one. Saif was incapable of love. *She* should know.

He took a deep, shaking breath. "That djinn last night did something to me. Did you feel it too?"

She didn't want to be in this conversation: he kept handing her bloody gobbets of his heart and she didn't want to be reminded that he was only another stupid mortal, with a heart, with a soul, with choices that were denied to her.

But oh, they were in uncharted waters now. Perhaps she might offer him her hand. Perhaps that chain might break. Perhaps, together, they might escape Khalil.

And perhaps, once the sultan conquered Tripoli, he'd confirm the liberties of the barons, distribute grain to the poor, and they'd all gather in the cathedral and perform *salat* prayers together. But Soraya didn't think so.

Instead she said, "I wasn't asking about your piffling self-doubts. I was asking what Khalil has against Watchers and Zakars."

The words hit him like a slap in the face. Saif straightened a little, and his cheeks flushed faintly red. Soraya felt a guilty relief flow through her as they found their feet on familiar ground again.

"The Watchers have always been the Master's sworn enemies, and the Zakars have always been the worst of the Watchers. I have standing orders to kill both." He gulped. "The only way this could be worse would be if the man turned out to be John Bessarion himself. The Master would have my head."

Another twinge of memory struck her. *Bessarion*—that *name*—but Saif was watching her, and she didn't dare to let him know it meant something to her. Even if she didn't know *what* it meant.

"I don't think you need to worry," she said with savage irony. "You might have omitted to murder him last night, but why brood on your failures? You still broke your word of honour and abandoned him to the Templars. I'm sure he'll be dead by nightfall."

Saif looked uncertain. "You...you think abandoning him was the right decision?"

"Oh, God." She lifted her eyes to the heavens.

He flushed again and spoke defensively. "What if I did break my word to him? God is merciful, and like you said, he'll be dead by evening. It's no shame to me."

Perhaps there was still a chance to save John Zakar, after all. "Isn't it? *You'll* know you broke your word, even if no one else does. *I'll* know. *God* knows. Every djinn, every afrit will see the breach in your spirit, and *they'll* know."

He shivered slightly.

"Don't you know that's how they get in?" she went on, remorselessly. "Remember what happened to you last night. Imagine being tormented like that again…"

"There is no God but God, the Alive, the Eternal…," he muttered through pale lips. It was the Throne Verse, a protection against evil spirits. "Are you trying to frighten me?"

"I'm warning you. What's the use of having a djinn as a slave if you won't listen to her?"

Outside, the sound of battle had gradually withdrawn deeper into the city. Now, before Saif could answer her question, someone called out from the courtyard below the house. Saif threw the window open again and leaned out, calling out directions.

Evidently, the signal he'd hung from his window had been answered.

As footsteps echoed in the house below them, Saif turned from the window, looking a little more like his old self again. Decisive. Confident.

"I didn't save John Zakar last night because he was injured, and the Templars were already on top of us. I meant to go back for him, and that's what I'm going to do, God willing."

Soraya couldn't risk letting her feelings show on her face, but she was glad to be sitting down. She felt weak with relief. "Even though he's a Watcher and a Zakar?"

Saif breathed deeply and nodded. "Everyone else in this city is about to be taken captive or put to the sword. I have sworn it to my master and I will faithfully perform it. But first, I will keep my word to John Zakar."

The door opened, and a pair of armed manservants staggered in carrying a chest. Having deposited it on the floor, they made obeisance to Saif. He threw back the lid, revealing silver mail, black silk, and a slim straight sword—the regalia of a warrior.

From the sound of battle outside, he would have to fight his way across the city. He would get a great deal of blood on his hands; and perhaps the temptation to abandon John would become too strong. "Let me come with you," Soraya begged. Frowning slightly, she manipulated the flesh of her body until it had taken the form of a man. "I won't be a liability to you, I swear."

He looked up at her quizzically—and then, to her great relief, he sighed and nodded.

Chapter XXXI.

John heard the sounds of pillage long before they reached the Templar commandery.

They came muffled to his ears through the grilles at head-height in his cell. These gave onto the street, allowing light and dust and screams to filter through into the small storage-room where he sat in company with dusky shapes that might have been hogsheads full of wine or preserved olives. Motes of dust drifted wearily in the thin stream of morning light, and a cacophony of shouts and shrieks echoed among them.

That was no battle going on outside. Instead, he could hear slamming doors, running feet, the crackle and roar of flames. The war drums had fallen silent as Tripoli gave up her people to the sack. In place of drums, a many-throated scream filled the air.

The Zakar children were somewhere out there in the midst of it. Hiding, he hoped, and safe for the moment.

Waiting for help that would never come.

John turned from the grilles and threw himself at the door, a stout oaken stopper in a room carved from stone. Pain shot through his ribs and up his arms as he pounded his fists against that unyielding surface. "Let me out! Let me go!"

No answer.

He fell back, cradling his ribs with a groan. He felt like an animal in a cage at a slaughterhouse, unable to do anything but wait as the butchers came closer. He'd heard what the Egyptian sultans had done to other cities they'd taken—the huge numbers of people enslaved or killed, the city left in ruins.

Al-Mukhtar had betrayed him. John gritted his teeth. He'd known it would end like this; yet he had still run his neck willingly into the noose. What had he been thinking, making alliances with the enemy when the Zakars' blood still called for vengeance?

Yet his sense of betrayal ran deeper still.

The Watchers had hoped he might save their city, and so, when Lilith had offered him the one thing he truly wanted in this world, he had turned her down. He had accepted that Soraya, the Watchers, the Zakars, and others here in Tripoli were *his* people, not just strangers he could abandon and forget.

And he had failed them.

He hadn't even been able to save the life of that poor old sand diviner. Again, guilt racked him. Who was he becoming? He had put his days of cruelty and bloodshed behind him; or so he had thought. When had he started going down this path? Was it yesterday at the House of Botron when he'd let the blood-drinker out of its cage? Or had it in truth been months ago, at Yarmouk, when he'd perjured himself for a chance at victory?

Outside, the nightmare went on. The scent of smoke and blood tainted the air, trickling through the vents. John covered his ears with his hands so that he could not hear the shrieks, and in the privacy of confinement, he shrank against the wall and wept.

A wave of utter exhaustion passed over him as the tension of the previous night dissipated. John felt perfectly empty, like a pot that had been scraped out. This was an exhaustion that went beyond his body and mind and into his very soul, for he realised now that he had been fighting a terrible battle for the last six weeks: Lilith exploiting his own weaknesses against him in his dreams.

He found himself, after a little while, speaking aloud to a hearer not physically present.

"But *why*, Sir?"

No answer came.

"I only meant to defend my people. I only *ever* meant well. And now two cities are destroyed because of me."

Not by his own hand, at least. John had not induced Khalil to destroy Oliveta. John had not promised to destroy Tripoli, nor stood by idle for years while Lilith created war and set all the Frankish factions at each others' throats.

Yet the things he *had* done, the people he'd tormented and killed, rose up before his eyes. Once he had comforted himself with the knowledge that he was no longer the same man who'd slain men coldly in battle, or thrown heretics in prison and confiscated their lands.

After Katsaros, he wasn't so sure. John dragged his hands down his face. Death would, at least, be a respite. Dead, he could do no more harm.

"What about my children, Lord?" he whispered, his gut churning with worry. "Who will care for them if I don't return? Who will care for Palestine?"

Leave thy fatherless children, I will preserve them alive; and let thy widows trust in me.

He leaned his head back against the hogshead, shutting his eyes. "All right. All right. I can leave them in your hands a little longer. But what good can I do when I am dead? *For the grave cannot praise thee, death cannot celebrate thee.*" He dug into his pouch, found the wax-sealed packet that he kept there, and held it out on his palms like an offering. "Is Rahel's vision never to be? Why would you give us such tools if we are never to use them?"

Why, indeed?

The silence echoed his thoughts back to him; echoed and echoed until he took them up. Why, indeed? There had to be a reason he was here in Tripoli at this moment.

He was hollow and spent in his spirit, but at least with Lilith gone he could think clearly again. Perhaps these people were not *his* children, *his* Watchers; but they were still his responsibility. It was surely no mistake, after all, that Elisa Zakar shared a name with his own child. She was not his blood, but she needed his help as though she was his own child—more, for she no longer had parents of her own.

As did the other Watchers trapped in this city. As did Soraya.

"But how?"

He opened his eyes and found himself speaking to an empty room. There was not even the faintest brush of another personality against his own now. Wiping the edge of his sleeve along his damp eyes, he shoved the sealed packet back into his pouch.

"Al-Mukhtar," he murmured, as all his terror fixed on a single focal point.

The Chosen had enslaved Soraya, slaughtered the Zakars, betrayed John and plotted against Tripoli. He had sold himself to Khalil, stolen the spear, destroyed cities.

If John had been brought to this time for a purpose, no doubt it was to destroy al-Mukhtar, Qeteb, and the master who linked them both. At present he was much too exhausted to face one such as Qeteb, and Khalil was far away in Cairo. But al-Mukhtar was here in Tripoli, and John prayed he would not die until he had faced the Chosen again.

The stench of smoke grew stronger as ash and embers began to fall like snow in the street beyond the grille. With it, the storm of chaos that had swallowed Tripoli reached the Templar commandery at last.

It began with shouts and pounding feet, a black storm of purposeful sound that flashed about the edges with high-pitched, terrified screams. At the commandery's stout gate, wood cracked and split under the blows of axes and the crash of battering rams. By now, every able-bodied man must have died on the wall or fled to the harbour, and there could be precious few men left to defend the Temple fortress. In less time than John would have believed possible, he heard heavy footsteps thumping through the courtyard. A cacophony of screams broke out as the enemy found their way into the infirmary.

Shakily, John got to his feet and paced the small room, caught between helplessness and frustration. How could he save himself? Even if his aching ribs allowed free movement, his bows had been taken by the Templars. He was practically defenceless.

Presently, muffled footsteps sounded beyond the door. A key rattled in the lock, and John turned to the door, making the sign of the cross.

The door burst open, but the man who entered was a Frank. Recognising him, John recoiled a step. Lilith might have bruised his ribs, but the black eye, the bruised throat, and more than a few other aches and pains were courtesy of Butros.

Now the Frank stared at him wildly down the length of a drawn sword. "You're in league with them, aren't you?"

John stood on the edge of death already, and he'd not yet laid eyes on a single Saracen. "Never," he said in a dry mouth.

"You're lying," said Peter of Alba between gritted teeth. He lowered his sword and lunged for John, grabbing him by the front of his tunic. "You caused this massacre; now you're going to get me out of here alive."

John tried to remain calm. "I can't. None of them know me from Adam."

The larger man shook him. "You *helped* them."

He had no answer to that. Perhaps he *had* helped the Saracens, but that didn't mean he was one of them, any more than yesterday's brief alliance with al-Mukhtar meant the Chosen was casting his loyalties in with the Franks.

That was something that Butros—Alba—had never understood. In his eyes, it seemed, you had to be either for him and his party or against them—as though he was the fulcrum on which the world turned.

Voices in loud Arabic floated down the stairs leading to the submerged corridor that held his cell. "He went down here! Maybe he's headed for the treasury!"

Alba muttered a curse and dragged John out of his cell, holding his sword like a bar at John's throat. Two blood-speckled Saracen soldiers in striped tunics and white trousers clattered down the stairwell to face him. They came to a stop when they saw John and Alba, surprise chasing curiosity across their faces.

"I want safe-conduct!" Alba shouted, much too close to John's ear. "Do as I say, or I'll kill your man here."

"Oh! He's one of ours, is he?" the foremost of the Saracens asked.

Without an instant's hesitation the second lifted a short bow of horn and loosed an arrow. John felt it hiss past his cheek and heard a wet crunch as it pierced Alba's eye. The sword clattered to the ground at John's feet, and a moment later the Frank fell to the flagstones behind.

It was not how he'd imagined meeting the besieging army.

"I'm looking for that treasury," the bowman said, lowering his weapon and brushing past John, stepping across the body. His friend faced John with a flash of smiling teeth. "So you're one of ours? Tell me, how many Gods do you worship?"

Here was something that remained the same, no matter the passage of time, John thought. In his youth, in the wars with the heathen Persians, it had been a question of emperors. Did you owe allegiance to Heraclius or to Khosrau? Later, when the emperor set him to hunting heretics, it was a matter of Gods and catechisms. What difference was there? He'd long ceased to believe that God really delighted in the slaughter of rival worshippers. Which meant that all his life, John had sent immortal souls to Hades, not in God's service, but in the service of a hubristic emperor who covered over his fear and weakness by claiming to be something close to divinity.

Well. He might not be required to kill for a creed, but he must still die for it.

"There is one God only, in three persons: Father, Son, and Holy Ghost."

"Well, son of a shoe!" the Egyptian said.

He looked John up and down, calculation in his eyes.

Briefly, John made some calculations of his own. The other man stood less than a lunge away, his bow sheathed and the point of his sword touching the floor. John might seize that wrist with his left before the man came on guard. With his right, he could snatch an arrow from the quiver at the Egyptian's side, plant it somewhere in the man's unprotected eye or throat. With luck, the rush of battle would dull the pain in his own ribs.

And then he might rush out the door and be instantly felled by the other Saracens without, having shed all that blood for nothing. So, when the other man reached out to grab him by the front of his tunic, John made no move to defend himself. He only braced himself for instant death.

Instead, the Saracen grabbed John and hauled him out of the cell, shoving him towards the steps that led up into the Templars' courtyard.

John went unresistingly. Outside, the sky was yellow and filthy with smoke: Tripoli was on her funeral pyre. The courtyard buzzed with activity. Egyptian warriors were everywhere, swarming throughout the massive fortress complex, breaking open doors and overturning furniture. There was a shout from above, and two men heaved a chest over the railing into the courtyard, where it split open to reveal documents and gold. Others swept it hurriedly onto a growing heap of plunder: armour, weapons, books and clothing. Crumpled shapes littered the courtyard in thickening, fly-speckled pools of their own blood—mostly the servants of the Order. Butros seemed to have been the sole knight in charge of an empty commandery.

His captor pulled him towards a ring of prisoners kneeling on the ground—human plunder to match the pile of armour and money. They hadn't yet crossed the courtyard when jubilant cheers broke out, and a shabby column of chained men emerged from an underground room. Despite their chains, their faces lit up in bliss as they emerged into the courtyard and the embraces of their rescuers.

Saracen slaves, John thought wearily. Of course.

At the forge, a Frankish blacksmith was ordered to start striking off their chains. Immediately, a burly Turkish mamluk dragged one of the Frankish prisoners over to the anvil, so that the irons could be transferred from one set of captives to another.

As the Saracen shoved John towards the kneeling circle of captives, one of their guards curled a lip. "What are you thinking? This one is worthless!"

The two men inspected him. John's captor's face fell. "He looked younger in the dark."

"They'll be selling boys for dirhems in the souks tomorrow. Good ones, young ones, cheap as dirt. Best put him down."

"He might be somebody," said the man who had killed Butros, hopefully.

"What's his name?" the guard asked.

He needed to stay alive—but how could he convince them? "I am John Zakar."

The first guard snorted. "Nobody. Thought so. You won't even get a ransom for him."

John's captor swore and stepped away. "Fine, you deal with him. I'm going to see if they've found the treasury yet."

With a grimace of annoyance, the guard took a step back, reaching for the short sword at his hip.

John had a wife and children, and a province that needed him, and he still meant to find his way back to them. Ten paces away to his right, the courtyard gates stood open like a promise of freedom; he must act now or die.

He lunged forward, driving his left fist straight for the Saracen's jaw. The other man's eyes widened and he dodged to the right—just in time to meet the piledriver of John's right to his gut, followed by a knee to the groin for good measure.

The Saracen's body was defended by strips of tough leather, and agony shot through his fist, as well as his ribs. Battling through the pain, John reached for the guard's sword hilt as the man collapsed. Within two heartbeats of his first movement he had the sword drawn and circled to face the nearest guard, the one that had asked his name.

"Listen, friend," John gasped, "I only want to leave."

Backing away, the second guard let out a piercing whistle that cut through the commotion in the courtyard and attracted the attention of the whole company. For an instant there was silence, and John went into a fighter's crouch, opening and closing his aching fingers on the sword's grip in the hope of restoring them to full capability.

He waited for the rush, but it never came. Instead, every man reached for bow and arrow.

If he couldn't turn the tables somehow, they'd shoot him dead where he stood. "Wait!" he called. "I am John Zakar, and I'm under the protection of the Chosen!"

Behind him, a bowstring twanged. In a desperate attempt to protect his vitals, John twisted towards the sound. Agony shot through his injured ribs, stealing his sight. At the same instant the arrow thudded home, nailing his right arm to his body just beneath the bicep. He'd thought he was prepared, but no one could really prepare for a length of barbed steel and wood through the body. The pain was cold, numb, nauseous.

His sword fell from nerveless fingers and clattered to the ground. John followed a moment later, sinking to his knees.

"Stop!" a familiar voice commanded. "Bows *down*."

With a groan of mingled pain and surprise, John looked towards the courtyard gate. Al-Mukhtar was dressed like a ghost or avenging angel, in a black silk tunic over shining steel vambraces, a vest of silver lamellar armour defending his torso. A pointed steel cap covered his head; from it hung a supple veil of linked steel that concealed his face, leaving only two green-grey eyes visible.

"He is telling the truth." The Chosen's commanding voice filled the silence his appearance had conjured. "This man is under my protection."

Bows creaked as they were lowered. John gasped again, fighting shock as his wound began to throb. Then a hand settled on his uninjured shoulder, and a new voice murmured, "Hold still."

John looked up into eyes he knew in a face he didn't. Young. Male. But clad in that familiar brilliant emerald green. The young Saracen reached down to pull his arm away from his body where the arrow had skewered the limb, its point wet with blood where it had dug an inch or so between John's already tender ribs. As the newcomer frowned with concentration, John's arm warmed, and the arrow moved: first the arrowhead dropped to the ground, and then the shaft drew smoothly from the wound. With it came a slow trickle of blood, but the Saracen was ready with a clean cloth to stanch it.

"Soraya!" John murmured, only faintly surprised as she wrapped the wound. He'd never seen her wearing a male body before. The face and voice were different, unrecognisable. But the eyes and the manner were the same, and John didn't know anyone else who could remove an arrow like this.

"Hold still," she repeated. "I've drawn out everything that wasn't already a part of you—it will heal clean, if you take care of it."

As Soraya finished tying off the makeshift bandage, the Chosen stalked through the courtyard to face him. With an effort, John clawed back his grip on consciousness and got to his feet—trembling, but wrathful. "Is this how you keep your promises? You swore me fifty souls."

"I am tardy," al-Mukhtar said with dignity, "not treacherous."

Soraya gave him an incredulous look.

Taking no notice, Saif twisted the carnelian ring from his finger. "Here is your token of protection."

Soraya's grip on his wrist tightened painfully, and John himself scarcely remembered to breathe. The ring in which Soraya was imprisoned—and al-Mukhtar was holding it out, as though he *wanted* John to take it.

"Choose your fifty and take them out to the orchards," al-Mukhtar went on in a level voice. "If anyone asks, they are my personal captives. You'll find my tent pitched with the rest of the army; my emblem—"

"He'll never make it with this hole in his arm," Soraya-the-boy said fiercely. "Let me go with him; I'll make sure they all reach the camp in safety."

"Very well," al-Mukhtar said after a moment's thought. His eyes narrowed at John, but he spoke to Soraya. "You have one hour, starting now. After that time, return for further orders."

"That's not enough time," Soraya objected.

John forced himself to concentrate, trying not to let the throb in his arm, the pang in his ribs distract him. "There are old. Feeble. Infants," he said. "Others who may be wounded. Please…"

"Two hours," al-Mukhtar said with a glance at the sky. "You have until midday prayers."

Abruptly he took John's left hand and placed the ring within the open palm. Then he turned on his heel and stalked towards the gate.

Beside him, Soraya closed her eyes and wilted a little in relief. Somewhat dizzy—whether with pain or with disbelief, he could not tell—John fitted the ring onto his own finger. "He just…"

"Gave it to us," she finished as his voice trailed away. "The key to my prison."

"Do you still feel the soul tether?"

Soraya nodded. "I'm bound so long as the ring is intact."

"Then let's get out of here so that we can destroy it." A moment ago, he'd been facing death. Now, perhaps, if he couldn't save Tripoli, he could at least save Soraya and the Zakar children—together with the other Watchers. Even better, someone had just dumped a familiar-looking pair of miniature crossbows onto the pile of loot. John limped over and collected one with his functioning left hand.

Instantly, Soraya was beside him. She grabbed the second weapon and the small quiver of bolts, loading it with a few quick, easy movements that would have been difficult even with two sound arms. John looked her up and down, noting that the jacket she normally wore had transformed into a man's tunic without losing either the embroidery or the intense colour.

"So green is your favourite colour, hmm?"

Her boyish smile was uncertain. "In the life I live, I don't get to hold onto many things." She glanced down at her unrepresentative body. "Not even my sex."

Handing him the loaded crossbow, she set to work on the other. John looked at the ring again, daring himself to believe. "Then come on. Let's build you a future worth keeping."

Her smile was hesitant, genuine, soft with hope; John had to wonder how long it had been since such a trusting expression had crossed her face. It pulled at his heart, filling him with fear.

Don't let me fail, he prayed as they ventured into the streets.

Following last night's storm, the wind had fallen. The smoke of Tripoli's burning brooded over her, a yellow veil before the distant sun. Beneath that covering, the Saracens went from house to house dragging goods and people out into the street. John's gut churned as he and Soraya passed huddled bodies crumpled on the cobblestones.

In his youth, before he had become husband or father, he'd seen similar things in the Persian wars at Jerusalem and Alexandria. It had been hard for a boy to bear then. Somehow, now, it was a hundred times worse.

He was only glad his stomach was empty.

"I don't understand Saif," Soraya mused aloud, as John turned down a narrow covered street in the hope of blocking out some of the sights, if not sounds. "First he was supposed to kill you, then he left you to the Templars, then he decided to let you go."

"Perhaps he's trying to salve his conscience," John rasped. "After all, he's responsible for *this,* isn't he?"

They emerged from the covered street, and John limped to a halt. It took him a moment to realise that the whimper of distress he heard was his own. A dozen children between six and thirteen had been herded into a line and roped together and now were being dragged down the street on their way to the Mamluk camp.

They'll be selling boys for dirhems... Good ones, young ones, cheap as dirt.

Suddenly his throat was dry. Matthias Zakar was just that age. He moved forward without thinking, until Soraya put a warning hand on his arm. "You've got Watchers waiting for you, haven't you?"

John took a deep breath, closing his eyes. Only yesterday he might have salved his conscience by telling himself they weren't his children. Now, it was nearly impossible to turn away and continue, but he took a deep breath and forced himself to walk on. There was nothing he could do to help them now. He had only fifty souls to save, and he had already promised to claim the Watchers.

A block of burning houses forced them to detour, as did a barricaded street where a small handful of Tripolitan citizens had chosen to die fighting. But at last they found their way to the dyehouse. It too was burning, flames crackling and smoke billowing from the lower windows.

John lifted both hands to his head and was instantly punished for it by the pain lancing through his wounded right arm. "Oh, God."

Soraya turned on him, her face blazing with purpose. "Where are they hiding?"

"One of the lower storerooms." John hurried into the factory courtyard, where the smoke made him cough, upsetting his ribs. Bursts of pain danced before his eyes; when it cleared, he took stock of the situation. The Saracens had certainly been here; all the carts were missing, and the windows were broken. Clutching his ribs, John headed towards the battered door, only to stop ten paces short of the threshold. Fiery heat radiated from the doorway, scorching his eyes even as he stared helplessly at the inferno within.

"Oh, God," he repeated in blank horror. He was too late.

"Wait." Soraya touched his arm. "I hear something."

John caught his laboured breath, and then heard it himself: a feeble cough. A moment later, he and Soraya were crouched over an iron grille at ground level on the other side of the courtyard. Making a fist, she punched through the metal as though it were paper. With a twist and wrench the whole grille came out. It was barely large enough for a child to get through.

"Hubert! Matthias! Are you in there? Are you safe?" John shouted into the thick, hot darkness.

"Prester," someone moaned.

John pulled back, nearly frantic with worry. "They'll suffocate. Is there anything you can do?"

Soraya cradled her bleeding hand to her breast. "Yes, but there's a chance I could bring down the whole building."

Better crushed in an instant than suffocated at tortuous length. John dragged a hand down his face with a whispered prayer. "Do it."

She gave a tight nod, pulling the turban from her head and wrapping her knuckles for protection. Then she knelt before the small opening, took a deep breath, and slammed her padded fist against the stone immediately above.

Cracks appeared in the cement. Soraya hunched over her fist, whimpering with pain.

"Soraya," John protested, but she shook her head at him. Her nostrils flared, and then her fist slammed home again. Mortar and rock cracked, and the stone moved an inch in its cradle. Instantly John called, "Stand away from the opening!" Swivelling onto his backside, he slammed his boot against the stone. Shockwaves travelled through his body, but the pain seemed far away. Once, twice—

The block came free and dropped into the darkness beyond. Instantly a crack ran up the wall, snaking between the stones with tiny puffs of dust and smoke. Beyond the wall came the grinding, cracking sound of a building settling under intense stress.

They must be using pretty inferior cement these days—and that meant he had no idea how much longer the building might stand.

"Quickly," Soraya said. Before John could move she had slithered feet-first through the enlarged space. "Stay there and help them out."

The Watchers were groggy and weak, half suffocated by the smoke. John pulled them out of that tiny hell one by one: men and women, young and old, from the Zakar children to Hubert himself. Elisa Zakar was nearly unconscious; he held her limp form for a moment, fiercely protective, before passing her to Anna. He counted forty-five rescues before a pale, muffled face reappeared at the opening and Soraya's male form squirmed through again.

"How are they?" she asked, pulling the tail of her turban more firmly around her mouth and nose.

"Sick," he said, nodding at the courtyard full of prone or sitting bodies.

The courtyard trembled under their feet. For a moment John thought it was an earthquake; but then a burning tenement on the skyline collapsed slowly in a cloud of stone, dust, smoke, and flames. In the roar of its falling stones, the dyehouse trembled and more cracks webbed across its wall.

Stone could not burn, but it would crack and warp in heat, and supporting timbers would be consumed to ash. John got painfully to his feet, clapping his hands like a shepherd with his flock. "Let's move," he said hoarsely. The Watchers did not argue.

Chapter XXXII.

By the time Gerard found his way to the palace, the evacuation was already underway.

As he charged through the gate into the courtyard—Marco panting at his heels—Prince Amalric of Cyprus kicked his way through the opposite doors, towing a protesting Lady Margaret by the arm. The young prince had evidently just arrived from the wall, for his armour was bloody and a horse bearing his emblem stood with heaving flanks by the open cistern in the courtyard.

"My dear boy," Margaret objected, "there's no need to haul me around like this. I was only waiting to see poor Lucy safely off."

"There's no time to lose, aunt. In another quarter-hour the streets will be jammed with people trying to save their necks, and Tyre can ill afford to pay your ransom." The prince spotted Gerard and pointed at him with an imperious snap of the fingers. "Montreal, get her to the harbour. I'll go back, try to stem the Saracen advance."

Gerard took her hand, but Lady Margaret wrenched it away. "Don't *you* manhandle me, Gerard! I will leave when Lucy does!"

Her words were swallowed up by the departing hoofbeats of Prince Amalric's horse, but Gerard understood their import.

"Please, my lady." He caught her elbow. "There's nothing you can do to help her now."

She slapped him. Not hard—she wasn't really trying—but Gerard still recoiled in shock. He might sooner have expected to be bitten by a lamb.

Lady Margaret took a deep breath, hardly less shaken. "Everyone else has left her, Gerard. Now more than ever…"

She didn't finish what she had to say. To Gerard's vast relief, Countess Lucy emerged from the palace ahead of the city's mayor, Sir Bartholomew Embriaco. White to the lips and nose, the sight of the courtyard seemed to do nothing to improve her mood, for when she saw Gerard and Lady Margaret, she stopped in her tracks and turned on Embriaco in fury. "Where are your men, Embriaco? Where are the bearers you promised me?"

Gerard glanced around the courtyard, registering for the first time how empty it was. Two litters and a cart of baggage stood waiting; but there were no bearers, no guards.

Gerard glanced at Marco, recalling the panicked people they'd seen running through the streets toward the water gate. "I presume they fled."

"You tarried too long, my lady," Embriaco said.

"I thought I had men of spirit around me, who meant to defend their lady like true vassals. *I* did not give you leave to retreat from the wall!"

"Oh, Lucy," Lady Margaret said reproachfully. "Amalric said there was no wall left."

Two bright spots of colour rose in Countess Lucy's cheeks, and for a moment she fell silent. Embriaco seized the opportunity to speak.

"We shall have to go afoot."

He bowed, presenting his arm, but the countess recoiled as though he'd offered to strike her. "So I am to trust my life to an Embriaco and a Templar? Do you mean to betray me together?"

In the incredulous silence, Lady Margaret snorted. "Now, Lucy, don't make a *complete* goose of yourself. Thank you, Sir Bartholomew, we accept your escort gladly. Come, Gerard!"

She turned on her heel and marched towards the gate on foot, leaving the others no choice but to follow. Embriaco seemed glad to fall into step behind her. Gerard snapped his fingers to Marco and ran to keep up. Last of all, the countess picked up her skirts of black damask and followed suit.

Outside, the street was full of chaos, as people streamed hopelessly towards the water gate. When Gerard caught up to her, Lady Margaret gave a wheeze of distress. "How will they all find places on a ship?"

"I don't know, my lady."

Marco spoke. "I don't think they've stopped to ask themselves that, sir. Didn't you feel it? The malice? The fear?"

Gerard remembered the terrifying apparition they had seen in the sky and hastily crossed himself. He couldn't see the hairy man now, but his gut clenched in remembered terror.

"Quiet, Marco," he said. The boy had a nerve speaking at all, when he was partially responsible for this unfolding disaster. With an effort, Gerard refrained from saying more. He'd leave his recriminations for a time when Lady Margaret could not hear.

She seemed too busy struggling for breath to pay any attention to Marco. As the street became more chaotic, Gerard pushed ahead of her to force their way through the crowd.

Behind them in the city was the sound of battle in the streets. Weapons clashing, voices crying out in desperation and rage, doors breaking open. Ever louder; ever nearer.

Ordinarily, had any small force of Saracens made their way into the city, Tripoli's narrow streets would become a death-trap, each window an embrasure where a determined archer might pour arrows into the enemy. But the people were at the end of their endurance, their resistance sapped by long defeat and the unseen creature that now descended upon the city to strike their hearts with a fearful chill. And thus, the Saracens flooded Tripoli's streets with sheer force of numbers.

As Gerard, the two ladies, and their escort approached the water gate, the crowd thickened until there was barely room to move. Yet move the people did, heaving and flowing like an angry living creature—many-headed, ugly, and dangerous. Old hostilities were in the air, heightened by terror. Somewhere ahead, Gerard caught the sound of an Embriaco war-cry. Behind him, Sir Bartholomew seemed to have heard it too. "Stand back!" he yelled at once. "If anyone wants to fight, I will personally cut his throat!"

Even with Lilith gone, her legacy remained in factional strife.

Realising they must get to the quay before things became any worse, Gerard began striking with the flat of his sword at the press of people before him. "Way! Way! Way for the Lady of Tyre!"

To his relief they gave way, generations of deference reminding them of their place. Slowly, Gerard forged a path through the water gate.

There were no longer any sentries guarding the narrow passage; the bottleneck was caused by the simple fact that, once outside on the quay, there was nowhere for the people to go. Those who could had leaped into the harbour in an attempt to swim to the galleys; others had been jostled in by the pushing and shoving on shore. In smaller boats at some distance from the crowded quay, sergeants and mariners awaited the coming of their lords from the battle.

Gerard elbowed his way to the quay's edge and hailed a rowboat flying the standard of Tyre. Beside him, Lady Margaret was mute; he saw her looking at the black mass of terrified people with tears in her eyes. As Countess Lucy and Sir Bartholomew reached the quayside, a boat bearing her arms followed Lady Margaret's dinghy toward the quay.

As the boats approached, the crowd jostled forward a little, threatening to tip the ladies into the water. Gerard turned, flashing his sword in warning, shouting at them to keep back as Marco helped Lady Margaret climb into her own small boat. She gasped as the tiny vessel wobbled beneath her, then collapsed ungracefully onto the thwart, splashing her mulberry silk gown with saltwater.

"Marco, you clown, watch what you're doing!"

The moment the words escaped him, Gerard remembered that he was trying to recommend himself to Lady Margaret by quite different behaviour. Worse, she seemed to have heard him, for she said, "Thank you, Marco; all's well. Lucy? Will you join me?"

The countess stood beside them, looking back toward Tripoli as though in a trance. Voices clamoured from the crowd: "Speak to us, Lady Lucy! Take us with you! Don't abandon us!"

They were in a demanding mood—fear trembling on the edge of violence—but Countess Lucy paid no heed, her young face pale and hard as stone. Gerard guessed what she was thinking; the same thought bothered him.

She could only save herself, and that was what she was doing.

"Lucy!" Lady Margaret called again.

The countess startled and turned. "I'll wait for my own boat."

Lady Margaret nodded. "Come, Gerard, there's room for you and your manservant."

Her mariners brought the little boat back to the quay. Gerard stepped down and turned to beckon Marco, but his servant stood on the quay above them with his mouth screwed into an uncertain line.

"What is it, boy? Hurry!"

With abrupt decision, Marco knelt down, undoing the cloak on his shoulders that bore Gerard's badge. "Sir, I beg leave to depart from your service."

"*What?*" The word escaped him involuntarily. A few scant hours ago, Marco had betrayed him—and by extension the whole city. Why should he protest if the fool wanted to leave his service?

Marco swallowed. "I...I can't go with you, sir."

Perhaps if Lady Margaret had not been sitting across from him, he would have bade Marco go to the devil. But she had asked him to recommend himself to her, and he was still stinging from the gentle way she'd responded to his outburst a moment ago. If he turned Marco away now, into a city that was being sacked, she would never think well of him again.

And nor, he realised with a jolt of surprise, would he.

"But I want you to come, Marco." It was strange how soft his voice had become. "You betrayed my trust, it's true, but we can discuss that later. In safety."

Tears rose in Marco's eyes. "Sir, God save you, but no. I need to try to get some of these people to safety."

"There *is* no safety, Marco. Please."

In answer Marco pulled his cloak from his shoulders, dropped it into the boat, and turned away.

There was an aching hollow under his breastbone, where his heart ought to be. Gerard turned to Lady Margaret, hoping for understanding or sympathy. Instead, he found her sitting very still with her eyes fixed on Marco's cloak at her feet.

As though she, too, was ashamed.

As though she, too, would have preferred to stay.

Gerard looked down numbly at her bowed head. There was a just and right order to things; everyone knew that and accepted it. It was right for the noble to hold high station, and for the mean to serve them. It was right for the ordinary sort of people to stand back while their betters made good their escape—a sacrifice by which they ennobled themselves in the way most appropriate to such persons.

But it was right, too, for people of noble station to protect and defend those of lesser status; and Marco, damn him, was making him look less noble by comparison.

"Marco! Wait for me, of your courtesy." He put an edge of sarcasm in his voice. "My lady, will you give me leave to depart?"

Lady Margaret's eyes lifted to his, widening in fear. Their blue depths put him once more in mind of the girl who had taken him to Tyre as a boy and become his dearest friend.

"Gerard, dear, if you go you will die, and then—"

She caught herself, as though she had meant to say something else. Her throat worked. "The next battle will be for Acre. You must be there, mustn't you?"

"It will take a miracle to save Acre." As the words spilled out, Gerard marvelled they did not leave his own tongue bloody, so bitter was the realisation. He had thought himself the architect of fate; but he was only mortal, after all. What kind of fool must he have been, to dream such power lay within his grasp? "The presence of a single man more or less will make no difference. Certainly not mine."

He picked up her soft hand and went to brush his lips across the graceful curves of her knuckles. At the last moment he thought better of it, plucked up his courage, and saluted her gently on the mouth. Was it only his imagination, or did her lips cling to his a moment before he withdrew?

"God go with you, my lady."

He scrambled onto the quay and looked down into tearful blue eyes. "Don't say that," she pleaded. "Say, *Until we meet again.*"

"Until we meet again, then."

He signalled the rowers to push off; as the boat pulled away from the quay she kept watching him, motionless, until at last she bent her head and ran a sleeve over her eyes. As Countess Lucy's rowboat nudged between them, Gerard shook himself and turned to find the countess, Embriaco, and Marco watching him with varied forms of astonishment.

Gerard took a deep breath and went directly to the point. "What's the plan, Marco? I presume you have one?"

Marco swallowed. "I think so, sir. Saint Thomas."

The scent of smoke wafted towards him in the air, and Gerard glanced towards the city. Already churning pillars of smoke billowed into the sky above. Qalawun had sworn to burn Tripoli if she failed to surrender; it seemed he meant to keep his word.

But the islet of Saint Thomas was small, out-of-the-way. At low tide, with the sea calm following last night's storm, it would not be difficult to reach. Meanwhile, in the chaos of the sack, the island might be overlooked long enough for victory to soften the sultan's heart and incline him to generosity.

Or, help might arrive. Lady Margaret's galley and many of the others in the harbour—whether royal, Templar, or Hospitaller—may already be loaded with fugitives, but the Genoese galleys were still anchored within sight of the city, empty save for their crews.

"My lady." Gerard turned to the countess. "If we lead all these people to the isle of Saint Thomas, will you send the Genoese to rescue us?

"It might work," Embriaco said. "Countess?"

At first, Gerard didn't know if she heard. The voices on the shore were still calling Lucy's name.

"Don't leave us, my lady!"

"My brother died to make you countess!"

"Are we not your people?"

At that the countess stiffened a little. "I don't know," she murmured, "are you?" But after a moment she turned, lifting a hand, and silence fell on the crowd. "Good people, you see that the harbour is small and the ships are few. If you will follow Sir Bartholomew Embriaco to Saint Thomas, it will be possible to board more of you more quickly."

"Thank you," Sir Bartholomew breathed, and Marco's shoulders drooped in relief.

The countess looked up at them as she prepared to step into her rowboat, and there was an odd note in her voice. "Don't thank me yet."

This time, Gerard didn't have to push or threaten his way through the crowd. The people stood willingly aside to let them pass, and pressed in eagerly behind to follow. Once back within the city walls, however, they fell into difficulties. Prince Amalric was there astride his horse with an exhausted band of knights and sergeants, shouting at the people to stand back and allow him passage to the quay. Embriaco caught his eye at once, shouting and signalling; the prince quickly picked up on the plan. "Pay attention," he roared. "Common folk, follow Sir Bartholomew! Keep the water gate open for the lords and fighting men to retreat. Remember, each man we lose here is one man less when we go to revenge ourselves on these damned Saracens!"

"What about us?" someone called.

"Follow us to Saint Thomas!" Marco shouted. "The countess has promised to send ships!"

Once again the effect was wellnigh miraculous. The people jostled back to let Sir Bartholomew and Gerard pass; soon the whole crowd was streaming up the Fish Street behind them. By the time Gerard turned into the narrow alley running towards the postern gate and the island beyond, Prince Amalric and a steady stream of lords, knights, and fighting men had the harbour to themselves.

Marco had left the postern unlocked a few short hours before, so there was no trouble leading the people through. With the tide at ebb, the strait was shallow, and the fugitives could reach the island without swimming. Gerard left Marco on the jetty while he and Embriaco oversaw the operation from Saint Thomas itself. At first he had hoped to hide the fugitives within the basilica, but the church quickly filled until there was no room left even in the sacred place behind the altar. Still the people kept coming. Gerard directed them to hide them on the rocks behind the church, an effort to keep them out of sight of the town; but still the fugitives crossed the strait, until there was no island left, just a black mass of people wedged tightly onto the land or sitting wetly on the submerged rocks.

At last, Marco shut the postern gate and waded to the island himself.

"I locked the gate," he said, offering Gerard the key. His face was pinched with fear as he trudged out of the water. Silently, Gerard made room for him on the rocks nearby, and together they watched the long, slow death of Tripoli. The galleys passing back and forth to the harbour; the fishing-vessels running short trips back and forth to the necklace of small islands stretching beyond this one; the bodies floating face-down in the slowly-rising tide—those who had thought to swim to a galley and found, too late, that they could not.

Towards the horizon, the Genoese galleys rode at anchor. Slowly, hampered by the incoming tide, Lady Lucy's galley pulled away from the harbour and advanced to meet them. Beyond the strait, Tripoli shrieked and burned. On the island, the only sound was muffled weeping and prayers.

Gerard found himself watching with clenched teeth and took a deep breath, forcing himself to relax, to wait. To surrender to fate. If this was his day to die, he would die doing a noble thing. If he lived, perhaps Lady Margaret would think better of him than she had before. Let him only sit and wait, resigned and ready.

Around noon, a fishing vessel stopped by the island, taking off two dozen people. It did not seem to leave the rocks any the less crowded. Gerard watched the sun redden behind a pall of smoke, watched a crowded Templar galley become the last to leave the harbour. He hid his face in his hands as it went past, oblivious to the cries of those on the island.

Less than twenty-four hours ago Lilith had waited on this island for the ship that would take her to Acre. Such a short span of time for so many things to change.

On the north shore of the island, a stir and a shout went up. Gerard heard voices calling the name of the countess and leaped to his feet with a dizzying rush of hope. There were too many people in the way, craning their necks and asking what had happened; Gerard fought his way through them and emerged on the north shore to find Sir Bartholomew Embriaco standing in the water with his hands lifted to his head. Those who could see, cursed, or wept, or shouted in a futile attempt to be heard.

Far on the horizon, Countess Lucy's galley had finally joined the Genoese—and they had hoisted sail, tacking slowly for the north and safety in Armenian Cilicia.

Don't thank me yet, she had said.

Gerard could only stand numbly and watch as the promised help crossed the horizon and vanished. There was little love lost between the countess and the people of the city; under Embriaco's leadership they'd stoutly resisted her rule; but how could she abandon them like this? Lilith might be gone, but her blight still ran thick in Tripoli, like poison in the water.

There was nothing left to do now but die.

Chapter XXXIII.

John didn't quite see how Soraya managed to produce a rope on such short notice, but from the colour and sheen, it might almost have been made of hastily-reassembled silk. Within moments she had the sick, dazed Watchers up on their feet and taking hold of it in imitation of a line of prisoners. As for John, he wasn't sure how much longer he could remain on his feet; but now was no time for rest. He told Matthias Zakar not to let go of his youngest brother, ruffled Elisa's hair, and limped forward to take the lead with a loaded crossbow ready in his good left hand. With Soraya bringing up the rear, they moved cautiously out of the dyehouse courtyard and into the streets.

By now, several hours into the sack, nearly everything that could plundered, had been. Those who were valued as slaves or ransoms had been taken, and half the city was on fire. The Saracens now moved from house to house with bloody swords, but John kept moving, willing himself not to look, hoping that some miracle might blind the children's eyes to the disaster unfolding around them. Yet no one challenged him, and the Watchers stumbled behind him like sleepwalkers.

As they came to the street where the barricade had been, John spied a huddle of bodies in the wreckage. For an instant his heart clenched, believing them to be dead. But then he heard a child's cry and a terrified hushing.

He limped to a halt and looked down at the little half-hidden group. A man and a woman stared back at him with haunted eyes, four children clasped in their arms. Franks, by their fair colouring, though not wealthy ones.

"We're friends," he said to the man in slow, clear Arabic. He sketched the sign of the cross. "We have room for five more. Send your wife and children with us."

The man could only stare at him, until Hubert, immediately behind John, cleared his throat and repeated the words in the Frankish tongue. Then the man nodded, but his lips went pale. Turning to his wife, he spoke in a rush of Frankish; she clung to him and wailed.

"John!" Soraya called from the back of the column. "One hour left!"

"A moment," he called back to her; but when he turned, he found that Hubert had said something to the family, and the wife was dragging her husband to the lifeline along with the children.

"This makes us fifty-one," John protested, but then Hubert turned to his own wife and kissed her through her tears, and his throat constricted.

"Hubert," he whispered. "Don't. The Coast needs you. The children need you."

The older man's face was streaked with tears of his own. "No, Tripoli needs me. Go."

"Keep moving!" Soraya shouted again from the end of the line. Wiping her eyes, Anna led the rescued woman to the rope, and the line shuffled forward again—past Hubert, past John, the Zakar children watching them both with huge eyes and pale faces.

John had no words left, and every breath hurt. It was all he could do to lift his hands in speechless, weary protest.

Hubert seemed to know what was going through his mind—the guilt and the grief—for he touched his left forearm in the familiar Watcher's salute. "Go in peace, friend. Find your wife and children."

"While you give up yours?" he cried.

Hubert did not reply. Instead, he stiffened and coughed, his eyes widening with surprise. He and John both looked down then, at the arrow-point that had suddenly emerged between his ribs. John reached out with a groan of horror, but it was too late. Hubert fell to his knees, then to the street, and the light left his eyes.

John looked up, numb with horror.

Half a bowshot beyond the Frank, a lone Saracen archer lowered his bow and stalked towards John. "No leavings," he said. "Sultan's orders. Kill or take prisoners. No exceptions."

His crossbow was an itch in his palm, a swift and vengeful death if he chose to use it. Deep inside him, the blood-drinker clawed at its bars. His hand was white with longing on the stock of his crossbow; but with a shudder, John turned away and hastened to follow the Watchers.

More death wouldn't bring Hubert back. The true blame for what happened here today lay with the man who had ordered the slaughter, the demon who had fanned the flames of mortal bloodlust.

"Are you all right?" Soraya murmured as he passed.

"Just keep them moving," John replied through clenched teeth. He could see from Matthias' face that he, at least, had seen yet another guardian die. John prayed he would get the rest of the Watchers to safety before any more disasters could fall upon them.

Yet Hubert had set an example, and the Watchers seemed to have awoken from their smoke-induced stupor. White-lipped and numb, Maryam exchanged herself for an old woman they found cowering in the shadows beneath a staircase. Others silently followed: a skilled weaver gave herself up for a wailing toddler, a young husband and wife for two waifs driven coughing into the streets by their burning home, a sturdy boy for a trembling young woman whose teeth had been battered out by some merciless fist. By the time they found their way to the broken city gates, as many as half of John's fifty Watchers were gone, replaced by the last broken victims of Tripoli's fall.

What good is it? a treacherous part of him wanted to shout. *Don't leave these people on my hands—I'm not their father! Stay alive and care for your own!*

He felt sick at his own reaction, at that part of himself that was so dark and ruthless. What praise was it, after all, if a man only cared for his own kind? What good was a Watcher who never looked beyond his own children, his own people, the people who needed his help least?

I ought to have stayed as well.

Yet if he stayed, he died; al-Mukhtar's promise was void and his fifty souls were forfeit, Watchers or no. He carried the carnelian ring; he must lead his fifty souls to safety, or there would be no protection for any of them. Pain of body and spirit made each step a torment; and yet John walked on.

At the city gate, he showed the carnelian ring to the Saracen guards and invoked the name of al-Mukhtar, the Chosen. They let the Watchers through without question. Beyond, the road was clogged with carts full of plunder and lines of shuffling slaves. Now Soraya handed over rear-guard duty to one of the remaining Watchers and came forward to John.

"This way," she said, touching his arm briefly, comfortingly, as she passed. The road wound slightly uphill toward the suburb of Mount Pilgrim, clustered beneath the fortress of Saint Gilles. Nearly two months ago when John had first walked this road, it was a peaceful journey through groves of fruit-laden trees. Now the landscape had been ravaged by war. The orange-trees had been splintered by stone missiles or hacked down for firewood, the bright scent of citrus replaced by the foul stench of latrines and livestock. In and around Mount Pilgrim itself sprawled the Egyptian camp: a muddy scar on the hillside, a sea of canvas humming with squalid crowds of camp followers, hectic with the pound, pound, pound of hammers on anvils, forging chains for the captives.

John's mind reeled at the sheer size of this encampment. There must have been a hundred thousand fighting men alone, perhaps even double or triple that number.

While he was still marvelling, Soraya nudged him, prompting him to show al-Mukhtar's ring to a sentry. Once again she took the lead and John followed through the camp like a sleepwalker, focusing only on putting one foot in front of the other. As they came to a tent of red and yellow silk, Soraya had him show the carnelian ring again. The flaps were opened; John walked numbly through and sank to his knees, cradling his arms around his aching ribs. For a moment, it was enough simply to rest.

Supported by a richly-carved and gilded central pole, the tent's inner curtains and carpets were woven with sumptuous geometric and floral designs. Colourful glass lanterns surrounded the tentpole in a ring, lighting the interior with a riot of colour. Cushions at the sides of the tent provided a place to sit or sleep, chests provided storage, and an empty armour-tree completed the tent's sparse furnishings.

That armour-tree seemed to loom over him, a gaunt and silent sentinel, an inexorable warning of just who had taken them under his protection. John turned away, unable to bear the reminder.

Behind him, his fifty souls crowded into the tent. The dazzling tent walls shut out the ghastly sights of blood outside, but not the sounds. Somewhere beyond the thin protection of silk and tapestry, a terrible wail lofted into the air. Inside, Elisa Zakar burst into tears, and John pushed himself to his feet again to find and comfort the child.

"Hush, it's all right." Somehow, Soraya was there first. She had been missing for a few moments, but now she had transformed back to her preferred female form and crouched in front of the trembling child with a smile, offering a basket of dried dates. "Don't be afraid. It's only the doctors pulling an arrow out of a man to make him better."

This, or perhaps the dates, seemed to reassure the little girl. She put one of the fruits in her mouth, and said with a woeful sniff, "I want Uncle Hubert."

Matthias scowled. "Uncle Hubert's dead."

I'm here, John thought, but he held himself back. He wasn't; not really. He still meant to go home sooner or later. Anna, Hubert's wife, went down on her knees and gathered the five of them into her arms. John watched the tears rolling down her face, and for a while, he could see nothing else..

"Eat something, John."

Soraya's voice cut into his daze. She was holding out a handful of dates, and he accepted them silently, knowing that the sweet food would revive him—whatever was left of him.

As he ate, Soraya watched the fifty salvaged souls. Some passed the dates around; others simply put their arms around each other and wept. John studied her face—was that grief, confusion, or something else?

"You Watchers…" she began in an undertone. "Who would give up a long and useful life for the sake of waifs and beggars?"

"Not us, but God in us." John cleared a rusty throat. "For the sake of God in them."

"There is nothing of God in me," Soraya said wistfully.

"Shall we test that?"

He slid the carnelian ring from his little finger, and Soraya came back to herself with a blaze of purpose. "The ring! Come!"

She left the tent in a delighted flurry of silk, leaving John to follow at an arduous limp. Across the way from al-Mukhtar's tent, a blacksmith hammered chains beside his forge, a steel brazier full of glowing coals. Soraya beckoned him toward it, but John hesitated.

"Soraya. Once this ring is destroyed, the Chosen will know we've betrayed him again."

"Yes, but this time he'll be mortal."

"And these fifty poor people will still be trapped in the midst of an army." John took her hand, looked into her eyes. "Will you protect us, when you are freed? Will you see us safely away?"

"Of course." Then her eyes darkened with sudden fear. "Perhaps I won't have it in me. Perhaps, if I'm free, I'll be heartless. Wicked. Perhaps you should—"

John tightened his grip on her hand. "Hush. I trust you, Soraya. I know you'll do as you promise. Here." He placed the ring in her palm. "Be loosed."

Soraya shot him a sharp, bittersweet smile and her fingers tightened on his with painful affection. Then she walked into the blacksmith's tent, and dropped the ring into the forge.

Busy at his anvil, the blacksmith paid them no mind at first, but the boy working the bellows watched curiously as Soraya stood over the flames, unflinching in the heat. John joined her and watched as the gold within the furnace first glistened, then glowed, then melted, leaving the carnelian isolated in a molten puddle.

Having finished the fetter he was working on, the blacksmith plunged it into a bucket of water to cool it, then turned to John and Soraya with a scowl.

"Look, I can't have people in my forge while I'm working," he began. But

Soraya was trembling a little with eagerness, intent on her task. Without speaking, she shouldered him aside and used a delicate pair of tongs to pick the hot crystal out of the fire. Shreds of gold still clung to its glowing surface as she tipped the carnelian onto the anvil.

John held out his left hand for the hammer, and the smith, after a brief hesitation, handed it over. He turned to Soraya, and managed a bow. "Lady."

She accepted it with a little smile. "No one has called me that before."

"You don't know that."

She raised the hammer, squaring up with the small gem—and paused. "There's something I haven't told you, John Zakar."

That stole his focus. "What's that?"

Her smile was very bittersweet indeed. "I'm sure I know you. I'm sure we've met. Long ago, before they stole my memories."

How could he have met Soraya before? Certainly not since Mosul; but that meant—

That meant it could only have been *before.* Six hundred years before.

Before he could ask, the haunting call of a muezzin cut through the camp, calling the Saracens to their midday prayer. Soraya stiffened.

"The time!" she gasped. Facing the anvil again, she lofted the hammer and brought it down with all her immortal might upon the cooling gemstone.

With a crack, the stone shattered into hot fragments. The handle of the hammer burst into splinters; and the iron head rebounded from the anvil, leaving a smoking crater and the sharp scent of hot metal.

The blacksmith gave a yelp of terror. Soraya gasped, putting a hand to her breast.

John lowered his protecting arm. "Did it work?"

"I don't know. I don't *feel* anything."

"What about the soul tether; do you still feel that?"

"I think—" She frowned. Gasped.

Forgetting his pains, John reached out to steady her. A useless gesture. For a moment Soraya stared at him from an agonised face. Her lips moved soundlessly; she rocked a little on her feet, then dissolved into dust that blew away on an eddying breath of wind.

The blacksmith swore explosively, but John stood numb, staring after her as she became one with the drifting smoke and ash from the burning city.

They had destroyed the ring, and Soraya was still enslaved.

Chapter XXXIV.

Crash.

Gerard started to his feet as muffled cries of fear rang out from the people crowded on the isle of Saint Thomas. That sound—it couldn't have come from the postern gate, surely?

Crash.

The gate was wrenched aside as though made of paper, and through it came not a phalanx of soldiers with a ram, but a single man with a spear. Gerard's blood ran cold. The man wore princely armour and a veil of linked rings concealed his face—but there was no doubt in his mind. Only one man in Tripoli could do a thing like that.

The Chosen reached back into the shadows and drew a horse after him. Mounting, he guided the animal into the water. After him followed another horseman—and another—and another.

Unsheathing swords. Stringing bows. Forging their way across the narrow strait toward the lonely island of fugitives.

At first, Gerard was stiff with fear, but then cries of terror from the people waiting beside him shocked him into action. Not to draw the sword at his side; he was only one man, and resistance was worse than futile. Instead, he waded waist-deep into the cold saltwater, waving his arms in a desperate attempt to intercept them.

"I am Gerard of Montreal, the personal aide to the Master of the Temple, Sir William of Beaujeu. I would like to negotiate a surrender!"

All his attention was on the veiled man with the spear. A moment too late, he realised another horseman was making straight towards him, a sword in his hand.

"We *surrender!*" Gerard screamed, trying to dive out of the way. But the water slowed every movement. He threw up his hands, receiving the full brunt of the sword's cut across his unprotected forearms. The blade scraped horribly along bone, the force of the blow driving him off-balance. Water closed over his head. Before his horrified eyes a red cloud flowered in the seawater, filling his mouth with the taste of his own blood.

For a terrible moment he was unable to find his feet, unable to breathe, paralysed by pain and buffeted by the incoming waves.

Then, as an arm snaked around his chest and heaved his head above the water, Gerard found he could breathe again. The salt blinded his eyes, but he could not escape the terrible sounds in his ears: shrieks, pleas, the wet chop and hack of great swords and battle-axes.

Nearer, a voice murmured in his ear. "Sir. Listen to me. Hold still."

Marco. Locking his flailing limbs into immobility with wiry arms.

"You're bleeding. Give me your hands."

Gerard fell back, panting. Slowly, shock began to set in, robbing him of his senses.

As his consciousness faded, Gerard felt Marco reaching for his mangled arms with fingers that had become somehow scalding hot. "Sir, listen to me. There may yet be time to save Acre. Tell Beaujeu he needs the angels on his side, not demons. Go back to Acre. Restore the Watchers."

Go back to Acre? Impossible.

Then everything faded away.

* * *

Some time later, Gerard opened his eyes and looked up into a blood-red haze.

After the pain in his arms subsided, the first thing he noticed was the smell—smoke and blood, bile and ordure. The second was the silence. He heard the shriek of buzzards, the splash of waves, and nothing else.

"Marco," he whispered in a raw throat.

No answer. His legs were cold, so cold. Out of the corner of his eye, he could see a motionless hand lying too close to his face. At first he thought the brownish flecks might be freckles, but as he turned his head, it became apparent they were speckles of blood.

He got an elbow beneath him and levered himself up with a groan. Water splashed as he moved, and he looked down at his prone legs. They were half in the water—red water—his hose and shoes soaked with a rusty spume. The smoke of Tripoli had settled over the narrow strait, blocking his view of the shore; and the sunset at his back had dyed it red.

Gerard sat looking at that red fog and poisoned sea for a long, horrible moment before he got his hands under him and turned.

The isle of Saint Thomas was a black mound behind him, its basilica a gaunt smoking wreck looming vaguely in the fog. All around that smoking heap, bodies lay piled on the stone. Tangled limbs, staring eyes, spilled guts; kites and buzzards stalked among them, pulling at exposed eyes and fallen innards. It was a charnel-house, an isle of the dead cut off from the mortal world by a pall of red smoke.

Marco had betrayed them. Prester John had doomed them. Countess Lucy had abandoned them. And finally, the Chosen and his men had carried out their sultan's orders with brutal efficiency.

"Marco," he whispered, glancing down at his forearms. A livid scar ran across each arm, but the skin was healed. It did not take much looking to find his manservant: Marco lay beside him on the shore, gazing sightlessly into the heavens over a slit throat.

Gerard felt nauseous, dizzy. For a while all he could do was sit on the rocks, watching the bloody spume. No tears came. His heart felt numb, as though cleft in two and as yet unaware of it.

It was darker now than when he had awoken, the redness fading from the smog as the sun fell towards the horizon.

Gerard heard a splash in the water toward the south end of the island. What was that he saw? A dark shape gliding through the water, a long low boat with a ferryman leaning on his pole? He blinked, and the apparition was gone; but terror seized him at the thought of being left on this cursed island in the dark. A moment later he was on his feet, plunging into the water.

The tide was going out again, and it was an easy crossing. The fire in the city must have died somewhat, but he couldn't face the postern gate, nor the destruction beyond. Instead, once across the strait he turned aside, circling the rocks at the foot of the outer wall. After skirting the harbour—its bloody scum, its floating bodies—he climbed to land at last and staggered beneath the aqueduct into the orange-groves beyond the city. Here, close to the harbour, were some untouched and unharvested trees. In the pall of smoke they loomed over him like ghosts, their fruit glowing bright in the dusk. At the sight his stomach growled, reminding him of his hunger. Gerard plucked a hanging orange, pierced the skin, and tore it open. The fresh scent of the fruit sprayed into the tainted air and, for a moment, he smelled Tripoli as she had once been: populous and rich and scented with citrus.

Instantly, Gerard threw the fruit from him and stood still, shivering. He could feel it at last, the wound at his heart. Marco. Marco was gone, his last action to give his master life. Tripoli was gone, rooted from the earth and burned. All those lives. All the beautiful things those lives had built, the legacies of Saint-Gilles and the Lady Hodierna and the Embriacos, were gone. Their future had been burned away, leaving a raw and aching pit behind.

How was it possible to find peace with such a terrible thing? Life was only worth living if a man showed foresight, moved great events, and left an immortal legacy. Gerard had always believed that: *each man the architect of his own fate.* How could he believe it any longer? He had tried to bridle his fate, and instead it had turned and trampled him.

He was too weak. He was not like other men; like the Chosen. He couldn't even convince the lady he loved to marry him.

He looked uphill through dusk and smoke, toward the Egyptian camp. He was shivering, hungry, and he no longer had the will to fight. If he was going to die, he might as well get it over with. If not, no doubt Beaujeu would ransom his worthless carcass. He had failed to master his destiny; so he would seek destiny out, and dare it to finish what it had begun. There was nowhere else to go, nothing else to do, and so he continued up through the shadowy orchards, working his way uphill in search of the Chosen.

In search of death.

Half blinded by smoke and darkness, Gerard found himself in the Saracen camp almost before he was aware. Al-Mukhtar's name acted as a password, and a sentry guided him to the mamluk's tent. Faces passed as though in a dream: artisans and engineers at work mending harness and machines, camp-followers stitching up rents in clothes, haughty mamluk lords leading retinues to and from the sultan's headquarters in the great fortress—and nearly everywhere he looked, the miserable faces of captives.

The sentry brought him to the entrance of a tent. Gerard knew Arabic, but he paid no attention to the words exchanged by the man with al-Mukhtar's servants. The tent flap twitched back, and Gerard looked into the silver-grey eyes of Prester John.

"Sir Gerard," the Prester said in amazement.

Gerard blinked in numb surprise. John Zakar looked much the worse for wear tonight, his clothing spattered with blood and his right arm in a sling; but he had survived the sack and was here in al-Mukhtar's tent.

A part of him was not even surprised. "You."

"Hush!" the Prester warned. "I only just got them all to sleep."

There was a slipper-shaped oil lamp in his left hand, and he beckoned Gerard into the tent with a jerk of the head. Beyond, the tent was dark and full of peaceful breathing; the lamp splashed light upon huddled shapes cocooned in blankets. There must have been dozens of people here. Gerard turned away from them with bleak disinterest, neither knowing nor caring who they were. Instead he sank onto a flat cushion at the side of the tent, and stared up at the Prester in dull fury.

"You're in league with that butcher."

The Prester knelt, putting the lamp on the ground between them. His lips were tight with something that might have been stubbornness, or perhaps even shame. "I exorcised Lilith because it was my duty as a Watcher, not because al-Mukhtar wished it. But because he did wish it, I was able to demand a safe-conduct for myself and fifty souls. Was I wrong?"

"Yes," Gerard snarled. "Lilith protected us."

"Lilith is a demon," said the other, dragging a hand down his weary, bruised face.

"Better every imp in hell than the mamluks of Egypt!"

Prester John looked up at him, expressionless. "Yes," he said softly, "I felt the same, for a while."

Once again Gerard reached for his anger—but it was already gone. He felt exhausted, and there was an ominous ache crawling up the back of his throat. Prester John, if that's who he was, watched him with calm pity. It occurred to Gerard that Marco, the soul of loyalty, had believed in this man; trusted him to the point of betraying Gerard himself.

He swallowed raggedly. "Because of you, Tripoli is gone. Acre will surely be the next to fall, and there will be no one left to protect the holy places. Tell me you plan to mend this. Tell me you will help us."

"I…" Now it was the Prester's turn to swallow; he shot a troubled glance at the sleeping bodies behind him. "Sir Gerard, I am only trying to find my way home."

"To your kingdom in the East?" Gerard prompted. "I know. Only promise to return if the sultan should attack Acre. We can no longer field an army, but with your help…"

His voice trailed away as he saw the look on the other man's face.

"My kingdom?" the Prester asked, his voice soft and flat. "You are mistaken. I have no kingdom."

There was a long, bruised silence. "But you're Prester John." Gerard's voice was weak and frightened, but he couldn't seem to give it any greater strength. "The great Christian prince. Ruler of the greatest kingdom of the east. Enemy of the Tartars."

John shook his head. "Sir, I'm only a Presbyter of the Watchers. That's all I've ever claimed to be."

Alba had warned him. Marco had warned him. Still he could not, *would* not believe it. "You have no kingdom? No army?"

"All I have is fifty poor broken souls I was able to save from the sack of

Tripoli."

"Then…no one can help us." Once again Gerard reached for anger and didn't find it.

Qalawun had done to Tripoli what Baibars had done to Antioch twenty years ago, and now the only great city that remained of the lost Frankish kingdoms was Acre.

Their last hope had been extinguished, and Gerard surrendered entirely to dread.

Chapter XXXV.

For a long time the Frankish knight did not stir again, staring at his grimy feet where they rested side by side on the opulent carpet. The lamp shed only a small and dim circle of light, but John could smell iron. If he was forced to guess, he would have said that Gerard of Montreal had waded through blood.

The taste of failure was bitter on his own tongue. This morning in the Templar commandery, he had comforted himself that he might yet rescue the Watchers and Soraya, and salvage some good from the terrible decision he had made upon the island of Saint Thomas the night before. All in vain. Many of the Watchers were lost, and Soraya was still imprisoned.

Now this Frank appeared to make yet more demands on his honour.

Because of you, Tripoli is gone.

It *wasn't* his fault. Tripoli would have fallen to the Saracens regardless of his intervention. Otherwise Lilith would scarcely have attempted to flee.

Tell me you will help us.

If one accepted that a man had duties beyond his own people, where did it end? Must John answer for the deeds of his distant descendants? What else was he expected to do before he would be permitted to go home?

How much easier it would have been, to accept a bargain with Lilith! Could she really have left him any worse off than he was now, practically a prisoner in a camp of victorious Saracen warriors? John recoiled the instant the thought crossed his mind, grateful that *that* temptation, at least, was now beyond reach.

It was no use worrying about finding his way home; first he must survive the immediate future. Al-Mukhtar's ring was broken; how would he react? Even if al-Mukhtar did keep his word and allow the fifty of them to depart, where would these broken people go? Where would they find safety in a calamitous world?

A scream pierced through the camp and fell away. John dropped his forehead on his knees. The wound in his right arm had stiffened the muscles, making it useless for any kind of action, and two nights of scanty and interrupted rest had left him exhausted. He just wanted to sleep, to see Rahel again even if only to tell her that he was sorry.

He just wanted to go home.

"Why?" Beside him, Gerard broke the silence. "What would Christ say to a thing like this, that his people should be slaughtered and led away captive, and his name disgraced? Why does God love the Saracens better than us? *Why?*"

John looked up. There was something expectant and quiet in the Frankish knight's face. He couldn't help but be reminded of the wide-eyed, trusting look in the eyes of a newborn child, and instinctively he tried to suppress the thought. He did not want to be a father to this man, too.

He closed his eyes so that he could not see the arrogant knight. Instead, he imagined his children, as they had sat over dinner a hundred times in the villa at Jerusalem. He imagined Rahel sitting calmly at his right hand, her hands folded on her lap and a warning arm around a squirming Elisa. He imagined Paulus cross-legged on the couch beside Elisa, staring into the middle distance in some kind of bored trance. He imagined Lukas slumped in a chair with arms folded and knees straddling, the characteristic moody look on his face; Marta sitting tidily on another with her nose close up against a tapestry-frame that held some brilliant design of her own creation.

A bittersweet pang of longing gripped him by the throat, and he began, not in the lordly Greek of the Septuagint, but stumbling through the Latin of Jerome, which a lost Frankish knight might possibly understand:

"How doth the city sit solitary, that was full of people! how is she become as a widow! she that was great among the nations, and princess among the provinces, how is she become tributary! She weepeth sore in the night, and her tears are on

her cheeks: among all her lovers she had none to comfort her: all her friends have dealt treacherously with her, they are become her enemies..."

It took him the better part of an hour to recite the whole Lamentation, with many trips and fumbles and some lacunae where there were gaps in his memory. The Frank was sobbing openly before he was halfway through, enormous racking sobs that shook his whole body.

When he finished, there was silence. Montreal lay face-down across the cushions, neither weeping nor speaking, although John thought he was not sleeping. He picked up his mantle, in which he had been about to wrap himself for sleep when the Frank arrived, and spread it over him with a sigh.

A tiny sound alerted him, little more than a breath. John looked up to see a man standing just inside the flap of the tent, tall and shadowy in the lamplight, reeking of blood.

The Chosen.

John startled, jarring a stab of pain from his injured arm and bruised ribs. He hadn't heard al-Mukhtar's approach; how long had he been standing there like an avenging angel? He could only hope that the young Zakars would remain asleep. He didn't want them to wake to this.

Despite the mamluk's bloody garments, his spear was bright and clean. "Do you have my ring?" al-Mukhtar asked quietly.

John's heart raced, but he kept his fear off his face. Wordlessly, he stood up, reached into his purse, and handed over a folded kerchief.

As al-Mukhtar unfolded the crisp linen, John touched the shaft of his left crossbow. Not that it would help.

The mamluk beheld the little cooled puddle of gold, the tiny crushed pieces of carnelian. His eyebrows lifted mockingly. "Glory to God, you were not very careful!"

There was nothing to say, and he wouldn't resort to flimsy lies. John only shrugged.

Observing his composure, al-Mukhtar gave a soundless laugh. "It was not so valuable as it seemed." Snapping the handkerchief clean, he handed it back to John with a flash of white, predatory teeth.

With a slow breath, John made himself release his crossbow and take back the cloth.

"And I have a replacement, anyway," al-Mukhtar continued, lifting his hand.

On his forefinger was a very large gold ring set with an amethyst, such as a bishop might wear. John looked from the ring to the Chosen's triumphant face, and his self-command cracked.

"Is this a game to you?" he asked softly. "Do you really pride yourself on what you have done today? It is one thing to capture a city; it is another to destroy its helpless people and burn it to the ground."

Al-Mukhtar's lips thinned. "They knew the terms. They had every chance to surrender."

"When the Zakars died, I thought it must take a devil to slaughter a man and his wife before the eyes of their children." John's hand returned to his crossbow. "God's mercy, I tried to believe you are men, but today you behaved like a nation of devils."

Al-Mukhtar's hand shot out, seized John by the front of his tunic, and drew him close. The lamplight illuminated only one small, furious sliver of his face. "One hundred and eighty years ago, these Franks you love so much slaughtered every man, woman and child they found in Jerusalem. They did not even take captives. Perhaps we are devils, Watcher, but if we are it is because we have learned from archdevils."

Strife. John glanced at the others in the tent, but the Watchers slept, and the Frank was still a motionless bulk beneath his mantle.

John swallowed. Perhaps he knew less of the history of this strange future than he should, yet he was in a reckless mood. "Is that what this is? Revenge for something that happened two hundred years ago? How is that reasonable?"

"It's no less reasonable than seeking to undo a conquest that happened six hundred years ago." Al-Mukhtar released him with a sigh; and suddenly his voice was wistful. "Man is weak by nature! All of us are bound by our past."

John gritted his teeth. He had been *there* six hundred years ago; he wanted nothing more than to return to that time, to fight that war and perhaps to win it. It was a mistake to forget that, even for a moment.

The Chosen turned away, raising the tent flap. "I did not come to trade threats. The Sultan wants you. Leave your weapons and follow me."

The *Sultan?* John tensed in a sudden involuntary urge to flee, but any such attempt would be futile. Laying his crossbows beside Gerard, he followed al-Mukhtar into the night.

Through the tents they wove, and once again the sickly reality of what had just happened hit him like a blow. Surely he had seen enough grief tonight; and yet all around him were new faces, new tears, new cries for help. In the distance, a bellowing voice was rebuking someone for drunkenness and fornication. John hoped bitterly that at least some of the Saracens would listen to their priests tonight.

Al-Mukhtar led him into the streets of Mount Pilgrim, past houses lit with lamplight and thrumming with dancing-music. The suburb's narrow streets sloped up sharply toward the swelling brow of the hill, where the massive citadel walls looked out over the suburb, the orange-groves, and the distant red glow of dying Tripoli. Nearer, the citadel revealed itself to be little more than a stronghold built for a single warlike goal, its walls thick and windowless. No wonder the princes of Tripoli had held their court in the more comfortable palace in the city itself.

An external staircase led to the citadel's roof, where potted plants and wicker screens, braziers, carpets and cushions transformed the rooftop into a stage where the sultan and his mamluks could feast and celebrate as they watched the city burn. At the centre of this space the sultan's tent had been pitched, its flaps open towards the sea. Within, in an interior no less sumptuous than al-Mukhtar's tent, though much larger, a ring of generals and scholars sat cross-legged surrounding a low, gorgeously-carved throne. Upon the throne sat an old man with fierce white whiskers wearing an elaborately brocaded silk jacket over his armour.

Sultan Qalawun. John's mouth went dry as he wondered what this man could possibly want with him.

For the present, he was left to wonder. A Frankish knight in chains stood before the low throne, answering the sultan's questions. Al-Mukhtar signalled John to wait his turn, and he silently reviewed what the Watchers had told him about Egypt. The Egypt he had known, the wealthy province that produced grain for the whole Roman empire, had fallen to Saracen rule shortly after Jerusalem. John could imagine how it had been: the Alexandrians, with their own theological traditions, resented the interference of Constantinople in their doctrines even more bitterly than had the churches of Palestine. Yes, they would have welcomed Saracen rule, and the freedom to hold their own beliefs without the threat of imperial persecution—persecution John recalled enforcing only too clearly.

Today Egypt was ruled by an elite coterie of military men: mamluks, or warriors who had been trained as slaves and then liberated to join their former masters in the government. Arabs, Turks, Circassians and even Tartars, they were bound together by loyalty to each other and to the men who had bought and trained them.

Most of all by loyalty to Qalawun, who now owned more mamluks than any other lord in Egypt. They were his power base, the threads by which he kept tight personal control not just of his brother amirs and their followers, but all the scholars, theologians, merchants, officials, artisans, nomads, and humble peasantry of Egypt.

Qalawun waved his hand, and the Frankish knight was led away.

"Al-Mukhtar," the sultan said, and John turned to find that all the force of the old man's attention had fallen upon them. He did not wish to bow before any such man, but as he and the Chosen stepped forwards to face the sultan, John found his defiance ebbing away. Prodigal splendour, absolute power, and the fierce pride in Qalawun's face compelled him to bend in unwilling homage.

"Is this the one you spoke of?" Qalawun asked al-Mukhtar. "The sympathiser?"

"Yes, my lord. This is the man."

"Is it finished?" the sultan asked.

That question was not directed to them. Instead, a man sitting cross-legged at a low writing-desk in the far corner of the tent quickly lifted a sheet of papyrus upon which he had been scratching with a quill pen, waving it in the air to dry the ink. "It is, my lord."

"Good." The sultan turned to face John. "Your name?"

Once more John felt an unseen pressure to answer, and he was too exhausted to recognise the danger. "John Bessarion, my lord."

He spoke the name without thinking; but at the word, Al-Mukhtar's armour chimed in a sudden startled motion. John looked up, meeting a wide-eyed, horrified stare.

Saint George help me, John thought, *what have I done?*

The sultan had not overlooked the Chosen's reaction either. "What is it, al-Mukhtar?"

Al-Mukhtar swallowed, regaining his composure with an effort. "I find I have misled you, my lord. I do not recommend entrusting your message to this man."

The sultan scowled. "Glory to God! This is a sudden reversal."

"My lord—his name…"

Strife. Strife. Strife. John slid another glance to the mamluk beside him. Al-Mukhtar's hand was knotted on the shaft of his spear, white knuckles showing through the flesh. John reached for his own belt, then stopped as he remembered that he'd left his crossbows in the tent.

The sultan's eyes narrowed. "What is the meaning of this, al-Mukhtar? You trusted him before you learned his name."

"Yes, my lord, but you have other servants you might send."

It was like the Lady Eschiva all over again. What a fool he was! Of course al-Mukhtar knew his name; of course al-Mukhtar knew what he had done. Khalil would have seen to that. Khalil had hunted him from Yarmouk to Oliveta—he and his servants would never stop hunting him so long as the two of them lived.

"Compose yourself, al-Mukhtar," Qalawun said contemptuously. "I am the king of kings; I am not afraid of this Syrian dog, and I mean to send one who was in Tripoli when it fell." He leaned forward with an ominous smile. "I want them to hear the story in every detail. If this Syrian will swear faithfully to deliver my message to the miserable Franks at Acre, that will serve."

John came back to himself with a jolt, his heart galloping like a racehorse. Khalil wanted him dead, Al-Mukhtar had learned his name, and the sultan was the only reason he wasn't already dead on the floor. Qalawun's errand might be his only hope. "I swear faithfully to deliver your message, my lord. I'll depart at sunrise."

The sultan glinted with grim humour. "Mind you do not stumble across him on his journey, al-Mukhtar, and end his life by accident, as it were."

"Your errand will not be impeded by *me*, my lord." But the Chosen's voice was stiff and expressionless, and John knew not to trust it.

The sultan held al-Mukhtar's gaze a moment longer, coldly imposing. "Very well," he said at length, and sealed the papyrus with his signet ring.

John tucked the message into his purse and bowed, this time with less reluctance.

As he turned to go, he found he was alone. Al-Mukhtar was a flurry of movement, already hurrying across the rooftop towards the stairs.

Where was he off to in such a hurry? Bright gaudy visions flashed into John's head. His fifty souls. The Zakar children. Asleep and helpless in the tent of a man who wanted to kill and could not.

A chill crept down his spine, and John hurried after the mamluk. "Al-Mukhtar!"

By the time he reached the foot of the stairs, the Chosen was long gone, swallowed up by the shadows. *Saint George, pray for us.* His ribs were aching after his hurried descent. Wrapping an arm around his side, John plunged into the darkness of Mount Pilgrim. The way back to the camp was long, lonely, and unfamiliar, and at each step he expected to meet a blade in the dark. By the time he made it into the Saracen camp and al-Mukhtar's tent came in view, he nearly wished he had. If al-Mukhtar had touched a hair of their heads—

He burst into the warm darkness beyond the flap. The lamp had gone out, and inside the tent was thick with steady breathing. Peaceful. Calm. Safe.

John closed his eyes, drawing in a shivering breath. That sense of relief passed as quickly as it had come, however, and he dropped to his knees, feeling for his crossbows. Yet even with their reassuring weight hanging from his belt again, he could not rest. For a long time, he lay himself across the tent flap, staring into the night beyond. It took him hours to fall asleep, but when he did, Rahel—the true Rahel—was waiting for him.

"There's so much to tell you," he greeted her sombrely.

She looked around her, noting the rich patterns of the tent. "So it seems."

The story was neither brief nor easy to tell, but at last he came to the end of it. Rahel sat beside him with her hands over her mouth, watching him sorrowfully.

"I thought something was wrong," she said, "but I couldn't get through to warn you."

John looked down at his hands. "I ought to have seen through Lilith's manipulation myself. I never knew how weak I could be without you. Even now..." His voice trailed away.

God help him, when would it end? At Yarmouk, the decision had been so easy. There was the warrior; there was the spear. All he had done was separate the one from the other. Even now he felt the exhilaration of battle, the glorious strength and swiftness the weapon had bestowed upon him. If he had known—if he had but *known* how that choice would follow him, how long and dearly he would pay for a few brief hours of futile strength!

Worse: Soraya had said that she knew him. John passed a hand over his eyes, wishing there was anything he might do to avoid facing the truth.

"There's something else," he said at length. "At Yarmouk, I did worse than steal a weapon. I made an oath to a heretic woman named Soraya. An oath I never had any intention of keeping."

There: that was his secret, his shame. No wonder the angels were silent. He might cast out demons and snatch children from death, but none of it mattered because he had done a terrible thing to a woman whose face he had never seen. All his self-righteous wrath at Khalil and al-Mukhtar that morning, when he had *this* on his conscience!

In a few words he told Rahel the rest of the story. Her eyes were gentle, but he could not meet them as he finished: "I owe a terrible debt. You understand, don't you? I must set things right, even if it means I never make it home."

She nodded, although her lips were tight with worry. "Of course I understand, John. You would not be my husband if you did not."

His sleep was broken after Rahel left him. Still, he saw no sign of the Chosen, not even by the time he and his fifty souls were ready to leave the camp the next morning at sunrise.

Chapter XXXVI.

The mountain was called the Face of Stone.

Eighty-five years ago—no, John corrected himself. Seven hundred and thirty-eight years ago, the road from Tripoli to Beirut had skirted the shore between this mountain and the sea, until the year of the great earthquake had shaken the mountain into the sea, destroying the road.

Now the road looped inland around the mountain, running through a dry, narrow gorge that blazed white in the noonday sun. Wiry scrub clung to the slanting sides of the gorge, speckling the rising slopes of the hills beyond.

Drawing his left crossbow, John turned to face the slow-moving column of weary, footsore, hungry fugitives behind him. "Take a short rest!" he called, and gladly they shuffled to a stop, throwing themselves on the ground. Most were still exhausted following the previous day's journey. Although the villages through which they had passed had been generous, freely trading food and medicine for the grisly tale of Tripoli's downfall and any scraps of news concerning family members lost to the sack, John knew only too well that the terrible events of two days ago would have left scars not just of the body but also the spirit.

"Will you load this for me?" He held out the crossbow as Gerard of Montreal limped up to him. Since the slaughter, the Frankish knight had barely spoken. Now, he simply nodded and wound the bow, replacing the bolt. Wincing, John reached for the second crossbow at his right hip. "I've never liked this stretch of road. Too perfect for an ambush."

"The bandits are not usually too bad down here on the coast." Montreal's voice seemed slow with disuse. "All the villagers along the coast here are Syrians, Armenians, or Franks. It's the Saracens further up in the hills that make the trouble."

He finished the second bow and handed it back.

Maybe we are devils, Watcher, but if we are it is because we have learned from archdevils. Al-Mukhtar's words returned to John, sparking his curiosity. "Why do they do that? Make trouble, I mean?"

"It's those damned Hospitallers and their constant raids on the local villages." At John's puzzled look, Montreal shrugged. "A previous count gave most of the mountain fortresses to the Hospital to garrison and rule. They haven't exactly endeared themselves to the Saracens."

Another of Lilith's gifts to her domain? Although, John's own experiences had given him a great deal of faith in the obstinacy of humanity, unassisted by supernatural corruption.

Still, it wasn't just native banditry that bothered him. Taking a scant mouthful of water from his canteen—given by a village woman in memory of a lost son—John nodded south up the gorge. "You say the lordship of Gibelet might still be resisting the Egyptians. How much further till we reach their territory?"

"I don't know for sure. The other end of this gorge, certainly."

Then they had only to survive the next few hours. John replaced the cork in his canteen and turned to call the fifty fugitives back to their feet, but the words died in his throat.

In the throat of the gorge behind them, a lone figure sat straddling a horse. He'd appeared silently, swiftly, and none of the fugitives had yet noticed him. John's scalp prickled at the sight of the black turban, the deftly-held lance.

A choking sound beside him told him that Montreal, too, had seen the Chosen. A ripple of surprise and terror ran down the whole line of fugitives as al-Mukhtar walked his horse through the white dust toward them.

It was no more than John had expected, even after al-Mukhtar's servants had escorted them safely out of the Egyptian camp the previous morning. Now that it had actually happened, a little of the tension in his body eased.

There was no need to fear the worst when it had already come.

John clenched his right fist where it hung in a sling, and regretted it at once. The weakness would cripple his wounded arm, even if the pain did not. As for his ribs, he didn't bother to test those. The pain had subsided in the last couple of days, but they still ached with every breath.

Determined anyway, he unhooked his left crossbow and strode past the line of frightened, murmuring fugitives until he faced al-Mukhtar.

"For expelling Lilith, you swore me fifty souls. Do you mean to break your word?"

"No," al-Mukhtar said coldly. "You have taken fifty-one."

It was true: since Montreal had stumbled into al-Mukhtar's tent, they had one man too many.

John let out a long, slow breath. So this was the end of it. He had done all he could to survive, to find his way home, to do some good. The first seemed impossible; the second he must give up; the third was still, perhaps, within his grasp. At least al-Mukhtar was still ready to honour their agreement.

"If I give myself up, it will be fifty again." John turned to find Gerard at his side. The Frankish knight had his dagger drawn, but his hands were shaking as he stared at al-Mukhtar, and his face was white as paper. John put a gentle hand on Montreal's shoulder, then reached into his pouch to extract the sultan's letter. "Take them to Gibelet, Montreal. Be sure they're cared for. Be sure this message reaches Acre. Can you do that?"

Stiffly, Montreal reached out and took the letter.

"I'm trusting you, friend. Swear you won't leave them until they're safe."

The knight took a deep breath and nodded. "I swear."

Protesting voices reached him from the ranks of the Watchers, and suddenly a pair of arms locked around his middle, sending starbursts of pain through his vision. "Uncle John!" It was Elisa Zakar, eyes full of tears. "Don't *you* leave us, too!"

John glanced up at al-Mukhtar, then threw caution to the wind and eased to his knees. The five children flocked to him, arms latching onto him from every side. Through dizzying pain, he felt someone wipe a sticky nose on his neck—but it wasn't just his ribs that hurt now. It seemed a paltry thing to die for them when they only needed someone to live for them.

"Oh, children. Forgive me. Be good for Aunt Anna."

He pushed them away and got up, but Elisa still clung to one leg. "Won't we see you again?"

"One day, little one." He smoothed her hair back from her upturned face, and forced a smile.

Matthias was watching him with dark, hollow eyes. "He means after we're all dead, Elisa. Come on."

John didn't protest as the boy shepherded his siblings away, back to where Anna stood waiting for them. The boy wasn't angry, only tired. Matthias had reason to know that an adult's promises could not always be depended upon. Perhaps he thought that honesty was better than comfort.

Perhaps it was better that way.

John turned to face the rest of his fugitives and cleared his throat. "Many of you saw your friends and family give themselves up for others. Now it's my turn to do the same for you. Go in peace, friends."

Montreal clapped his hands at them. "Let's go! Now!"

Evidently, the Frank was eager to clear the scene before the Saracen warrior changed his mind. Montreal did not look back, but many of the fugitives trudged away reluctantly, their heads slewed around for a doleful last glance.

None of them expected him to survive. John felt that he might have appreciated a pretence. Well, perhaps that was a luxury none of them could afford after the nightmare of the last few days. He stood and watched, keeping his back to al-Mukhtar until the column had crested the slope and vanished from sight.

Silence and wind replaced the sound of tramping feet. And then al-Mukhtar's hoofbeats came closer.

John turned, lifting his left crossbow. The Chosen raised an eyebrow.

"Glory to God, you know very well those can't hurt me."

"Habit," John said. "I take it you have come to kill me."

Al-Mukhtar shrugged. "My loyalties belong to my Master, not to Sultan Qalawun."

I've faced your master before. Yet here I am. The words were on the tip of his tongue; but it would be a childish taunt, especially when there was still something he wanted from this man. John's throat was dry, but he pointed toward the spear and forced the words out. "A dying request. Before you use her to kill me, let me say goodbye to Soraya."

The half-smile wiped off al-Mukhtar's face. Slowly, he straightened in the saddle, his hand clenching on the weapon.

"What?" John added. "It's obvious, isn't it? The two things you were never without were your ring and your spear. The ring, which was not magic…and the spear, which is. Let me speak to her."

Al-Mukhtar's eyes were murderous shards of green ice. "Why? So that the two of you can betray me one last time?"

John held that gaze without flinching. "I gave you Tripoli. I was the one who completed the mission you could not, and my people suffered for it. Are you not strong enough to be generous?"

The challenge hung in the air for a long moment. John held himself still and expressionless, although deep inside he was begging. Only let him speak to Soraya, only let him make this small sliver of recompense, and he could die in peace.

Al-Mukhtar's lips thinned and he studied the landscape with a long, measuring look. At last, he descended from the saddle and tethered his horse's halter to the low branch of a sycamore tree. Stamping the spear against the stone beneath his feet, he spoke. "Soraya, come forth."

A wind blew up clouds of dust, resolving into a whirlwind which condensed into the shape of a woman. Within moments, Soraya faced him. "John!" She glanced back at Saif, confused. "What is happening?"

"Say what you like to her," al-Mukhtar said. "It doesn't matter; she'll forget it all, anyway."

Soraya was still staring at the Chosen. Little by little, realisation dawned in her eyes, and her teeth bared in a snarl. "It was the *spear*? All along, it was the *spear*?"

"Time was it took you just days to figure it out." His voice was hard as stone. "The more we erase your past, the more foolish you become, it seems."

Soraya's fingers sharpened to claws. "I may be a fool," she bit, "but I can make you bleed." She lunged forward, but instantly al-Mukhtar clenched his fist. Soraya crumpled to the ground, gasping as though he was about to tear the spirit from her body.

"Stop. Please." John fell to his knees, taking her hand. "Hear me, Soraya. I know why it is that you remember me."

Al-Mukhtar's hand unclenched in surprise, and Soraya clawed back enough strength to lift her head, eyes wide with fear. "No! I don't want to know," she choked. "God be merciful—please don't make me remember..."

"It's all right." John closed his eyes in shame. It wasn't only the burden of her servitude she'd had to contend with. It was the guilt. *His* guilt. "I am the one who should ask forgiveness."

"For what?"

"For what I did at Yarmouk, at the great battle, six hundred and fifty-three years ago, when you saved my life."

Chapter XXXVII.

The River Yarmouk, A.D. 636

The battle had raged for days already. One day of preliminary skirmishing between lancers; three days of desperate struggle across the land between the two river valleys; one of exhausted truce as the men tended their wounds and the commanders plotted.

In late August, the Syrian highlands east of Lake Tiberias were hot and dry. Even at night, the heat lingered. John crouched by the river to splash water on his sweating face, but before he could reach the water, the crackle of something heavy in the undergrowth brought him to his feet, sword out.

He'd left the Roman sentries behind some time ago—a quarter of an hour, judging by the tilt of the stars. "Give the watchword," he whispered in Syriac to the silent darkness.

A wild beast, a gazelle or jackal, should have fled at the sound of his voice. A friend should have responded.

Instead, silence.

That silence told him everything he needed to know. This steep gorge protected the Roman camp from the heretics' attack, but it also provided a hidden passage for a man on foot who wanted to creep from one camp to another.

"Give yourself up, and we'll let you live," John growled, switching to the heretics' language.

A voice answered from the shadows. "But there's only one of you, and you can't even see me." It was a silvery female whisper, unafraid. Amused, even.

The heretic women had joined the fighting more than once in the last four days, and John was taking no chances. He moved forward, sword ready. "Well, that makes two of us. What are you doing out here?"

"Shouldn't I be the one to ask that? You're right underneath our camp."

Saints. John glanced up. It was too dark, the valley's edge too indistinct to show the shapes of sentries, but he realised he could see a faint red light of campfires reflected from the thick clouds covering the sky above him. She was right: in the dark, he had travelled further than he thought.

A question occurred to him. "All right. So why aren't you shouting for help?"

"Oh...I suppose I could." She let out a sigh, her voice weary. "Maybe I will."

John scowled into the darkness, confused. Nothing about this made sense. Why wasn't she frightened of an enemy warrior? Why, with his life on the tip of her tongue, did she hold her breath?

The longer he kept her talking, the more likely she'd be to let something slip. "You don't sound terribly interested in the result."

"Why should I be? It's not as though I'm here by choice. Incidentally, do you have any idea how your commander has disposed his cavalry for tomorrow?"

John nearly choked. "I beg your pardon?"

"I only thought to ask. It would save my having to trudge up this valley and find out for myself. Likely get shot for my trouble."

"Well, I'm hardly going to tell you, am I?"

"Oh, you needn't tell me the *truth.* All I was told to do was find a Greek and charm it out of him. My orders left me with a certain amount of—elbow-room."

John blinked, but he was beginning to understand. *I'm not here by choice.* "Why don't we make a deal? I'll tell you whatever you need to hear, so long as you get me into your camp."

"Oh no," she said with a chuckle. "If something went wrong, it would be at least as unpleasant as going to the Romans."

He could understand the difficulty, but he needed the help. "You can't get something for nothing, my lady."

A weary sigh. "Shall I call out to the sentries, then?"

"No!" John scowled in thought. There was something else he needed much more than a free pass into the camp. "All right: I need to know a man's name, that's all. Can you do that for me?"

There was a short silence while she considered it. "That seems fair."

John closed his eyes, calling to memory the battle's first day. "The man I need to find…he was skirmishing on the first day. He wore a white headdress and a black tunic, and…" John shook his head in unwilling admiration. "He didn't lose a *single* fight."

Later, on the second day when the Romans had come within a hair's breadth of victory, it was the lancer in the black tunic who had spearheaded the heretic countercharge. For days John had watched the man doing feats of incredible strength. Watched, and been ready to gnaw his fingers for envy.

Despite vastly superior numbers, the Roman offensive had made little impression on the heretic army. Now, they were trapped between two deep gorges, cut off from retreat, and staring defeat in the face. Vahan and the other ranking officers had spent the whole day's truce trying to plot, bargain or threaten their way out of the trap in which they had been caught. To no avail.

John had done what he could to help, but privately his thoughts had been occupied by the invincible lancer. Without him, the battle might have been won three days ago.

Without him, the battle might yet be won.

The woman had been silent so long he wondered if she was still there. At last she whispered softly, "You saw?"

"Yes."

"Khalil ibn Hassan," she said, still in the same thoughtful tone.

"That's his name? Thanks." John wiped sweaty palms on his trousers, quickly inventing a plausible lie that would benefit their true battle plans. "Vahan has put the cavalry in—"

"It's his spear," the woman interrupted.

John hushed. "I beg your pardon?"

"Khalil's spear," she repeated insistently. "That's what makes him invincible. Take the spear, and he's just an ordinary man."

The spear. "It's…magic?"

"It's *cursed*," she hissed, the word sputtering violently into the night air. "To make it, Khalil sought the help of a demon named Qeteb. Promise me that once you have it, you will expel the demon and destroy the lance."

Entranced by the possibilities, John barely heard. Remove the lancer from this tale, and the heretic trap might yet be sprung…but what if the lance itself could be captured? With it, John himself might be the hero. Did they tell stories of John Bessarion's exploits at Nineveh? They would tell far greater things of his deeds at Yarmouk. Victory for his people. Death to the invaders. Peace for his fatherland.

It seemed almost too good to be true. "Why are you helping me?"

"Because Khalil is my master, and I hate him. Promise me you will destroy it."

He couldn't afford that; not while the army balanced on the knife's edge of destruction. "After the battle is won."

"What part of *cursed* don't you understand?" Her whisper became higher-pitched, more sibilant as her apathy flowered into passion. "How many immortal souls have been sent staggering prematurely to the hereafter because of that weapon? How many mothers have lost their sons, children their fathers? How much longer will this war last for its sake?"

John shut his eyes and hardened his heart. "I will destroy it; you have my word. But not before the battle is won. My children also have a father," he said, and in the darkness, she sighed.

"Tomorrow?" Her voice was small and reluctant.

"When the battle is won."

"Very well, then," she said. The passion had faded away again into weariness. "Khalil keeps the spear close to him at all times. The only exception will be at sunrise, when he is due to attend council in the general's tent, and weapons are forbidden. At sunrise, then, you must enter his tent and take the spear."

"To do that, I must be within the camp by dawn."

"Yes." There was a long, determined breath. "My name is Soraya. Come with me."

* * *

The Lebanon, A.D. 1289

Soraya's face was buried in her hands; her body so still that John wondered if she had forgotten to breathe. Was she aghast? Disconsolate? Furious?

He drew a deep breath. "It was a promise I did not keep. Even after the defeat, I told myself that the battle was not yet won. That I could wield the spear until it was." He dragged a hand down his face as though it could wipe away the bitter shame he felt. "If I had kept my promise, you would have been freed centuries ago. Khalil might have killed me in revenge, but with no hope of regaining the weapon, he would never have burned Oliveta." He took another deep breath and continued. "All this is my fault, my most grievous fault. I dare not ask your forgiveness."

Soraya looked up at him—the djinn of the spear, who had drunk blood for six hundred years because he had not freed her. Her face was wet with tears. "But then—I wasn't trying to kill you."

Clearly, she remembered nothing of their meeting in the gorges of Yarmouk. "No."

She scrubbed away the tears with her hands. "I only wanted the bloodshed to stop."

"Yes."

"And to be free."

"Yes."

Her face crumpled again. "Then this *is* who I really am. I have *always* wanted better."

There was no longer anything he could do to set things right; but at least he had spoken. John forced a smile, and offered his handkerchief. "I presume it was you; I never actually saw her face. So many of the things that puzzled me then…why you weren't afraid…the manner was the same, but the voice was different."

"Yes. I think I would craft a different body for a mission like that." She blew her nose loudly, then laughed ruefully. "I…I keep doing terrible things to your kerchiefs. I'm sorry."

He tucked the damp cloth away with a shake of his head. "It's the least I could do."

"Oh, John. Maybe I'll be angry at you later. But right now…" She threw her arms around him, whispered in his ear. "Thank you."

Startled, John looked beyond her to the Chosen. Al-Mukhtar waited patiently; the breeze tugged at his lightweight tunic, but his face was stern as stone.

"Maybe I'm *not* one of the evil djinn," she breathed at last, pulling back. Her lips seemed to taste the words carefully, and then a smile split her face as she turned it to the sky. "I seek forgiveness from God for all my sins and turn to him."

Al-Mukhtar was waiting for him. John tried, but failed to return her smile. "I hope one day you'll learn more." Another piece of memory drifted back to him. "I remember one thing you told me. We spoke of our families. You said you were one of seven sisters."

"I did?"

"The youngest, you said."

Her gaze unfocused. "I have sisters," she whispered. Another glowing smile lit up her face, and she pulled him back into a fierce hug. "Thank you," she whispered into his chest. "I never thought to find hope in my past."

With that, the hopeless present intruded on them. John turned to where al-Mukhtar stood watching, spear in hand. "This was all the parting gift I could make, Soraya. I'm sorry I didn't free you when I had the chance at Yarmouk. I'm sorry he's going to take even this away from you."

Al-Mukhtar moved like a statue coming to life. Coming on guard, he pointed the spear at John. "Are you finished?"

Horrified understanding dawned over Soraya's face. "You're going to *kill* him?" Incredulous, she stepped between them. "What are you doing, Saif? He gave you Tripoli! You *promised!*"

"Surely you heard him." Al-Mukhtar's green eyes shifted a shade closer to silver. "This is the thief who stole you from the Master. And if he was not a thief, he would still be a Watcher. And if he was not a Watcher, he would still be a *Bessarion.*"

"I don't understand—He's a Zakar—"

"He lied! He's a *Bessarion.* He's *the* Bessarion; the one who began it all." Al-Mukhtar took a deep breath and pointed his spear at John. "I was wrong to spare you when I thought you were only a Zakar. But if I spare you now, John Bessarion, I am dishonoured forever." Al-Mukhtar's lips thinned, and he lifted his chin with a show of bravado. "For as long as I've served Khalil, there have been three standing orders. Eliminate the Watchers. Eliminate the Zakars. And never, on any account, permit a Bessarion to live."

John stared at the other man, stricken. His descendants. His *children.* "How many?"

"Not enough." Al-Mukhtar poised his spear to strike.

Soraya darted between them and fell to her knees. "Saif, I *beg* you…"

"Step aside," he snarled.

"Please." Soraya's hands dropped to her side, clenched in the white dust. "Don't do this."

Even as she spoke, her hands flashed up, and she hurled a handful of sand and gravel with all her strength straight into al-Mukhtar's eyes.

"John," she screamed, *"the spear!"*

Her fists clenched, perhaps in an attempt to wrest all the strength she could along the soul tether. Al-Mukhtar staggered back a step, one hand reflexively clutching his face. John, on his feet and momentarily more agile than Soraya, was already lunging towards al-Mukhtar. A stab of pain shot through his ribs; but John grabbed the spear behind the point and twisted it swiftly from al-Mukhtar's grasp.

It fit into his hands with familiar comfort, and with it came a familiar rush of power. His right arm warmed suddenly—stronger and not so painful as he moved.

"Break it!" Soraya shrieked.

He already had the shaft above his head, lashing it against a nearby rock. No matter how tough, the ash shaft should have cracked at the least. Yet it was as though he'd struck the rock with a bar of iron. The shock jarred his arms; agony pierced through his wound. John gasped. Reflexively his hands opened; he dropped the spear.

What did he expect? Spears broke all the time. The only way this one could have lasted six hundred years was if it was spelled not to break. That must be why Soraya had told him to exorcise Qeteb as a preliminary.

Al-Mukhtar clawed the sand from his eyes, blinking furiously through the grit. "Soraya!" he roared as she rose from her knees into a fighter's crouch, her hands splayed wide. He snatched his sword from the sheath and pointed it at her. "Stay where you are, devil!"

"I'm not a devil," she said with a grin feral enough to belie it. "And without the spear, you can't order me around."

Shock played over al-Mukhtar's face as he realised the truth of what she'd said "No," he conceded, "but I still have the soul tether." His hand shot out and clenched.

John snatched the spear up again in the same moment, letting its power—*Soraya's* power—spark through him once more, pushing his aches to the back of consciousness. If he couldn't break it, he'd have to exorcise Qeteb.

And for the opportunity to do that, he'd have to kill the Chosen.

Teeth bared, Soraya fell to her knees again, fighting for control of the soul tether. No time to lose. John levelled the spear and rushed al-Mukhtar. The Chosen dodged aside; but the effort must have dislodged his grip on the soul tether, for instantly Soraya charged to her feet and launched herself across the space between, colliding bodily with the mamluk. They went down together in a cloud of white dust and John followed, the point of his spear feinting as he tried to find an opening.

"Now," Soraya gasped, and she must have loosened her grip on the soul tether because suddenly al-Mukhtar was on top of her with his hands around her neck, providing a stable target.

John lunged.

Al-Mukhtar's eyes widened and he moved faster than John would have thought possible, throwing himself aside. John's thrust pierced uselessly through thin air. In the same movement, al-Mukhtar took Soraya by the jacket and threw her with astonishing force: she flew through the air behind him for fifteen paces or so before hitting the ground in a cloud of dust.

John hesitated just a moment, his attention stolen by Soraya's flight. In that unguarded moment Al-Mukhtar charged. By the time John realised his danger, the mamluk was inside John's guard and reaching for his sword, dropped in the sand at John's feet.

John stamped on the fallen blade, reached for his left crossbow, and pulled the trigger. The bolt drilled through al-Mukhtar's right shoulder and lodged precisely in the hollow between collarbone and neck, disabling the arm. That bought him a breathing-space, and John stepped away, bringing the spear to guard.

As he did, something plucked at his belt.

The Chosen rose to his feet, raising John's second crossbow with his good left arm. Time splintered. Beyond al-Mukhtar, Soraya's mouth opened in a futile warning shriek. Just as he had in the Templar courtyard, John twisted to provide a smaller target.

He half expected the bolt to go through his temple, but al-Mukhtar evidently preferred a surer target. The bolt punched through his right leg, skewering the thick muscle in front of the bone. The pain was hot and sickening. With a groan, John collapsed to one knee.

Al-Mukhtar took a deep shuddering breath, threw down the expended crossbow and pulled out the bolt that still jutted from his body. Only then did he climb to his feet and yank the spear from John's slack hands.

Half blinded by the pain—it seemed to burst throughout his whole body now, unfurling from ribs and arm and leg and muscles he didn't even realise he'd strained—John looked up into the blazing eyes of his death.

Rahel, he thought. *I'm sorry.*

Before the blow could fall, the ground shook. An immense shadow fell over them. An enormous hand fastened around al-Mukhtar's body, swept him up and hurled him away. Up, and out of the valley altogether, spear and all.

John peered speechlessly at the gigantic figure as it knelt before him. *"Soraya?"*

As he and al-Mukhtar battled, she must have drawn the white dust of the valley into a body three or four times the mass of his own. Now as she towered over him, the sparks of her power crackled in her hair. She passed an immense hand over his leg and the arrow turned to particles, flowing from the wound.

Her voice boomed like thunder.

"You're wounded. Take the horse and go while you still can."

Under the sycamore tree, al-Mukhtar's animal pulled against its halter in panic. Clearly, giants were beyond the scope of its experience.

John let out a groan of frustration, a hand pressed to the hot trickle from his thigh. "The spear! I swore I'd free you!"

"Then *live,* and keep that promise." Something soft shone in her great eyes: hope. "Did I not say I could return you to your own time, if only we had met in the past?"

Home. Soraya could take him home! He'd been so wrapped in shame, so focused on his imminent death that it hadn't even occurred to him. Now—it was like coming out of prison and seeing the stars again, the boundless horizon.

He had been so very certain that Lilith was his only choice. Yet now it seemed so plain, so simple. He was meant to free Soraya; and then she would send him home. If he had not been in so much pain, he might have laughed for pure delight.

Instead, John took the scrap of green silk she handed him, and twisted it around his leg to stanch the flow of blood. "You would do that for me? You said you meant to be angry with me."

She only laughed, soft and low, but deep enough to make the earth shake. "Free me, John Bessarion. Restore my memories. And I *will* take you home."

She picked him up as easily as a child, setting him down atop the frightened horse. With one yank, she snapped the halter like a thread.

John clung to the saddle horn as the maddened animal bolted south up the gorge.

Before reaching the crest, he glanced over his shoulder. Where Soraya had stood, a column of dust blew in the wind.

* * *

"The terrible thing," John whispered, "is that now I know why there were no Watchers in Damascus."

John's sleeping body lay shrouded in a blanket, hidden in the undergrowth in a fold of the hills above Botron. Al-Mukhtar's horse was tethered nearby, so exhausted after its reckless gallop that it had lain down to sleep. A little way up the slope from both of them, his dreamself watched Rahel as she paced through the trees, her hands clasped under her chin as she tried to grasp everything he'd told her.

"This al-Mukhtar has been killing them all systematically. All the Watchers. Anyone who bears the name Zakar or Bessarion." John dragged his good hand down his face. "Saints, not even Soraya and I could kill him, working together."

Rahel turned to him, still wringing her hands. "Could…could he perhaps be persuaded?"

John stared. *"Persuaded?"*

"To let you go. To free Soraya."

"You're serious?"

She smiled faintly, and gave a shrug. "Do you remember what you said to the Watchers at—"

"Of course I do," John said uncomfortably. Unbidden, his mind supplied the words. *Not to condemn the world, but that the world through him might be saved.*

"Well." She gave him a hopeful smile. "You're John Bessarion, the man who hunted heretics and now cares for them as his own. Aren't you?"

"Yes, and that's why I'm helping Soraya. But…you've never met this man, Rahel."

"I know. Some people can't be helped." Rahel's face fell, and she took a deep breath. "You look terrible, my love. You need to get that leg cared for."

Even in his sleep, his wounds were a hot insistent ache. "As soon as the sun rises, I'll go into the village to buy salve." Earlier that afternoon, he'd emerged from the gorge of Theoprosopon to espy his fifty fugitives trudging their way through the hazy hills towards Botron and the low coastal city of Gibelet. Instead of following them, he'd turned away, plunging into the hills. His heart had protested, but he could find a safer way to let Matthias and the other Zakar children know he was still alive. If he rejoined them, he'd only put them in danger: he was confident by now that al-Mukhtar meant to hunt him to his death.

John looked down at his ghostly hands. Until now he'd been reluctant to tell her; their hopes had been dashed so many times already. "There's one more thing. Since Soraya knew me in the past, she could bring me home. If she was free. If she regained her memory."

Rahel stared, and he saw the look in her eyes: hope against hope, clouding over again in a moment. "But surely, in order to do that you would have to free her from the spear and exorcise the demon that bound her and took her memory. You would be walking right back into a fight with the Chosen—and Khalil." She swallowed. "Don't do it, John. I'll go back to Antioch. I'll free Soraya and destroy the spear in *this* time."

"No," he said quickly. "Please. It's too dangerous—there's a war on, and you only just survived the last journey."

"Still, John! Six *hundred* years! The poor girl!"

He lifted a hand to his forehead, and was surprised when the clammy feeling of sweat didn't meet his ghostly hand. "Rahel…if you free her in your time, before I get home, she won't be here to help me in mine."

"I can speak to her. Ask her."

"Of course." It was still a risk, though he had long since forfeited any right to defer Soraya's freedom.

"Listen," he said at length. "It's dangerous for you to return to Antioch. Especially with times the way they are; especially with Paulus and Elisa depending on you. It was *my* promise, not yours. If I can get Soraya free in this time, and find my way home, I'll go to Antioch myself and free her in yours."

"And if you fail? If you can't free her in your time?" Rahel asked, her voice low.

He took a deep breath. "If I fail…then when the war is over and it's safe to travel, and the children are grown, you must go to Antioch." He let out the breath with a deep sigh. "Ten years. If ten years pass and I don't come home, you must do what you must."

Rahel nodded, and made a sound like a sob. "I wish I could do something to help."

"Keep the children alive, and safe, so that I have something to come back to." He swallowed. This afternoon he'd had ample time to think, to lay a few more stones in the wall of things he understood. "One more thing. Before I banished her, Lilith called me *the last of them.*"

"The last of…?"

"The last of the sacrifices of Oliveta. The last of the Bessarions." John ran a ghostly hand along the ache in his thigh. "If Paulus and Elisa's descendants go by Zakar, yet the Lady of Beirut recognised the name Bessarion, then…" He took a deep, deep breath. "Lukas and Marta—one or both of the children are somewhere *between* us, Rahel. And if Lilith knew them, then there's just a chance that Soraya might have known them too." *Even if only at the moment of their deaths.*

He waited for her to say something, but she could only nod mutely. Hope against hope. He took another breath.

"I know there's danger, dear heart, but if there's a way to put our family back together again, I have to face it."

Chapter XXXVIII.

"The King of Kings, Lord of Lords, al-Mansur Qalawun, the Powerful, the Dreadful, the Scourge of Rebels, Hunter of Franks—"

William of Beaujeu cleared his throat. "I think it will be sufficient to skip the sultan's greeting, Montreal."

Gerard glanced up from the sultan's letter, swallowing nervously as he met the eyes of the Acre council. Directly in front of him, King Henry II of Cyprus and Jerusalem sat leaning forward with his chin on his hands. Upon hearing of the fall of Tripoli, the young king had rushed from Cyprus to meet with his delegates in Acre.

The canopied, carved, and gilded throne was flanked by the king's younger brother Prince Amalric and his aunt, Lady Margaret. Others in the frescoed council chamber included the Lady of Beirut and other great barons of the kingdom's few remaining fiefs; the Masters of the Temple, the Hospital, and the Teutons; and those commanders who had been in Tripoli when it fell: Marshal Geoffrey of Vendac for the Temple and Brother Matthew of Clermont for the Hospital; John of Grailly, the seneschal of the kingdom and commander of the elite French Regiment; and Otto of Grandison, a great lord and representative of King Edward of England.

Only Countess Lucy was missing. She had gone north to her mother's kinsman, the king of Cilician Armenia. As stubbornly as she had fought for her county when it was there to be enjoyed, she seemed to have little ambition to regain it now.

Not that regaining Tripoli seemed to be on anyone's mind.

From her place beside the king, Lady Margaret sent Gerard a warm, encouraging smile, and he returned it hopefully. Once he'd led John Zakar's motley collection of fugitives to Gibelet, the local Watchers had taken them in. They'd helped the fugitives find a place to stay, even raising the passage money for those who had family to join in other cities. Having discharged his obligation to Zakar, Gerard had been able to arrange his own passage by ship to Acre. He'd reached the city only a few hours before, so recently that he still felt queasy from the journey. At least the horrors he'd experienced in Tripoli were beginning to fade, lost for the moment in the exhilaration of his safe escape.

Not to mention the warmth of his welcome in Acre; even Master William had pulled him into an embrace. More importantly, however, Lady Margaret had been overjoyed enough to kiss both his cheeks in front of the princes, her nephews.

Now they and the other great lords waited to hear what the sultan's letter contained. Gerard lifted the paper again, pausing every few words to translate the meaning from Arabic to French.

"To the noble king of Cyprus, the true and wise: Greetings and our good will! Because you have been a true man, so we are sending notice that having defended our trading interests and snatched the whole land of Tripoli from the hands of those miscreants who have used it in the past to prey upon our people and threaten the security of our kingdom, we are now ready to hang up our bow and sheath our mighty sword."

The Arabic word for *sword* was *saif.* Gerard thought of the Chosen, and hoped that the figurative language was meant to hold a double meaning. He would be glad to see no more of al-Mukhtar for a little while.

"For that purpose, we direct you to send ambassadors to conclude a truce between ourselves and Syria and Cyprus, so that we may swear oaths of peace towards each other."

The whole council-chamber seemed to hold its breath until Gerard folded the letter away. Then it breathed a collective sigh of relief, and the whispers started. The king sat back, drumming his fingers on the arm of his chair. Even he looked deeply relieved. "Master William, will you go as an ambassador, since the sultan likes you so much? And…" his eyes scanned the room before settling on Grandison. "You I can trust, my lord Otto. Make ready to depart by Ascension at the latest."

He stood, signalling an end to the council.

"My lord," Beaujeu objected. "Don't you want to confer about this?"

"I don't see that there's anything to confer *about*," the young king retorted. "Do you think we can afford *not* to have a truce?"

There was a bitter edge in the king's voice. For years the Master of the Temple had supported a rival claimant to the kingdom of Jerusalem. That lord had died four years ago in Italy, leaving the path clear for the Lusignans of Cyprus to claim the throne. With that, Beaujeu had gracefully yielded his opposition to Henry's rule, but a certain measure of discomfort persisted between the two men. Gerard sighed, reminding himself that the Templars were little better trusted in Acre than they had been in Tripoli before its fall.

"Of course not," Beaujeu said, respectful despite the young king's thinly-veiled hostility. "Still, we can't afford to hope that such a truce will last long. First Antioch, then Tripoli. Logically, Acre will be next."

His words silenced the room, destroying the sense of relief that had descended upon them all.

"Which we will discuss another time, Beaujeu," the king said brusquely, stepping down from the throne. In his absence, the High Court gathered into knots of conversation, hungry for more details of the fall of Tripoli; desperate for news of the dead or missing; questioning whether the English king's projected crusade would come in time to save them, or whether an exodus to Cyprus or Frankish-ruled Greece might be wise.

Once, Gerard would have listened to them in confidence that something would change, that some clever enough plan would save them. Today, he felt only a sour sense of dread churning in his gut as Marco's words echoed in his mind. *Tell Beaujeu he needs the angels on his side, not demons. Go back to Acre. Restore the Watchers.*

Beaujeu stood alone in the crowd, only his tight mouth betraying his anxiety. Gerard made his way towards the Master of the Temple and asked, without much hope, "Have you any plans, my lord?"

"I had *planned* to have Katsaros' help."

Gerard swallowed. He'd had to confess to Beaujeu just how badly his mission had failed, but that morning, the Master had only been happy to have him alive and well and back in Acre.

He needs the angels on his side, not demons. Gerard wasn't sure he wanted to risk giving his formidable master any such message. Instead, he took a deep breath. "I'm not sure how much help Katsaros would have been, my lord."

"Was your Prester John any better?"

His jaw clenched, but Gerard said submissively, "No, my lord."

Beaujeu grunted and stalked away. Gerard sighed. Tomorrow morning's debriefing would be uncomfortable, but he could fight that battle when the time came.

In the meantime—the memory of Lady Margaret's smile tugged at him, hinting at better things to come. A squire-attendant pointed him toward the council-room antechamber, but Gerard's heart sank as he made it through the double doors into the quiet space beyond. Lady Margaret was there, but not alone; she stood close to Eschiva of Beirut at one of the traceried windows, speaking in an undertone. Gerard hesitated.

Go back to Acre. Restore the Watchers.

Weren't the Ibelins involved with the Watchers, once?

The two ladies smiled as he approached. "Oh, Gerard," Lady Margaret reached out with a little pleading gesture, as though she could not be fully at ease unless he was near. "When I think of what Lucy did to poor Marco, and all those poor people on the island!"

"I told you she was a little hussy," Lady Eschiva said with a shrug.

"Oh, Eschiva."

"What? I did, and you know it. *Oh no,* you said. *Tripoli needs a woman's touch. We are more compassionate by nature.* Ha!"

Gerard was scandalised, but Lady Margaret spoke before he could. "I misjudged her." She turned towards him. "Gerard, I am so ashamed. It never crossed my mind that she would abandon you."

"You judged her by your own kind heart, my lady."

"You'll have to be more suspicious in the future, my good gossip," Lady Eschiva put in. She glanced from Gerard to Lady Margaret, not missing their clasped hands. A mocking eyebrow lifted. "Well, my ship is leaving at the next tide. I should go, and…pack my songbirds."

Gerard reddened. "One moment, by your leave. I meant to ask a question. What do you know about the Watchers?"

She shrugged. "They're a sort of devotional lay order. My family were Watchers for generations, as it happens. My great-grandfather, the Old Lord, was one of their most powerful Presters."

The Old Lord, a Prester? A sudden blaze of illumination took Gerard's breath away.

Not noticing his astonishment, the Lady of Beirut went on. "To tell the truth, we haven't kept the family tradition going. I think my father was a Prester—at least, I remember him telling me that he credited the Watchers for his grandfather's success—but the title lapsed when my sister Isabella inherited. No Prester has been a woman, you see." For the first time she noticed the look on Gerard's face, and her languid demeanour sharpened a little. "Why does it interest you, Sir Gerard?"

"The Old Lord," Gerard stammered. "Forgive me, my lady, but you mean your great-grandfather was a Prester of the Watchers? Prester…John of Ibelin, in fact?"

Beside him, Lady Margaret made a startled sound of understanding. John of Ibelin, the Old Lord of Beirut, was a legendary figure in the history of the kingdom. Born to a Frankish lord and a Greek princess before the loss of Jerusalem, half-brother to the first Queen Isabella, the Old Lord had been a warrior, a diplomat, a leader and a builder. He'd ruled two kingdoms as regent, repelled the Holy Roman Emperor's determined efforts to usurp the thrones of both Cyprus and Jerusalem, and died as a Templar at a good old age.

Could it be that the legends of an eastern monarch, all along, had sprung up in their own soil?

"Oh, yes." Lady Eschiva smiled. "We of Ibelin don't like to sing our own praises—" she ignored Lady Margaret's good-natured chuckle, "but yes, I believe the stories about Prester John might originally have been inspired by my celebrated ancestor."

"Saints," Gerard muttered. It had been the Old Lord he'd looking for all this time. What if the Watchers really did hold the secret to John of Ibelin's greatness?

Lady Margaret watched the hope dawning on his face and said quietly, "Gerard, you know the Watchers can't raise armies or produce wealth."

"But what if they could bring…" He struggled to find a word encompassing all that he hoped for. *Luck? Success? Blessing?* "It would take a miracle to save us now. Aren't Watchers in the business of working miracles?"

Eschiva hummed thoughtfully. "There was a time when all the greatest and most powerful people in this kingdom were Watchers, but these days, they've practically disappeared. I should have to learn more about my great-grandfather's achievements; what exactly his connection *was* with the Watchers."

"We must revive the Watchers' councils," Gerard breathed. Visions of hope danced through his mind; the kingdom restored to the days of its old glory. "My lady, I don't have the influence to do that, but you…"

Lady Eschiva put her head to one side. "The Ibelins might yet save the kingdom, you mean? Well, it's better than sitting in council watching Henry and Beaujeu peck at each other. I'll let you know what I find."

She kissed Lady Margaret fondly on the cheek and walked out into the courtyard, humming a song under her breath. In the silence, Gerard turned to Lady Margaret.

The room seemed suddenly very large, very empty, and very still. Margaret looked up at him, and then down at their clasped hands, as though she was suddenly conscious of his touch; but she didn't try to move away.

So Gerard cleared his throat and said, "You told me to recommend myself to you in a way that went deeper than clothes and flattery, my lady."

He couldn't read the look in her blue eyes as she glanced up at him. Her voice was very soft and a little pensive: "Is that why you went to Saint Thomas, then?"

She had seen. "Yes. For you."

Her mouth twisted, something between pride and sorrow. "And how did it make you feel, Gerard?"

It wasn't the question he expected, and his smile vanished away as he unwillingly remembered all—the blood, the stench, the corpses.

Marco, staring into the sky with blind eyes.

The corpses of all his hopes were piled on that island together with the dead. He said bleakly, "It didn't work. It wasn't worth the effort. If we'd gone with you, Marco would still be alive."

"Ah," she said very softly, looking at the floor between them.

The silence stretched out, and Gerard gave a gusty laugh. "A man should provide for his own, otherwise he's worse than the heathen; isn't that true?"

She looked up at him then, with a frown, and somewhere deep in Gerard's belly, he knew he had made a mistake. "You helped them for my sake and Marco's, because you knew and loved us."

"Yes." He didn't understand why she looked so disappointed.

"But not for theirs." She drew her hand from his. "That's not true compassion, Gerard."

He opened his mouth to protest, but she forestalled him. "What you did was noble, and I honour you for it, dear. I hope you know that."

Her words hung flat and dead in the air. "But?" Gerard prompted numbly. He still didn't understand. Hadn't he done as she asked?

She looked at him with a sharp twist at the side of her mouth. "I never mean to marry again. The truth is…I've never told this to anyone. Not to a man, that is. But I'm not well, Gerard. No, don't fear for me. I'm in reasonably good health. But there are things that don't work for me the way they work for other women. One of those things is…" She sighed. "The act of love has never produced life in me. Only pain."

He'd never seen her look so sad, or so humiliated.

He'd never felt more ashamed of himself. For pressing her. For demanding to know why she refused him. For holding up the possibility of children like a lure. "Margaret," he said through numb lips, "I never knew."

"I know," she said gently. "I never told you."

"You didn't…" He swallowed, his face suddenly on fire at the thought of forcing such a secret out of her. "You didn't owe me that explanation."

She gave him a bittersweet smile. "No. I make a gift of it, dear. The truth is, I don't need a husband, and I think I am happier without one. But there is something I do need, if you're willing to give it."

"Anything," he said, raggedly.

Her eyes closed briefly in longing. "A *friend.*"

He had lost so many things in the last few days; what was another hope to add to the pyre? He could not force her to take him, any more than he could master his fate. Gerard bowed and kissed her soft hand. "You may depend upon me for that."

He did not know how they took leave of each other; nor how he left the palace, and made his way through the busy streets of Acre towards the Templar commandery. He was in too much of a daze, numb with this new disappointment.

The worst of it was what she had left unsaid. He knew her well—better, perhaps, than anyone else in the world. Lady Margaret was a princess, a ruler, a diplomat; but she was also a woman, with a woman's desires and a woman's love to give. He saw now that her manner towards him had, for a short time, been that of a woman towards the man she favoured. Only at the end of today's meeting had she withdrawn again into simple friendship.

He might have had her—but instead, she had slipped through his fingers. A word, a look, a foot placed wrong; and she was lost to him forever—lost so irrevocably that she had chosen to tell her most unhappy secret, knowing exactly how solemnly it would oblige him never again to renew his suit. Never even to think of it, because although she thought him lacking in compassion, she knew he could not stomach the thought of hurting her.

He could not blame her; he could only hope, one day, to understand. Until then—well, he was the richer for her friendship. He could content himself with that.

He was still wrapped up in these thoughts when he stepped through the massive gate of the Templar fortress and emerged into the courtyard. It was a sunny day in late spring, and the enclosure was flooded with light, its honey-coloured arches stark against the clear blue of the sky. A round pool with a fountain graced the centre, and on the other side of it Brother Reddecoeur stood next to a man leaning on a walking-stick. As Gerard circled the water, the man's face came into view.

John Zakar.

Gerard paused mid-step, his mind stuttering to a halt and all the bitterness of his failures rushing in on him again. John Zakar, the false Prester who'd expelled Lilith, destroying Tripoli.

Gerard was alive because of him, he reminded himself. So were the poor, ragged Watchers he'd extracted from Tripoli. The last he'd seen of the man, he'd been bargaining his life away for Gerard's sake.

Saviour or foe, knight or villein; Gerard still didn't know what to make of this man. Only one thing was certain: he could not rejoice to see him again.

Zakar's gaze slid past Reddecoeur and lighted on Gerard with a smile. "Ah, Sir Gerard. You reached Acre safely? And the others?"

He spoke like an equal, and Gerard swallowed his distaste. There was always a chance the man genuinely was of knightly birth. "They will be safe in Gibelet. I hear the new lord is bargaining with Qalawun for an independent peace. What brings you to Acre?"

"Your Order is dedicated to fighting the Saracens." Zakar limped past Reddecoeur, and Gerard wondered how he had survived a confrontation with the Chosen with little more than a wounded leg. "Brother Reddecoeur here thinks that my particular gifts might be useful."

Reddecoeur smiled. "He wishes to take service with the Temple."

"In what capacity?"

Zakar didn't answer straight away. Finally, he said quietly, "Al-Mukhtar is a threat to this city and to me. I don't believe in being prey. I'd rather be the hunter. When Qalawun returns to Egypt... well, I would imagine the Master sends men to Egypt often. Eyes and ears."

A spy, then. Zakar *did* seem to be a man of gifts when it came to such things, and whatever his relationship with al-Mukhtar, it certainly seemed to have gone sour. Gerard nodded curtly. "I'll mention your name to the

Master."

He headed for the stairs that led to the loggia and his own cabinet. He wanted to immerse himself in his work; there was a new passage of his history to write, and he meant to sketch his impressions of the downfall of Tripoli while they were still fresh.

At the door to his cabinet he stopped, recalling Lady Eschiva's pledge to restore the Watchers as they had been in the Old Lord's day. Zakar was a Watcher—a Prester even. Perhaps…

Gerard grunted in self-reproach. It mattered not a jot if he'd had the best intentions in the world: this man had brought Tripoli to destruction. Such a man was hardly the right one to restore the glorious Watchers of old. He must remember not to let Zakar catch the faintest hint of what he and Lady Eschiva had in mind.

So determined, he closed his door and sank gratefully into the cool detached apostrophes of his history.

Epilogue.

It might have been weeks later, or years. Locked inside the spear, Soraya had no way to measure time, and when the command to manifest forced her out of it and into bodily shape again, Saif gave her few clues either way. As always, he held the spear clasped firmly in his hand. He was dressed informally in a crisp, clean shirt that hung open to expose his chest, woven from many fine iridescent strands of silk. Blended together they constituted a muted eggplant colour, punctuated by a wildly swirling pattern of golden spirals and starbursts. It was such a unique piece of work, so different from the rigid geometries the Egyptians typically used to adorn their tents or clothing that Soraya blinked at it in momentary surprise.

"Soraya," he greeted her coldly.

Soraya glanced around her. She was back in the echoing lower room beneath Saif's house in Cairo. Racks of weapons lined the walls, but Saif didn't seem to be in a sparring mood. He only leaned on the spear and glowered at her.

"You turned on me," he said harshly. "Again. Your lust for the Bessarion has blinded you."

Soraya's heart clenched with anger. "It's not lust," she said between her teeth.

"Glory to God, don't lie to me! I've seen the way you look at him."

When she'd first met John, she'd thought him well-favoured, that much was true; but it was a long time since that kind of thought had even occurred to her. He was her friend, that was all. He wasn't even one of her kind. Soraya scowled. Why was it that mortals so easily believed an immortal might conceive a passion for one of them?

It was too much to explain. "He's a pretty man, but what I love in him is his honesty."

"What is he to you, then? Tell me the truth."

"A *friend*." The words marched off her tongue without her leave. *The one who will free me from your grasp.* She reached for other thoughts to keep that truth off her lips as long as possible. "Hope, salvation, kindness, everything *you* are not."

"Stop." The command struck her into immobility. Saif tilted his head back, sighing deeply. The next moment a knock came at the door, startling him. He wheeled, jabbing a finger towards her nose. "Stay there and don't, for *anything*, utter the name *Bessarion*."

Soraya let a startled snort escape her as he stalked toward the door. Khalil must hold John in the deadliest enmity if Saif meant to conceal his name from his master. Well, it was all to the good, if it meant John's mortal enemy remained ignorant of his presence.

Saif flung open the door and Soraya studied the young man who entered, bracing herself for the sense of power and dread he carried with him. Apparently in his late twenties or early thirties, Khalil wore an exquisitely embroidered tunic and the ornamental golden belt of a high ranking official. Soraya's mouth dried as realisation struck her. She had seen that belt before—she knew the shape of the nose, the breadth of the forehead, the black beard trimmed like velvet.

She'd seen all of them on the prince she'd poisoned seven months ago. This must be his brother and successor.

Memories fitted together into a dreadful pattern.

I asked about the next heir last night. Al-Ashraf Khalil. A pleasure-seeking idiot.

Saif, wiping blood from the blade of his spear. *He'll change now.*

She knew, then, that more than one prince had died that night. While al-Salih Ali had gasped his final breath with a belly full of bad honey, al-Ashraf Khalil—the *real* al-Ashraf—had been bleeding out to the tune of a black ritual, the magic of shared names and flowing blood changing the appearance of the sorcerer to match that of his victim.

Soraya's blood froze as the meaning of this struck home. Qalawun was an old man and the first heir was dead.

Khalil ibn Hassan was positioned to take the throne of Egypt.

Khalil stopped before Soraya with dark eyes full of ruthless intelligence. She had the feeling that he could read the thoughts stumbling through her head; that her memories were a plaything to him.

"Did Saif have any trouble with you?" the sorcerer asked.

Soraya didn't answer. His commands were not binding upon her, and she didn't care to incriminate herself. Let Saif speak, if he liked; let him tell their master how she had fought and conspired against him, how she was the one to save John Bessarion's life when Saif had him at the point of a spear.

Saif answered for her, and not quite as she had expected. "No more than usual, my lord."

Of course—he was already in enough trouble.

Khalil turned back to Saif. "The sultan spoke well of you. Qeteb tells me that in the sack of Tripoli you fed him more blood than any other single warrior."

Soraya couldn't restrain a groan of horror at this revelation. It earned her Khalil's piercing gaze, and she fell silent, pressing a hand to her mouth to stifle any further sound.

Saif's throat bobbed as he swallowed, and bowed without looking at her. "Thank you, my lord. May God reward you with all good."

Khalil grunted, unimpressed. After an ominous silence, he spoke again. "You never failed me before, boy."

"I was never pitted against Watchers like these before, my lord."

"Do you dare to make excuses?"

"No, my lord."

The sorcerer's eyes narrowed. "You made the mistake of allying with one of them. I presume you brought me his head?"

Now it would come: Saif would explain that she, Soraya, had turned against him in an effort to kill him, and had helped the Watcher to escape.

She would be subjected to whatever punishment this dark sorcerer could devise.

Instead, Saif bowed his head, almost like a victim before the executioner's sword. "No, my lord. I promised him safe-conduct in exchange for performing the exorcism. He did so, and I allowed him to depart once the city was taken."

"You *let* him depart?" Khalil's voice cracked like a whip in the still underground room. "Even after I told you to destroy the city and everyone in it?"

"You've taught me many times about the importance of keeping my oaths with honour, my lord."

Soraya wanted to laugh. Was Saif pretending to be an upright man? Did he have any idea how hypocritical he seemed beside someone like John Bessarion?

Or perhaps his words were calculated. Perhaps he was trying to trick her into trusting him for some reason. Their conversation moments ago made it clear that he was jealous of John, jealous of her. Not for the sake of lust, she thought; he could have satisfied that at any moment the last seven months, if not long before, and she could not have resisted him. No, Saif wanted something different, something he'd sworn never to accept from her.

Friendship.

The Chosen, the Sword of Egypt, the fabled killer whose lance drank blood with ruthless appetite, was lonely.

Good.

"Ought I to have broken my oath?" Saif persisted, as the silence stretched out.

Soraya expected Khalil to erupt into a rage. Instead, his lips thinned. "There is a difference between oaths made to fellow believers, and oaths made to deceiving *thieves.*"

"Then may God forgive me." Saif bowed. "I will wait for this Prester John, and finish him off with a clear conscience." He turned to look at Soraya. "I think it will be easy, my lord. God willing, I think the Watcher will come to us."

Soraya's eyes widened. *No.*

"Good. Be ready for him when he comes." Khalil kept his eyes on Soraya, and she found her assumed body was sweating. He added softly, "It's not long since the last time, but I think it is best to purge her memories again."

Soraya blinked in horror. Take from her those shards of the past which she had recovered—render her senseless and ignorant for the time when John would come in search of her. "No. Please!"

"Quiet," Khalil whispered, and although he couldn't control her like Saif did, it was as though her tongue shrivelled inside her mouth. He turned to Saif with a shrug. "She has a history of joining forces with Watchers. We can't be too careful. What about you? Would you be the lighter for your... doubts?"

"I have no doubts, my lord." Saif glanced at Soraya, his face unreadable. "And I would be honoured to keep the memories."

"Tell me if the nightmares return again." Khalil waved them to a door. "Wait outside. I'll call you when the ritual is prepared."

Saif led her into the next room; the closing of the door loosened Soraya's tongue. Abandoning all pride, she threw herself onto her knees before him. "Don't let him do this to me. *Please!*"

He stared down at her, and his lips thinned to a harsh line. "Get up and stop grovelling. I've already done as much as I dare for you."

She had no choice but to obey. He hadn't commanded her tongue, however, and that she could still use. "Oh, I see," she spat with all the venom she could muster. "You knew he was going to steal my past from me, so you thought you could afford a little benevolence. A pat on the head before you gut me."

For a moment, it struck her just how dead and hopeless his eyes seemed. "Yes," he said levelly, "exactly that. Now be silent."

* * *

A door slammed, waking echoes. One woke slowly, groggily, in the centre of a sigil. There was a strange rushing in one's ears, a sough like distant water, a steady drumbeat at one's centre that quickened as one's confusion increased.

One was embodied, but did not seem quite at home.

Images fluttered around the edges of one's senses. Things that had happened in the past. Faces one had known. Sounds one had heard. A taste of salt and iron and death that made one shudder instinctively.

"Soraya."

The word pierced one's foggy memory, triggered a thought.

Soraya. Me.

Shakily, still plagued with fading memories, Soraya got to her feet. Footsteps sounded, echoing across the great dim room. Smooth flagstones paved the floor, racks of swords and spears lining the walls.

Light filtered in through high windows, lighting the grim face of the young man who stood opposite her in silence.

She studied her captor a moment. With an aquiline nose, a carefully-trimmed beard and smooth, pale, unwrinkled skin, her master could have been any age between eighteen and thirty-five. His fine silk tunic was woven from many fine iridescent strands of silk in a wildly swirling pattern of golden spirals and starbursts, and it struck a strange chord of memory within her.

She snatched at the fading images. They trickled through her grasp like water, but it seemed terribly important somehow to remember. Before the memory faded entirely Soraya caught a name. "That shirt," she murmured. "That's one of Marta's patterns…" Another effort. Another prize, snatched from the fading memories. "Her name was Marta Bessarion. *What did you do to her?*"

She looked up to find her master watching her in something like terror. His tongue flicked over his lips, and he shot a glance toward the newly-closed door. *"What did you say?"*

"Marta Bessarion," she repeated. "And there were…others?"

The man's face hardened in a ferocious scowl, and he jabbed a finger in her direction. "I forbid you ever to speak that name again." There was a spear in the crook of his arm, and now he swept it up, taking a stance. "On guard."

She tried to hold on to the name, but the last fleeting shadows of her memory had already fled. Soraya's eyes fastened on the amethyst ring on his finger, and instinct took over.

That has to be it. The vessel that he uses to imprison me.

The thought came unbidden into her head. She knew this intuitively, the way she knew that she rode this body lightly rather than truly inhabiting it. She was only a spirit. A djinn.

There were only three ways a djinn could escape such a prison. The master of a ring could set the djinn free, if he so desired, by commanding her to go. The ring could be destroyed.

Or the master could be killed.

Perhaps, if she could injure him badly enough…

Soraya backed away as he advanced. Suddenly, she whipped around, raced for the wall, and seized a short sword.

He was right behind her when she turned and thrust the length of the blade into his exposed chest, cleaving his heart open.

He groaned in pain, but he didn't falter. Instead, he wrapped his hand around the hilt as she let go, and drew the sword from his own body with a grunt. The blade came away glistening with blood, but before her eyes the wound sealed over leaving smooth, unmarked skin.

At the same moment, dizziness swept over her. Well, of course if she could actually *hurt* him, he'd never let her inside this room, within reach of all these weapons. That dizziness suggested a drain on her power: he had her on a soul tether. Her own immortality, her own strength and speed flowed to him through the ring that connected them.

He moved closer and spoke in a commanding voice. "Your name is Soraya, and you answer to me."

Something about his words made her stomach cramp with a rage so consuming that she realised she must already know this man well.

Know him, and hate him.

He glanced away, seeming to debate something. Finally, he turned back to her. "You are one of seven sisters. You are here because you gave up everything you wanted for the life of..." he looked at her oddly. Half suspicious, half jealous. "The life of a *friend*."

She understood the words. It was their significance that escaped her, and the chilly, resentful way he pronounced them. "What?"

He turned, stalking away from her towards the centre of the room. "My name is al-Mukhtar Saif al-Din, but I want you to call me Saif. Choose yourself a weapon. It's time we practiced."

S.D.G.

John Bessarion will return in **The Shadow of Egypt**

Wondering what happened to the other Bessarions?

Read Rahel, Paulus, and Elisa's story in
Children of the Desolate
Available free at suzannahrowntree.site

Lukas' story began in
A Wind from the Wilderness
Available now!

Marta's story began in
The Lady of Kingdoms
Available now!

Historical Note

There was a nasty moment when I sat down to begin writing this novel and thought: *Oh dear, I seem to have forgotten everything I might have known about the thirteenth century in the crusader states.* Somewhat rattled, I turned to Christopher Tyerman's *God's War: A New History of the Crusades* for a quick refresher. Here, not entirely to my relief, the following words greeted me: "The internal politics of the kingdom of Jerusalem in the thirteenth century presents the observer with an almost impenetrably dense pointillist picture of confusion, competition and conflict."

Never was a truer word spoken. By the end of the thirteenth century, the political history of the crusader states was hopelessly muddled by dynastic disasters which in turn led to rival claimants to the throne of the kingdom of Jerusalem (which was now ruled from Acre). Meanwhile intermarriage had created a dense web of interrelation among the ruling families of Antioch, Tripoli, Cyprus and Cilicia. Complicating matters is the fact that the crusader East had now become simply one small part of a much broader world. For example: Eschiva of Ibelin, the Lady of Beirut, was of native Greco-Frankish crusader settler stock on her father's side; but she was the granddaughter of the Frankish duke of Athens on her mother's side, and her husband, Humphrey of Montfort, was the second cousin of that Simon of Montfort, Earl of Leicester who is famous in English constitutional history. It was the age of Marco Polo's expedition to the court of Kublai Khan, with the Mongol conquests opening up the Silk Road and making travel across Asia easier than ever; but people were moving around Europe much more freely too, and the history of the thirteenth-century crusader states thus becomes inextricably intertwined with the endless wars between the great Italian trading states of Venice, Pisa, and Genoa; or the ambitions of the Hohenstaufen emperors of Germany; or even the cold war between Mamluk Egypt and the Mongol Il-Khanate of Baghdad.

For these reasons I have tried to keep the historical details in this novel fairly focused. Since the loss of Jerusalem proper a hundred years previously, the kingdom of Jerusalem had been ruled from Acre, mostly by *baillis* or regents, the most prominent of whom was John of Ibelin. A Frankish kingdom in Cyprus, and an Armenian kingdom in Cilicia, acted as important allies to the mainland crusader states. Following the overthrow of Saladin's dynasty in Egypt at the hands of the remarkable queen, Shajar al-Durr, the Mamluks had risen to power: a military junta that recruited slave-warriors, then freed them to hold high rank in government. The Mamluks consolidated their power in Egypt and Syria ruthlessly; having stemmed the tide of Mongol advance at the battle of Ayn Jalut in Galilee in 1260, they seem to have decided (with some justification) that as potential allies of the Mongols, the crusader states were too dangerous to be left in peace. Accordingly, in 1268, the Mamluk sultan Baibars took and sacked Antioch with great slaughter, ending the principality formed during the first crusade a hundred and seventy years before. He, and his eventual successor Qalawun, spent much of the following two decades systematically mopping up crusader fortresses both from the dwindling kingdom of Jerusalem, and the independent county of Tripoli in today's Lebanon.

By the time of this story, crusader politics was dominated by two great military Orders—the Temple and the Hospital—which manned the majority of the crusader states' border fortresses. Despite being independent entities, answerable only to the Pope, they usually took opposing sides on any given question. The endless petty warfare of the Italian trading cities of Venice, Genoa, and Pisa was just as predominant, as was the factional strife between the supporters of Charles of Anjou's claim to the throne, versus the claim of Henry II of Cyprus.

As usual, my goal has been to follow the historical record as closely as possible, embroidering in the gaps rather than changing anything. This has been a challenge for this book, since there are fewer sources and less commentary on the fall of the crusader states than there is on their rise and zenith. Additionally, there is a terrible paucity of English-language academic study on the history of Mamluk Egypt during this period. Had I arranged to start learning classical Arabic twenty years ago, this book might have been better researched.

Countess Lucy, Benedetto Zaccaria, Margaret of Tyre, Eschiva of Ibelin, William of Beaujeu, Sultan Qalawun and the Embriaco family are all real historical figures; and Lucy's brother Bohemond VII really did execute the Embriaco rebels by walling them up inside their moat. Gerard of Montreal was a real person about whom we know little, unless he is the possible identity of the chronicler known today as the Templar of Tyre, whose history is the only major eyewitness account of the late thirteenth century in the crusader states. The name is somewhat misleading, since the so-called "Templar" was a secular knight in the service of William of Beaujeu, the Master of the Temple, and not a full-fledged member of the Order. We know that he served Margaret of Tyre as a page and he was clearly devoted to her; he records that she was very beautiful in her youth but later became extremely fat, and it was these little details that gave me the idea for their relationship in this book. The "Templar" was also highly trusted by Beaujeu; it's thanks to him that we know so many tantalising details about the Templar intelligence network, which included a double agent embedded at the highest levels of Mamluk government. Even for a medieval chronicler the "Templar" left a particularly strong impression of his personality in his work, which has informed the character of Gerard of Montreal, just as his history supplied the details of the fall of Tripoli. Here I have taken a liberty with the historical record. Although the "Templar"s account of the siege is vivid, he likely drew on the experiences of eyewitnesses; unlike later events, he leaves us with no impression that he himself was present during the siege. Lady Margaret, however, was certainly there; she had served as *bailli* at some stage before Countess Lucy's accession.

Thanks to the brevity of knightly life expectancy in the crusader states, it was quite common for women to rule in their own name, as Margaret did in Tyre after her husband's death, and as Eschiva did in Beirut at the same time (having inherited the title from her scandalous sister Isabella). It's not completely impossible that Countess Lucy's difficulties in convincing Tripoli to accept her rule, and the "Templar"'s somewhat unflattering portrait, had to do with her gender; but undoubtedly the most important reason was that following the civil wars that had racked Tripoli in the previous decades under the rule of Lucy's father and brother, the barely-subdued nobles still wished for a change of regime.

Lucy managed to play the differing factions against each other and win her birthright by threatening to hand over larger and larger concessions to Genoa, but this ultimately led to her downfall when a pair of (probably Venetian) merchants went to Egypt to warn Sultan Qalawun that the Genoese might be about to gain an important maritime base in the eastern Mediterranean. If the Genoese dominated the seas, this would threaten the slave trade via Cilicia, whence Qalawun sourced the mamluk slaves who formed the basis of his power. According to the "Templar", it was this that motivated the sultan to besiege Tripoli. His campaign was originally scheduled for late 1288, but had to be delayed when his son and favoured heir al-Malik al-Salih Ali died unexpectedly after a sudden illness. Early in 1289, with second son al-Ashraf Khalil named heir in his place (who, in historical fact, was most likely *not* being impersonated by a mad sorcerer), Qalawun marched for Tripoli.

Beaujeu's spies warned him that the sultan was on his way to destroy Tripoli, but Countess Lucy refused to believe his warnings due to Beaujeu's interference in the civil wars of her brother's reign. I have stuck pretty closely to the "Templar"'s account of the back-and-forths that occurred. When it became clear that a siege was about to happen, however, allies were summoned from around the eastern Mediterranean—and given the factionalism so rife in the crusader states, the predictable result was that, according to the "Templar", "there was an evil hatred constantly between them." After a punishing seven-week bombardment with siege engines, the walls of the city were breached in several places. The crisis came when the Venetians decided to retreat to their ships, and the Genoese followed them out of distrust, fearing to be cut off if the Venetians should attack their own fleet. The end followed quickly: Tripoli was levelled to the ground.

For dramatic purposes, I have taken the liberty of implicating Countess Lucy in what happened on the isle of Saint Thomas, but this is my own invention. The historical record is as follows: Two Arab historians, Abu al-Fida and Maqrizi, agree that a large number of Franks fled the city to the small island, where they were followed and slaughtered. Abu al-Fida states, "After the looting I went by boat to this island, and found it heaped with putrefying corpses; it was impossible to land there because of the stench." A large number of prisoners were also taken: according to Maqrizi, 1,200 of them had to be kept in the Sultan's arsenal.

Due to the events depicted in this book, and the rebuilding of the modern city atop the ruins of the crusader city, it is impossible to reconstruct pre-Mamluk Tripoli with any accuracy. However, I have made a number of educated guesses using historical maps and the comments of medieval chroniclers from Raymond of Aguilers to the "Templar" himself; and the isle of Saint Thomas is still there, now reachable across a footbridge. Maqrizi states that "the population was extremely wealthy, and 4,000 weaver's looms were found"; we know that white silk was a major export, and for this reason I made the Zakars weavers. They, together with the Watchers, Katsaros, Peter of Alba, al-Mukhtar Saif al-Din, Soraya, Khalil ibn Hassan and John Bessarion, are fictional.

While the 636 battle of Yarmouk, and Emperor Heraclius' subsequent departure from Syria, were real historical events, I should also note that Oliveta is a fictional town, and that in reality atrocities of this nature did not characterise the seventh-century Muslim conquest. The population was neither slaughtered, nor compelled to convert to Islam: in fact, the population of large parts of the Levant would continue to be majority-Christian until well after the fall of the crusader states.

I would like to acknowledge the people who gave generously of their time and insights to make this story the best it could be. I'm tremendously thankful, as always, to Christina Baehr, Schuyler McConkey, and Stella Dorthwany for their endlessly challenging literary critique; to David Noor and Abigail Hartman for challenging me on theological questions; and to my Muslim sensitivity readers Leila Ammar and Shoohada Khanom, for helping me get the Muslim calendar right and ironing out some of the details on djinn. Intisar Khanani and Jamie Wheeler also acted as ministering angels, connecting me with the people and resources I might not have been able to access otherwise. Finally, my editor, Lucy Holdsworth, and my cover designer, Jenny Zemanek, have once again risen to the occasion. I'm so deeply grateful to all of you.

Suzannah Rowntree
November 2020

Further Reading

Without a doubt my most important historical source in preparing this novel was Paul Crawford's recent translation of *The 'Templar of Tyre', Part III of the 'Deeds of the Cypriots'.* This, the first English translation made directly from the original manuscript, only appeared in 2016. The manuscript itself was rediscovered and lost to history several times over, and for centuries was known only through rumour and bad copies until the real thing was finally unearthed in the Royal Library of Turin in the late 1970s. I feel incredibly privileged to be able to use it as a source today.

Other essential books that helped me understand the history of the thirteenth-century crusader states include: Christopher Tyerman's *God's War: A New History of the Crusades,* Peter W. Edbury's *John of Ibelin and Kingdom of Jerusalem,* and David Nicolle's *Acre 1291: Bloody sunset of the Crusader States.* Jonathan Riley-Smith's *The Knights Hospitaller in the Levant, c1070-1309,* and Malcolm Barber's *The New Knighthood,* provided more information than I could possibly use for the military Orders of the Hospital and the Temple. Meanwhile, Robert Irwin's *The Middle East in the Middle Ages: The Early Mamluk Sultanate, 1250-1382,* Linda S. Northrup's *From Slave to Sultan: The Career of Al-Mansur Qalawun and the Consolidation of Mamluk Rule in Egypt and Syria (678-689 A.H./1279-1290 A.D.)* and David Nicholle's *The Mamluks, 1250-1517,* were the most helpful resources I could find on the Bahri Mamluk sultanate. John Man's book *The Mongol Empire* was a wonderfully readable (if inexplicably laudatory) introduction to the earth-shattering history of the Mongol conquests. Finally, the *History of Tripoli* website written by Dr. Ghazi Omar Tadmouri—now accessible only through the Internet Archive's Wayback Machine—was invaluable in helping me fill in a picture of the long-vanished thirteenth century city.

The background for the seventh century events was helpfully supplied in part by Judith Herrin's *The Formation of Christendom* and *Byzantium: The Surprising Life of a Medieval Empire;* by John Julius Norwich's *A Short History of Byzantium;* Sir Stephen Runciman's *A History of the Crusades, Volume 1* (although his work on the crusades themselves is now largely superseded, his expertise in Byzantine history was helpful); and David Nicolle's detailed study of the battle of Yarmouk, *Yarmuk AD 636: The Muslim Conquest of Syria.*

I continue to return to several foundational books for help understanding the crusader states in general: *Medicine in the Crusades* by Piers Mitchell; *Crusader Archaeology: The Material Culture of the Latin East* by Adrian J Boas; *The Atlas of the Crusades* edited by Jonathan Riley-Smith; *The Crusades and the Christian World of the East: Rough Tolerance* by Christopher MacEvitt; *Western Warfare in the Age of the Crusades* by John France; and Carl Stephenson's *Medieval Feudalism* and Marc Bloch's *Feudal Society.* As always, van der Toorn, Becking, and van der Horst's *Dictionary of Deities and Demons in the Bible* provided helpful inspiration for writing Lilith, Qeteb, and other fantastical elements.

No historical research is complete without reading original source materials. In addition to the *Templar of Tyre,* I consulted Francesco Gabrieli's *Arab Historians of the Crusades* for the Mamluk take on the siege of Tripoli, Malcolm Barber's *Letters from the East* for useful commentary from the crusader nobility, and the delightful, irrepressible John of Joinville's *Life of Saint Louis* (in M.R.B. Shaw's translation in the Penguin Classics *Chronicles of the Crusades*) for essential background on thirteenth century attitudes and the legends of Prester John.

About the Author

Suzannah Rowntree lives in a big house in rural Australia with her awesome parents and siblings, reading academic histories of the Crusades and writing historical fantasy fiction that blends folklore and myth with historical fact.

You can connect with me on:

🌐 https://suzannahrowntree.site

Subscribe to my newsletter:

✉ https://www.subscribepage.com/srauthor

Also by Suzannah Rowntree

The Watchers of Outremer Series
Children of the Desolate
A Wind from the Wilderness
The Lady of Kingdoms

The Pendragon's Heir Trilogy
The Door to Camelot
The Quest for Carbonek
The Heir of Logres

The Fairy Tale Retold Series
The Rakshasa's Bride
The Prince of Fishes
The Bells of Paradise
Death Be Not Proud
Ten Thousand Thorns
The City Beyond the Glass